Elvis's Beauty, Barber, Bait & Bakery

Elvis's Beauty, Barber, Bait & Bakery

A Dozen Fathead Minnows With Every Perm

Rita Haag

Wood Lane Books

CONTENTS

CONTENTS

CONTENTS

CONTENTS

CONTENTS

This novel is dedicated to Gregg Malaczewski

Gregg is the real-life barber who cut my hair for
years and kept me laughing with his
tongue-in-cheek plans to open
a small-town business:
Gregg's Beauty, Barber, Bait, and Bakery:
A Dozen Fathead Minnows With Every Perm.

He is the inspiration for this story,
although beyond a love of fishing and hunting,
the Brent Wallace character
is a complete fabrication of my imagination.

THE CROW STARTED IT

Brent Wallace was not the type to initiate a conversation. The crow started it. On any other day, that's where the conversation would have ended, since Brent Wallace was also not the type to talk to animals. But the morning had gotten off to a such a bad start that by the time the piercing "CAW" echoed out over Little Pine Lake, Brent figured if he didn't get a few things off his chest the whole day would be ruined. Besides, he was the only fisherman on the water so no one else would hear his rant, and it wasn't like the crow would care what he said anyway.

"Don't get me wrong," he called out in the general direction of the woods on the west end of the lake where the crow apparently lived. "I like women. I own a salon, for Pete's sake. I spend half my life with them. I even married one. But I like fishing more. Fish are predictable. You know where you stand with fish. They don't flirt, they don't cry, and they don't ask you to cut their hair like Jennifer Aniston's."

To Brent's surprise, the crow cawed back. He'd never spoken to it before. In fact, he seldom saw it, since the woods featured a heavy growth of bird-hiding evergreens, but one morning he realized that every time he took his old Lund 1700 Pro Sport out on Little Pine Lake and cut the power on the Evinrude, he heard a familiar caw. He also noticed a fuss every time he reeled in a walleye. If it was a lunker, the crow let loose a series of sharp, bold caws, but if the catch was puny, Brent heard a disappointed *awwww.* Not the ideal fishing buddy, but not bad, either, although he'd never imagined actually having a conversation with it. On the other hand, people talked to themselves all the time, so was this so weird? Besides, what the crow lacked in comprehension it made up for in dependability, and Brent Wallace was definitely the type to value dependability. Even in a crow.

After a quick scan of the lake to make sure he was still alone, he grabbed his new Pflueger President Spinning Rod and aimed his voice out over the water. "I'm just frustrated because it's my fiftieth birthday. And it's the opening day of walleye season, so," he continued as he searched the tree line for movement, "I decided to give myself the perfect gift: a day on the lake!"

He eased onto the boat's swivel seat and pulled his bait bucket closer. But he still hadn't made his point, so he picked up where he'd left off. Even if the crow didn't understand, it felt good to let it out.

"I had the day all planned," he said as he scooped out a fathead minnow and baited the hook. "Hang out on the water. Catch a few walleye . . . have a few snacks . . ."

"Caw! Caw! Caw!"

Brent looked up and watched the bird fly kitty-corner toward a bank of willows on the northern shore. It settled in a branch facing him—as if waiting for the rest of the story—and Brent let loose in a tirade he'd been holding in way too long.

"But do I HAVE any snacks? No! Because while I was at the gas station deciding which kind of potato chips I was in the mood for, this clerk—a *clerk*, mind you, not even anyone I *know*—comes up and nearly runs into me. No regard for personal space. I'm backing away but she keeps marching at me. Finally she stops and plants her hands on her hips and hollers out, 'Well aren't you just a big hunk a' handsome.'"

He felt the heat rise to his face again as he recalled the three heads jerking up from across the aisles and staring.

"I hightailed it out of there without buying a thing. No chips, no candy bars, no jerky. I love snacks. Fishing without snacks is like movies without popcorn." Slamming the lid on the bait bucket, he vowed never to stop at that gas station again.

"Okay. Done venting. Time to fish."

He stood and cast out, his eyes following the end of the line as it snapped in the air, then dove in the water. He imagined a school of walleye gliding along several feet below the surface and suddenly doing an about-face to go after the lively minnow. It was a great image, but his mind started churning again.

"Also, Lisa got up at four a.m. She never does that. I think she's up to something."

He was considering whether or not it was important to mention that Lisa was his wife when he felt a pull. He jerked the rod and welcomed the adrenaline rush, but when he reeled in the line the minnow was gone. He baited the hook again, cast out, and the feeling of dread returned.

"So, can I relax and enjoy myself today? NO! Because when I walk in the door tonight people are going to jump out from behind furniture and yell, "Surprise!"

Lisa loved parties. He hated them.

"Maybe I'll just stay out here until midnight. If I don't get home 'til two in the morning the party will be over, and everyone will be gone. What do you think about that?"

No word from the crow, but the bobber wobbled, grabbing Brent's attention. He stared at it thinking he could be wrong about the party since Lisa hadn't asked when he'd be returning. In fact, he couldn't recall discussing if he'd even get home tonight.

The crow was still quiet. Maybe it had heard enough complaining. He eased back onto the padded seat and pretended he didn't have a job or a wife or a birthday that had been ruined. Soon he felt another nibble, saw the bobber dip, and yanked the rod, setting the hook. He wound the reel, and the fish leapt out of the water, a mid-sized walleye with a lot of fight. Brent played it for several minutes, then brought it in. Although his heart was thumping like mad with the thrill of the catch, he felt a sudden rush of empathy. No amount of flipping, jerking, or pitching was going to save the struggling fish.

"You know," he called out as a thought clarified, "I think that's my problem. Being around women makes me feel more like a fish than a fisherman."

The crow swooped from the willow, flew overhead, and cawed. Brent cawed back and held the fish up to give the bird a good look and called over: "See? You catch a fish, you're in charge. You catch a woman, and . . ."

He left the sentence hanging and the crow let out a barrage of cackling as it headed back to the edge of the woods and flew off noisily through the trees. Brent eased the hook from the walleye's mouth and threw the fish in the live well. He grabbed the minnow bucket but decided to change things up. He searched his box of lures for a Wally Diver, tied it to the line, and cast out. He looked out over the water for a few minutes thinking about that struggling fish, then felt a rumble in his stomach.

He put the rod back in the holder and sat. As he pulled the cooler closer Lisa came to mind again, and he realized she *was* a good woman. Just not good for him.

"The only reason I ever got married was because Lisa asked me out, arranged our dates, proposed, and took care of all the wedding plans. I was honest about things. I told her I liked her a lot, but I wasn't sure I loved her."

Jeepers, he thought, *saying it out loud makes it sound terrible.* As silly as it was, he felt the need to explain. "She really wanted to get married, and I was already forty-two at the time. And the only bachelor in my poker club."

He took a deep breath. Although this was the last thing he wanted to think about, maybe on his fiftieth birthday he should be making some sort of plan for the rest of his life.

"I never should have married her, that's for sure. By our first anniversary it was clear she had more in common with her wardrobe than with me."

Even though the crow hadn't returned, it felt good to put his thoughts into words, like maybe his mouth could say things his brain wasn't ready to admit.

"We talked about divorce, but we'd both worked so hard fixing up our house, neither of us wanted to leave."

He took out a ham and cheese sandwich and when he pulled the plastic wrap apart he found a small piece of perfumed note-paper, which *he* certainly hadn't put there. He sniffed the sandwich to be sure it hadn't taken on the lavender scent and set it on the cooler, unfolded the paper, and read the note: *Dear Brent, Just wanted you to be the first to know I'm "engaged." Ray proposed last night! I'm filing for divorce tomorrow. Love you! Lisa.*

Engaged? So *that's* why Lisa had gotten up early.

This is too good to be true, he thought, and he read the note again looking for the flaw. The quotes around engaged? Was this tentative? Was the "engagement" dependent on something which, whether it happened or didn't, might cause Ray to un-propose?

Then he realized Lisa had probably used quotes because they were still married, so she couldn't be "officially" engaged. Well, good for her, he thought. Then it hit him: If she was engaged, he was off the hook. And if she and Ray got married, they'd have to buy out his half of the house.

And if they bought out his half of the house . . .

2

201 SOUTH STREET

It could work.

But not just a beauty salon. As crazy as it had sounded at the time, Uncle Thad's idea suddenly made a lot of sense. "You gotta go bigger," he'd said, when Brent had shared his dream to semi-retire in Pine Lake. "A small town like that? You set up a beauty salon *and* a barbershop. And bait. Gotta have a bait shop with all the lakes up there, cabins everywhere. You could sell a lotta bait. Heck, you throw in a bakery, then you got something."

Brent was tempted to leave the lake that very minute, but the fish were biting and his brain was humming. Just before dusk he packed up and headed to shore. As he cut the engine, the crow cawed and soared overhead, flapping in such a way that Brent could have sworn it was waving its wings. He waved back and cawed a goodby as the crow flew off into the distance.

Well if that isn't a good omen, I don't know what is, Brent thought. He winched the boat unto the trailer, hopped in the truck, and checked the time on the dash: 8:45.

He must have driven that road a hundred times before but had never paid attention to exactly how long it took to get from the lake to the little downtown area. Twelve minutes? Fifteen?

When he pulled to the curb across from the vacant building he checked the time: 8:52. Only seven minutes!

He peered out at a large plate glass window etched with the words *Havisto's Market* and broke into a smile as he read the two large words on the billboard out front: FOR SALE.

The building was big enough to accommodate four shops and battered enough to be in his price range, not to mention that the For Sale sign had been there as long as he could remember. A banner slapped across the bottom read, "Land Contract Option." The seller was probably very motivated. Maybe even desperate.

He shut off the ignition, grabbed his cell phone, and headed to the building. Stopping in front of the realtor's sign, he entered the number for Pine Lake Realty. After the fifth ring he heard the beginning sounds of a recorded answer, ended the call, and slipped the phone back into his vest pocket. There was a cell-phone number . . . but it was Sunday night. Maybe he should wait and call in the morning. On the other hand, he was a serious buyer. He pulled out his phone and entered the second set of numbers listed on the sign, hoping the guy would be up for an impromptu showing.

After four rings, deafening music filled his ears. "Hello?" Brent hollered.

"Who is this?" a voice on the other end shouted.

He shouted back: "I'm looking for someone from Pine Lake Realty. Sorry, I must have the wrong—"

"No! Wait. Wait!"

The music stopped.

"It's me. I'm Pine Lake Realty. I mean, like, I work there."

I mean, like, I work there? Maybe she was her father's answering service. Regardless, this obviously young girl needed a lesson in phone etiquette. "How old are you?" he asked.

"Why? Are you some kind of pervert?"

"No . . . NO!"

She suddenly sounded a lot older, and he broke into a sweat picturing his arrest. He nearly hung up, but . . . could this be the opportunity of a lifetime? He took a deep breath and continued.

"I'm standing in front of a commercial building on South Street. It has a Pine Lake Realty sign in front with this number on it. I'm not a pervert, I'm a potential client. I was hoping I could see it tonight while I'm in town."

"You actually want to see that building?"

"Well, I know it's late, but I work six days a week and—"

"Wow! You mean the building at 201 South?"

"Yes. Is there a problem?"

"No. No! But it's been on the market so long I kinda gave up on it."

This couldn't be an actual realtor. Must be an assistant. A very young and unprofessional assistant-in-training. "If you aren't able to show it, is it possible to locate someone who could?"

"I can show it. I just want to make sure you aren't some lunatic. Hey, wait a minute. Did Binky Todd get you to call me? This is a joke, right?"

"No! I'm definitely interested in the building."

"Great! I'll be there in five."

Five minutes passed, then ten, then fifteen. He considered leaving, but now when he looked at the FOR SALE sign it seemed to have spawned an invisible line that read SEVEN MINUTES TO WALLEYE. He walked around the old building again, peered in a couple of windows, imagined closing up at five o'clock on a weekday afternoon, and easing his boat out onto Little Pine Lake a mere seven minutes later. That would be the life!

As he was about to give up, an aging purple Honda Civic with a dented driver's-side fender roared into the lot, muffler rattling. It squealed to a stop and the door opened releasing a fairly tall, formally-dressed—but shoeless—purple-haired girl.

"Hi," she called out. Whoever she was. Definitely not the realtor.

"Hi. I'm just waiting for a realtor," he said.

"Yeah. I figured. That would be me. Dana Novicki."

Not likely, he said to himself, thinking he'd interrupted her at her high school prom, or maybe a wedding since she was wearing a slightly-stained, shiny, light purple gown with a dark purple shawl. As she came closer he wondered if it hurt to have that many holes poked in your ears and face. And if she always went barefoot. It wasn't even summer yet.

She held out her hand which had a thing on the back that seemed to be crawling up her arm.

"Is that a tattoo?"

"It's a yeti crab."

"Oh." He stared at it for a second then remembered his manners and shook her hand, surprised at her strong, assured grip.

As she pulled her hand back she flipped it. "It has these hairy pincers . . ." She pointed at them and continued, "and scientists think—"

He lost track of what she was saying—something about food and protection—because now she sounded like a ten-year-old explaining a science project. No way this girl, who couldn't have been out of high school yet, was a realtor.

"Do you have some form of identification?" he asked.

"You mean like a driver's license?"

True, he thought. She was driving, so that meant she was at least 16. And she was tall, about five-eight he guessed, although he didn't know what—if any—correlation there might be between age and height.

"No, I meant something to show you really are a realtor."

"Yoo-hoo!" she said, ramming the jangling keys in his face.

Startled, he jerked back, throwing his hands up for protection.

"Duh!" she said, her purple-ringed eyes growing huge. "I have the keys. I must be the realtor."

He considered getting back in his truck, heading home, and calling Pine Lake Realty the next morning when most likely an actual realtor would answer, but she was walking in the direction of the building, which, he reminded himself, was *only* seven minutes from walleye. If he could get it for the right price he'd be seven minutes from walleye, too. So, "Duh!" he said to himself and followed her for several yards when her bare feet caught his attention again.

"Miss . . . what was your name again?"

"Dana. Dana Novicki."

"Okay, Miss Dana Novicki, we're heading into an old building and you're barefoot. What if there's broken glass or nails on the ground? Shouldn't you put some shoes on?"

She turned and looked at her car, then looked back at him. "Yeah. You're probably right. I might have something in the trunk."

She headed back to her car, her dress swishing with each step. She opened the trunk, pushed things around, then threw something on the ground. Seconds later she clomped in his direction wearing a too-large pair of men's black dress shoes.

"My lucky day!" she said. "I get all my clothes at thrift shops and on my last visit I picked these up for Binky. That's my boyfriend. Good thing I have big feet. They're still a little loose, but you're right. I really should have shoes on to walk around in there. Thanks," she said, as she continued clomping and swishing in the direction of the building. When she got to the door she turned and said, "That is one muckraking outfit!"

For a split second he was confused, his mind connecting the word muckraking with old-time journalism and pushy reporters. He glanced down, just to be certain he was wearing what, in his mind, didn't look at all "muckraking" considering it was his fishing vest with all the pockets, his fishing hat onto which he'd attached a variety of carefully chosen lures, and the lucky belt with the fish-shaped buckle he'd inherited from Uncle Thad who'd won it at a fishing tournament.

The young woman looked down at her feet, causing a purplish hank of beaded hair to break loose from the rest of her tousled coif and swing in mid-air. "I usually wear shoes when I'm showing a house but I couldn't find them."

So she does normally wear shoes, he thought. And she does have the keys.

She put the key in the lockbox but before she opened the door she turned to him again. "Do you have a girlfriend?"

Jeepers! Was she coming on to him, too?

Then, recalling her pervert comment earlier, he thought of entrapment, and looked around. Although they were completely alone in a quiet neighborhood in a totally secluded parking lot at the back door of an abandoned building . . . and despite the fact that she was a realtor (supposedly), and he was a potential buyer (hopefully), he wondered if there was some kind of surveillance going on and asked: "Are you wearing a wire?"

"You mean like an underwire bra?"

"What? NO!!" He felt the heat rise to his face. "You just asked if I had a girlfriend." He'd put every bit of innocent exasperation he could muster into the words.

"Yeah . . ."

He had to assume the obvious. "Don't you think I'm a little old for you?"

"Oh, WAAAY old. I'm not asking for me. It's just that you're kind of cute. In a traditional sort of way, I mean. And my aunt just got a divorce. No wedding ring so I just wondered if you were putting yourself out there?"

"Out where?"

"You know. Like . . . like dating."

Walleye. Remember the walleye, he told himself.

"I just want to look at the building," he said, suddenly aware of the contrast between that nearly lifeless sentence and Dana

Novicki's fancy dress, quirky coif, ridiculous shoes, unusual demeanor, and yeti crab tattoo. For a split second, he envied her.

As if reading his mind, she shot him a 'thumbs-up,' said, "Sure. No problem," and to his relief, she turned around and opened the door.

He considered telling her he was married, but decided against it. Bottom line, she gave him the creeps. All that purple. Maybe she was in some sort of cult.

No, mentioning Lisa wasn't a good idea. But now that unsettled feeling—along with thoughts of his soon-to-be-ex-wife—conjured up scenes from one of the Twilight Zone reruns she used to watch. Of course, in that episode the embodiment of evil was a scruffy, blank-eyed, six-year-old boy. Still, there was something about the darkening skies, the lightning and thunder in the distance, and the intense silence in the quiet little town that made him hesitate before following this tall, formally-dressed girl —with hairy pincers crawling up her arm—into the old building.

3

FOUR LITTLE SHOPS

Dana Novicki banged on the entrance door of her boy-friend's little house hollering, "Binky Everlovin' Todd, get out here." When he didn't appear she hammered with both hands, screaming, "Binky, Binky, BINKYYYY!"

Several seconds later the door flew open. "What the hell is wrong with you?"

Dana jumped up and down in place, clomped down the two porch steps, clomped back up, and threw her arms around the young man who stood before her in a t-shirt and zebra-striped pajama bottoms, with his hands on his hips and a scowl on his face.

"Every time I think you've finally grown up you pull some-thing like this. It's almost ten o'clock. I was in bed. I told you, I have to work tomorrow. EARLY!"

"Guess what!"

He put his hands up as if to stop her, and she grabbed them and tried to pull him into a dance, but he held his ground and she bobbed around him.

"You lost your shoes," he said, staring at her feet.

"NO! Now *guess*! Oh, and these are for you," she said, bending over and unlacing the black shoes.

"I don't feel like guessing."

"Binky Poop-Face Todd, you are no fun." She handed him the shoes. "They're your size. And they're still in really good shape! Look at the soles."

"Dana, I'm tired!" He took the shoes and looked them over. "I work construction. What am I gonna do with these?" He shook his head and set them down inside the door. "This better be important, because I am seriously considering breaking up with you about now."

"Frog flippers! Think how BORING your life would be without me." She smiled a big smile. "Okay. The 'what' that I was asking you to guess about is that I . . . just . . . showed—wait for it—HAVISTO'S!"

"It's Sunday night. Who looks at real estate on Sunday night?"

"He's gonna buy, I just know it." She closed her eyes, twirled on the little porch, and ended on her tiptoes. "Do you know what this means?"

"That you can pay back the three hundred bucks you owe me?"

"C'mon, Binky." She tossed her head from side to side, and stuck her lower lip out. "Aren't you excited for me. I'm going to make my first sale!"

"Babe, I could have been just as excited—NO!—actually, I would have been far more excited if you'd waited until tomorrow to tell me. I need to get some sleep."

"He's going to turn it into four little shops and he's going to call it Brent's Beauty, Barber, Bait, and Bakery."

"You're kidding."

"No. Seriously. Won't that be cute? And we really need a bait shop around here."

"Okay, Babe. I'm happy for you. Goodnight." He grabbed the doorknob.

"Don't you want to celebrate with me?"

"Yes. I do. Just as soon as you actually sell the building. You can take me out for a steak."

"Okay. That sounds like f—"

SLAM!

"C'mon, Binky. Open up. Oh, come on. At least give me a hug."

Dana stood on the doorstep for a minute. "Oh, poo. BINKY TODD, YOU ARE THE WORLD'S WORST MUCKRAK-ING BOYFRIEND!!"

She waited another minute then turned around and got back in her car, wondering how early she could go to Grace with the offer. This was going to be tricky. Stubborn old Grace Havisto would have to ease up on her terms a little. Mom would know how to handle this, she thought. I'm really gonna need to tone down the 'Dana.'

4

ELVIS ON THE COUCH

Grace Havisto typed in her bid for the professionally framed and certified-authentic Elvis Presley-autographed album cover and hit the enter key on her computer. As if by magic, Elvis's smoking rendition of "A Hunk A Hunk of Burnin' Love" filled her ears. For a split second she sat back, nodding her head to the music and then, with a start, realized where the sound came from. She gave her desk chair a shove and as it hit the wall behind her, the jolt—along with a strategic push off the armrests—gave her sufficient momentum for a graceful rise to standing position.

"Ooo, ooo, ooo, I feel my temperature rising," Grace sang with the music as she sashayed to the front door, moving to the beat. She was smiling right up until she pushed aside the curtain panels and peeked out at a triple-pierced ear bisected by a beaded braid of mottled purplish hair, and whispered, "Fiddlesticks!"

"It's me, Grace. I've got an offer."

It was Dana, the irritating realtor girl. Grace hollered through the closed door, "You need a touch-up."

"Yeah. Soon as I make a sale in this godforsaken town maybe I can afford one. C'mon, Grace. Let me in. I've got good news."

"Just wanted to make sure you are who I think you are."

"Who else around here has purple hair?"

Grace opened the door and as Dana entered she reached back and pressed the doorbell again, then wrinkled her nose. "What's that?"

Grace just gave her a look. What kind of idiot wouldn't know that was Elvis?

"Oh. Yeah. Mom told me. That's Elvis, right? How did you get your doorbell to do that?"

"It was a birthday present from my grandson. Smart kid." At least he knows who Elvis is, she thought. "Are you getting married today?" she asked.

"What?"

"Your dress. If I'm not mistaken, that's a wedding dress."

"Oh. Right. Isn't it great! I got the best deal on it because it had a purple tag. Purple is my lucky color."

"Really?" Grace said, feeling only slightly guilty about the sarcasm in her voice. "So when's the wedding?"

"No wedding. I just love beautiful, old, cheap dresses."

Grace took a brief moment to ponder how on earth a sweet, normal, poised businesswoman like Audrey Novicki could have spawned a wacko kid like Dana, then headed into her living room. "Well, c'mon in, then. You can sit over there by my sweetie."

Dana stuck out her tongue and shuddered. "What is that? It gives me the creeps."

"That's Elvis!" Wacko *and* moody, Grace thought. "Fine," she said, plopping down next to her cloth-and-plastic idol and pointing to the love seat across from her.

Dana looked around and made a face.

"Oh, for heaven's sake, sit down, Dana. There's nothin' here gonna bite you."

If Grace had known Audrey was going to let her daughter join the realty office, she would have specified that only Audrey would handle her listing. "Where is your mother again?"

"She's in Greece. But, listen. I have an offer on your building! Can you believe it?"

"You found a buyer who'll turn it back into a grocery store again, right?"

"Grace, we are so lucky to have found this man. He—"

"He married?" It was the eager look on Dana's face that got Grace to thinking that silly girl was holding back key information.

"I don't know. Are you in the market for a husband?"

"Dana, you may have some kind of realtor's license, but you're practically a child and I question your ability to judge a man's character. Married men are better businessmen. They're more responsible and more likely to make good on a land contract."

"I don't know if he's married."

"Does he wear a ring?"

"What do you care if he wears a ring or what he does with the store? You've had two offers in three years, and not even one the year before that and—"

"Land contract! Grocery store! Amen!"

"Grace, you're killing me here. I've finally come up with a buyer, but you've got to be a little flexible. The guy I'm working with likes the place. He likes the location and he's got the down payment all saved up. I don't know if he's married, but he's run his own . . . his own . . . place . . . in Green Bay for several years. Learned the trade from his dad and took over the family business, but he likes fishing at Little Pine Lake so he wants to move up here. Can't figure out why, since this town has been dying for years."

"Well, we certainly need a decent grocery store."

"This guy even wants to put in a bakery as part of the whole . . . thing."

"Hmmm . . . A real whipper-snapper, huh? Did he meet my terms?"

"He's willing to pay one hundred fifty thousand dollars with fifteen thousand down and sign a land contract at six percent interest on the remainder. Where else can you get that rate right now?"

"I made it very clear!" Grace paused to pound her fist on the end table to her right. "I want one hundred eighty thousand dollars with twenty percent down and the rest on a ten-year land contract at ten percent."

"This is the best offer you've had. I don't know if he'll go for—"

"I'll go to nine percent and that's it."

"O-M-G! Do you want to sell or not? I gotta tell you there's another party eyeing the place and they're getting a little feisty."

"Another party? Who? What's their offer?"

"It's a family of rats and the talk around here is they're look-ing into hiring a u-haul."

"Ha ha. Very funny."

"Go see for yourself. It's not a pretty picture. Wise up, Grace! You have a good offer from someone who can see beyond the cobwebs and rat turds—"

"Mice. Mice! You have a grocery store, you have mice. When my dad ran the place from 1932 to—"

"Twenty-three people have looked at that rundown building since you listed it with us eight years ago. I checked the records. Twelve of those people gave you reasonable offers which you refused. We've been forced to drop the price several times as the building deteriorates, and the last time anyone even showed interest was over six months ago. Again I ask: Do you want to sell or not? Because I am seriously considering terminating our contract."

"I'll tell your mother."

"Hah! Mother could care less."

"Your mother was the most attentive realtor I've ever worked with."

"You're right. *Was.* But now she's basking in the Greek sun-shine with some guy she met online, can you believe, who's a postmaster in Iowa. Or was. The dude wears a muckrakin' cowboy hat everywhere he goes, which my mother apparently believes is charming. She says she's in love, she may never return to Pine Lake, and I'm stuck here, playing realtor. I mean, you know, *being* a realtor."

"Well, my social security isn't quite covering everything and my savings are running low. I'll take one hundred eighty thousand, twenty percent down, and the remainder at ten . . . nine percent for ten years."

"Grace, you're, what . . . ninety years old?"

"Hmmph! I'm eighty-three. So what?"

"Why don't you just sell and be done with it? You might not even live ten years."

"Since I'm not poisoning myself with purple dye and risking infection by poking holes in my body I'll probably outlive you. You've got my terms."

"So this is your counter offer?"

"My firm terms. Grocery store. Land contract. One hundred eighty thousand, twenty percent down, nine percent interest, ten year land contract."

"Fine. I'll see what I can do."

"He probably drinks."

"Doubt it. When he rode in on his Harley with his motor-cycle gang I checked out one of his tattoos and it read 'Drink kills. Do drugs instead.'"

Grace's hand smacked her chest, and she pulled in a breath.

"I'm kidding, Grace! He's a clean cut guy. Runs his own busi-ness. Has a chunk of cash to put down, remember? Not your typical outlaw."

"I miss your mother."

"Not as much as I do. See you later, Grace. I'll let you know as soon as I hear from him."

5 |

YOU LOOK FAMILIAR

Brent heard his salon door open and checked his watch. "Be right with you, Ginger," he called out. He took one more swipe with the broom, sweeping the last of the hair into a pile. As he bent to grab the dust pan a voice yelled, "I'm not Ginger!"

At that he let the broom drop, raced to the door, and cringed at the young woman standing there in a tight, purple, off-the-shoulder dress. "What are you doing here?"

She glared at him. "Well, I'm sure not here for a haircut."

"I figured you'd call."

"I was in Green Bay, so I thought—"

"In here, quick," he said, hustling her into his office. Although he'd been alone in the salon, he couldn't keep from taking a nervous peek around to make certain no one had seen her, then closed the door. "Okay. Give me some good news."

"Boy, mister, you better chillax or you're gonna blow a gasket." She looked around, then plopped down in the chair opposite his desk, and he grimaced.

"Sorry, but I have a good reputation with a . . . a more conservative clientele. If they see you here . . . as if you were a client or . . . " Or worse, he thought, thinking her little dress looked a size too small and her makeup a size too large. "So. What did she say?"

"You might have to come up some."

"Aw, crap." He planted his hands on his hips and let out a frustrated sigh. "Who wouldn't take that offer? I'm having a hard time believing you even told her about it."

"I gave her your offer. Begged her to accept it. I actually went to her weird house to try to talk some good-old-fashioned sense into her." She groaned. "Oooh! I hate it when I sound like my mother! I gotta get out of that town. I probably want to sell even more than you want to buy."

"Did you tell her I'm ready to put a fifteen-thousand dollar check in her hands?"

"Are you deaf? Yes, I told her. Over and over and over. She's the most stubborn client I've ever had."

"Oh? And how many clients have you had?"

Her face took on a haughty look, as if insulted by the question, but he stared her down until her resolve melted and she groaned and muttered, "Okay, one! Her. But it's still the truth."

Brent checked his watch hoping Ginger would be late as usual, and looked back to see Dana scowling at him as if he'd turned green. He did a quick zipper check, but that wasn't it. "What? Why are you staring at me like that?"

"Do you have a brother or . . . or dad, or some relative in Pine Lake?"

"No. At least I don't think so. I was adopted, so I guess it's possible, but not very likely. Why?"

"I swear to God you look familiar."

He pulled his chair out, sat, planted his elbows on the desk, and rested his forehead on his palms. Maybe he should give up the salon, rent a chair, work four twelves, and spend every weekend up north. As if he could afford that and saving for retirement, too.

He looked up. "Is there anything else for sale up—"

"Shush!"

Her harsh tone and penetrating stare unnerved him, but then she popped up and leaned over the desk. As her hand shot out, finger pointed at him, he pulled back and winced.

"Sit still!" she commanded. He froze. "You are such a baby," she said as her hand flicked a few strands of hair down over his forehead. "Hmmmm." She pulled her hand back, sat again, and cocked her head.

"What's wrong?"

"There's some . . . thing-g-g-g . . . " Scowling, she stretched out the last part of the word. "What the heck is it?" she asked, looking at him one way, then another, finally skewering him with a narrow-eyed gaze.

"That's it!" she screeched, jumping out of her chair.

"You know of another place?" he squeaked. He would have been embarrassed by his mousy response, but she seemed lost in a trance, her big eyes darting across his face, and then they opened even wider. She pumped her fist and hissed, "YES!"

"Another place?" he repeated, his still-subdued voice barely above a whisper.

"No. No, no, no. But I've got a great idea. You need to talk to her. You! You, you, you. In person! Do you have a white jacket?"

"Do I have a white jacket?"

"Like a dressy thing. Sort of a blazer? But not so formal. More like a shirt. Maybe with sequins on it."

"NO!! Of course I don't have a white jacket that's . . . are you nuts? No one has a shirt like that."

The way Dana squinted and peered at him gave him the creeps. She wasn't bad looking, but she was at least twenty-five years too young and at least fifty ways too, too . . .?

"Listen! Seriously!" She narrowed her eyes and now aimed both pointer fingers in his direction. "You gotta go talk to her."

"But it's your job. I can't talk to her." He should have hired his own realtor for this. An actual professional with some experience. "Can I?"

"Oh, you most certainly can. I won't tell a soul. You go right ahead."

"I don't know. I've never heard of realtors operating this way."

"You've never dealt with crazy Grace Havisto before. But I think I'm on to something. You just play along with it."

"Okay, fine. When?"

"How about tomorrow?"

"My busy day. I'm completely booked every day this week, only free on Sunday."

"Perfect."

"Okay. I can be in your office by nine a.m. Or even earlier, if you—"

"No. Go right to the building. Noonish. Look around. Act like it's the first time you've seen the place. If I know Grace, she'll have her eye on you. Between her and her nosy friends they always know what's going on in that town. In fact, if she had already seen you, this would never work."

"What would never work?"

"Never mind. Not important. Just do what I said."

"Should I tell her I'm the guy who made the offer?"

"No. No way! Go along with whatever she says, and don't tell her we've met."

"What about the white, the white . . . whatever you called it?"

"Hmmm . . . a white jacket would help, but . . . unless it's perfect it won't do us any good. And if it's too perfect it might give her a heart attack."

"WHAT??? I don't want to scare her."

"Nah. You won't. Just don't wear anything too hunterly. No plaid flannel. Wear the hippest thing you've got."

He looked down at his clothes. A simple brown, tan, and olive green plaid shirt, a neat pair of khakis. "I'm not a dressy guy."

"Borrow something! Maybe a darker shirt. And a pair of sleek black pants. You need to look hip. You know. Cool."

"Why those clothes?"

"You want the place, right?"

"Of course."

"Then go with me on this. Just dress in the hippest, coolest, dating-type clothes you've got."

"Dating-type? Oh, come on. You said she's ninety years old."

"Eighty-three. And could you put a little something in your hair to make it shiny? Make it look darker. Kind of slick it up but let a few strands hang down on your forehead."

"You're getting creepy."

"Oh, I'm sure you think I'm already way past creepy, but trust me. If she doesn't agree to sell to you within a week, I'll . . . I'll, I'll take out all my piercings. Ethen thith one," she said, sticking her tongue out and pointing at a tiny chunk of gold perched on it.

"Is that a frog?" He winced. "Oh, god, it's a frog. What if you swallowed that thing?"

"O-M-G! If you ever decide to quit doing hair, you'd make a wonderful mother."

"And if you ever decide to . . . to . . . " Damn! He couldn't think of a clever comeback. If he didn't want that building so badly, he'd . . . well he didn't know what he'd do, but he wouldn't be sitting here seething.

"Take a deep breath, cowboy. Fact is, the seller is not all that motivated. But I am. So Sunday morning you get all duded up and make like Mr. Nosey Pants and give that building a good looking over."

"Okay. But she won't get the wrong idea, will she?"

"Just do what I said. Hang around the building and check it out. Let her see you're interested. In the building, I mean."

"What if she doesn't show?"

"Oh, she'll show. And remember not to tell her you've been working with me. Or what you're going to do with it. But if she asks, tell her it looks like it would make a nice grocery store. Those words. Exactly. Say them: It looks like it would make a nice grocery store."

"I'm not going to—"

She closed her eyes and shook her head. "I'm not letting you screw this up. Say the words."

No way was he going to say those words. He pushed his palms out and shook his head.

"Well, I'm not leaving until you say it."

"IT LOOKS LIKE IT WOULD MAKE A NICE GRO-CERY STORE!"

"Good. That was a little loud, but that way she'll be sure to hear you." She scowled. "Seems like there should be something else we could do to make sure this works. Hmmm . . ."

Brent glanced at the clock, torn between wanting to hear more and getting her out of his salon before Ginger Crosby showed up for her wash and set. Of all people to be next on the schedule. The old gossip could do a lot of damage if she saw him walk out with Dana wearing that tight little sheath and purple-ringed eyes. Especially from a closed-door session. He hopped up, opened the door, and peeked out into the waiting area. "You'd better go. I have to finish cleaning up before my next client."

"Okay. So do like I said."

He glanced out the window at the parking lot and as he turned back she shot out of her chair and let out a shriek, hollering "OH, OH, OH," and hopping up and down.

"What? WHAT? Are you okay?"

"Fine. I'm fine, fine, fine"

"Damn, kid. You scared the hell out of me."

"Sorry, but I just thought of something. You told me you were adopted, right?"

"Yeah. So what?"

"O-M-G!! This is so MUCKRAKING PERFECT!!!"

The way she shook reminded Brent of a wet dog and re-kindled his doubts. "Are you sure you can handle a real estate transaction? I mean, actually, as well as legally?"

"Of course! But listen. If at some point in the conversation you can mention that you're adopted, you are SO going to get this place. In fact, look for a way to bring it up. And, remember . . . this is TOTALLY IMPORTANT . . . if she says anything about you putting in a grocery store, don't deny it. Just say those words we rehearsed. And DON'T tell her what you're planning to do with it. Play it cool. Once you buy it, you can pretend you changed your mind."

"I don't want to do anything mean. Or sneaky."

"Not mean." She scrunched up her face. "Maybe a little sneaky but in a good way. You're going to make her day."

Just then a car bumper scraped the cement abutment outside the window and Brent shouted, "Out! NOW! If old Ginger sees you—"

"Okay, okay, I'm leaving." She headed out of the office toward the salon's entrance.

"BACK way," he warned, pointing her in the opposite direction. "Through the supply room."

She groaned and rolled her eyes but spun around and headed out the door.

ALIVE AND WELL

Dana read the headings from her online search and nearly rolled off her exercise ball. Elvis Presley's son, alive and well in the Midwest! Well, sons *plural*, according to the articles, some with his last name, one creepy character actually calling himself Elvis Jr., others bearing their supposedly adoptive families' last names. Would it be so implausible for one of them to want to escape the constant harassment and fade into some nice little community like Pine Lake?

Of course, this son-of-Elvis stuff was all conjured up by nut jobs with too much time on their hands, but still, it looked authentic enough.

She highlighted the article, pressed the copy button, and opened her email account. Before her conscience could talk her out of it, she typed a quick note explaining she'd seen the article on a website for real estate agents that talked about the growing trend of celebrities moving to small towns. Which was an actual thing. Or should be an actual thing. Whatever! She sent it off to Grace with a simple *FYI* in the subject field.

Taking a last look at the photo she realized there was one more detail that would improve the odds of success, and she scribbled two words on a notepad.

7 |

THE PERFECT BUYER

Grace ran her magnifying glass over the photo on her computer, memorizing as much detail as she could, then trotted back to her picture window and peered out at the man looking at her old grocery store. It couldn't be! But even his shirt was the same as the one in the picture.

Back at her computer she zoomed in on the face. "Oh my good gracious," she shouted and patted her chest. Should she call Evie now? And Betty? But they'd never believe her. They'd have to see for themselves. So all those years of holding out for the perfect buyer had paid off. And maybe that Dana wasn't such a light-weight after all. It was sweet of her to share the article. You just couldn't judge a person by their looks!

She raced to the front door and peeked out. Oh dear. The young man was kicking at the lower boards on the side of the old store. She might have to lower her price. There was a tad bit of rot on some of the siding. Grabbing the door knob, she remembered she hadn't brushed her hair that morning. Or her teeth.

Not to mention a little lipstick wouldn't hurt. Just because she was 83 years old didn't mean she shouldn't look her best.

She brushed her teeth, washed her face, and applied moisturizer. She pulled a tube of lipstick out of the medicine cabinet, took off the cap, braced her elbow on the mirror's frame to steady it, and applied the rosy plum color. Fiddlesticks! Was that a car taking off? She hustled back to the front of the house, relieved to see the car still parked out front. Glancing at Cloth Elvis on her way through the living room, she whispered, "Pull some strings for me, Sweetie," and headed out her front door.

8

ADOPTED?

Brent checked his watch. Where was the old lady? He'd begun to lose hope this crazy plan would work. The sleazy-looking shirt was driving him nuts. He felt silly showing so much chest and had been grabbing at his collarbone all morning trying to locate the non-existent top button.

Then he noticed an old gal racing at him, clearly a woman on a mission. He put on his best smile and greeted her. "Hello, ma'am. I was just eyeing this old building. You don't happen to know if it's still for sale, do you?"

He felt a little sheepish asking since he was less than fifty feet from the For Sale sign, so he'd thrown in the "still," but based on the cobwebs visible in the front window, he figured no one had been inside for at least a year. Several seconds passed and he feared his cheeks would cramp from over-grinning. Was she hard of hearing? He spoke up: "If it's available I might be interested."

She wobbled, then grabbed a rickety No Parking sign for support. He stepped closer, keeping a respectful distance, yet ready to lunge if the old sign—or the old gal—gave way. He tried again, practically hollering. "DO YOU HAPPEN TO KNOW WHO OWNS THIS PLACE?"

"Oh, yes. Yes. I own it."

He could have sworn he saw her eyelids flutter. Was she flirting? He stifled a grimace just in time.

"Are you interested? It's a lovely building and it's at a very good price."

"Well, I'd like to see more of it, but . . . yes . . . I'm very interested."

"Wonderful. Let me get the key. I'll be right back."

Brent nodded and waited for her to move, but she kept looking at him as if he was her long lost son. Yes. More that than flirting . . . he hoped.

"I'll go get that key then," she said, giving him another wistful look.

If she kept it up, Brent was thinking, maybe he could talk her down to one hundred fifty thousand.

Minutes later she hustled back and let him in the building, muttering about the fact that it hadn't been cleaned in awhile. Even she seemed surprised at the accumulated filth. He acted as if he was seeing it for the first time, which wasn't difficult since he noticed a few flaws he hadn't seen earlier. Not only had it been evening then, but the dim bulbs had clearly masked a lot of damage. In the bright light of day he began to wonder if one hundred fifty thousand was still too high. It would need complete rewiring, as opposed to updating. New plumbing. Walls replaced. On the other hand it was the perfect size, and maybe here in a small town he'd have a better chance to pull off his plan for a strip mall without a bunch of zoning restrictions. When her voice rose he realized she'd been talking, and he tuned back in.

"I said I'd be particularly pleased to see a grocery store here."

He nearly suggested he had other ideas, but remembered Dana's warning. Still, she seemed like a nice lady and with her living across the street, he decided to straddle the line between the truth and a flat out lie. He repeated "the phrase" in his head and then spit it out. "It-looks-like-it-would-make-a-nice-grocery-store."

A long minute passed and nothing happened. Okay, she took that well, he thought, and decided to go with the idea and expand on it.

"Is there anyone in town who could run a bakery? I mean, a nice grocery store should have a bakery." Which was the truth. He considered adding more true-sounding words, but feared he might stick his foot in his mouth, so he waited for her response.

"Now, let me think. Well, there's Mrs. Belisky. She's a whiz with baked goods. Bread, pies, doughnuts. Widowed young. She might consider it."

"Well, I'm *definitely* interested," he said, before she got caught up in plans for a bakery. "Of course the place needs a lot of work." He kicked the base of a board coated with grayish slime and his foot left a splintery dent. "I'll need to put some money into it." He noticed a crack in the ceiling that had obviously resulted in some serious water damage and waited for her to talk price. He turned his attention to a deep gouge in one of the floor boards and when he looked back, she was staring at him.

"You don't happen to be related to anyone who . . . ?"

Hmmm . . . Same question Dana had asked, although the way the old lady let the question dangle in an almost accusatory manner made him wonder if he bore a resemblance to some nefarious local bad boy.

"No relatives in the area. I like to fish and hunt, but running my own business means I don't get much time off. I figured if I lived up here, I could be on the lake or out in the woods shortly after I closed up."

"No . . . I meant . . . I was just wondering if perhaps you have a . . . well . . . if there is someone in your family who . . ."

What was she insinuating? Although the damned shirt Dana sent him *was* making him feel like a criminal. He was crazy to have let that purple-haired teeny-bopper tell him what to wear, especially since he was trying to impress this older woman, not flirt with her. He should have been wearing a suit---something that made him look more trustworthy.

When the woman stepped closer and squinted, he felt the need to defend himself. "I don't know what you're getting at, but I'm an honest person. Learned the business from my dad. Bought him out when he retired."

"You took over from your father?"

Seeing the look of utter disappointment on her face he quickly added, "My father was a good man, too."

"Oh. I'm sure he was." Her smile was back but her face radiated pity. "Do you . . . do you look like him?"

"Not really. I was adopted. I'm not sure who my real father is." There. Just as Dana had suggested.

"You're adopted?"

Oh, damn. Had that been a mistake? "But, I'm—"

"Of course. Oh, that's wonderful! That's perfect. Oh yes. All makes sense now."

She reached over and patted his arm as her smile crept up the sides of her face. Her steady grin unnerved him and he headed for the door. This lady is nuts, he decided. Probably dementia. "I should get going," he said, hoping to nudge her into action.

"So you run a grocery store now?" she asked, her voice suddenly strong, her posture perfect, her attitude all business.

He'd anticipated the question but hoped by the time she asked they'd have discussed the price. "I'm sorry. I have to . . ." He took a very obvious look at his watch, and tapped it. "I have another appointment."

Well, he did. He was headed over to Dana's office with a progress report.

"You're looking at another building?"

He nodded and grunted in a way that he hoped she'd interpret as yes. The building in question was merely the real estate office, but he would definitely be looking at it before he went into it, so it really wasn't a lie. Fortunately, the very thought of losing the sale seemed to have spurred her to action. She jerked as if she'd been goosed, and her hand shot out as if to stop him.

"But we haven't talked price," she said, taking a step closer.

"You're right. Did you have something in mind?"

He could almost see the wheels turning. He'd made it clear the place needed work, but she didn't know he already knew the price. She'd probably take advantage of his expressed interest and shoot it up to two hundred grand.

"How about one hundred sixty thousand. I'd take a land contract over ten years with some money down, but I'm sure we can work out the details."

"But that's—" Less than Dana quoted, he nearly said.

"Too much?"

Would she drop it more?

"Well . . . for you . . . I'd go to one hundred fifty . . . but I'm afraid I just can't go lower."

"One hundred fifty thousand?"

"Okay. One hundred forty thousand! But that offer is only good today. Tomorrow it will go back up to . . . to . . . the asking price. We'd have to get over to the realtor's office and make it official. My realtor is . . . well, I'm sure she's free."

He'd heard that the clothes made the man, but considering he looked like a cross between a mafia hit-man and a peacock, this was ridiculous.

She offered her hand and he took it. She put her other hand over his and patted it. He was about to snatch it back when he realized the look on her face now had a more motherly cast to it, and he had a moment of foreboding. With her living right across the street, how long would it take to realize he was not reviving the old grocery store, especially if she was as nosey as the ersatz realtor claimed?

"I'll call the realtor," she said, all business again. "Maybe you'd like to cancel your appointment?"

He raised his eyebrows and nodded, as if to suggest that was possible and followed her out of the building. As she locked up and headed back to her house, he hopped in his truck, slammed the door, and punched numbers into his cell phone. "She's about to call you. We've got a deal. She doesn't know anything. Let her tell you about it."

One hundred forty thousand! Far less than Dana had quoted. Either she had been trying to pull something over on him or the old lady realized that decrepit building wasn't such a steal after all. A shrill "YOO HOO!" caught his attention and he turned to see the old lady waving a white scarf, which seemed appropriate based on Dana's description of Grace Havisto's stubbornness. But she also had quite a set of vocal cords, and Brent could see she wasn't a pushover. He rolled down the window.

"I just reached my realtor, dear. She'll meet us at her office in fifteen minutes. It's just around the corner. Halfway down the block on the left." She pointed to the end of the street, her bright pink nail polish shining in the sunlight. "Pine Lake Realty. You can't miss it."

9

A RAT-INFESTED MUSEUM

Brent drove past Pine Lake Realty again. The "Closed" sign still hung in the door, although he'd spoken to that weird young woman just minutes earlier, and she'd told him to come right over. He circled the block once more, then eased his truck along the curb and parked, chastising himself for not contacting an actual, professional, card-carrying, non-frog-pierced realtor. As he pulled the key from the ignition he heard a banging sound. Leaning toward the passenger side window he looked out in the direction of the noise. The door to the realty office was now ajar and a hand came out and beckoned him.

He left the truck and hurried up the short walk. As he reached for the knob of the partially opened door, a hand grabbed him, yanked him inside, and slammed the door behind him.

"She thinks you're Elvis Presley's son!" Dana squealed. Her head went back, her arms went out, and she shimmied up and down, then stopped mid-shake and winked. "Illegitimate, of course."

Brent stared at her. In the semi-darkness her wide eyes and purplish hair gave her a demonic look, and the black dress with the football-pad style shoulders and bright 4-inch-wide purple belt didn't help. He instinctively took a step backwards and grabbed the door knob.

"Sheesh. You're acting totally freaked out." She flipped on the light switch. "Don't you hang out in the middle of the woods all by yourself?"

"Yes, but then I have a gun."

She shook her head. "Well, listen, tough guy, we got about two minutes to get our stories straight. Like I said, Grace thinks you're one of Elvis Presley's illegitimate sons who's hiding out in the Midwest."

"Why does she think that?"

"Because you're practically the guy's twin! Hasn't anyone ever told you that? Especially in that shirt. Nice job with the hair, by the way. C'mon."

She hustled off and Brent self-consciously ran his fingers through the few strands that had been tickling his forehead all morning. He followed her into the room that was apparently her office. Or someone's office. It was unlikely she had selected the creamy wall color, homey framed landscapes, and old-fashioned wooden desk. The chairs could have come from his grand-mother's dining room, complete with little round brown-and-yellow braided rugs on the seats. The desk was clear except for a phone, a mug of pens and pencils bearing a yellow smiley face, and a three-ring binder spread open to reveal a somewhat un-attractive photo of the building on which he was about to make an offer.

"Sit."

He positioned the little rug in the middle of the chair's seat and held it in place as he settled onto it, while she rifled through a purse the size of a suitcase, finally pulling out a laptop. "You gotta see this," she said, as she opened it and booted up.

He watched her work the computer muttering instructions to herself, periodically opening her mouth far enough for him to see the miniature gold frog lolling on her tongue. Although it was a squat little guy it looked like it would rub the roof of her mouth raw. He considered asking about it, but she turned the computer in his direction and shoved it at him.

"Here. Look at this."

"Could this be Elvis's secret son?" he read aloud, and stared at the picture. He could definitely see the resemblance, and the hair and the purple shirt—almost identical to the one in the photo— added to the illusion.

"You got it," Dana said. "One of many claiming to be. That's why Grace is finally going to sell that rat-infested museum."

He grimaced, and Dana slapped her hand over her mouth. "That's just an expression."

"An expression?!"

"Oh, for muckraking sake. It was originally listed at two hundred twenty-five thousand, so you're getting a good deal at one hundred forty. I told you this would work."

She pulled the computer back, hit a few buttons, then slammed the top down. "God, I can't believe I'm actually going to make a sale," she said as she tucked the laptop into her purse. Or suitcase. Or whatever it was.

He glanced at the photo in the three-ring binder again, re-played Dana's "rat-infested museum" comment in his head and sat back to think. Maybe the place was still over-priced. It could easily cost another hundred thousand or more to make repairs, update the utilities, and turn it into four smaller shops.

"Rat-infested museum, huh?" Brent shook his head, irritated at what this mess had become, but mostly irritated with himself for getting stuck with no way out. Since he hadn't re-upped on his lease, three months from now he would be without a place to work. He needed this darned building.

On the other hand, there would be walleye.

Dana huffed. "Hey, I'm just frustrated with old Grace. It's NOT a rat-infested museum. It needs work, and you know it, but it is everything you want in a building. That's what counts. You're not going to find anything else in this price range. You wanna spend three hundred grand, I can come up with some-thing better. Or somebody could. Well, maybe. But it's still not going to be a turnkey operation. Property taxes here will be less than just about anywhere else and everything you want to put in that building is needed here. We've been through this."

"Yeah, well people have been getting by without a bait store and a bakery. And you've got two beauty salons here already."

Dana pretended to gag, then snorted and rolled her eyes. "Myra is, like, one hundred and eight or something. Way older even than Grace and, crap! Have you ever been in her place? Her chair is an antique, the closest electrical outlet is in her kitchen, which, by the way, smells like Limburger cheese, which, further-more, by the way, is how you smell when you leave. And Mike and Michelle—they're *M and M Beauty*—they hate each other.

You don't need perm solution there. Just listening to them will curl your hair. Heck, I'll be your first customer."

He looked at her hair and scowled, thinking there's no way he'd have purple dye in his salon.

She rolled her eyes again. "I *know* what you're thinking. Sheesh, you'd better not play poker around here."

"Well, excuse me, but I was trained to respect hair, to honor it. Not beat the heck out of it with cheap dyes."

"You'd rebel, too, if you grew up here. There is NOTHING to do. In fact, the way to really make that place pay off is to open some kind of dance club."

Brent put his hand across his cheek and rubbed it. "Look. I'm stuck with this place. I no longer have a choice. My salon in Green Bay has already been rented. Besides, that old lady is going to show up any minute, so we can't act like we've had this big discussion."

"You're right. Go sit in the waiting room."

She glanced at the clock behind her, and Brent followed her eyes. Only the 12 and the 6 were on its face. The letters of Pine Lake replaced numbers seven through eleven, and the word Realty replaced the numbers from one through five: It was now about K minutes to R. But the pine cone in the middle had an oddly reassuring effect, reminding him of photos of the cabin he'd been lucky enough to rent every weekend until the end of September.

Still, this was a big step. Things weren't going to fall into place as if a fairy godmother were pulling strings. Whatever little obstacles he had to overcome, this had been his dream: to work where he could fish and hunt every minute he wasn't in the salon instead of hustling like a maniac so he could get a few precious days on the lake or in the woods.

"Out! I'll start drawing up the papers for an offer. Oh, and when you see her, say, 'Hello, ma'am,' like that. With your voice kind of low and southern. A little drawly."

"Drawly?"

"Yeah. String out the words a little, like you're a southern gentleman. And pull your upper lip a little to the right."

As stupid as that sounded, he found himself doing what she asked.

"NO. Don't sneer! Here." She dug in her wastebasket, found a crumpled piece of paper and ran her hand over it to smooth out some of the wrinkles. "Like this," she said, pointing at the Elvis lips in the photo. "Wait." She pulled a mirror out of her carpet bag/suitcase/purse and held it up for him. "Try it again. Just a little pull."

"Oh, for crying out loud." Brent grabbed the mirror from her. "This is getting ridiculous."

"No, THIS, as you so disparagingly refer to our preparation, is what got the price down to ONE HUNDRED FORTY K!!!!" she yelled. "But we still have to negotiate the down-payment and interest rate and stuff so don't forget to curl that lip."

What an irritating little snit! He imagined telling her to go fly a kite and stomping out and getting in his car and laying rubber on the way out of town.

But after a bit of negotiation and a closing in a couple of weeks, she'd be history and he'd be seven minutes from walleye, so he just walked out and took a righteous bit of satisfaction in slamming the office door behind him.

10 |

THE DEAL

Grace eased up behind Elvis's son's truck, shifted into park, cut the engine, and pulled her keys out of the ignition with a little too much vigor, causing the mini-Elvis on her key chain to fly up and wrap itself around her official (or so the packaging promised) Elvis Presley Steering Wheel Cover. She took that as a good omen and smiled as she disentangled it. Whenever the King brought attention to himself, something good happened to her. His own son!!! Running a remake of the very grocery store she used to run with her father and then her husband. That dear young man would certainly need help and advice—lots of it no doubt—and she was eager to assure him she'd be there every step of the way.

This new development in her life was just what she needed, and further proof (just look at him!) that Priscilla Presley was not the only woman to have played an intimate role in the King's life. In her heart she had always believed Elvis to be a gentleman, but how could a man like that be held to the same standards as the rest of us? It just wasn't possible. In fact she wouldn't have been surprised if he'd sired scores of children by young women throwing themselves at him. She knew what went on with celebrities and movie stars like Elvis Presley.

And now one of his sons was about to buy her building! Perhaps that young man *didn't* know who his father was, or maybe he just wanted to escape the limelight, like it said in the article Dana had sent her. Either way she'd respect his privacy and let him decide when (if ever!) to let the cat out of the bag.

As she entered the real estate office he turned to her, and she took a quick little breath. The spitting image, he was. Maybe even more handsome than his father.

"Hello, ma'am."

Oh, goodness! She could almost hear Elvis's voice.

"Hello Mr. . . . Mr. . . . dear me, I seem to have forgotten your name."

"I don't recall that I gave it to you. It's Brent Wallace."

"Brent Wallace?" The name seemed entirely too ordinary for such an extraordinary man.

"Yes, ma'am. Brent Wallace."

But . . . that curl in the lip. Oh, my. She hadn't noticed that before. There just wasn't any doubt.

"Well, it's nice to properly meet you Mr. Wallace, and I want you to know that I'll be avail—"

The office door flew open. "Grace, Mr. Wallace, come in and we'll make this official."

He stood, bowed ever so slightly, and swept his hand out, palm up, indicating she should enter first.

More proof, as if she needed it! The son was as mannerly as the father.

"Grace, dear, have a seat."

Grace couldn't help but notice the lilt in Dana's voice, and the generous smile that softened her face. Was it possible she also knew Brent's true identity? She'd never seen Dana so mannerly.

On the other hand, maybe the little sneak was up to something.

Thank goodness she was closer to the end of her life than the beginning. She'd never get used to purple hair, and it was difficult to trust someone so young and unprofessional and covered with tattoos and piercings. If she'd met her on the street in some big city, she'd be frightened to death of her. Not that she couldn't take care of herself. She'd just have to be on guard, a thought that made her wonder what the heck Dana was doing now, putting her hands on the back of the chair Grace was about to sit in. She brushed Dana's hands away and grabbed the chair back, holding it tightly as she sat.

"I understand Mr. Wallace happened upon your building this morning and it appears to be exactly what he was looking for."

"Yes! And I'm looking forward to the day I can just cross the street and—"

"I also understand you've agreed upon a price."

Grace was speechless. How dare that brash young woman interrupt her like that!

"I don't want to hold either of you up," Dana continued, appearing to purposely avoid looking at her. "Mr. Wallace said he has a busy day, so . . ."

She cleared her throat and looked down at a sheet of paper on her desk, then up at Elvis's son and rattled off a string of words as if the building were on fire. "Okay! Grace said you went to look at the building, and after a brief discussion you've agreed on a selling price of one hundred forty thousand on a land contract."

Why was Dana talking so loud and so fast? One minute she's Little Miss Business Woman and the next she sounds like she's running an auction. Goodness. Young people had no manners anymore.

Then she became aware that Brent was looking at her and she couldn't help but think of the way Elvis looked at Joan Blackman in *Blue Hawaii.* As if he was waiting for something. And then he said, "As I recall, she did agree on that amount," and she realized his voice was fairly loud as well.

"Oh. Yes." Grace reminded herself she needed to pay attention so Dana wouldn't mess up the deal.

"So. We have a mutually-agreed upon price, correct?" They both nodded. "Then we can get right to the official business and skip the offer stuff. I mean . . . presenting an offer and counteroffer. Okay?"

They nodded again. "Good. Now for the terms. Mr. Wallace has only fifteen thousand to put down. Now Grace, uh, Mrs. Havisto, you said that for a down payment you wanted twenty percent, so—"

"Fifteen thousand is fine."

Dana's jaw dropped and Grace noticed the little gold frog perched on her tongue. She had the urge to gag just imagining how that thing could tickle the back of your throat. And what if your saliva dissolved whatever was holding it in place and you swallowed it? The thought made her woozy and when she slapped her hand on the desk for support, Dana's mouth slammed shut, and she scowled. "Did you just say 'fine'?"

Grace recovered, smiled at Brent, then turned to Dana, raised her eyebrows to suggest this was a ludicrous question and in a demure voice responded: "Yes. I'll take fifteen thousand down."

Noticing Dana's obvious and very amateurish look of frustration, Grace sighed and imagined what it would have been like if Dana's mother was across from her. Audrey would have offered them coffee, chatted a bit about the weather or some other inconsequential topic, then completed the transaction amidst gracious conversation. Instead, Grace held her tongue as Dana flipped her pen-holding hand in an exaggerated arc, aimed it at the page, and repeated in crisp, clipped, snotty-sounding words as she wrote with animated strokes: "Fifteen . . . thousand . . . down."

11

HER FIRST REAL SALE

Dana hit the period at the end of the sentence and couldn't help but glance at Brent, who seemed blissfully unaware of the minor war she had previously waged on his behalf trying to get Grace to accept anything close to these terms.

Although pretending to look at the paperwork in front of her, she grew irritated thinking about how it had taken three years to get her first sale. True, she hadn't tried that hard. It was a lot more fun to tend bar at *Cap's Corner*, although since that was one of the few places that *was* fun to work at, everyone her age who hadn't left Pine Lake for college or bigger opportunities was trying to get in there. She could only get a couple shifts a week and she was barely making ends meet. Well, actually, those muckraking ends weren't meeting at all.

The more she let her mind wander, the harder it was to resist screaming to these people that she hadn't ever wanted to be a realtor. It was probably the last thing she'd wanted but she was stuck here because there wasn't ever anything else to be. She'd hated high school (BOR-ing!), which no one could understand because she'd been a mostly straight-A student . . . except for that one tousle with chemistry, and even there she'd managed a B plus which she doubted even Madame Curie could have pulled off in Radcliffe's class.

But if you're already smart and learning is easy, what's the point? Not to mention that her high school counselor made her take the MENSA test, then paid for her first year of membership. That pushy woman kept tossing college brochures her way and sending her emails on all the great jobs in law, medicine, and technology, despite the fact Dana had made it clear she had no intention of repeating the agony of the last four years by enrolling in college, only to get mired in law, medicine, or technology.

Although real estate was as boring as everything else, it had been easy enough to work under her mother's lax supervision and earn the realtor's license. Beyond tending bar, there was no other appealing form of employment anywhere on the horizon, and her mother had made a fairly decent living in the business until she met the postmaster who whisked her away to Greece.

Eventually she planned to move to a bigger city but until she had some idea of what she wanted to do with her life, it made more sense to stay in Pine Lake. She liked having her mother's house to herself, and, with only a high school diploma, the bar experience, and no other skills (despite being smarter than ninety-nine percent of the people she'd ever met), there weren't many opportunities out there. Every job she'd ever applied for demanded some college, if not a degree, and the only other local jobs open to her—cleaning, babysitting, and senior care—were definitely worse than working for her mother.

These thoughts raced through her mind as she stared at the papers, resisting the urge to tell them that since she got only a small salary for keeping the office going (although she wouldn't tell them she was living in her mother's house rent-free), this commission, although not much, would basically be hers, and they could both go suck eggs.

Except for that one little problem, she reminded herself. Well, not so little . . . but she didn't need to think about that now. No, now was all about her first real sale. What a stroke of luck that the guy looked like Elvis Pres—

"Hey! You're supposed to be conducting a real estate sale here."

She jerked to attention, realized she'd been staring at him, stifled an urge to stick her tongue out, and picked up where she'd left off.

"Okay. The terms of the land contract will be-e-e . . . " And here she paused and looked at Grace, her mouth still open from pronouncing the word 'be,' which she had already strung out into three syllables. Grace had insisted on ten years and nine percent, but now Dana didn't know what to think. The only certainty in her world was that she must get this sale. After a moment of uncomfortable silence, her excitement spilled out in a harsh demand. "Grace! How many years?"

"Mr. Wallace, would ten years work for you?"

"Certainly," he said, and Dana pinched her thigh. This was actually happening.

"Then, the percentage would be-e-e . . .?" And she looked at Grace again, leaning a tad forward, eyebrows raised, fingers crossed beneath the desk.

"I'm thinking sevv . . .ah . . ."

Grace looked at Brent, and Dana held her breath. Brent's upper torso also seemed to be moving ever so slightly in Grace's direction as if to telepathically affect her answer, and Dana wondered if there was a way to add a percent to her commission considering the huge success of the Son of Elvis ploy.

"Five percent!"

Brent glared at her. Dana lifted her shoulders and eyebrows and threw her hands up in the midst of a not-so-discreet shrug. She wanted to scream that she never would have quoted nine percent if Grace hadn't insisted.

"If that's acceptable to Mr. Wallace," Grace added.

Dana figured that by now Brent was pinching his own thigh. The decrease in the sale price had already saved him a bunch, and this reduction was going to lower his monthly payments even more. She had totally earned that extra one percent, and in truth, it was only fair considering how much she'd lost when Grace dropped the price.

"That's fine," Brent said, and Dana realized she'd been lost in thought again and snapped back to the business at hand.

"Right. I'll just fill everything in, then, with a closing date of . . .?"

"How about three weeks from Monday?" Brent suggested, and Grace nodded her approval.

"I should be able to get an attorney to draw up the land contract by then." She flipped the desk calendar to the next page. "That would be June eighth. Unless I let you both know otherwise."

Dana filled out a few more papers and several minutes later Grace shook Brent's hand. When Dana reached her own hand across the desk, she saw Grace start to pull hers back, but, obviously, she didn't want Brent to think she was an old biddy. Grace's hand landed in hers for a quick second and then she yanked free.

Fine, Dana thought. We'll be out of each others' hair forever. Well, almost. Frog flippers! She had to get that other situation taken care of. "Okay. I'll get this filed with the register of deeds and get copies to each of you," she said, shaking Brent's hand.

Grace put her hand on Brent's arm. "Like I said, I'll be there to help you every step of the way. I can't wait to buy my groceries there again."

Dana saw a frown appear on Brent's face and when he began, "Well, I—" she slammed a drawer and hollered, "NICE SWEATER, GRACE. SEE YOU LATER!"

"I'm not deaf," Grace said, glaring at Dana as she stood. Grace then turned to Brent, nodded, grinned as sweetly as an angel, repeated she'd be available to help in whatever way she could, and headed out of the room.

Dana held her breath until Grace had gone through the waiting room and she heard the bell jingle on the outside door.

12

UNOFFICIAL CONDITIONS

Dana pumped her fist. "Woo-hoo! My first sale! And it only took three years. Three long and frustrating years." She shook her head as she re-gathered the stack of papers and bounced them on the desk.

"She really thinks she'll be buying her groceries there?" Brent asked.

"Oh, she'd definitely like you to re-open Havisto's."

"But I never said I would. In fact I've made it clear to you that I'm NOT going to open a grocery store."

"Don't worry about it."

"Did you tell her I was going to open a grocery store?"

"No."

"Then where did she get that idea?"

"She's had that idea since she put it up for sale. That was one of her conditions. Well, unofficial conditions, not written in the contract since that building is more likely to be struck by lightning than bought by someone who wants to turn it into a grocery store. Gary's Groceries is just around the corner and there's no way this little town can support another one. I mean, newsflash, we've had that building listed for eight years already. That's probably some kind of record for a real estate office, one for which we will not win any prizes."

"So she's really going to be disappointed. I thought all that talk about a grocery store was just her being nostalgic."

"What she may be is dead by the time you open for business. No worries. She signed the papers and there's nothing in them about opening a grocery store."

"But, after she came down on the price and the terms, I almost feel like I owe her."

"Speaking of which—I mean the owing part—I lost quite a chunk of commission with the price drop, which was a big savings for you, not to mention the terms were far better than I thought they'd be, so . . . it might be nice of you to offer me a little something for coming up with the Son of Elvis idea. Without that, you probably still wouldn't have a deal."

"On a rat-infested museum."

"O-M-G!!! Let it go already. Slip of the tongue."

"I'll have to hire help to get the place ready to open in three months. Hell, I probably won't be able to open then. So maybe you'd consider tossing a couple thousand my way to cover the weeks I won't be getting a paycheck."

"Oh, fine. It was just a thought." She turned off the lights and shoved him out the front door. "Gotta go. See ya' in three weeks."

13 ▌

THE CABIN

Brent wound along the dirt road, turned onto Lawson Lane, and followed it to a small parking lot. He shut off the ignition, pulled a key from the glove compartment, and headed to the path marked CABINS, eager to see if the real thing lived up to the photos on the website. He hadn't been comfortable renting it sight unseen, but the reviews were good, and the owner had overnighted the key and a brochure before he'd even received Brent's deposit.

His life would soon become a blur of perms and haircuts Monday through Friday and long days of remodeling on the weekends. But with any luck, next summer he'd be living in his own cabin and spending every night amid the scent of pine and campfires.

With that thought he became aware of a strong smoky odor. He followed the path according to the directions on the brochure, the acrid smell growing more intense with every step, until he came to an opening in the trees that revealed a smoking pile of rubble. He looked at the brochure, mentally retraced his steps, and realized the cabin he intended to live in on the weekends over the next few months had burned to the ground.

"I'm still in a state of shock myself," the owner said when Brent reached him by phone. Then he explained how his eighteen-year-old son, unbeknownst to him, had hosted a post-prom party at the cabin. Someone had thrown fireworks into the burning fireplace, and minutes later the whole thing went up in flames. "Your cancelled check's in the mail," he added, sounding genuinely sorry he couldn't offer any other options, explaining that his other three cabins were booked through summer.

Brent ended the call, wondering what the hell he was going to do. There were no other cabin rentals available, and the only motel that had any openings charged an exorbitant rate which he couldn't afford and wouldn't pay on principle. Besides, it advertised itself as a "lovers getaway with romantically-themed rooms" and he'd be darned if the first impression he'd present to Pine Lake would be the vision of Brent Wallace in a room with wall-to-wall mirrors or sitting in a heart-shaped hot tub. With no time to waste, he called Dana.

"Well, there's kind of a sleazy motel north of town."

"Yeah. I already scratched that off my list."

"I can't think of anything else. Hey, why don't you ask Grace?"

"What does she own?"

"Her house."

"So?"

"Well, for Elvis's son she might consider renting a room."

"You're kidding."

"Me kid you? I was just thinking that since she knocked down the price on her building, maybe she'd like to make a little money on the side."

"You think so?"

"Of course not! Sheesh. Does she look like a lady who'd try to make a little money on the side?"

"You're the one who suggested it."

"Not because she needs the money! It's because SHE THINKS YOU'RE ELVIS'S MUCKRAKING SON! Or have you forgotten how we got you such a great deal on that building?"

"No need to scream. She really thinks that?"

"You don't catch on very fast, do you?"

"Well, you, you . . . "

Damn. Why couldn't he ever think of even one clever retort? Just let it go, he told himself. After next week you'll never see her again. In the meantime, he'd take the high road. "Okay. There's probably a faint resemblance, but that bit about me being Elvis Presley's illegitimate son is ridiculous."

"I know that. You know that. Why not let old Grace have her fantasy? Give her a thrill?"

"Your choice of words is not helping."

"Well quit taking everything I say the wrong way. Hey, you called me for help, and I'm trying to help you. Help, which, by the way, I am not even charging you for although with all I've done for you, you really owe me."

"All you've done for me? I made a good, solid offer with reasonable terms. You insisted you presented it, and yet I ended up with a better price, a lower interest rate, and less money down, than what you quoted me. I can't believe you even gave her my offer."

"Are you nuts? Of course I gave her your offer. Surely you picked up on my desire to off-load this piece of . . . of . . ."

"Well, how did I end up with a such a good deal?"

"BECAUSE YOU LOOK LIKE ELVIS!"

With that he heard a loud CRACK, like a phone hitting a wall.

Maybe she was right. Still, living in the house of the woman from whom he'd just purchased a building that he had no intention of developing into the business she'd expressly requested it become, seemed like a bad move.

On the other hand, he sure needed a place to stay.

14

WELCOME TO GRACELAND

Brent rang the doorbell and tried to pull the edges of his collar closer together. The deep "V" of the shirt's front was bad enough, but the fact that it was purple made it even sleazier, albeit more memorable. Once he was certain she recognized him, that shirt was history.

A minute passed and he pressed the buzzer again. Hearing musical notes through the door, he figured she must be hearing it inside. Maybe she wasn't home. Maybe he should have made his request over the phone, but since he hadn't even seen her house, it seemed like a good idea to look it over before asking if he could rent a bedroom there. Unlikely she was one of those crazy hoarders whose houses are filled to the brim with old furniture and piles of newspapers and memorabilia, but he'd seen enough horror stories on television to be wary. Besides, if he was going to spend his weekends there, he intended to come clean on how he'd be using the old grocery store, and that was definitely an in-person conversation.

Seconds later the front door opened and an energetic rendition of Elvis's, "A Hunk A Hunk of Burnin' Love," charged his eardrums. The old lady must be hard of hearing. Considering her supposed love of Elvis, the musical greeting made sense; he just wasn't prepared for that decibel level.

"Well, hello, dear. What a pleasant surprise."

"Brent Wallace," he said. "I'm—"

"Oh, yes! I remember your face but forgot the name. Come in. No need to stand in the doorway."

He followed her through an archway into the living room and froze. As far as his eye could see, some version of Elvis, or things connected to Elvis—in the form of photos, statues, posters, prints, replicas, and souvenirs—covered every surface, vertical and horizontal.

"Welcome to Graceland," the old lady said.

Speechless, his eyes traveled from one Elvis to the next, again recalling episodes of the Twilight Zone he'd watched a few years ago with his wife.

"Get it? GRACE-land?" she said with a wink. "Why don't you have a seat. Can I get you a cup of coffee?"

"That sounds . . . good." He caught himself before he said 'normal.' "Black, please."

"You can sit over there by my sweetie. I just made a fresh pot so I'll be right back. How about a couple of cookies? Not home-made. I can't tolerate the sugar like I used to but I keep them around for my grandson. He still visits once in awhile. In fact he's the one who set up my doorbell. Clever boy. Come, come." She motioned to him. "Sit anywhere you'd like."

Brent nodded and looked around. He could sit next to Elvis, under Elvis, or on Elvis in a rocker where it looked like the fabric on the seat had been replaced by an embroidered likeness of the man. He chose the Elvis-afghan-covered love seat and started to sit, but moved over one cushion so as not to be staring into what now appeared to be a judgmental pair of eyes set in a pasty, flesh-toned plastic face, which sat atop a cloth body dressed in a white suit dotted with blue and red sequins. So *that's* what Dana meant.

He smoothed the Elvis afghan he'd wrinkled and looked up at the poster-sized black-and-white photo of Elvis in a leather jacket sitting on a motorcycle. At the bottom of the print a tiny plaque-style banner read: *A Gift from Graceland.*

Graceland! Was it possible her parents had actually named her Grace? What were the chances?

Looking around again, he wondered if he'd be able to stand being in the house for even a few minutes. The thought of possibly climbing into bed with Elvis on top of him really creeped him out. Elvis on his pillowcase? The walls? How had her husband put up with this much stuff? Photos of the man everywhere, a huge metal Elvis trash can holding umbrellas at the door, Elvis doilies, clothing, framed album covers?

It wasn't just the eerie presence of the man on every surface that was unnerving, but also the question of what kind of person would choose it. He hadn't spent much time around Grace. Maybe she *was* crazy. And if she thought he looked that much like Elvis, would she find some way to keep him here? Forever? A la the Twilight Zone?

He leaned forward, ready to stand up and sneak out when Grace returned with a tray holding two Elvis Presley mugs, featuring Elvis Presley's mug, below which just a hint of purple shirt showed. He shuddered and clutched the lapel of his shirt, deciding to ditch it that very afternoon.

"So nice of you to visit. Have you begun work on the store yet?"

Stalling, he focused on the tray she'd set on the coffee table, which featured Elvis wearing a lei, and the words Blue Hawaii spelled out in blue letters. The tray also held a small plate of macaroons partially concealing Elvis strumming a guitar.

"The store?" He eased back onto the love seat as he took the cup of what he now feared might be Elvis-flavored coffee from her slightly shaky hands. He sipped and smiled, relieved to find it refreshingly bland and ordinary. "Well, maybe we should talk about that."

Grace had already set her mug on the Elvis coaster on the end table between the miniature guitar and the miniature pink Cadillac, no doubt a replica of one owned by Elvis. Pink? As Brent wondered if that was where Bruce Springsteen got those lyrics, he saw Grace lean forward on the loveseat, clap her hands together, and leap into verbal action.

"How silly of me. Of course you can't get started until we close, but I'm so excited. It will be wonderful to walk across the street and pick up my groceries again. My dear husband, Harvey, and I ran that store together for nearly thirty-five years."

"That long?" Brent said, thinking this meeting could not have gotten off to a worse start.

"Oh, yes. I don't suppose that little girl told you any of this."

"Little girl?"

"Dana. The realtor's daughter. I thought any interested party would like to know the history of the building but whenever I suggested the idea Dana turned and walked away. Harv and I loved that store. We had wonderful customers. They came from all the little towns around here because we carried such a nice variety and our prices were reasonable."

"It sounds very—"

"Now you have all these big, impersonal supermarkets and it's like walking into a warehouse. I get tired just stepping in the door. I get my groceries in Burnham north of here."

"Isn't there a grocery store near the realty office around the corner?"

"Hah! Gary's Groceries. I wouldn't feed their goods to my dog. Not that I have a dog. And his mother, Ethel? Well, we used to be good friends, but about ten years after Harv and I took over the store from Dad, she bought that little building, turned it into a grocery store, and priced everything below cost, trying to run us out of business so her son would have a job. No one else would hire him and he was running the streets like a hooligan."

She picked up her mug, took a sip of coffee, swallowed, and started in again before Brent could frame his next sentence.

"Had this truck with wheels taller than me and he'd race it down Main Street and Broadway and South Street, all the windows rolled down, and the noise from the so-called music blaring so loud you couldn't hear yourself think. Not to mention that he took off the muffler. Well, maybe it fell off. A kid like that, running wild, terrorizing the neighborhood! One day he got so drunk he smashed into a UPS truck. Fortunately the driver was out of the truck and making a delivery at the time so no one was hurt. Then she made him the store manager!"

"The UPS driver?"

"No. Gary! You can be sure I'll never put one foot inside that grocery store."

Here was his opening, and he jumped right in. "When I was first looking at real estate around here I stopped in and didn't think it was so bad. Produce looked pretty good. He has one heck of a meat department, and the prices didn't seem exorbitant."

"I'll have you know they practically doubled since we closed Havisto's."

"But prices do go up over time," Brent said, testing the waters. He didn't necessarily want to stick up for Gary and irritate Grace, but where she saw a competitor, Brent saw a solution.

"Lots of kids are a little crazy when they're young, but they grow out of it. Besides, there are inspections, permits, laws and codes. If it doesn't meet certain standards, they'll shut it down. Maybe you should stop in some time and check it out. It's within walking distance for you."

"Never," she said, pounding her fist on the end table, causing the miniature pink Cadillac to shoot forward and ram the miniature guitar. "You'd have to kill me first. Besides, when you open up I won't need to. Just make sure to keep your produce well-stocked and tidy. Customers will walk away from a whole display of grapes if they see a spoiled one."

"Well, I'm not sure how well another grocery sto—"

"I suppose that coming from the city you'll do things differently but I'll be glad to help you any way I can. I could still handle a checkout. Not all day, but a four or five hour shift would suit me fine."

"Mrs. Havisto, the thing is—"

"Oh, there's the phone. If you'll excuse me, I'm waiting for a call from my friend Betty. I won't be a minute."

"I can leave and come ba—"

"You sit right there, young man. No need to rush off. I'll just let her know I have a visitor and I'll be back in a jiffy. Have a cookie!"

"Maybe another time would be—"

But Grace raced off, watched over every step of the way by Elvises of every age and size, in cars, boats, buses, and on beaches, stages, and movie magazines. He thought about leaving, but had the eerie feeling one of the Elvises would tell on him, or maybe another song would break out and alert her as he opened the front door. He hadn't more than a minute or so to think about it when Grace came racing back into the room.

"I'd love to have you, dear. And if you could just help me with a few small chores, like installing the air conditioner, why you could stay here for nothing. Maybe a few dollars for meals, but the room would be free."

"I'm not sure what—"

"Now don't be shy. That irritating little realtor girl just called and explained all about it. It's settled. I keep two guest rooms ready for my daughter and grandson, so it's no problem at all. Do you have your things with you?"

"No, Mrs. Havi—"

"Grace, dear. It's Grace. My goodness, Elvis, if we can't—"

"It's Brent! Please!"

"Oh, I'm sorry." She swatted the air with her left hand, blushing ever so slightly. "I know your name, but you . . . well, you look like him. I may forget once in awhile. Brent, Brent, Brent. There. That should keep me straight. This way, Brent."

Despite his many misgivings, he followed her up the stairs, both impressed at her stamina and disconcerted by the modestly framed photos that climbed the wall in uphill fashion. He'd seen this type of thing before, where the kids were babies on the first step and by the time you reached the top you saw the current model, maybe sporting a mortarboard or in wedding attire. But here, Brent's eyes followed baby Elvis, kid Elvis, teen Elvis, teen-idol Elvis, white-clad Elvis, and heavy Elvis until he got to the top of the stairs where he came to an abrupt stop and stared at the man's head at rest on a silvery pillow in his casket. The photo looked like a black and white that had been retouched with color in a last-ditch effort to revive the guy.

Grace had moved a few steps into the hallway, then turned and looked back, cocking her head to one side. "Ah. Such a shame," she said. "He left us too soon." Then she resumed the tour, beckoning him with an impatient wave of her right hand, and Brent noted she was no more breathless than he was. She led him down an Elvis-flanked hallway (more photos, posters, magazine covers, etc.) to a door on the right, and as she opened it, light seemed to explode from inside. He held his breath, (could Elvis be lying in state, his embalming fluid giving off a bright glow?) but stepped into a south-facing room where bright sunshine forced a sea of PINK to bounce off the walls. Neon pink. As if he'd fallen into a bottle of that weirdly pink medicine. But where was Elvis?

"I would put you in my grandson's room, but there was a little leak in the roof and it's torn up right now. I know the color in this room is intense—it didn't seem that bright in the store—but on sunny days it's a bit overwhelming."

Yes, he thought, on sunny days you could be temporarily blinded.

"But at night," Grace continued, a tinge of apology in her voice, "you can't tell what color it is, and the bed has a nice, comfortable mattress. This is Jenny's room. My daughter. She put the kibosh on Elvis. I respected that. She always liked the color pink. Well, not this color, as I found out, but I didn't think it was worth redoing after all that work. One of these days I'll get around to changing it."

It even smelled pink. It reminded him of the awful strawberry-scented gum one of his rare young clients favored. Then he noticed the odor seemed to be emanating from several pink candles adorning the dresser.

"Well, it is fairly bright," Brent began, "although I suppose at night, as you said, it wouldn't be noticeable. But it seems to have a strong odor."

"It's been closed up because Jenny hasn't stayed here lately. She's dog-sitting for one of her neighbors who's in Europe for couple of months. I'll get the windows open and . . . well, any little changes you'd like to make, go right ahead."

He was thinking that if he could stay here for a few weeks it would give him time to find another place. Only Friday and Saturday nights. Free with a few chores. A matter of yards from where he'd be working. And since Elvis wasn't allowed in here, he could probably handle it.

"Thank you. It will be fine, as long as you're sure it won't be a problem."

"I'd welcome the company. You stay as long as you like. I think they'll be finished with the work in Jeremy's room by the end of the month. Then you can move into that one if you prefer. He doesn't stay overnight much anymore. Maybe at Christmas."

"Oh, I'm sure I'll find something else soon. This is only temporary."

"Do you mind if I get a little nosy?"

He shrugged.

"I just wondered why a handsome young man like yourself never married?"

"I did marry, but she wasn't the right one for me. My life is pretty much split between work and hunting and fishing. Lisa was more interested in socializing. I had a hard time keeping up with her, and it got to the point where I didn't even want to try anymore."

"Lisa?" She smacked her chest. "Her name was Lisa? Oh my goodness!"

He waited for her to explain her surprise, but she seemed dumbstruck so he continued his explanation, trying to put his marriage and himself in as non-threatening a light as possible. "Yes. A very nice woman, but a little too high maintenance. She recently got engaged to a good friend of mine."

"I'm sorry to hear that."

"It's okay. I'm actually happy she found someone. No hard feelings. We're still friends."

"Good. I don't understand why there are so many divorces these days, but I know it happens. Jenny's marriage lasted just long enough for her to get pregnant, but Jeremy is a good kid. Never gave her a day's worry and he's been the best grandson I could ask for."

"Would you mind if I put those candles in the closet. The smell is . . . it's pretty strong."

"Of course not. In fact, I'll put them in the basement."

"I don't want you going to any trouble for me."

"No trouble at all."

"There is one other thing we need to talk about."

"Tut, tut. Not a penny. I won't take a penny. You can pay . . . let's say twenty dollars for the weekend meals, and give me a hand once in awhile. I always wait for Jeremy to put my air conditioner in, and sometimes he doesn't have a chance until summer's practically over."

"I'd be glad to do that, Grace. That sounds more than fair, but what I was going to talk to you about was—"

"Oh, there's the phone again. I bet it's that roofer. He said he could finish in an afternoon, but he's cancelled twice on me already. He's supposed to call today."

She hustled down the steps ahead of him and he intended to follow but caught himself stopping at the top and staring at dead Elvis. Is that what he'd look like in his own coffin someday? Would it be unsettling to live in a shrine to someone who looked so much like him?

But the price was right, the pink wouldn't show at night, and maybe he could find a way to break the news about his plans for Havisto's Grocery a bit at a time. Ease into it.

He started down the steps, then stopped for a closer look at white-clad Elvis, wondering if there was a way to use his lookalike status to break the news to Grace. He'd had honorable intentions, but it seemed like every time he got up enough courage to say something, she took over the conversation or the phone rang. Just as well. Breaking it to her gently made more sense.

This way he could do odd jobs for her here and there over the next few weeks, so she could see he was responsible and respectful and a pretty good guy in his own right. A guy who could turn a dilapidated old building into an attractive addition to South Street, even if it wasn't what she'd had in mind. How could Grace not see the wisdom in that?

He took one last look at teen-idol Elvis, and followed the sound of Grace's voice into the living room.

"So, that was the roofer. Some problem with his truck. Who knows when he'll get here? But Frank—that's Betty's husband —he recommended him and said he isn't the type to take advantage, so you'll just have to stay in that pink room awhile longer."

"Well, I appreciate that you're willing to put me up for a few weeks."

"Weeks, months, whatever. It's fine with me. Now, let's see. I know you'll get keys from Dana, but I'll go get mine. Last thing you want is to be locked out of your own store, so I had plenty made. Gave one to my daughter, and Betty, and—"

The litany of names continued as she disappeared around a corner, and Brent realized half the people in town must have keys. Once he started actually remodeling, he'd change the locks, but until then, it probably didn't matter.

Soon she returned, her outstretched hand revealing three marked keys. "Now, this is for the shed at the back of the parking lot. If you want to bring up some tools and such you can store them there. The darker one is for the store. And this one, with the pink string tied on it, is for the house."

"Thanks. Maybe I'll drive up Friday night with a load."

"And bring your overnight bag so you can start settling in."

"I'll try not to be a bother."

"You'll be no trouble at all."

"One more thing. This will be messy work. Is there a spot in your basement where I could change?"

"Certainly. In fact, there's a shower down there. And Harv used to store his hunting clothes in an old dresser. You're welcome to use that."

"Good idea. Remodeling is messy work, so I'll try to keep the worst of it in the basement. I'll see you next Friday night, probably around eight o'clock or so, if that's not too late."

"I stay up and watch the news so that will be just fine."

As Brent left, he felt the burden of time lighten knowing he could get started next weekend. He had to quit worrying so much. Everything would fall into place just fine.

15

THE SURPRISE

Grace charged through Evelyn's front door without knocking and was barreling toward the kitchen when she tripped over little Shep. The dog yelped, and Grace jerked and lost her balance. She grabbed at one of the dining room chairs, tipped it over, and went down with it. Seconds later Evelyn and Betty rushed in, Betty brandishing a yellow-coated bread knife.

"I'm okay!" Grace yelled, as Evelyn picked up and consoled little Shep who had backed himself into a corner, whining and trembling. "Easy with the knife, Betty, it's only me," Grace said as she pushed up on all fours.

"Was someone chasing you?" Evelyn asked, looking toward the front door. Shep licked her face.

"No. But you'll never guess what happened today." She stood, uprighted the chair, straightened her blouse, and rubbed her right elbow.

"Are you alright?" Evelyn approached her and Shep growled as if to point out the perp.

"A little shaken, but otherwise okay." She reached out and swiped her finger across the knife and stuck it in her mouth. "Lemon meringue pie?"

"I told you I made one yesterday," Evelyn said, as Betty flipped the knife over and swiped the other side herself.

"Well in all the excitement, I forgot."

"Grace, you'd better watch your blood pressure," Evelyn said. "Ever since you got a buyer for that building you've been riled up. What excitement?"

"Well, ladies, I didn't want to spoil the surprise but . . ."

Something about that "but" caused her to realize she had nearly wasted a perfectly good opportunity.

"Never mind," she said.

"What?!" her friends screamed in unison.

"You'll find out soon enough."

"Bet you got more than you expected for the building!"

"Yes. That's it. I got a whole lot more than I bargained for."

"I told you," Evelyn said to Betty, then resumed her interrogation. "You've been acting like you just won the lottery. How much more?"

"I can't talk about it. Not now. Besides, it's part of the surprise."

"What do you mean?" Betty asked. "You have a bit of lemon filling on your lip."

Grace licked her lips. "That's delicious Evelyn. Every bit as good as Mrs. Belisky's. I'm ready for a piece."

"First give us a hint about the surprise," Evelyn said.

"Okay."

Evelyn and Betty leaned their heads toward her.

"Well, it's . . . " Grace searched her brain for something to say.

"Well, what?" Evelyn barked, startling Shep who let out a frightened little squeak.

"It's that . . . I'm inviting you for breakfast next Saturday morning."

"That's not much of a surprise." Evelyn said. She put Shep down and followed the other two ladies into the kitchen.

"Wait 'til you see what I'm serving before you say that."

16

A CLEAR CONSCIENCE

Brent looked up from his computer and groaned. Mavis was now fifteen minutes late for her haircut, his last appointment of the day. The truck was packed and he was eager to head north. He answered another email, shut down his computer, and was about to turn off the lights when the bells hanging over the door announced Mavis's arrival.

"Sorry I'm a bit late. My daughter forgot I had an appointment."

She gingerly made her way through the salon, taking baby steps, rocking side to side, and setting each foot down cautiously as if the floor were littered with land mines. After six complication-free years with an artificial hip, she still feared that, "one of these days it's gonna crumble like a stale muffin, and I'm gonna end up on the ground."

He thought about grabbing a scissors and snipping on the way, figuring he could complete half a haircut by the time she made it to the chair. He even considered picking her up and carrying her, but fortunately he'd resisted because when she revealed that in addition to a cut she'd also like a color—"A nice, rich, reddish blonde"—he surely would have dropped her.

He peeked at his watch, realizing a dye job would add considerably more time to his already twenty-minute-late exit. He suggested—not only because of the hour, but also because "a nice, rich, reddish blonde" was a horrid idea—that with her mature complexion a softer shade would be more attractive.

"This is a big decision, Mavis. Why don't you think about it, and I'll do the color at your next appointment."

Either she didn't hear him or chose not to. Time slowed as she settled in her chair, brought her purse to her lap, unzipped one of the compartments, and removed a wrinkled, palm-sized piece of paper, which she then painstakingly began to unfold. Brent stole a glance at the wall clock. Since this was his first night at Grace's house, he wanted to arrive as early as possible. His anxiety crept higher until finally a full magazine photo was laid out on Mavis's lap.

She placed her palm in the center of the page and pressed out in every direction until the creases were less noticeable, and the blood vessels in Brent's forehead began to throb. Still looking for a way to avert the 'rich reddish blonde' disaster, his hand floated toward the mirror. He was about to suggest she take a good look, but caught himself. Alerting her to reality via her reflection wouldn't help. Thirty years from now he might not see himself clearly either, and here was a sweet old lady who still had some spunk and wanted to express it.

On the other hand, he owed it to his clients to talk them out of making terrible mistakes.

As he stared at the magazine photo he considered pointing out that they were looking at a barely-out-of-her-teens starlet whose long, lovely, reddish-blond tresses had likely been manually attached, glossed to a deep shine, then professionally primped for an hour. Not to mention that the hair in question framed a dewy complexion, huge, heavily made-up eyes, and deep red lips. Did Mavis realize that the longest strands of her thinning hair were shorter than her pinky?

Remembering his own dear grandmother and how he hoped hairdressers (and everyone else!) had treated her, he held his tongue while Mavis tapped optimistically at the various waves and curls.

"Maybe I could let my hair grow out a bit?" she offered.

He was tempted to gently suggest that two very different realities were at play here and they were hanging out at opposite ends of the spectrum. Were, in fact, just barely hanging on to each end of the spectrum. But realizing an argument would consume more precious minutes, he grabbed a color chart and suggested the subdued 8B, but she went all out for the incendiary 7R.

He did his best, even cutting the coloring time short. Despite his efforts the resulting fiery-red highlighted the bags under her eyes and make her ashen complexion look even more pallid, but she was delighted and left with a more sprightly, albeit still guarded, step. The minute she was safely in her daughter's car, he shut off the lights, closed, and locked the door.

At seven-thirty-eight, nearly a full hour and half later than planned but with a clear conscience, he headed out to his Ford F-150.

17

THE WINK

It was after nine-thirty when Brent drove into Pine Lake, so rather than unloading his tools and supplies and storing them in the shed behind Havisto's, he decided to wait until morning. He parked in the glow of the street lamp in front of Grace's house where the bright light would likely deter a potential thief.

Although he had the key to her back door, he wondered if coming in that way might frighten her, especially since he hadn't had the presence of mind to let her know he'd be so late. Wondering if she'd already gone to bed since the front of the house was dark, he hesitated to ring the doorbell but decided that was better than peering into windows like a peeping Tom.

Grace appeared in a matter of seconds. As Brent walked into the foyer, discreetly noting that Elvis' temperature was— once again—rising, he wondered if Grace had many visitors. It wouldn't take him long to tire of this song, especially since, rather than picking up where he left off, each time the doorbell rang Elvis apparently sang the same few bars over and over at an ear-piercing volume.

"Sorry to bother you so late, but it took longer to pack than I thought," he said by way of apology.

"No problem. I've just been watching a movie. *Blue Hawaii.* That's the one where Elvis sings, *'I can't help falling in love with you,'* to Joan Blackman.

Grace had sung the words, upper body swaying, her face taking on a dreamy look. Just as Brent was about to back out, never to return, she stopped. "That was our song. Harv's and mine. No matter what they say, you really don't get over losing your one true love."

Relief flooded over him. Of course she wasn't singing to him. He blushed at the thought, then recovered with a smile, not sure what to say.

"You're welcome to watch the movie with me if you'd like. Or maybe you're hungry? I can fix a little snack."

"No, thank you. I stopped for a bite on the way. If it's okay with you I'd like to get settled so I can get an early start tomorrow."

"Certainly. Would you like me to wake you around six-thirty or so?"

"I'll just set the alarm on my cellphone."

"In case that doesn't work, if you're not up by say . . . seven a.m. . . . should I wake you?"

"I'll be fine. I'm always awake by seven," he assured her.

"They do say the early bird gets the worm. See you tomorrow then. Goodnight."

And just before she turned to walk away, she winked.

Why would she wink? And why would that wink be so unsettling? It wasn't really a flirting sort of wink, but more of an I've-got-something-up-my-sleeve wink.

He headed upstairs, reminding himself that Grace was the one who should be concerned, considering she was giving the keys to her house to a total stranger and allowing him to spend the night.

After unpacking and getting ready for bed, he climbed in under the blankets and pulled the flowery pink comforter up to his chin. The feather pillow was just the heft he liked, the mattress was comfortable, and the room was a touch cool, perfect for sleeping. But every time he was about to nod off, Grace's wink appeared in his mind's eye.

He eventually dozed off but awoke several times as the wink resurfaced in his dreams until he convinced himself that Grace was as harmless and sweet as Grandma Newsome. She obviously still loved her husband, Harv, and had no interest in him beyond the man who was going to re-open the old grocery store. Of course, he really had to straighten *that* out.

Wink.

THE WELCOME COMMITTEE

Grace frosted her homemade tart-cherry and cream-cheese-stuffed kringle, then prepared a bowl of pineapple chunks, orange sections, and kiwi quarters. She coaxed a pan of perfectly set eggs onto an Elvis-crooning-at-the-microphone platter, cozied the bacon alongside, and put the dish in the oven to keep warm. She scanned the kitchen: counter clean, floor swept, glass surfaces sparkling, coffee brewing. A cardinal sang out, and she decided to open the kitchen window a crack, welcoming the cheerful sounds of an early summer morning.

As she set the pitcher of orange juice on the table, "A Hunk a Hunk of Burnin' Love" burst through the house. Grace looked at the Elvis clock over the sink and headed to the front door. Evelyn and Betty had argued that a seven o'clock breakfast was unheard of, especially on Saturday morning when they liked to check out the local garage sales, but Grace held her ground. "It will be worth it!" she had insisted, and Evelyn said that would be possible only if Grace were serving Fountain of Youth smoothies.

"You'll see," Grace had said, her eyebrows jumping up and down. "Now, be here a few minutes early. No later than ten to seven."

Grace listened at the base of the steps and heard water running in the sink on the second floor, so Elvis likely hadn't heard the doorbell.

She opened the front door and was pleased to see both women nicely dressed. Evelyn had even put on a bit of blush. Well, a lot of blush. She looked as if she had just run a mile in the sun. Or maybe like she had a fever. Regardless, she had clearly taken pains with her outfit, a striped-red-and-white shirtwaist, very flattering to her still slim figure. Betty, muttering about some people's lack of consideration, was wearing a summery blouse of navy dots on white, a pair of navy slacks, and a grumpy face. Grace couldn't wait to turn that look around!

"Right on time," Grace said, hustling them into the kitchen. "Betty you sit by the refrigerator and, Evelyn, you can sit next to her. Good."

Grace had arranged the table and seating so that both ladies had a perfect view of the kitchen doorway, and as soon as she heard footsteps on the stairs, she intended to situate herself for a perfect view of their faces.

"Four place settings? Is Jenny here?" Evie asked.

Grace shook her head, enjoying the intrigue.

"Jeremy?"

"No, my grandson is doing some kind of training in Chicago."

"Well, for goodness' sake, Grace, you dragged us out of bed at this ridiculous hour on our garage-sale morning and you have an extra place set. The least you can do is warn us who's coming.

It's not that new lady we saw at the church picnic last week, is it? That one with the low-cut dress? My goodness, she's near as old as we are. She had no business being in that dress and at a church picnic, no less."

"D'you mean Martha Plimsey?" Betty poured a good half cup of cream into her coffee and Grace grabbed the carton from the refrigerator to refill the little pitcher.

"No. That other lady. She's new in town. You know who I mean. She was flirting with Pastor's father." Evelyn had leaned forward in her chair and was scowling her impatience at Betty's inability to read her mind.

"Pastor didn't look so good, did he?" Betty took a sip of coffee and set the cup back on the saucer. "You know he took a tumble down the church steps just two days—"

"I smell bacon!"

Evelyn and Betty fell to a hush and their eyes opened wide, as Evelyn grabbed Grace's arm. "Did you have a man over last night?" Betty's hand went to her mouth, and Grace broke into a big, self-satisfied grin.

All three faced the kitchen door, and when Brent appeared Evelyn whispered, "He's so young."

Brent came to a dead stop. "I'm sorry. I didn't know you had company. I'll just leave—"

Grace's arms flew up. "No, dear, you haven't had breakfast. It's all ready. Besides, this is for you. We're your welcome committee."

She held her breath as Brent's gaze slipped from her face to Evelyn's, to Betty's, to the kringle on the counter, to the many Elvises staring at the ceiling from all the plates. He took a step backwards. "I was just going to grab a cup of coffee and maybe a piece of toast, Grace. I didn't mean for you to go to all this trouble."

"No trouble, and if you're going to put in a long day's work, you need your nourishment. Now, you just sit down, and I'll get you a cup of coffee and set the food on the table." She turned to her friends and announced, "Ladies, I'd like you to meet the new owner of Havisto's Groceries, Elv—I mean Brent Wallace."

"My goodness! Is . . . is . . . he . . .?" Evelyn asked. "The resemblance is uncanny!"

Of course, after meeting Brent, Grace had forwarded Dana's son-of-Elvis-living-in-the-Midwest email message to Evelyn and Betty. As fans went, they weren't as dedicated as she was. But they both liked his music, although Evelyn always stipulated it was his hymns she enjoyed the most, despite the fact that her CD collection included his *Golden Records* album which had plenty of rock'n'roll tunes on it. Grace later regretted passing on Dana's email. She didn't want them to figure out why she'd sent it until she was able to choose the method of introduction that would garner the most excitement, but clearly they had been surprised at the guest of honor's entrance.

For his part, Brent still appeared uncertain as to whether or not he should join them. Seconds later Betty jumped up as if awakening from a trance. She pulled out the chair next to hers and patted it. "You sit right here, sweetie."

Grace, feeling particularly pleased at creating such a commotion, suddenly remembered her manners. "Brent, these are my very good friends, Evelyn Tarwood and Betty Gagnon."

"A pleasure to meet you, ladies. I apologize for my work clothes. I wasn't expecting breakfast."

Grace felt like she'd just won the lottery. The morning was turning out even better than she'd hoped. She popped two slices of Mrs. Belisky's homemade bread in the toaster and set the fruit salad on the table. "Help yourselves to some fruit and I'll have the rest of breakfast on in a minute."

"My goodness," Evelyn said. Grace watched her glance at the Elvis plates then back to Brent several times. "He's the spitting image," she said, looking up at Grace in awe as if she had been responsible for Brent's looks.

Betty patted the chair again and said, "Now don't be shy, Mr. Wallace. We won't bite." But judging by the look on Betty's face, Grace got the feeling she would have given him a good chomp just to make sure he was real.

While the toaster did its number on the bread, Evelyn and Betty grilled Brent. Grace would have reminded them of their manners but she was curious, too. They asked several questions about where he lived, what the store he owned now was like, and why he was moving, but his answers were frustratingly brief.

Probably just shyness, Grace thought. And what a lovely trait it was in someone who could have developed quite an ego because of his looks, although he seemed most comfortable talking about hunting and fishing. In fact, he seemed to go on quite a bit about that and even returned to the topic each time they asked about his plans. Grace made a mental note to give him a bit of advice on the importance of making a good first impression. It was fine to take advantage of the area's recreational opportunities, but if he hoped to establish a loyal customer base he'd need to keep the store open until at least seven in the evening, handle the stocking, straightening and cleaning after it was closed, and do a little public relations work every chance he got. This morning, he'd just missed out on a good opportunity.

When the toast popped up, Grace applied a generous amount of butter, cut the slices into triangles, and set them on a salad plate in the middle of the table. She pulled the bacon and eggs from the oven, set them on Elvis hot pads, and stood back to survey the feast. "Oh. Almost forgot," she said, and with that she picked up the kringle, took a quick second to admire her handiwork, and placed it directly in front of Brent.

"Thank you," Brent said, nearly an hour later as he drained his coffee cup and pushed back from the table. "I surely didn't expect such a spread. I'm afraid I ate too much to unload my truck."

Grace beamed. "Nonsense, dear. I'm just so happy our store will be back in business. I'll do whatever I can to help. What time would you like lunch?"

"Oh, this will be more than enough to last me the day. No need to go to the trouble."

"Goodness—it's no trouble. It's nice to have somebody to do for again. And if you need anything else today, you just come on back. The door will be open. If I'm not here, you help yourself. When you're in town, this is your house."

"Thank you. You're very kind. Ladies, it was nice meeting you."

"Oh, the pleasure is all ours," Evelyn said, and she and Betty stood and shook hands with him. Betty seemed unable to let go, and Grace noticed that Brent had to finally give a little tug to get his hand back.

While she had been a bit sorry to have embarrassed him with the fuss, it had been worth it. Grace loved Evelyn, but the woman had enough grandchildren to form an army and wasn't shy about keeping her and Betty up to date on everything from new teeth to soccer trophies. Betty's son was an attorney and her daughter an architect, so Betty and her husband, Frank, always seemed to have something to brag about. Grace figured with Brent living at her house, she was solidly in the race, and she would never forget the look on her friends' faces when he had stepped into the room. To her way of thinking that alone was worth a year of breakfasts. Not that she'd mind the work. Life had been way too dull, but suddenly things were looking up.

Elvis's son! Right in her own kitchen!

19

THE TRUTH-DEMANDING LIGHT OF DAY

Brent headed east on South Street, turned into the former grocery store's parking lot, drove through, and pulled in across from the back door. He turned off the engine and let out a deep breath. So Grace really thought he was one of Elvis Presley's sons. Which explained the wink. And why she'd been so adamant about getting him up by seven o'clock.

Should he have told her he had no intention of reviving the old grocery store in front of her friends? Should he have said he was fairly certain he was no relation to Elvis Presley? Should he have made Grace promise there would be no more fancy Saturday morning breakfasts? Or Sunday or Monday morning breakfasts either, for that matter? Even if she loved doing it, he was taking unfair advantage of her mistaken impression of his parentage.

He'd already grown fond of her; she could have been one of his regulars. He hadn't planned to end up with such a focused clientele, but he'd learned a lot from the older women who'd become his friends through the years. They were generally calmer and more likely to find their smiles after having to wait several minutes past their scheduled appointment while he satisfied a particularly fussy customer. And they knew a lot about life. And they laughed more. And they didn't make passes at him. Well, rarely.

Grace and her friends were perfect examples, and he was fairly certain he could count on having each of them and any of their friends for customers, but under the circumstances, he couldn't help but wonder at what price.

He pulled down the visor and took a good look at himself in the mirror, moving his head up and down and side to side so he could see his whole face. Since he really didn't know who his father was, it was possible—in the same way it was possible to be struck by lightning—that he was Elvis's son. Grace was clearly enjoying the possibility, and that in itself wouldn't cause any harm. He should let her retain bragging rights, since that's clearly what that gourmet breakfast was about. As long as it had been a one-time thing. He couldn't afford to while away an hour every morning he was in Pine Lake just to be polite. Maybe he'd have to get started earlier. Surely she wouldn't drag her friends over for breakfast at *six* a.m.

He turned to grab his hard hat off the back seat and accidentally hit the horn, causing him to jerk and knock the hat to the floor. When he reached back for it, his hand landed on the box of papers dealing with his plans. He picked it up and brought it to his lap, paging through the little pile. So far they were just a series of rough sketches dividing the building into four separate businesses, each with its own entrance.

The bait shop would sit on the southwest corner facing South Street with the barbershop behind it. The beauty salon would be on the northeast corner, with the bakery in front where the plate glass windows were now. He would have to put extra insulation between the two areas and some kind of exhaust fan to mitigate the problem of perm odors wafting through the bakery.

The parking lot east of the building was still in good shape with plenty of space for the four shops. He grabbed a pencil and was about to jot down some notes when a sudden loud rapping to his left startled him, and he whipped around to face the assailant.

It was Grace, her hand inches from the window, apparently ready to rap again if need be, her forehead wrinkled with concern. Similar looks etched the faces of her friends, who stood a few feet behind her.

"Is everything okay?" she shouted.

Brent rolled down his window.

"We heard the horn beep and thought you might have had some trouble." This from the one in the dress. Evelyn? Or Betty? He was normally very good at remembering names and faces, but in his surprise at breakfast he hadn't been focused.

"Betty thought we'd best check since you're new in town."

"I'm fine. I hit the horn accidentally when I was reaching into the back seat."

"Alright then. We just wanted to make sure."

"Thank you."

"You're welcome."

Betty and Evelyn, or Evelyn and Betty, had moved out from behind Grace and now all three were standing in a row outside the truck smiling at him as he smiled back. He hesitated to leave the truck, fearing that action would be interpreted as an invitation to continue their visit, so he busied himself with a tour of his glove compartment.

"Have a good day, then," one of them said. He turned back and smiled again, this time needing more force to keep his lips in position.

"You, too. Thank you again for breakfast, Grace. I'll see you later." He waited a few seconds, thinking it had been rude to go for the glove compartment. It was probably even ruder not to tell this dear, sweet, concerned, generous lady his intentions for the old store.

"Be careful, now. Do you have a cellphone in case you have some kind of accident?" Evelyn said. Or was that Betty? Whichever one was in the dress.

"Yes. If I happen to have an accident, I can reach 911."

"And you have my phone number," Grace said, her face taking on a very serious aspect, as if he were about to traipse off into dangerous, wild-animal-infested territory in the dark of night, rather than enter an empty building in the piercing, truth-demanding light of day.

"Would you like mine, too?" the one in the navy slacks said. "In case Grace isn't home? I live just two blocks down and I have a very reliable car."

"Betty! That car must be 20 years old."

Oh, good. That one's Betty. Betty with the bonnet hair. It was more rounded than Evelyn's so that would help him remember.

"Yes, it's old but Frank keeps it in very good condition," she said to Evelyn, clearly peeved that the woman would disparage her car. Then she turned to him: "Frank is my husband. He was a teacher, but his hobby is fixing up old cars, so he learned how to repair engines. It's very reliable, so should you ever need to be taken to the hospital or anything. I mean, the ambulance isn't that close, and since I'm just down the street, I could certainly—"

"Thank you, ladies. I appreciate your concern, but I'm sure I'll be fine." He put his hands on the wheel and turned his head for a quick look behind him, then faced the them again. "I need to move the truck closer to the shed for unloading. I don't want to run over you, so I'll see you later."

At that Grace put out her arms and backed the ladies up toward the wall of the shed just east of the door. He drove forward and to the right, then made as if to back up directly to the door which any fool could see would merely give him the benefit of about three feet less to walk, but the ladies stood their ground, baby-stepping ever closer to the wall until they were up against it.

"You're doing okay," Grace hollered. "You've got maybe another foot." She began waving him closer, and he gritted his teeth and backed up until he felt a thud as the rear bumper hit the door, then a crack as the trailer hitch punched a hole in it.

"GOOD!" Grace hollered.

20

BORING!

Brent sat in Dana's office, the check for fifteen thousand dollars in his hand, heart thumping in his chest, turmoil swirling in his stomach. An uncomfortable silence filled the room, disturbed only by Grace's nose-blowing. She had the sniffles and periodically pulled a tissue from a pocket in her sweater, wiped and apologized, insisting it was "Allergies . . . nothing contagious," then re-pocketed the tissue.

They'd been sitting there nearly ten minutes watching various looks of confusion cross Dana's face, although these were quickly followed by raised-eyebrow-ahas of understanding as she read through the papers in front of her.

Around the fifteen-minute point, Brent asked if there was a problem.

"Nope," Dana said, not even looking up.

"Well, I thought we were here to sign papers."

"Right-o."

"So why aren't we signing papers?"

"Just hold your horses, bucko."

Grace huffed in disgust. "Young lady, you are so disrespectful."

Dana looked up and eyed first her, then Brent, as if she just realized they were sitting there. "Sorry, but I have to read through all this and make sure we're doing everything right."

"You mean this is the first time you're looking at those papers?" Brent asked.

"NO! I started to read them last night, but they are so boring."

Grace turned to Brent and rolled her eyes.

"Do you really know what you're doing?" he asked.

"Of course. I said they were boring, not that I don't understand them. Sheesh. This is my first sale, you know."

"You're supposed to have all this done before you meet with us," Brent said.

"Didn't you hear me a minute ago?"

"Oh, right. Boring!" Brent shook his head and looked over at Grace, whose folded arms and clenched jaw suggested the tremendous restraint it was taking not to jump over the desk and beat Dana silly. He felt sorry for Grace but also didn't want her to have a stroke or something. He looked back at Dana, who was now running her finger across one of the pages. If Grace did have a stroke, would Dana even notice?

"Grace and I are going out to get a cup of coffee. We'll be back in . . ." Brent pushed his sleeve up to consult his watch, ". . . in half an hour."

"I don't think it will take that long to fin—"

"Well that's when we'll be back!" He shot the words out in a raised voice, then hesitated, searching his angry brain for a "bucko" type word to throw back at her, but all he could come up with was "babe," and that was definitely not representative of his feelings at the moment. Several epithets came to mind but were vetoed by Grace's presence, so he kept his mouth shut. "Buy you a cup of coffee, Grace?"

"Hmmmph!" Grace looked ready to spit, but she stood, turned, and stomped out of the realty office ahead of him.

Half an hour later when they returned, Dana's laptop was out, but she closed it as they walked in. Brent waited for her to make a smart remark about how long she'd been waiting, but Dana just smiled and said, "I'm ready," as if she hadn't just wasted nearly an hour of their time.

Brent had been rehearsing a few choice words as they walked back from the coffee shop. Based on her silence, Grace must have been doing the same. But minutes from now he'd be through with Dana. Finally! Once she got her hands on the commission from this sale, she would likely get as far from Pine Lake as she could, so he was eager to end this deal and be done with her.

Ten minutes later Grace picked up her check, stood, and told Dana that the next time she saw her mother, that woman was going to get an earful.

"We all do what we gotta do," Dana said, stuffing papers into her big whatever-it-was, and Grace stomped out again.

"You weren't very nice to her," Brent said, wondering how Dana would manage to get through life with that attitude.

"Well, now I have a headache."

"Weren't you taught to respect your elders?"

"Why are you still here?"

Brent searched in vain for a biting remark, but tried to put some sting in his response. "I assumed you'd come with me to get the lockbox and give me the keys."

Dang it, he thought. She deserved to be put in her place, but clearly he wasn't the guy to do it. Later he'd probably come up with all kinds of smart remarks, but now he just stewed, feeling somewhat emasculated by his inability to produce an appropriate put-down. Not to mention that her lack of professionalism made him wonder if he should hire his own attorney to verify that this transaction was legal.

21

GOOD RIDDANCE

Brent drove to the back of the building, parked, and looked out at his "dream come true." Instead of excitement, he felt like he'd just lost the biggest poker game of his life to a card shark who'd taken his money and run.

Did that tattooed, pierced, tongue-frog-toting child fill out the correct forms in the proper manner? Did he bear some of the blame for being in such a hurry? He was a pretty fair weekend carpenter and felt he'd accurately assessed the building, but now Dana's "rat-infested museum" comment came back to him. Was that the moment he should have backed out?

Dana appeared, screeching to a stop next to him in the parking lot. Stepping out of the car, she looked like a wild high school kid on the verge of gang membership based on the weird tattoos on her neck and arms. All of which (with the exception of the yeti crab), according to her, were positive symbols concerning peace and love and good fortune, but they could have been satanic verses for all he knew.

He met her at the door where she was removing the realty's key box. "You know, eventually she's going to realize I'm not re-opening her grocery store."

"Not your problem."

"She's also going to figure out I'm not Elvis's son."

"But you're adopted!"

"So?"

"Maybe you are his son. Do you know who your real dad is?"

"No."

"So you could be Elvis Jr."

"Not likely."

"Not impossible."

"Fine. But I am NOT turning this building into a grocery store."

"You don't have to."

"Well it really seems like she's counting on it."

"And I suppose life has never disappointed you," she snorted, dropping the keys into his outstretched palm.

Brent nearly told her to go to hell but restrained himself in consideration of the fact that this last glib remark from Dana would be the last glib remark he'd ever hear from her. But he couldn't resist one more jab, so he shook his head as if to chastise her for a lack of compassion. Her response—which was pretty much what he expected—was to roll her eyes, do an about-face, and wave her hand wildly in the air as she walked away.

Good riddance to you, too, he thought, pulling a small pad of paper and a pencil out of his pocket. He headed to the front of the store to revisit his plan for remodeling the entrance. Approaching the plate glass window, he reached up to rub his hand over the letters of Havisto's Market emblazoned near the top in a semi-circle, wondering how to remove them. As he pulled his hand away, he glanced out the window and realized he could see Grace's front porch, where she just happened to be sitting.

He jerked back, then carefully leaned forward and peered out again to see if she was looking at him. Her head was down. Reading? Napping? Suddenly she looked in his direction, and he jumped back.

Damn! Didn't he have enough on his mind without worrying about Grace's feelings? Not that he owed her anything. He'd paid her asking price. This was his place to do with as he wanted, and he didn't need her permission. Although moving forward would have been a lot easier if she'd been a mean and cranky old lady instead of a sweet and generous woman who reminded him of his own grandmother.

He forced his attention back to the arc of letters, wondering if he should consult a glass specialist. Maybe someone at a hardware store would know how to remove them. And maybe he should just confess his plans to Grace and be done with it so at least he could stumble through the next few months in peace.

On the other hand, there was nothing in either the purchase agreement or the land contract that limited or stipulated how the building would be used. Besides, he'd be so busy he wouldn't have time to worry about Grace's feelings.

But what if she was out there every day watching every move he made? Maybe he should march right over, tell her his plans, and be done with it. But what if she cried?

No, he should just let it be for now. He'd have plenty of time to set her straight, and it might be better to put a few days or weeks between the sale and the confession. He also had to quit thinking about explaining his plans as a confession. Surely she must be relieved that she no longer had to worry about the old building. Once she had a chance to celebrate the sale and enjoy the down payment she'd likely be more open to his plans.

Reposition walls, he wrote on his notepad. He glanced at the floor. Remembering he'd brought a large push broom, he went out to the shed to get it.

After picking several spots at random and sweeping away the layers of dust, dirt, and rodent droppings, he realized most of the wood floors were in pretty good shape, needing only a sanding. Although he'd have to put tile or linoleum in the beauty salon and barbershop. They'd be at the back of the building so he could keep the wood flooring across the entire front half for the bait shop and bakery.

This would work. One step at a time he would make his dream come true.

22 |

A LITTLE SELF PEP TALK

Brent walked back to the northwest quadrant of the building, stopping every few feet to make note of something. Coming upon a set of swinging double doors, he was about to raise his hands to push through them when they came at him, revealing a figure silhouetted in dim light, and he stumbled backwards.

"Sorry, dear. I noticed you were here and thought it might be helpful if I gave you a tour of the place. Show you how we had our store set up."

So she *had* seen him.

"Not that I expect you'll do everything the way Harv and I did it. I'm sure you'll have wonderful ideas of your own."

Tell her now. Tell her now, you idiot. END THIS!

"Let's start at the front."

She took off, and he followed her, working up his courage, until she stopped.

"Grace, I need to clarify some—"

"Oh, you'll need to change this right away. Unless you still want the name Havisto's."

She scowled at the etched letters in the plate glass window, then brought her left arm across her belly and rested her right elbow on it and massaged her cheek with her right hand. What on earth was she thinking? That he might actually leave the name?

"I think we had those letters etched right in the glass, not just printed on it. I can't recall. Either way, I imagine they could be rubbed out somehow. Hmmm . . . This brings back such memories. A store like this helps you get to know everyone in the community. In a way I envy you, just starting out. So much to look forward to."

He let out a sigh and she turned to him. "I know, dear. There's a lot of work ahead, but you're young and ambitious, and—" She slapped her hip. "Ohhh! There's my new phone. I just got it. I keep accidentally putting it on vibrate."

She pulled the phone from her pocket, slid her finger across the front and rolled out a lilting, "Hello-o-o. Grace here."

He couldn't do it. He couldn't tell her. Not now. Later. He'd let her show him how she and her husband had set the place up, let her reminisce. But over time, as it became clear to her what was actually happening, he'd tell her he thought she'd *hoped* it would become a grocery store, not that she was *counting* on it, and when she started to argue he'd—

"That was Evelyn. She's invited us over for pie."

"Us?"

"I told her where I was."

"Grace, I really need to get started—"

"Oh, not this minute. I told her we'd be over in half an hour or so."

"But I don't—"

"Don't worry. She doesn't expect you to bring a thing. Just your handsome young face. You know we old ladies are harmless, but as Jimmy Carter said, it's okay to enjoy looking. Or something like that. Now, where were we? Oh. The letters. There must be a way to change them. Then the checkout aisles. With computers the way they are now . . ."

The tour continued, Grace surging ahead, sharing memories with every step, offering explanations that were hardly necessary. It was pretty obvious how Havisto's Market had been laid out. They covered the entire store then pushed back through the double doors to a large room where three walls and part of the fourth were lined with shelves from floor to ceiling. Along the wall on the right was an old walk-in freezer, the door lying on the floor in front of it.

"We had to do that. Rules. Although it does open from the inside, so I don't know that we *really* had to do it. Betty hounded me until I had the door taken off, but I think the laws actually applies to refrigerators and such left out on the curb."

They left through a doorway next to the freezer, passed the exit doors that opened to the parking lot, then entered a door beyond to what had been the employee break room. An ancient chipped and yellowed porcelain sink with a built-in drain rack abutted an equally ancient counter, its surface marked by water rings, knife gouges, and peeling laminate. Brent felt his mood slip again. In the middle of the room stood a rickety table and several mismatched chairs, none of which, for safety's sake, he'd venture to sit on.

As if reading his thoughts, Grace chimed in. "You know we had six employees at one time, before Gary's Gross opened. That's what I call it, because it was terrible what they—oh, there's my phone again. 'Hello-o-o. Grace here.'"

She put her hand over the phone and whispered, "It's Evelyn." She took her hand away and nodded a couple of times. "Well, thanks for the warning. Okay, sweetie. See you soon."

Grace checked her watch. "Still have twenty minutes. She said Betty would have felt left out if she didn't invite her, so she just wanted to let us know she'll be joining us."

Brent had no intention of 'joining them.' Not the way he was feeling now. In its current state the building was downright depressing, the detritus of its past life scattered here and there like rotting carrion. If he'd been trying to sell the building he'd have cleaned it up a little. Taken that old sink out. Donated that old table and chairs. On second thought, who'd want them? No, this was a job for a bonfire. Even the wood shelving in the store room had seen better, certainly drier, days. Although some of that might at least be salvageable.

Grace pushed open a narrow door in the northeast corner of the break room which led to a small bathroom housing a sink, toilet, and shelving lined with rusting cans, miscellaneous containers, and the shredded remains of a roll or two of toilet paper.

"Oh, this will need to be cleaned up a bit."

He nearly responded with "a LOT!" but caught himself. After all, she was trying to be helpful.

She moved to another door on the east wall, which opened into what had obviously been the office. That room had a second door on the south side leading into the body of the store. The doors—all scarred with cracks and marked with divots—would need replacing. He couldn't help but notice Grace had grown quiet. Was that a look of disgust on her face? Maybe she was finally losing the rose-colored glasses. He'd have to keep that in mind when he broke the news about his plans. Play on her sympathy a little. Maybe tell her that after he realized how much work needed to be done, he'd decided to come up with something different. Clearly his own rose-colored glasses had been deeply hued to hide the filth and deterioration that now met him at every turn.

On the other hand, he thought—as Grace suddenly came to life again and rambled on about how wonderful it was to run a business in such a nice little town—where else could he find a deal like this? It might take awhile, but eventually he'd close at five o'clock and be fishing minutes later. There *was* a lot of work to be done, but he'd known that from the start, and this way he wouldn't be tempted to cut corners by salvaging questionable material. But the bones were solid, the roof still in good condition, the load-bearing walls all sturdy and intact. In just a few short months, this place would be bright and cheery, inviting and successful, and he'd never have to put away his hunting and fishing gear again.

After his little self-pep-talk he felt better and decided to complete the tour later on his own. With Grace there it was difficult to make notes, and her constant comments seemed to re-affirm her notion that this would soon be a grocery store. "Grace, I appreciate the tour, but I need to get to a hardware store and lumber yard and price a few things so I can get started."

"You're still coming to Evelyn's, right?"

He intended to say no, but recalled how disappointed Grandma Newsome had been when he couldn't make Sunday dinner at her house. "Alright, but I can't stay very long."

"We understand. But remember! You need to stop and smell the roses. Or the lemon meringue pie, as it were. Evelyn's specialty. I'd be happy to drive you over."

"I thought she lived just down the street."

"Yes. She's at 410 South St. I planned to run a few errands afterwards and thought you might like to come with me. I can show you around town, and—"

"Thanks, Grace, but I can walk." He checked his watch. "I'll meet you there in a few minutes."

23 |

ENERGY AND ENTHUSIASM

Back in the room that had been the grocery's office, Brent read several old notes tacked to cork boards advising of incoming shipments, damaged goods, a note about an upcoming birthday. He thought it strange that they'd still be there, as if someone didn't have the heart to remove them. An old beige metal desk took up a corner of the room, rust marring several surfaces and several shallow dents along one side.

He pulled out the wooden, slatted-back chair in front of it, noting it had no rolling wheels, no comfort-providing armrests. He scooted the chair back a few inches so he could pull the top middle drawer open. Amid the dustballs and pencil shavings, he found pens and pencils sporting the names of suppliers and service companies, an ancient Tootsie Roll, some wrapped mints, paper clips, rubber bands, and two Lincoln pennies.

Next he opened the two drawers on the right, the bottom one for files, the top one holding a yellowed pad of paper, business-sized envelopes, and three 34-cent postage stamps. The top left drawer was empty, but the one beneath it held a large metal box. He tried to pull it out, but it was wedged in from side to side and wouldn't budge, although there were about two inches of space between the front of the box and the drawer. After fighting with it for several seconds, he pulled out the entire drawer and set it on the desk. Examining it closer he discovered a hasp on the far end secured by a keyed padlock.

He checked all the drawers again, feeling around the edges in case a key had been taped there, but found nothing, nor was there anything above each of the doors in the room except thick layers of grime. He supposed it was possible Grace had a key, although surely she'd have taken the box if it had anything of value. But why was it locked? It wasn't easy to shake the whole drawer, but he slid it back and forth on the desk and heard something move inside.

He made a mental note to bring bolt cutters from home, then replaced the drawer, and wandered through the rest of the building. He'd probably underestimated the amount of time and money it would take to make his dream come true, but he'd made the commitment. He couldn't back out now. Instead he imagined the renovation completed, customers and clients passing through, and Grace touring the finished product with a huge smile on her face.

People at home had laughed when he told them his uncle's idea. It had spawned some clever slogans, like: *Whether you're in the market for nightcrawlers or French Crullers, get 'em at Brent's Beauty, Barber, Bait, and Bakery*. No body had taken the idea seriously, but here he was!

As excited as Grace had apparently been to take over from her father years ago, he was that excited to create his own version of success. He couldn't let himself be discouraged. This was his dream and he'd make it come true.

Maybe that's how he'd have to break the news to Grace: not with excuses and apologies, but with energy and enthusiasm. He imagined explaining his vision to her and suddenly he could have sworn he heard her voice. "Mr. WALL-ace!" he heard again, and realized she had returned.

"I'm in the office, Grace."

Seconds later she walked in. "Hello, again. I couldn't recall if I gave you Evelyn's address."

"410 South, right?"

"Oh. Then I did. Well, you said you'd meet me there, and when you didn't show up, I assumed I had forgotten to give you the address."

"No, I just got distracted. Say, do you happen to have a key for this old box?"

Grace looked at it. "Oh, no. That's where Dad kept the money. Harv and I used banks. If you're ready, dear, as long as I'm here, I'll give you a ride."

A GOOD IDEA

Brent opened the passenger side door, glanced in, and froze. "Wow," he said, taken aback at how Elvis had invaded the little car. "You really must be one of his biggest fans. I can't believe they make all this stuff." He brushed his hands over the Elvis Presley seat cover to smooth out some of the wrinkles.

"It's not a perfect fit. I had to do a few alterations."

"Looks like you had better luck with the floor mats. Sorry to step on you, old boy," he said as his left foot landed on Elvis's head, making a crinkly sound. As he brought his other foot in, he heard the noise again. "Aren't they kind of slippery with the plastic still on them?"

"My daughter made me take it off the driver's side, but I figured it was safe to leave it on the other mats. Keeps him clean."

"Wow! A steering wheel cover, too."

She dangled the Elvis key chain in front of him. "Harv gave this one to me. He thought I'd be a better driver if I was chauffeuring Elvis around. Ooo! Ironic, huh?"

Brent just nodded, wondering how anyone could justify spending hundreds—or maybe even thousands—of dollars on tacky Elvis merchandise. "You must have been collecting for a long time," he said. It was the most neutral comment he could come up with.

"I didn't have most of this stuff when Harv was alive. But after he passed I didn't think it would hurt anybody. It gave me something else to focus on. Seatbelt," Grace said, putting the key in the ignition.

As they walked into Evelyn's kitchen, Brent caught a whiff of the lemon meringue pie before his eyes spotted it in the middle of the table. He'd have to set down some serious rules or he'd put on the pounds quickly around these ladies.

"Welcome to my home," Evelyn said, with a big smile. "Betty, Frank, they're here."

Brent looked in the direction of the voices as Betty and a younger man walked in the room.

"Elvis," Grace began, then covered her mouth with her hand, mumbled "oops" and continued, "I mean Brent, this is Betty's husband, Frank."

"Husband?"

Betty laughed. "You aren't the first to wonder how this old broad landed such a handsome young man."

He blushed but was relieved to hear he wasn't the only one who noticed the age difference.

Frank held out his hand. "Yes, I was trapped by a cougar. That was long before anyone used that word. I'm actually older than I look, and about thirty years ago Betty caught my eye and the rest is history. She'd been turning down marriage proposals for years, so I figured I was the lucky one when she said yes to me."

This comment led to a closer look at Betty, and Brent could see why Frank had fallen for her. Still, he figured she was at least ten years older than Frank, who was staring at her with obvious adoration.

"Okay, let's have some tasty pie and juicy conversation." Evelyn said, grabbing a knife from a drawer. She cut into the pie, put the first piece on a plate, and handed it to Brent.

"So you're the one who bought Havisto's," Frank said, placing his napkin on his lap.

"And if I remember correctly, you were a teacher." Brent thanked his brain for delivering that bit of information as a way to change the subject before it got uncomfortable. "What did you teach?"

"Shop. More recently known as Industrial Arts. I put in my time and retired at fifty-five. It was okay, but retirement is a lot more fun. Mostly."

Brent nodded and kept the conversation going. "I seem to recall Betty mentioning you like working on old cars."

"Well, this is not juicy conversation," Evelyn piped in, with an impish grin.

"Sounds like it might be to your guest," Frank said, eyebrows raised in mock disagreement.

Evelyn laughed and turned to Betty. "Did you ever find that pair of shoes you bought?"

Betty shook her head and began an explanation clearly aimed at the other two ladies, so Frank turned back to Brent.

"I'm re-doing a '64 Ford Mustang. You're welcome to stop by and take a look sometime. Lotta work but I like it. You into old cars?"

"No, I like fishing. Walleye especially. Hunting, too, in the fall. That's why I wanted to relocate." Not wanting to bring the focus back to himself, he quickly added, "Know any good fishing spots around here?"

"Well, I'm not an expert, but I'll get you Jim Bermeister's number. He's the top fisherman in this area. Knows all the good places, best times to go, best bait . . . all that stuff."

"Friend of yours?" Brent figured if he could keep the conversation moving for another couple of minutes, he could chow down, thank Evelyn for the pie, and get out before any more potentially awkward questions came his way.

"More of an acquaintance. I used to manage a bait shop north of here during the summer, and that's when I got to know Jim. My dad and uncles were serious fishermen, so I grew up with it but once I turned sixteen I bought my first car. Old as the hills, but I learned to keep her running. After that I lost interest in fishing, but I knew enough about it to run the bait shop. It was a good summer job for a teacher. The owner liked me because I never asked for time off to go fishing."

"Bait shop, huh? I haven't noticed any around here. Except for the stuff they sell at that little gas station north of town."

"Yeah. Tourists go there. Nobody else. His stuff is pretty poor quality. Usually old and I've noticed the temperature in his tanks is either too warm or too cold."

"Is the bait shop you worked at still open?"

"Sam's still got the store, but his health isn't so good. It's just something for him to do when he feels up to it. He has a couple of high school kids working for him, but it's not the same."

"So where should I buy my bait?"

"West of here there's a little town, Burnham. About 15 miles or so out on Highway V. Burnham Bait is about the best you'll do. Somebody should open a bait shop around here!"

"That sounds like a good idea," Brent said, pulling the napkin off his lap and setting it next to his plate. "Well, I've got work to do. It was nice meeting you, Frank."

"You, too. Welcome to the neighborhood."

"Ladies," Brent said, pushing his chair back and standing. "I need to get going."

"So soon?" Evelyn asked.

"Right now, the only time I have to work is on weekends, so I need to stick with it. But thank you for the pie, Evelyn. It was delicious."

"You're welcome. I'm happy you could join us. I'll show you to the door."

"And I can give you a ride back," Grace said.

"It's an easy walk. I'll be fine. Evelyn, you just sit and enjoy your visitors. I can find my way out."

25 |

GUILTY

Dana had decided she'd tell Binky her situation that night. He'd reassure her it was okay, and they'd be fine. Maybe he'd even offer to loan her some money.

They had heated up a frozen pizza and watched a noisy, bang-up, car-crashing kind of movie. It was even stupider than she had expected, but she had let him choose so as to start the evening on a positive note. When the movie finally ended, she flicked off the remote and dove in before she lost her courage.

"Binky, you know I've been trying to budget my money, but there have been a lot of expenses lately. I had to buy that dress for Sammy's wedding and the shoes to go with it. And I hate to admit it, but you were probably right about the coat."

She really didn't think that. She loved the coat, a vintage wool in deep purple, flared at the waist, with covered buttons down the sleeve. In her size! She'd never seen another one like it. Even though it cost more than it should have (she really had to quit searching Etsy's vintage clothing) it totally rocked. And she *had* compensated by picking up a silky lavender shirtwaist on eBay for only twenty bucks. But she wasn't going to tell him all that. At least not now.

"But the coat looked so cute with—"

She stopped, realizing what that funny little noise in the background was. "Hey!" She kicked Binky in the shin, then reached over and turned on the light on the end table.

He came to with a start. "What?" He blinked and rubbed his eyes.

"You're snoring, is what. How long have you been asleep? Did you even see the end of the movie?"

"Yeah, I saw it. I couldn't believe they let that guy go after all that. I just fell asleep a second ago."

"So what have I been saying?"

He let out a huge sigh. "I'm sorry!"

"You never listen to me."

"In my defense, I've just put in six twelve-hour shifts, it's been hotter than hell, and I don't have air conditioning in my house. So give me a break. You're the one who was so excited about me getting this job."

"Yeah, because I thought you got three-day weekends, so maybe we could have some fun once in awhile."

"It's construction. Three-day weekends only happen in winter."

"Fine." She folded her arms and pouted as convincingly as she could. She had been practicing in the mirror putting her lip out just enough to make it clear she was unhappy without looking ridiculous. After a fair amount of time she discovered that by emphasizing the slight downward turn at the outer lips, she had nailed it.

"Okay." He'd been slumped in the corner of the couch, but now he sat up and yawned. "What were you saying?"

"Never mind."

"Dana, you're acting like a baby. And quit with the lip. I'm listening."

"Well, you know I sold that old building. The one that used to be a grocery store."

"You mean the *only* building you were trying to sell."

"Don't be sarcastic. I'm trying to get more listings, but every time I start talking to a potential client, they want to know about my sales record and all kinds of realty stuff."

"So maybe you'll have to move to a bigger town and work in an actual real estate office for awhile."

"I *do* work in an actual real estate office."

"No comment."

"Binky, my mom is an actual realtor."

"Who ran off to Italy."

"Greece! See, you never listen."

"I listen when it's important. That's why I'm listening now. You might also have to let your hair grow out to its regular color, and take Percy out, and—"

"I thought you liked Percy."

"Percy is cute. The fact that he lives on your tongue is, is—"

"You said it was sexy."

"No! *You* said it's supposed to be sexy, and I said I suppose it could be, except that every time I think about it I remember how your tongue bled and I have to say that a mouth dripping blood is definitely not sexy. Unless you're a vampire."

"You are so un-romantic."

"Okay, you lost me. We talked about you selling the building, and Percy, and now we made it all the way to me being un-romantic. I'm not a flower-buying kind of guy. Besides, you aren't exactly an I-want-flowers kind of girl."

"Binky, I'm in trouble."

"Oh, no!" He turned to her, a look of panic contorting his face.

"Oh, yes."

"How far along are you?"

"How far along with what?"

"The baby!"

"What baby?"

"I thought you just said you were pregnant."

"Okay, this is what I'm talking about. I never said I was pregnant."

"Ooo, that's a relief." He fell back against the cushion. "When you said you were in trouble, I assumed that's what you meant."

"Why would you think that?"

"Babe! I'm too tired to play this game."

She tried the lip again.

"For Pete's sake!" He groaned and she nearly kicked him, but he sat up again so she let it pass. "So how are you in trouble?"

"Okay. Well. I took . . ."

No, that's not how she wanted to say this. She hadn't really taken, she'd just borrowed.

"You took what?"

"Hold on. Be patient. This isn't easy."

"Why don't I go home and get some sleep. We can talk about it tomorrow."

"Just let me finish. I need to talk to someone about this."

"Maybe this is girl stuff."

"NO!" She punched him in the arm. "Shut up a muckraking minute." She blew out a sigh and faced him. "You know that old building?"

"Haven't we just been through this?"

"You're hopeless."

"Sorry. As far as I know, there is only one building, so I assume you are speaking of the one you JUST SOLD!"

"Yes. You don't need to yell. The thing is, Grace didn't do such a great job of cleaning it up."

"You already told me that. And when you started working with your mom she said that if you spent a few hours cleaning up the place she'd pay you twenty-five dollars an hour."

"Right."

"Stop! Do you realize what just happened?"

"What?

"*Do* you?"

"What are you talking about?"

"Did I not just remember you got paid twenty-five dollars an hour for cleaning?" Before she could answer he continued. "Good! Just making a point. I *do* listen, when I'm not dead-tired. Okay. Back to your story. And FYI, I'm not buying the lip. If you were three years old, maybe, but since you're sixteen, it's not working."

"I'm twenty-two!"

"No comment."

"UGH! Where was I?"

"You spent a couple hours cleaning . . ."

"Yeah. Well, actually, most of the day. It was really bad in there. Still all kinds of stuff left. So I took a lot of it back to Grace."

"Ah, yes. I remember. Some clothes. A coffee pot. Dishes. Pretty good memory, huh? So then . . ."

"Well, there was that old cash register. It was just a piece of junk, and Grace said she didn't want it, and Mom told me to take it to my Uncle Milo, because he buys all this old crap and sells it in his friend's antique shop."

He half-heartedly stifled a yawn, which she made a point of ignoring but before she could continue, he groaned and put his hands up as if to stop her. "Again, I ask, why can't we talk about this tomorrow?"

"LISTEN! Because before I took it in, I was messing around with it, pressing the buttons and stuff. It was kind of funky and old-fashioned and . . .and . . ."

She stopped. This was the really hard part.

"Okay. I'm holding my breath. And . . .?"

Dana made a face and pulled her arms in across her chest.

"And you broke it?"

"NO!"

"Well, WHAT?"

"Well, see, when it opened it looked empty." She released her arms so they'd be free to fly about and help her with her story. "There were all these slots for the money, like they still have, and there was nothing in any of them. But then I lifted that part out, you know like they do when you've been standing in line to pay for a jar of mayo, and there are five people in front of you, and then just when you get there another cash register person comes up and tells the one who is just about to check you out that she should go on break, so then you have to wait while the new one types in some code and slips her cash drawer in that spot and gets all organized?"

"Maybe if I wasn't so damned tired I'd find this interesting." He sunk back into the couch.

"Okay! I found almost nine hundred dollars underneath that drawer thing with the slots for the money."

"Oh?"

"Yeah. Eight hundred eighty. Mostly fifties and twenties, but a couple of hundred-dollar bills, too."

"And . . .?"

Dana scrunched up her face and pulled in a breath through her teeth.

"You didn't give it to the lady who owned the building?"

"Not yet."

"Dana, we're way past yet. What was that? Like, three years ago?"

"I kno-o-o-w." She got really whiny, which she knew Binky hated—and even she hated—but she couldn't help it. "Okay. The thing is, I owed some money on my credit cards and there are always so many expenses. I meant to pay it back as soon as I got a good job."

"So you don't have any of the money?"

"Nope."

"And it never bothered you before?"

"Yes, it bothered me, but I've never made enough money to pay it back, so I kind of felt I wasn't obligated to worry about it, but now that the building is sold it kind of seems like I need to get this settled."

"But now you'll get a commission from this sale, so you can take care of it."

"Well . . ."

"Well, what?"

"The thing is, I'm broke. And I've got about two thousand in credit card debt, and I can't charge anything anymore."

"Look, Babe, I love you but I've got my own bills and my own credit card debt. We talked about this, and you always said you'd be fine once this sale went through."

"Because I thought by the time I sold the darned thing I'd have a couple more sales under my belt."

"Dana , you stole nine—"

"BORROWED! I intend to pay it back."

"You need to tell that lady and give her an IOU or something. That's a lot of money and she's probably on a fixed income. My grandma is and she'd love to find out she had an extra nine hundred dollars coming in."

"Only eight hundred eighty. And Grace isn't really poor. She's doing okay."

"But it's still her money. You have to tell her the truth and let her know you're going to pay her back."

"I know. I've been looking for more work, but they won't give me any more shifts at the bar, and there's nothing else here."

"That guy who bought the building is going to need help. Probably like painting and cleaning and stuff. You can paint.

You can clean. And didn't you say he wants to put in a couple of different shops? Maybe you could work in one of them."

"I don't know. He's pretty straight-laced. He already thinks I'm weird and he also thinks I never gave Grace his offer because he ended up talking to her in person and she gave him a really good deal. I mean REALLY good. He got it for nearly thirty thousand dollars less than she was asking. Which cut into my commission, of course."

"Why'd he get it so cheap?"

"Because Grace thinks he's Elvis Presley's son."

"No, seriously."

"Seriously! I am totally serious. He actually does kind of look like Elvis."

"Elvis, as in the guy you told me about? The singer who got old and fat and died?"

"Yeah, but Grace is nuts about Elvis. She's probably his biggest fan in the whole world."

"So you're telling me some famous wealthy guy's son showed up and wanted to buy a crappy old building. That doesn't even make sense."

"But Grace thinks he's Elvis Presley's *illegitimate* son."

"Where did she get that idea?"

26

GOOD INTENTIONS

Grace awoke with a start to the sound of the doorbell. She'd been sitting on the couch, keeping an eye on the progress across the street. This morning all the activity was visible through the large plate glass window where she and Harv used to spell out the daily grocery specials with fat, bright-colored washable markers.

The last thing she remembered was wondering why Elvis's friends ("He just doesn't look like a Brent," she had told Evelyn and Betty. "I keep slipping. He'll have to get used to it.") were installing the counter that way. It seemed to her the counters should run perpendicular to the window to keep the traffic moving, not parallel to it. And then she'd apparently fallen asleep.

Elvis sang out another chorus of "A Hunk A Hunk of Burnin' Love," and she pushed herself up off the couch. At the door she shoved the window curtain aside to see a deliveryman holding a notepad-sized contraption.

He'd been looking behind him, but when he turned back and saw her, he held up the notepad thing and shouted: "I've got a delivery but there's no one across the street to sign for it."

Grace opened the door and stepped out onto the porch. "They've been working all morning. At any rate they were working last time I looked. I fell asleep. They must be at lunch."

"I just need a signature, ma'am. I already called the phone number listed, but there's no answer, and I can't wait for a call back. I got this place as a second address. Is the owner here?"

"No. Only here on weekends." She checked her watch: 1:30. Elvis's workers did seem to take late lunches.

"Well, I need a signature. Are you the owner's mother?"

"No, he's staying here while he works on the building. He just comes up from Green Bay for the weekend. What are you delivering?"

"Chairs. They're in crates so I can leave them at the back door, but I should have a signature."

"Chairs?"

"Yes, ma'am." He hit a button on his note-pad thing and said, "Looks like . . . barber chairs. Four of 'em."

"Oh, barber chairs? That can't be right. He's remodeling a grocery store."

"Well, I can't leave them without a signature."

"Oh, no. I can't sign that. That would be a mistake. You just write down they were refused. It has to be some kind of mix-up. Are you sure you have the right address?"

He held the little machine up for her to see.

She shook her head. "The address is correct, but that order is wrong. There's a salon around the corner. Could be they ordered something. Can't you call your office?"

"I already did. Crabby guy hollered at me to get a signature and unload 'em. They're in crates and they're heavy. It would take a real smart aleck with a big truck and lots of muscle to steal them, so I'm sure if I drop them off, they'll be safe. I just need that signature, ma'am."

Grace thought about it for a minute but didn't want Elvis to end up having to pay to return them later. She shook her head. "No. This is definitely a mistake. You have to take them back."

He stared at her for several seconds, then heaved a deep sigh. "Okay. Refused!" he said, stabbing a key on his little machine. "At least I haven't unloaded them yet. Sign here."

27

TRYING NEW ADVENTURES

Brent was gathering the day's accumulation of towels when he remembered he still hadn't called to find out what had happened to the barber chairs. As he headed to his office to jot down a reminder, the bells at the salon's front door jingled. He was about to check his appointment book when he recalled that Scotty had arranged for a potential renter to see the salon that evening. He did an about-face, finished stuffing the towels into a laundry bag, then headed to the entrance where a woman waited just inside the door.

"Mr. Wallace?"

"Brent. Nice to meet you," he said, extending his hand.

"Monica Seaquist. I hope this time is okay."

"It's fine. I'm finished for the day. Scotty's a good landlord, by the way. If you take the place, you'll find he's easy to work with. Come in. Feel free to look around."

"I'm still thinking this over. I rent a chair now, but . . . well I've recently become an empty nester so I have a little more time on my hands. Thought I'd put it to good use while I'm still young enough to try a new adventure."

"That's sort of what I'm doing."

"Mr. Danbury . . . well, Scotty . . ."

She let out a little laugh, as if she felt uncomfortable using the owner's first name. Her tentative smile hinted at her shyness and she took a little breath—as if to steel herself—then started again. "Scotty said you were going to open a salon up north."

There was something endearing in her manner, and he was drawn to her, but when she ran her left hand through her hair, he spotted a wedding ring. As surprised as he was that he had noticed, he was equally surprised to feel a hint of disappointment.

"That's my dream. I like to fish and hunt. I figured if I moved up north I could be out in a boat or in the woods a few minutes after I closed instead of trying to fit a year's worth of fun into a few days here and there."

"Oh, I know! I really like working with hair, but it seems like you have to put in long hours to make a living at it."

"No kidding!" He turned and led her into the salon area. "Well, this is the place. I've got these three chairs, a small office back there to the right and the bathroom off to the left, storeroom behind. There's a back door that opens to a small parking lot, but most people just park out front."

"You're leaving the chairs?"

"Yeah. The guy who was originally going to rent the place wanted them. When he backed out I offered to leave them. Scotty said he'd just as soon try to rent the salon as is. With the plumbing in place it made sense."

"Hmmm . . . It's a great location but . . . I don't know if I can afford it ."

"What about renting one of the chairs to another stylist?"

"I suppose. But I'm afraid there'd be a lot more paperwork."

"That's the one drawback to the new venture for me, too. But I'm planning to get an accountant. As long as I can find one that doesn't charge a lot. Setting up a new business is so expensive."

"That's why I was hoping this place would work for me, with everything already set up. But these chairs are . . ."

"Old! It's okay. You won't hurt my feelings. But the mechanics work. The upholstery's in good shape. I've recovered them when they needed it, but, yes, the style is definitely . . . retro."

She laughed. "That's probably a better way to describe them," she said, running her hands over the fabric on the arms.

After a few awkward moments of silence he realized he was searching for something clever or interesting to say to keep the conversation going. "Scotty's a good landlord."

Neither clever nor interesting, he thought. Maybe Dana was right. But apparently Monica Seaquist hadn't noticed he was a dork, because she turned back to him, smile intact.

"I got the impression he hates to see you leave."

"Well, I'm not leaving because I'm unhappy here. If I had known about the problems I was going to run into with my move I might have stayed, especially when the guy who was originally going to rent it backed out. But by then I'd already bought a building for my new business. Once I get settled and finally have time to go fishing and hunting, it will be worth it. Kind of exciting to start something new. Come on. I'll show you the office and storeroom."

28

THE APPLICATION

Dana stacked the three books on the left side of the table in Millie's Cafe, arranging them so the titles faced away from her. She pushed her tongue across her upper teeth, still unaccustomed to the strange sensation, then stuck it out as far as it would go and looked down, trying to see past the cross-eyed version of her nose, when a voice startled her.

"What the heck are you doing?" Brent stared at her as if she were contemplating murder.

"Oh. Hi. I'm. . . I'm trying to see what . . . never mind."

"Are you trying to see your tongue?"

"Yeah. I ditched Percy." Dang. The confused—or was it shocked?—way Brent was looking at her seemed like an unfortunate beginning to the interview. She pushed the books a few inches toward the center of the table to take Brent's attention away from her face.

"Sorry. I can't remember . . . is he your boyfriend?"

"Is who my boyfriend?"

"Percy."

"No. Percy is the frog. Was." She stuck her tongue out again. "Thee? I took hi ou."

"Why'd you do that?"

She scraped her tongue across her upper teeth again. She couldn't resist. It was so weird. "Because I'm applying for the job."

"What job?"

"Your accountant."

"You're kidding."

"I am totally serious. Look." She took the top book off the pile and set it in front of him, giving him just enough time to read the title before she set the next one beside it, and seconds later she placed the third one on top of the other two.

"Okay. I see three books on business and accounting." He eased into the booth, then picked up the top book, turned it over in his hand, then set it back down.

"They're textbooks." Surely he figured that out, but she wasn't taking any chances.

"You're going to school?"

"Nope, just reading them."

"Why?"

"I told you. I'm applying for the job."

He looked around the cafe as if he were searching for a response.

"I can read, you know."

He shook his head and looked at the books, opened each one, flipped through the pages, and finally said, "Yes, but you need to be able to do a lot more than that."

"I'm smart."

"Well . . ."

"No, I'm serious. I'm *really* smart. I'm halfway through this book already." She grabbed the one to his left, *Tax Accounting Practice*, and held it up for him.

"I don't think you understand what I'm looking for. I'm opening four small businesses. I'll be hiring several part-time employees and—"

"I'm willing to take part-time work."

"No. What I'm saying is this . . . this venture . . . will be fairly complicated. I need someone to keep me in business and out of jail."

"And here I am, right in front of you."

"How much college have you had?"

She blew a puff of air through her lips. "College? Seriously? That will take four muckraking years, and you need someone now."

"Exactly! Which is why I'm going to hire someone who already has a degree."

"Mmm, mmm, mmm." She raised her eyebrows and shook her head slowly, doing her best imitation of her mother's reaction the day she told her she was getting Percy. Well, the day she told her she had already gotten Percy. "Gonna cost you a lot of money."

"Dana, I think it's . . . admirable that you are trying to . . . to better yourself, but I need a professional. Someone with the right education. And experience. And I don't mean to be rude, but I am a very busy man. Thank you for your time."

He started to push up from the bench and she looked for something to keep him there. "You mean I ditched Percy for nothing?"

"I'm sure your life will improve with Percy . . . gone."

"Wait. Wait, wait, wait. Sit back down. Just give me two minutes."

He huffed, his hands on the table, his stance half way between standing and sitting. "Fine. But I doubt there's anything you can say to make me change my mind." He fell back onto the seat.

She leaned across the bench to her left and unzipped her monstrous carrying thing, pulling out a stack of papers. "Okay. First, here's a business plan." She loved the sideways look of doubt on his face. Oh, this was perfect. The less he believed she was capable of, the easier it would be to convince him.

He took the sheets of paper and began reading. "Where did you get this?'

"I created it. Wrote it up. Whatever. I did it myself."

"You just took this off the internet and filled in the blanks."

"No way. I read a chapter on business plans in this book. See?" She located a bookmark and flipped open to the chapter: *How to Start Your Own Business Without Ending Your Life.* "So you can see that not only can I read, I can handle a computer and do spread sheets. C'mon. I'm perfect for this job."

"Pffft." A scowl of disbelief contorted his face.

"Hey, I know your financial situation. You can't afford any-one else."

"If you think blackmail is going to work on—"

"OMG! This is not blackmail. This is . . . inside information that enables me to help you."

"Like I said, I'm impressed that you've gone to all this trouble, but—"

"Give me a week."

"You've got purple hair."

"I'll grow it out."

"You wear . . . weird clothes."

"I'll expand my wardrobe."

"You have enough holes in your head to . . . to . . ."

"So I'm not only smart, but also creative. That's good in business."

"You're covered in tattoos."

"I have a *few* tattoos! But that doesn't mean I'm not smart and capable."

"YOU'VE NEVER EVEN HAD A REAL JOB!"

"Of course not. This is the first interesting opportunity that's come my way."

"Interesting?"

"I love math. Check my grades. Check my SAT. Just because I don't want to do the traditional march of boredom through four long, agonizing years of college does not mean I am not capable. You give me a library card and a couple of weeks and I bet I could teach just about any muckraking class out there. I'm really smart. MENSA-smart!"

"MENSA?"

"MENSA is—"

"I know what MENSA is. That doesn't mean you can handle this job."

"I'm just asking for a chance. Give me one week. I'll even work for free."

"Fine. One week. You work for free. If at the end of the week I like what you've done, I'll hire you. And I'll pay you for the week."

"Twenty an hour."

"Minimum wage to start."

"Eighteen."

"Fifteen. Then if—and it's a big IF—if I hire you, I'll review your work after one month. Then we'll talk about a raise."

"Deal!"

She put her hand out to shake his, and although he hesitated a minute, he finally reached across. She saw the look of surprise when he felt something land in his hand, then watched a scowl erupt on his face as he turned his palm to see the little gold frog.

"That's just a reminder of the first step, a really BIG step, that I took to get this job. Just so you know I'm serious."

He didn't move. She could tell he was struggling to decide whether or not to accept it.

"If you need to fire me, you can give it back."

29

THIS WOULD NEVER WORK

Brent tried Pine Lake Realty's door, but it was locked. Back in the truck he fumed, thinking that if Dana expected him to trust her with his finances, she had better be on time.

Ten minutes later he went back to the door, but it was still locked, so he walked around the side of the building. On the far end he saw light through the blinds and rapped on the window, but there was no response.

That did it! He stomped back around to the front and was on the way to his truck, ready to fire her when he heard a door open. At the entrance a young woman with short blonde hair, wearing a white blouse and dark slacks, called to him.

Dana hired an assistant? She didn't even have any listings! How irresponsible. What a mistake! She was finished.

As he got to the truck he heard a loud, "Hey!"

Dana???

He took a deep breath. Fire her now? If he didn't need her so badly . . . but he did.

She waved him in, and he took another deep breath. Shook his head. One more chance!

He seethed as he stepped inside, setting his face in as angry a look as he could muster. "What happened to your hair?"

"Cut it. Dyed it. Faster than letting it grow out. What do you think?"

It was taking every ounce of self-control not to scream, "YOU'RE FIRED!" and she was oblivious. He counted to ten, let his shoulders drop, and tried to focus on one of the pictures on the waiting room wall. In it a young girl with a pink bonnet sat atop a horse in a meadow, but his brain wasn't falling for it. He wondered what would happen if he actually did scream, "YOU'RE FIRED!" and stomped out. Did she think if she did all this for him—for this job—it would be more difficult to let her go?

She tousled her hair and launched into an explanation. "I don't have the coloring to be a blonde, but I figured as long as I was ditching the purple, I might as well try it and see. And did you notice my clothes?"

"Okay, let's get one thing straight. All these changes won't matter if you can't do the job. I won't be guilted into keeping you on the payroll just because you took the frog out and changed your hair color and wardrobe." There. Not as dramatic as it had been in his head, but he felt a bit better.

She appeared ready to respond, but he stopped her with a raised hand and an "Uh, uh, uh!" then paused and continued. "One of the first things I will expect, no, DEMAND, is that when we have a meeting, you'll be on time."

"You're the one who was late!"

"I was here," he checked his watch, "nearly fifteen minutes ago."

"Why didn't you knock? You can see on the door that the office doesn't open until nine a.m. Mom's rules. The door stays locked until nine. I've been here since quarter to eight."

"O-KAY! FINE!" This would never work. One short interaction as her employer and he was already losing his temper. "Do you have the paperwork ready?"

"Aye, aye, Captain. C'mon back."

"Just call me Brent. Please."

He followed her into the office, sat, and checked over the forms she handed him, doing his best not to let on how impressed he was with her work. After all, this was only the first assignment and a simple one at that.

"These look good. Thank you."

"You're welcome. How tall are you?"

"What?"

"How tall are you?"

"Surely you can see how tall I am."

"Five-ten?"

"And a half."

Her face came close to his. "Greenish eyes. Dark brown hair. You weigh . . . what? One-sixty?"

"There is no form anywhere that asks for that information."

"Ooo . . . beg to differ. Dating sites ask for it, and I know a lot of people lie, but I think it's best to be honest."

"Dating sites??? I'm not on any dating sites."

"Not yet."

"What?! Now, listen here. I hired you as my financial and tax advisor. Nothing else. I am paying you for those business services only."

"Of course. But you need a girlfriend."

"That is my business. And you are dangerously close to getting fired."

"Aha! It *is* your business. Just as this form stuff is your business, but you are not good at it, and you are not attending to it, and you're grouchy and acting all bachelor-y. You need a woman in your life."

"I just got rid of a woman. I was—actually I still am—married, and it was a mistake."

"Yes. You picked the wrong woman. Obviously that's a problem, so how can you trust yourself to find the right one? You need help with that, too, and my services in that department are free."

"I forbid you to . . . to mess in my personal life."

"There you go again. Mess!! Yes, your personal life may be a mess, but I can help."

"You put me on one website, or set up one blind date, or do *anything* remotely connected with bringing another woman into my life, and I will fire you on the spot."

"Whoa! Pretty touchy on the subject!"

"I'm moving up here so I can hunt and fish every minute I am not at work, and I don't intend to limit even one of those non-working minutes with a romantic relationship."

"What about just hooking up?"

He felt his cheeks grow hot and quickly made the angriest face he could to cover his embarrassment. This was looking more and more like a mistake. "One more word on this subject and I will walk out the door, and you will be out of a job."

"Fine. But the fact that you're so crabby all the time, suggests that—"

"You know—from a job security standpoint—you're still on strict probation here, so if I were you, I'd stick to the accounting aspects of the beauty, barber, bait and bakery business."

"Fine." She shuddered and whinnied like a disgusted horse, but she whipped a piece of paper off the top of a pile on the right side of the desk and slapped it down in front of him. "I need more information to fill out this one. It's an estimate of your living expenses. I guessed at these numbers to get started, but I wanted to go over them with you."

"You have eight hundred a month for an apartment."

"Yeah. So?"

"Well, I'm planning to build a cabin near Little Pine Lake."

"You don't have time."

"What do you mean, I don't have—"

"I mean you are going to have to spend every minute between now and the first of October just to get these stores open and then you'll be working your ass, I mean butt, off for at least another six months, so no way will you have time to build. Nope! Your finances are in horrid shape, and even though you might be able to find a cheaper place, bottom line, you can't afford to spend anything on an apartment. That's my point. You have to stay at Grace's."

"Living expenses at forty thousand dollars a year?"

"If you moved to an apartment."

"Do I really need four hundred a month for phone and internet? Or six hundred for food?"

"Not if you stay with Grace. That's why I'm telling you to look over these numbers."

He looked at the rest of the sheet. "You have all these crazy high numbers for clothing and food and . . . ? What's this? You've got $10 a month for travel and entertainment! That's kind of insulting."

"All you do is work and hunt and fish, which doesn't cost you anything. You might hit the video store a couple times a month . . ."

"Three thousand a year for car insurance!!! Who pays that? Other than someone who's really reckless. I sure as hell wouldn't give a loan to anyone with these numbers."

"OKAY! Like I said, you need to go over these yourself, but I guarantee you *still* won't be able to afford to live anywhere else right now. Sheesh! You have to admit, I did a great job on the rest of the forms."

"Yes. But! . . ." He stopped, looked her straight in the eye, and pointed a finger at her. ". . . you stay out of my personal life, do you understand?"

She dropped her hands to her side as if giving up, and nodded.

"Let me see your hands. No. Hold them up so I can see you're not crossing your fingers, and promise me my name will not end up on some dating site. And I don't mean just today, or just this week, I mean forever! Got it?"

"Okay. Whatever you say."

But the way she said it made him think she was already up to something.

30

HAND IT OVER

Dana rang the doorbell again, hollering, "C'mon, Grace. I haven't got all—"

The door swung open, Elvis howled, "Burnin' Love," and Dana took a step back. Grace had a towel around her head, but the hair sticking out was wet and foamy, as if she'd just sudsed up. Maybe she'd been washing her hair at the sink. She dabbed at her eyes with a little red- and white-checked towel, and Dana noticed they were red and tearing.

"Whoa! Are you okay?" Dana felt a stirring of sympathy until Grace hit her with a mind-your-own-business sort of scowl.

"What are you doing here?"

"I came because . . . um, I'll get to that." This was not starting out well, so she tried to put some genuine concern into her voice. "First, I want to know if you're okay."

The towel fell off and Grace grabbed it. "What do you think?"

Well, crap, Grace, I'm really trying to be nice here, Dana thought. She rearranged her face with a little scowl that she hoped looked like sincere interest and cocked her head. The more she looked at Grace's hair, the more confused she became.

"Your hair looks a little . . ." Greasy is what Dana wanted to say. REALLY greasy, and foamy at the same time. In fact the sodden mess on Grace's head suddenly struck her as hilarious but with the nasty look on Grace's face, she didn't dare crack a smile.

"Sorry, Grace, it's just that it looks . . . really awful. What happened?"

"Tile cleaner." She wrapped the towel around her hair again.

"Tile cleaner? I don't get . . . OHHH! . . . you mean in your hair!"

"Thought it was hair spray."

Then Dana couldn't help it. No wonder Grace's eyes were red. Hairspray in your eyes was bad enough, but tile cleaner!? She burst out laughing, and Grace slammed the door in her face.

"Crap!" Dana screamed. She had rehearsed this meeting several times with various scenarios but it had never turned out like this. "SORRY!!!" she hollered through the door, pressing the doorbell again. "GRACE, I'M REALLY SORRY!"

The door shot open. "What do you want?"

"Oh, Grace, I . . . it just looks so . . . it must have burned your eyes. I'm sorry. I shouldn't have laughed."

"You aren't just a kidding. I thought I was going blind. I ducked my head under the kitchen faucet, and then I heard the doorbell."

"Do you want to give it another rinse?"

"No! Let's just get this over with. What do you want?"

"Well, I need to talk to you. It's kind of an apology."

"For what?"

"Can we sit down?"

Grace let out a disgusted sigh but waved her in. This time Dana held her tongue and dropped down next to Elvis, as sort of a public relations move.

"Told you he wouldn't bite," Grace said, pushing the towel back onto her head. "But since you insist on sitting, I need to give my eyes another wash."

Several minutes passed during which Dana had time to note there were eighteen versions of Elvis scattered about the room along with miscellaneous stuff, most of which seemed to be unrelated, like a tiny pair of blue shoes and a miniature pink Cadillac. The Elvis crap was one thing, but the random items plopped at various spots around the room were beyond tacky.

"Now, what is this about? There's no problem with the sale of the building, is there?"

Grace had returned with a fresh towel on her head, but her eyes were just as red and her scowl just as angry. "No. Not the sale, but I owe you some money."

"Fine. Hand it over." Grace's hand came out, palm up.

"I can't. Not right away. I don't have it."

Grace tsked and shook her head, and the towel fell off, revealing her unsuccessful attempt to rinse out all the tile cleaner. The way her foamy, sticky, icky-looking hair was plastered to her head nearly made Dana bust up all over again, but she couldn't afford to irritate Grace more than she was already planning to.

"Let me explain." Dana took a deep breath and reminded herself that this conversation would be over in a few minutes, and she'd feel a lot better. Probably. "Remember when you first listed the place with my mom?"

"Of course." Grace re-wrapped the towel and held it in place with her hand.

"And you wanted to leave everything the way it was, but it didn't sell? Then a few years ago Mom suggested clearing some of the stuff out?"

"And?"

"And you were feeling sort of overwhelmed and sad, and you said we should go ahead and get rid of everything, but we still brought some things back because we weren't sure you *really* wanted to get rid of everything."

"Young lady, slime is dripping down my back. What is your point?"

"Okay. Sorry. You remember that old cash register?"

"Hurry up. What about it?"

"You said you didn't want it, but I thought it was kind of interesting, so I decided to take it to my uncle whose friend runs an antique store."

Grace started tapping one of her feet and her obvious irritation and impatience made Dana feel a little sick to her stomach. She looked for a way to say she took the money without actually saying she took the money. Grace reached back with her free hand and rubbed the nape of her neck with the towel, which loosened it enough that it fell off again. "Fiddlesticks," Grace said, rewrapping it. "Dana! Boring story!"

"Okay, okay. There was some money in it."

"Money in what?"

"In the bottom part. Under all those slots."

Grace looked confused. "You mean in the bottom of the cash drawer?"

Dana nodded. "You must have forgotten about it."

"That was years ago."

"Yes. Yes it was. I'm really sorry, it's just that I had so many bills and never in my whole life did I think about *not* giving it back to you, and I never forgot that I owed you that money, it's just that I always needed it, so since I couldn't pay you back right away I *made* myself forget about it. I mean just temporarily. I actually have a note, an I.O.U. note, written in HUGE black letters on my dresser that says I owe you . . ."

And then she stopped. Admitting she'd kept the money was easier than saying how much she had kept, which, considering the amount, suddenly made it sound a lot more like stealing. She was tempted to lie. Temporarily, of course. Some day she'd tell her the truth. Definitely! Just as soon as she was able to pay it all back. She pondered the possibility, but then realized that when she finally owned up to the total amount, Grace might wonder if she was lying again. After thinking it through she realized she had to tell the whole truth.

"I'm listening. You owe me what?"

"Eight hundred—"

"Eight hundred?"

"Eight hundred-eighty dollars."

"EIGHT HUNDRED-EIGHTY DOLLARS!?"

Dana was amazed at how loud Grace could yell. She tried the lip pout, but Grace wasn't buying it.

"Does your mother know about this?"

"Calm down, Grace. I don't want you to have a muckraking heart attack."

"I'M NOT GOING TO HAVE A HEART ATTACK! Now does your mother know about this stolen money or NOT?!"

"No. Of course not." Dana realized she was practically whispering, hoping it would calm Grace down. If Grace had a heart attack now, she'd *really* be in trouble. "Mom would have made me pay it back."

"I should think so. That's stealing."

"But, Grace, I'm telling you now because I just got a job and I'm going to give you fifty dollars of each paycheck until it's all paid up."

"Why didn't you just pay me out of the commission you got on the store?"

"Because I owe money on my credit cards, and the interest is so high."

"Interest?"

"Yes. They don't care if you have a decent job or not. Those credit card companies just keep charging you, like a gazillion percent."

"Well, shouldn't you be paying me, like, a gazillion percent, on that eight-hundred-and-eighty dollars since you've been using it all these years?"

Dana squeaked in horror and clenched her lower jaw. She hadn't thought about that. Oh, crap. The old lady was probably right. "Okay, Grace. You're right. I should probably pay you some interest."

"What number, exactly, is a gazillion?"

"For muckrakin' sake, Grace. It's a credit card company."

"What's a gazillion?"

She groaned. "It's eighteen percent. That's a lot."

"I'll take nine."

"But—"

"I could probably have you arrested."

"Well, I didn't have to tell you."

"Well, why did you tell me?"

"Because I have a job."

"You mean you have another house to sell?"

"No. I have an actual job. I'm an accountant."

"Since when? Did you even finish high school?"

"Despite what everyone around here seems to think, I got A's in just about everything except chemistry, in which, even though I hated it, I got a B plus. I'm really smart and I have just become the accountant for Brent's Beau . . . beau . . . beautiful new business."

OMG, she'd just about let the cat out of the bag. Brent had been very clear that until the day he opened the door for business, she was not to mention the name. Unless a miracle occurred, at which point he had promised to contact her immediately.

"Okay, I gotta go. I just wanted you to know I intend to pay you back by the end of the year."

"At nine percent interest."

Dana tried to think of some logical argument against paying nine percent, but her mind was a complete blank. She stood and tried her poor little girl face pout again.

Grace rolled her eyes. "Oh, please. What do you take me for?"

Dana let out a throaty sigh of frustration and stomped out.

"Interest accruing quarterly," Grace called after her. "As an accountant, I assume you can figure that out."

"FINE!" Dana yelled over her shoulder and slammed the door behind her.

31

MAYBE

Brent stared at the credit card statement on his computer, office phone to his ear. "Would you please repeat that."

He listened, frowned, and shook his head. "Do you have a record of who exactly it was that refused delivery?"

He waited while the person on the other end checked whatever she had to check to determine who was responsible for causing the four chairs he'd ordered for the barbershop and salon to be sent back to the supplier. Not only had they charged him a return fee—in addition to the original shipping charges—but also a ten percent re-stocking fee.

"But she didn't have the authority to refuse them. Didn't anyone try to reach me first?"

It was not the fault of the nice lady in customer service that Grace had refused to sign for his chairs, but he was having a hard time maintaining a pleasant voice.

"That was the—" He stopped. Nice lady couldn't care less that he'd forgotten his cellphone that day. He probably hadn't listed his salon office phone number, either. Another lesson. What were the chances that none of his crew would be on-site when the truck arrived the one day he'd forgotten his phone?

"But no one even left a message." It wasn't likely he'd get them to cover return shipping charges, but he certainly intended to try. There had to be some reward for being cordial when he wanted to scream obscenities.

"Yeah, yeah. I understand. But what if I'd been able to call back in five minutes? I really think you should make it a policy that only the person who orders can refuse a delivery."

He listened to her explain that after several drivers had waited as much as an hour without anyone arriving to sign for a delivery, they'd had to revise their policy. Now, for costly items requiring a signature, drivers had to wait only fifteen minutes for said signature from an authorized person over the age of 18 at the address listed, unless other arrangements had been made, *and,* she emphasized, this information was included on all order forms.

"But if Mrs. Havisto hadn't been home, what would the driver have done?"

She began to repeat the fifteen minute rule, but he interrupted her. "My crew would have been back from lunch within half an hour." She said her driver would not have known that. "Yes. I realize he wouldn't have known that, but obviously people were working there, so wouldn't it have made sense to assume they were at lunch?"

When she launched into the fifteen-minute rule again he let out a frustrated sigh. "No. Don't re-ship at this time." He was about to end the call when she told him they'd also sent an email the day before alerting him to the delivery with a four-hour window.

"I didn't get an email." There was a brief pause, the sound of paper rustling, and then she told him they'd attempted to send an email to BRNET. . . and he tuned out her voice. He'd transposed the "n" and the "e." Again. He typed BRNET so often that he usually checked, but of course, that day he hadn't. It was never questioned since anyone who paid attention assumed that since he owned a salon, the letters were shorthand for "brunette."

All in all, the unfortunate string of errors and mishaps had added up to over three hundred dollars in shipping fees with nothing to show for it. He recalled his earlier fears that Grace might somehow sabotage his plans, although if that did happen, he figured it would be *after* she found out he was not planning to reopen the grocery store, not before.

"Fine. Whatever. If I decide to reorder, I'll . . . reorder."

Maybe he could find something second-hand, something used but newer than the decades-old chairs he'd been too cheap to replace. He'd have to keep an eye out for salons and barbershops going out of business around Northeast Wisconsin. Another hassle to deal with, and although it was discouraging, he was also feeling guilty. This was his own fault for not being honest with Grace. If she had known what was really going on with the old grocery store, she would have signed for the darned chairs, and he'd have them.

On the other hand, he thought by now he would have been forced to tell her his plans. After Dana's description of her nosiness and Grace's own insistence that she would be there every step of the way, he had been surprised she hadn't shown up at the store. In fact, she hadn't so much as asked about his progress since the day she had given him the "tour" and they had ended up at Evelyn's for pie. Had he somehow made her feel unwelcome? Or maybe she just didn't want to be a bother.

Either way, once he opened his shops the reality would be so far from her expectations that it would come as quite a shock, and he couldn't let that happen after her kindness toward him. It was time to confess. He would tell her Saturday at breakfast, if only to prevent another shipping disaster. He had really liked those bright red chairs with the chrome trim and had tentatively planned a simple red-and-white color scheme around them.

He went out to look at his old chairs, trying to see them as if he were a stranger walking in for the first time. Like that Monica. He rubbed his hands over the arms, the seats. There were nicks in the fabric, frayed spots at the seams. The hydraulics worked well, but visually, the chairs were pretty unimpressive. It wasn't just the color, it was the style. They were old. Utilitarian. He had inherited them and had never given a thought to replacing them. He had always assumed he'd re-cover them as needed and use them until either they were useless, or he was.

Walking through the salon, he realized it was in desperate need of updating. He hadn't redecorated in ages, the linoleum tile had cracked in several places. The shade trees had grown tall and limited outside light so that the once inviting rosy-taupe walls looked dingy. Giving the chairs another look he realized there was no way he'd put them in his new salon. If he had told Grace the truth right from the start, he wouldn't be cursing his lousy luck, and those shiny red chairs would be in storage in Pine Lake awaiting installation.

The phone rang halfway through his last appointment of the day. Still in a funk, he considered letting it ring, but his conscience made him march across the room, and answer in a cheerful voice.

"Oh, hello, Monica," he said, glad he'd put the extra effort into his greeting. "Sure. I'm in the middle of a perm. How about we make it forty-five minutes."

"Good news?" his client asked, when he returned. Brent realized the thought of seeing Monica Seaquist again had put a smile on his face and nearly made him forget about the chair fiasco.

After his client left, he tidied the waiting room, straightened shelves, and swept the work area. As he set the broom back in the closet, he heard the jingle of the door bells and rushed to the front to greet her.

"I hope this isn't a bother," she said, and he wondered if everyone thought she was the kind of person who lit up a room or if this was the blossoming of some repressed midlife crisis.

"No bother. I'm happy to help Scotty find a new tenant."

"I wanted another look because a friend in the business told me a guy has some barber chairs from the fifties for sale. I was wondering how this place would look as an honest-to-goodness retro salon. The guy who owned them had a barbershop near the stadium, and he set it up in Packers colors. My friend said they're in good shape, a soft green and gold."

"Really? That sounds like a great idea." So great, in fact, that he began thinking about the possibility for himself. Small Wisconsin towns were usually full of Packer fans.

"How many chairs are there?" he asked.

"I'm not sure, she just said several. I'm trying to build up my client base, and setting myself apart with a Packers theme might help. I thought maybe I could put up signs with the players' names and what they do. Like, so-and-so is a fullback. Fullbacks are the players who . . . well, I don't know what they do, but I could have kind of a glossary on banners around the shop to explain all the terms."

Suddenly she laughed, and the way she put her hand over her mouth he realized she hadn't been teasing him with the idea, she'd been embarrassed.

"Oh my goodness," she said, and chuckled again.

"I'm sorry, but—" He'd tried not to look shocked, but clearly he'd failed.

"No, you're right. It is a TERRIBLE idea. Now that I've described it out loud I can't believe I ever thought of it. By the way, you probably shouldn't play poker."

"Not very subtle, huh?" Damn, he liked this woman! "I hated to burst your bubble, but I don't think a salon is the best place for a class in football basics."

"You're right. I guess I envisioned those chairs and lost my sense of reality."

"But you found your sense of humor. You can laugh at yourself. That's wonderful."

Her silly grin faded into a shy, blushing smile, and he was tempted to hug her. Except that she was wearing a wedding ring and he barely knew her, and now the lull in the conversation had become awkward. To her credit, she smiled and shrugged her shoulders in an "oops" sort of way.

"So! You're really interested in this place?"

Although nothing could come of meeting Monica Seaquist, he was encouraged to know there were still some decent women out there. Maybe Dana was right. Maybe he should look into dating again. Maybe.

32

A BROWN PAPER BAG

Brent had been rehearsing his confession all the way to Pine Lake. As he entered the back door he called out, "Grace, we have to talk." But when he walked into the kitchen he saw the table had been set for one and there was a note on the plate: *Gone to Green Bay to visit my daughter. Back by noon tomorrow. Breakfast casserole in glass container, top shelf of refrigerator. Microwave with lid ajar for two minutes on Power Level 5. Orange juice in door, grapes in fruit drawer. Brown bag lunch on bottom shelf. Pastries (not homemade) and cookies (homemade, but not by me) on counter. Fondly, Grace*

Damn! He needed to get this over with. Tomorrow!

He headed upstairs to the grandson's bedroom. Painted in shades of tan with curtains in a deep blue- and-brown pattern, this room was more to his liking, thankfully, since his search for another residence was not going well.

He turned on the overhead light, dropped his travel bag on the floor, and noticed the dresser held two new earthy brown candles and a small vase of dried flowers next to a photo he'd seen before but hadn't paid much attention to. He picked it up. A studio pose, it showed a young woman with a little boy: Grace's daughter, Jenny, he assumed, and her son, Jeremy. The woman looked familiar in an ordinary way, like the so-called moms you saw on television commercials for plastic wrap and cleaning products. Nice looking, pleasant smile, pixie haircut. The little boy was missing two teeth. Cute kid.

He set the photo back on the dresser and checked his watch. With Grace away he decided to get right into his work clothes and head over to the building.

After grabbing the bolt cutters from his truck, he walked across the street and made his way to the storage room where he'd left the rectangular green metal box in the drawer. Although Grace said she and Harv had never used it, there was definitely something inside. A wad of money? Enough to allow him to abandon this project, and spend the rest of his life hunting and fishing? Not likely. But he allowed his brain a few seconds to play with the idea, and in the image that formed, he was on a boat in the middle of Little Pine Lake—with Monica Seaquist beside him—reeling in a wildly flipping walleye.

Surprised at the audacity of his imagination, he mentally brushed it away, pried the metal box out of the desk drawer, snipped the combination lock, and yanked it off. Lifting the lid he discovered a brown paper bag. He pulled it out, opened it, and found another little plastic bag, inside of which was a small, rectangular gift-wrapped box with a tag that read: *To my dearest Grace, With love, H.*

A bracelet? A necklace? A watch? It was most likely some little piece of jewelry that he'd bought for her birthday or some special occasion. If it *had* been a wad of money, he would have returned it but he was still disappointed. On the other hand, maybe giving this to Grace would soften the blow of learning what was really happening to Havisto's Groceries. Although, what if he revealed the truth first? Then, when she was about to vent her anger, or cry, or whatever, he could casually announce, "Oh. By the way, I found this last night." He suddenly felt a pang of guilt thinking he'd considered using, for his own selfish purpose, what was most likely the last gift Grace's husband had purchased for her.

Having put in a couple of hours nailing in place several studs which would be the foundation of one of the new interior walls, he picked up the little package from Grace's husband. He left by the back door, locked up the building, and headed across the street, realizing he was far more exhausted than usual. With Grace out of town, he had worked an extra long day, and every bone in his body ached.

He went directly to the basement intending to clean up and change into comfortable clothes. He set the gift on the old dresser he was using to store towels and work clothes, then opened the top drawer and remembered he'd taken his towels home to wash. He brushed himself off, untied and kicked off his boots, and took the two flights of stairs to "his" bedroom. He pulled clean towels from his travel bag, ran back down to the basement and tossed them on the dresser. He stripped off his dirty clothes, grabbed a towel, and took a long, hot shower, feeling his achy muscles slowly relax. Stepping out of the shower he decided he was too tired to watch the news. He wrapped a towel around his waist, headed up the two flights of stairs, slipped on pajamas, and went straight to bed.

While the breakfast casserole was heating the next morning, he remembered the gift and returned to the basement. Although he was certain he'd left it on top of the dresser, it wasn't there, nor was it in any of the drawers. He'd been thinking about several things last night. What should he do about barber chairs? Would he get that variance? Did he have enough studs to finish the wall the next day? In his preoccupied state he must have left the gift in the office. He went back upstairs to the kitchen, took the break-fast casserole out of the microwave, and poured a glass of orange juice. Noticing that Grace had left a thermos on the counter, he made a pot of coffee, then sat down to eat. And think.

He'd be silly not to use that gift to his advantage. It wouldn't hurt anyone, and it might help Grace accept his plans. In fact, it would mean using the gift to her advantage as well. Besides, it wasn't as if he could revive Havisto's. That had been decided years ago when Gary's Groceries opened around the corner.

After breakfast he searched every inch of the office and retraced his steps back to Grace's house. He kept his eyes on the ground in case he had dropped it along the way, then checked the basement again. It was a mystery, but he had no time to think about it since minutes later his crew showed up with coffee and donuts. He explained what he had found in the lockbox, and asked them to keep an eye out for the small brown paper bag.

On their lunch break he tried to join in the conversation, but his heart wasn't in it, and the loss of the gift was weighing on him. Piper read his mind and asked: "Have you told her yet?"

He shook his head. "She was visiting her daughter last night, but she's probably back by now. I'll tell her today."

"Aren't you making this out to be a bigger deal than it is? It's your building."

"Well, actually it's a land contract, so it's not really mine yet. I'm beholden to her in a way. Not to mention that I'm living in her house and eating her food." He held up the half-eaten sandwich. She had layered ham, salami, and provolone cheese with lettuce, tomato, and some kind of dressing. As delicious as it was, he could barely swallow it. He re-wrapped the sandwich, pushed up from the folding chair and took a deep breath. "Guess I'll go get it over with."

He was about to climb the steps to her front porch when his cell phone rang.

"Hello, Grace," he answered.

"Is this El . . . Brent Wallace?"

"Yes it is," he said, smiling at her slip of the tongue.

"I'm sorry to bother you, dear, but I was hoping it would be alright if I didn't get back until tomorrow night. Jeremy is in town and wants to take Jenny and me out to supper with his first paycheck from his new job."

"Of course it's okay. I'm fine and there's no—"

"You just help yourself to whatever is in the refrigerator. I had planned to bring back a small roast and make you a decent dinner, but I think there are cold cuts."

"The guys were talking about going to a supper club in Burnham tonight, so this will work out just fine."

"Oh, good. I'll make it up to you."

"You're doing a lot for me as it is."

"And you're doing a lot for me. I'm so grateful you bought the building and are bringing it back."

"Well, Grace, we'll have to talk more about . . ."

But he couldn't do it. Not over the phone.

" . . . about meals," he said. "I'm putting on weight, so you don't need to keep making so much food for me."

"I'm sure you're working it off as fast as you eat it. Now I'll be back tomorrow for sure, later in the day, and I'll fix dinner before you leave. Jenny is making two apple pies tomorrow morning, one for me to bring to you. She's nearly as relieved as I am to see Havisto's come back to life. Well, not necessarily Havisto's. Of course you may call it something else. Oh, and I forgot to tell you. Someone tried to deliver some chairs—barber chairs, I think they said—last week. They wanted me to sign for them. The deliveryman was quite pushy, even a little rude, but I stood up to him. Lord knows what it would have cost to send them back."

Oh, damn! He couldn't keep this up. But the next little fib rolled right off his tongue. "Grace, it looks like the guys ran into a problem, so I gotta go. See you tomorrow."

Maybe a few beers with the guys would help him sleep. Otherwise it was going to be a long night.

33

CONSIDER COMING HOME

Grace tucked her phone in her purse.

"Mom, I'm proud of you," Jenny said. "Not every 83-year-old is willing to get a cellphone and learn how to use it. I don't like being so far away, but knowing you keep your phone handy is reassuring."

"Betty and Evie and I keep tabs on each other, so you don't need to worry. But I wish you'd consider coming home."

Her daughter let out a sigh and shook her head. "I'd love to, but I need to make good money so I can retire there eventually."

That's what Jenny said every time, but Grace kept hoping there was something she could say to change her mind. "What about coming back to the store?"

Jenny stepped closer and hugged her. "You are such a pushy mother." She said it with a smile on her face, but stepped back and folded her arms so Grace would know she was serious. "It won't pay as much. And I like what I do. Besides, I'm sure the man who bought it has his own plans."

"I can hardly believe it's been nearly thirty years since you worked there. Dad and I were lucky to have you and Jeremy around as long as we did."

"We never would have made it without your help. Josh was a big mistake. I still can't believe I was so stupid."

"You weren't stupid. You loved him and you thought he loved you. I think he did. He just wasn't ready to have kids. Besides, without him I wouldn't have my wonderful grandson."

"I hate to think what would have happened if I'd gotten dependent on Josh. At least this way I was forced to go out and work right from the start. I don't think it hurt Jeremy."

"Of course it didn't. Even though you had to do it alone, you couldn't have raised him better. But I have to admit I miss the boy he used to be. Remember how he loved to hide? He'd get so antsy we'd hear giggles when we got anywhere near him. Then he'd jump out and we would screech as if he'd scared the daylights out of us. He'd grab us and give us the sweetest hugs."

"Don't get all melancholy on me, Mom."

"Oh, I won't. I know I have it good. Got my health, got two of the best friends a gal could have. That nice young man bought the store. Did I tell you he looks—"

The doorbell rang, and Jenny checked her watch. "Jeremy's a little early. Are you hungry?"

"Oh, I suppose I could eat," Grace said, realizing it was probably a good thing Jeremy's arrival had interrupted her before she explained how much Brent looked like Elvis. Jenny still didn't have much patience with her on that subject.

34

AWKWARD

Brent was installing metal shelving in the storage room when he heard a voice. It was after five, the guys had just left, and he didn't expect Grace for a few more hours. He fitted another shelf into brackets then heard it again, the voice sounding closer and feminine.

He started for the door when a nicely dressed woman appeared. "Can I help you?" he asked.

"Oh. Hi. I thought I heard someone working here."

"And you are?"

"Kathy Westby"

She offered her hand but Brent shook his head. "They're pretty dirty," he said, presenting his hand palm out. "I'll skip the handshake."

"Sorry to barge in on you like this, but I heard you purchased this building and were going to open a new business here."

There was an awkward pause, as if she'd forgotten whatever it was she intended to say, then she took in a little breath, grinned, and gave a slight shoulder shrug and continued.

"Sorry. I didn't expect you to be so . . . so . . . the thing is, I'm an Interior Decorator and I wondered if you needed help with any of that."

"I think I can handle it."

Another awkward silence, one he'd experienced enough times that he felt a blush coming on. "I really need to get back to work," he said nodding toward the wall behind him.

"You *do* know how important it is to make a good first impression?"

"Yes, I understand about first impressions, but . . . how did you know I bought this building? The For Sale sign is still up."

"Small town. I was driving by and saw the truck, so . . ."

"I have some ideas. It'll be awhile before I need to make any decisions." He was about to thank her for stopping by when she jumped back in the conversation.

"The thing is, I'm just starting up my business so I'm offering my services at a substantial discount. I'd appreciate a chance to show you what I can do. My fees are quite low."

"Thanks, but I'm pretty strapped for cash. I'm afraid the only thing I could afford would be free."

"Could I at least show you my portfolio? I think you'd see what a great deal you'd get by hiring me. Most interior designers would charge you seventy, eighty dollars or more an hour, but I'd be willing to accept half of that to get the experience."

"Look, I wish I could help you out, but I just . . . I'm not thinking that far ahead. I'm doing as much work on my own as I can."

"Let me buy you a cup of coffee sometime."

He put his hand up to stop her. "I'm not even living in Pine Lake yet. I'm still working at my salon in Green Bay."

"Could I meet you there? For lunch? I could bring something in and show you my portfolio."

A firm "NO!" was on the tip of his tongue, but he hesitated, trying to put himself in her shoes. "Fine. But you'll have to call next week so I can check my schedule. I'm really busy with appointments so I won't have more than a few minutes."

"Do you have a cell phone?"

"I'll give you the number at the salon." She cringed and he felt sorry for her, knowing how difficult it was to start a business, so he tried to offer an explanation to clarify. "That way I'll have my appointment book handy."

She pulled out a notepad, wrote down the number, then handed him a business card. He took it, glanced at it to be polite, then took a backwards step. "Okay. I already know I'm booked up early in the week, so call me Wednesday. Sorry," he said, nodding in the direction of the shelving, "I need to get back to work."

After she left, it struck him that although most of the building was not very well lit, she headed out with what seemed to be a great deal of confidence. He tiptoed to the doorway, peeked out, and watched her quickly navigate the shortest route to the back door.

While the business card suggested she actually was looking for work, he also got the feeling she had been in the building before. And the way she kept pushing after he made it clear he wasn't ready to think about decorating made him wonder . . . had she been hitting on him?

Dana!

ALL THIS ELVIS STUFF

The following Saturday evening Brent thanked Grace for a lovely dinner, determined that—gift or no gift—tonight would be the night he'd come clean.

"You're awfully quiet," she said. "I hope nothing's wrong."

"I need to talk to you about something."

"Please don't tell me you've found another place."

"No. Not that."

"That's a relief. I know this arrangement won't last forever, but . . . well, I have something to tell you, too. Have a seat in the living room, and I'll be in in a few minutes. The newspaper is on the end table. And just so you know, I'm more than happy to have a little company around here. I mean besides Evelyn and Betty. It's nice to hear a man's voice again."

"Speaking of which, I just have to ask . . ."

"Ask what, dear?"

"All this Elvis stuff. Didn't that ever bother your husband?"

"Oh, no. He used to tease me about Elvis, but Harv knew he was the only man for me. Right after he died, I didn't know how I'd go on. I missed him so."

"That must have been a rough time."

"Yes, but Evelyn and Betty pulled me through. They made me go out shopping with them to thrift stores and rummage sales and such. That's where I picked up most of my treasures. Once word got out, people started looking for Elvis items and giving them to me as gifts. When you're as old as I am, you have everything you need and just about everything you could possibly want, but people still like to give on special occasions. They say it's fun to look for some Elvis thing I haven't got yet. Elvis helped me look forward to life again."

"I'm guessing you've been to Graceland, then."

"Funny you should mention that. It's the only thing on my bucket list, and I decided it's about time I went. Since I sold the store, I decided to treat myself with some of the money from the down payment. That's what I wanted to talk to you about. I'm going to rent one of those nice SUVs and Betty and Evelyn and I are going to Graceland."

"Are you sure you're up to that trip? That's not an easy drive."

"Well, that's the best part. My daughter's going with us. She works so hard, I never thought I'd be able to talk her into it, but I'll pay for the car rental and gas—since it's my dream trip—and for Jenny's hotel rooms as a gift from her dad's estate. Harvey was the youngest. All his brothers and sisters are gone. My brother—I didn't have any sisters—moved out west years ago. It will be sort of a family trip since the only aunties Jenny knows are Evelyn and Betty. They've always been so good to her."

Grace smiled and paused. Likely thinking ahead to the trip with her daughter and her two best friends. Brent had a brief pang of regret that he never had children. Every time a friend had to cancel a hunting or fishing trip because of family demands, he had counted himself lucky. But hearing Grace talk about her daughter and grandson with such love and pride made him wonder if he hadn't missed out on something.

"We'll leave next Friday for a ten-day trip, take our time traveling to Memphis, and do a little more sight-seeing as long as we're that far."

"Would you like me to move out while you're gone?"

"Goodness, no. In fact, part of the reason I've never taken this trip is because I hate to leave the place empty. I'm *counting* on you to be here and keep an eye on things. You'll have to get your own meals, of course, but surely you know your way around my kitchen by now."

"Grace, you're so kind."

"Kind, pshaw. You could also say I'm selfish because I've enjoyed your company tremendously. There's no need to find another place to live. You stay here as long as you like. Now, didn't you say there was something you wanted to talk to me about? Oh, there's the teakettle. Would you like a cup? I have some delicious lemon ginger tea. Good for settling the stomach after a meal."

"I'll pass, thank you."

"Let me make myself a cup, and I'll be right back."

36 |

BEING THOUGHTFUL?

Brent sat back on the couch and breathed a sigh of relief. What an interesting development. By the time Grace returned, he'd have made a lot of progress, and she'd be in a great mood. He pictured her telling him about the trip to Graceland. As she was winding down, still basking in the glow of the experience, he'd tell her he had a surprise for her, too.

In fact, maybe he'd been looking at this all wrong. Maybe he should act as though he had *assumed* she'd be thrilled to see what a wonderful job he had done turning that dingy old building into four attractive little businesses. Having lost the gift her husband had hidden, he felt even worse having to break the news since he had nothing to balance it with, nothing to take the sting out of it. But maybe the only reason she wanted it to be a grocery store was because she figured that was all it could be. Maybe she had never realized there were options. And since she really liked him, wouldn't she also really like what he had done with the store? Especially if it was bright and cheery and the best-looking place in town?

Besides, if he told her the truth and she *did* end up being incredibly angry, it could ruin her trip, so wasn't he just being thoughtful by not breaking this news to her now? She had just told him it set her mind at ease knowing he would be there to keep an eye on the house while she was gone. If he told her his plans now, maybe he wouldn't seem so trustworthy. Good thing she shared her plans first.

"I'm getting really excited about the trip," she said as she walked in, accompanied by the tempting smell of ginger. "Just getting away and seeing someplace new will be such fun," she said, as she settled next to the big, weird Elvis doll. "And I meant what I said. There's no need to move."

"Well, being right across the street *is* saving me a lot of time. Eventually I plan to buy a cabin near Little Pine Lake, but I need to sell my house in Green Bay first. In the meantime I'd feel better if you let me pay some rent."

"Don't be silly," Grace said.

"But I leave my things here week after week. I really feel like I should give you something for letting me—"

"No. Not another word on this. The money you give me for meals is plenty. But I am concerned about something."

Oh, no. Did she figure out he wasn't opening the grocery store? Before he could organize his thoughts, she spoke.

"Is that little realtor girl working for you? As an accountant? I didn't even realize she had a high school diploma."

"She's not really working for me. Well, she is, but it isn't a job as such. Not yet. I'm having her work on a trial basis. She's actually quite intelligent, although don't ever let her know I told you that."

"She may be intelligent, but her manners are atrocious, and she can be sneaky. Underhanded. Why, her mother would have fainted if she saw the way Dana handled our real estate transaction. That girl has no tact at all. I'd be careful if I were you. Did you know she stole from me?"

"What?"

"I suppose I shouldn't be talking about her, but you're new around here, so it only seems fair that I warn you. She can be a little wild. I wouldn't trust her with anything too important. When I put the building up for sale I wasn't in the best frame of mind. It felt like I was saying good-bye to an old friend. That store meant so much to Harv and me. It was difficult to be there, going through everything, selling things as if they had no meaning. But what was I going to do with all of it? So I had a sale, but of course not everything went. Audrey—that's Dana's mom— she told me she'd take care of it, the dear one. She hired Dana to help clean it up and . . . well . . . "

Grace took a deep breath and folded her hands in her lap as if she was about to make a huge confession. "I told you I wasn't as attentive as I should have been. Evidently there was a cash register that didn't sell. Dana found some money hidden underneath the main drawer, and she kept it."

"She did?" He'd have to fire her tomorrow! "How did you find out about it?"

"She told me. Just a few days ago."

"She did?" So, in the end, she was honest. Maybe he wouldn't fire her, because, *damn!* she'd been doing a bang-up job, even clarifying things he hadn't been able to figure out. He'd just have to be very careful.

"Said she's going to pay me back. With interest. She fought that idea at first, but it seems only fair."

"Was it a lot of money? Not that it's any of my business, but . . ."

"Eight-hundred eighty dollars! That's a lot of money to me."

"Oh. Wow. Thanks for the warning. I'm going to keep a close eye on her from now on."

"I would if I were you. Oh! I almost forgot. There was something on the doorstep with the newspaper this morning and I think it was meant for you. I'll go get it."

She returned holding a small, gift-wrapped package and for a quick second, Brent thought it might have been the one he had found. His stomach tightened until she handed it to him.

It had been wrapped in light purple paper, was square rather than rectangular, and on it was handwritten, "Happy Father's Day!"

"I don't have any kids," he said, handing it back to Grace.

"I know, dear. But I suspect it's from that religious group that's sprung up around here. They do random acts of kindness, and this is just the sort of thing they come up with. I found a certificate for a free car wash under my windshield wiper when I came out of the thrift store a few weeks ago. Here. You open it. Unless you want to wait 'til tomorrow."

He shook his head, still thinking it wasn't his place to accept whatever it was.

"You may not be a father, but since I could never be one, it must be for you. Go ahead."

He took off the ribbon and wrapping to find a small box of chocolates. "Hmmm . . . no message inside."

"That's the way that random-acts-of-kindness group does things, but they probably didn't want to write on that pretty box."

"I suppose we might as well try them out," he said, removing the lid.

"Happy Father's Day, dear," she said, lifting her teacup to him.

37

NOT OKAY, NOT SURE WHY

Brent set down his scissors, excused himself and picked up the salon phone. After rattling off his usual greeting, he heard: "Hi. This is Kathy Westby. About the decorating interview?"

Wednesday! He'd forgotten about her. "I'm pretty busy today. I've got another haircut in five minutes and I'm booked back to back after that."

"Could I stop by after your last customer? I don't mind if it's late."

"Let me check my schedule." He stalled, hoping that by some miracle she'd pick up on his lack of enthusiasm.

"Are you still there?"

"Sorry, yeah, just checking. Okay, can you stop by at eight?"

"Yes, thank you. I appreciate the chance to show you some of my completed projects."

"It has to be quick. Been working since nine this morning and I have another long day tomorrow."

"I'll be there at eight."

At seven-forty-five he cleaned up from his last client and considered turning off the salon's main lights and the "Open" sign. Maybe if it looked dark inside, she'd take the hint and drive by without stopping. But she had driven down from Pine Lake, and he'd have to deal with her at some point. Might as well get it over with.

Minutes later he heard the jingling of the bells on the front door. He let out a sigh and headed to the entrance, but his face brightened when he saw it was Monica Seaquist.

"Looks like you're ready to leave," she said.

"No, no, come in. What a nice surprise!" He was about to take a step toward her, thinking for one ridiculous, unguarded moment that he'd hug her, but caught himself. He also felt sheepish about that overly exuberant hello and tried to take some of the oomph out of his voice. "So you're still thinking about renting here?"

"Yes. Still sifting through the pros and cons. I was driving by and saw you were still open. If it's no problem, I'd like to have another quick look around. I'm taking some vacation time and thought that if I had a clearer picture of the salon in my head, maybe being away would help me make the decision."

"You're welcome to take photos if you'd like."

"Oh. Good idea. Thanks." She opened her purse and pulled out her cell phone as he headed to the bank of switches to turn on the rest of the lights in the building.

"Apparently he's had two other people looking at it so I need to figure this out, one way or the other."

"Oh? Well, I think I know who he means, and I didn't get the impression either one of them was that interested. But of course, they didn't say much to me."

As the salon brightened it seemed to Brent that Monica Seaquist was glowing, and his heart took a little leap. Seconds later he realized he'd been staring and said the first thing that came to mind. "The place could use a new coat of paint. I'm sure Scotty would pay for it if you did the work."

"Seems like he'd be a good landlord. Right now I have to drive across town to get to my salon. This would be a lot closer for me."

"It's a great location. I've actually had to turn away business at times."

He was steps behind her and kept an appropriate distance although he felt as if some invisible magnet was drawing him closer. She bent to look at something and when she stood again, her honey-blonde hair took on a luster in the overhead lights. It hung to her chin and curved in, was shorter in back. It looked so soft and clean, and he wondered what it smelled like.

He also wondered why he was wondering, but it felt so good, he let himself say the next thing that came to his mind.

"Your hair looks very nice. Do you do it yourself?"

"Oh, thank you."

She'd turned to look at him and blushed and for some reason, that really got to him. Was she always this sweet and pleasant?

"Tuesday is our slow day, so we take turns doing each others' hair."

"It's a very flattering cut."

"Good genes. My dad always had great hair. Thick and wavy."

He had a sudden, dizzying desire to touch her hair and the very thought evoked a self-conscious wave of embarrassment. What the hell was wrong with him?

She walked ahead of him toward the storage area and he glanced at her reflection as she passed the mirrors along the way. Beauty had been his profession and yet he realized he'd always thought of it as an external thing. This woman might never win a beauty contest and yet she radiated beauty. He wanted to tell her, but how could he say out loud what he'd just been thinking without sounding crazy?

She turned back to the salon area and he followed. "Can I show you anything specific? Answer any questions?"

"You said you recovered the chairs yourself. Was that difficult? I'm not very handy."

"The first time a friend helped, but I've recovered them my-self twice since then. I can't say it was easy. Unless you know someone who'll give you a good price, it might be cheaper to replace them. Is your husband handy?"

She looked confused for a moment. "Oh. The ring. My husband is . . . he's not in my life anymore. It's . . . it's easier to wear a ring."

No husband? He nearly hugged her out of relief but caught himself again and picked up the thread of conversation. "If you already have a good client base, you could probably get by with these. I guess if I was starting out—well, I am starting out—then it's more important to make a good first impression. But since you'll be bringing most of your clients with you, you could put it off awhile. Like I said, they work fine. Here, have a seat and I'll give you a ride."

Another blush threatened and he backed away, shocked at what he'd just proposed. But there was something unexpectedly reassuring in the way she laughed and hopped into the chair.

"Up," he said, with a lilt in his voice as he raised the chair to its highest point. "And down," he added, letting his voice drop in a playful way.

"One more time, please, kind sir." She smiled at his reflection, and for a few seconds he felt like a carnival-ride operator, bringing a little crazy joy into someone's life.

He raised the chair again, and lowered it, repeating, "And do-w-w-w-n," as if the words were the last notes in a song.

"This certainly seems like a fun place to work," she said, but before he could respond the bells on the front door rang.

"Hell-o-o!"

He had forgotten about the interior decorator. If he didn't respond, maybe she'd go away. Then she repeated her greeting, her voice sounding overly familiar and making him even sorrier he had agreed to see her.

"Bre-ent," she called out, in nearly the same tone he had just been using with Monica Seaquist. "Bre-ent! Are you here?"

He was considering how he could get rid of her when Monica hopped off the chair.

"I should go. Thanks."

"You don't have to—"

"It's fine. I just wanted a quick look. Thanks!"

She hurried toward the exit and offered a soft "Hello" as she passed Kathy Westby on the way out.

"Was I interrupting something?" the woman said as she walked up to him.

"No," Brent said, wishing his answer had been yes.

"We did agree on eight o'clock, didn't we?"

"Yes. Yes we did." He felt his mood darken as he nodded at the door. "She's considering renting here after I leave and wanted to see the space."

"Oh. Good. I mean . . . how nice that it will be rented. Do you own this building?"

"No. Renting." He answered in a monotone, and let his mind wander back to Monica Seaquist. Why her? It had been years since he'd given any woman more than half a glance and suddenly he's smitten? He pictured her again, and looked back toward the door.

"Brent? May I call you Brent?"

You may call me irritated, he thought, especially since you've already been calling me Brent. He shrugged in answer to her question, as if he didn't care either way.

"Are you okay?"

No, he thought. *I'm not okay, and I'm not sure why . . .* but he motioned her to follow him. "It's been a long day."

"I picked up some decaf coffee, and brought some cookies— just made them this afternoon—if you'd like a little something before we get started. Since you worked so late I thought you might be hungry."

Homemade cookies?

He entered his office, waved to the second chair, and sat. "I'll just have coffee, thanks."

"There's cream and sugar," she said, pulling out a cup and handing it to him.

"Black is fine." He felt a sudden tinge of regret for his rudeness, but as he took the lid off the coffee he couldn't resist making a very obvious check of his watch. "I'd like to be out of here in twenty minutes, so let's take a quick look at your portfolio."

She pulled a small photo album out of her purse and flipped through a handful of pictures: a couple of obvious classroom projects, a few shots of what appeared to be small businesses, then some living, dining, and bedrooms. Although the rooms were attractive, he saw nothing that shouted 'fine design.'

"I didn't have a chance to ask before, but what business are you going into?"

As eager as he had been to get rid of her, after seeing the pitiful little portfolio he reverted to feeling sorry for her, so he tried to soften his tone. "I'm putting in sort of a mini-mall with a beauty salon, a barber shop, a bait shop, and a bakery."

"My goodness. That sounds ambitious."

"You know how small Pine Lake is. I knew I'd have to diversify to make it. But . . . I'd rather that word didn't get out about my plans. I still haven't figured everything out and I don't want to set any expectations. In case I change my mind about anything."

Damn! He hadn't wanted to talk about his plans yet. He checked his watch again and managed to produce a breathy yawn, then apologized. "Sorry. These long days tire me out."

"Do you have any idea how you're going to decorate all those stores? Are you thinking of a common theme or something completely different for each business?"

How could she have overlooked that hint?

"Decorating isn't what concerns me right now. When the time comes, if I need help, I'll let you know." He stood, rested his fingertips on the edge of the desk in what he hoped appeared to be impatience, and smiled.

"Okay. Thank you." She packed her mini-portfolio into her purse, but didn't stand.

After several seconds he said, "You're welcome." She still didn't move.

"Guess I'd better get going," she finally said.

"Goodnight. Through the door and left." No way was he going to walk out with her and risk several more awkward moments of silence.

He turned off his computer, stacked a few sheets of paper and stepped to the door to make sure she was gone, and saw that she was standing at the exit looking back. She waved. He was tempted to duck back in his office but it was too late. He waved. Then she smiled and turned and, finally, left.

Could he have been right earlier? Was she really hitting on him?

And was it possible he was actually, for the first time in his life, falling in love?

38

RELATIONSHIP ADVICE

Dana recognized the number, and answered in a cheery voice: "Hey, Auntie. How'd it go?"

"I don't know. Not very well, I guess."

"I told you he's not great with women, and you'll probably have to give him lots of hints and opportunities and a couple of chances. Do you think he picked up on anything?"

"Not really. But I don't think he likes me."

"Oh, that's just the way he is. Kind of grumpy-grouchy, but I think he's just lonely and doesn't know what to do about it."

"Well, he is cute."

"Do you think he looks like Elvis Presley?"

"Yeah, he does. I mean, in some of the younger pictures anyway, before Elvis put on so much weight."

"I think Grace Havisto actually calls him Elvis. So what's your next move? Are you going to do any decorating for him?"

"He thinks he can do it himself and he doesn't want to spend the money."

"Figures. Well maybe in a few weeks you can come back and actually give him concrete ideas. In the meantime I'll sneak in some comment about budgeting for decorating. Bring up the importance of creating great first impressions in a new business."

"I was wondering if I should try to get a job working in one of his shops. Maybe running the bakery? I did manage that little cafe in Green Bay for nearly ten years."

"Hmmm . . . I'm surprised he said anything about the businesses. He's really trying to keep it hush-hush. But, yeah, why not try it? Can't hurt. And he'll definitely need help."

"Might as well. It doesn't look like I'm gonna land any interior decorating projects around here."

"You should have told him about your experience in the cafe."

"I didn't think of it at the time. Which was probably for the best because I got the impression he'd had enough of me. There were a few awkward moments."

"Tell me about it. I've sure had my share of what you'd call really weird and awkward moments with Mr. Brent Wallace. But he is totally single so at least you don't have any competition. I'd say leave him alone awhile, then stop in and say you were curious about his progress. Or, better yet, you could say that when he talked about all those shops, you thought about it and realized you'd be a good one to run the bakery."

"Okay. That would give me another excuse for dropping by since he made it pretty clear he's not that impressed with my portfolio. Thanks, Dana. Who would have guessed you'd be giving relationship advice to your Auntie Kathy?"

"No problem. As long as I don't have to offer any guarantees of success. I'll talk to you later. Hey, wait! You know what might work . . .?"

39 |

ARGUING WITH HIS CONSCIENCE

Brent unplugged the table saw and checked his watch, shocked to find it was nearly seven-thirty. He was tired and hungry, his back ached, and he still had a two-hour drive home.

He locked up and headed back across the street. In the kitchen, he was about to open the refrigerator to grab a quick snack when he heard the garage door rise. Grace back already? He was certain she had planned to spend the night at her daughter's.

He glanced at the clock and looked out the kitchen's side window, thinking it had been a good idea to take care of the breakfast dishes. It wouldn't have mattered to Grace, but he was more concerned than ever with making a good impression. Despite the time, it would only be polite to let Grace tell him about her trip.

The garage door rumbled to the ground. Seconds later the entryway door opened and he heard, "I'm home!"

"Welcome back, Grace."

"Hello, dear. Oh, it's good to be here. I had a wonderful time but all that traveling wore me out. And it's so nice to see you. May I give you a little hug?"

He held out his arms, and she charged in and squeezed.

"You know, I dread the day you'll leave. In fact I was afraid you'd have gotten a little tired of hanging around an old lady by now. And I know all this Elvis stuff can be a bit much. Speaking of which, I saw the most interesting thing. Did you know your fa . . . oops . . . oh dear."

Grace blushed and teetered in the process.

"Are you alright? Here." He pulled out a chair for her. "You'd better sit down."

"Thank you." She grabbed a piece of mail from the stack on the counter, took two steps and flopped into the chair, then fanned herself with the envelope.

"Now, what was that interesting thing you were talking about?"

"Oh, yes. Well, did you know that Elvis Presley was a Packers fan?"

"He was from Tennessee, wasn't he?"

"Yes, but in the museum at Graceland one of the tour guides asked where we were all from. When we said Wisconsin, she said, 'Oh! Elvis was a Packers fan!' She also told us they had a Packers helmet in the archives."

"Well, I suppose that could make him a fan. It seems odd he'd like the Packers. Doesn't seem like he'd be much of a sports fan."

"I wouldn't think so, either," Grace said. "But the tour guide said she tells this story to all the Wisconsin people who come through. Apparently his security manager, who was also a Packer fan, knew that Elvis actually followed the team for awhile in the 1960's and he wrote an article about it. Not Elvis. *He* didn't write it, the security manager did."

"Interesting! Shows he was a smart guy. So I take it you had a good time?"

"Oh, we had the most marvelous vacation. We all got on so well, and everything just fell into place. Sight-seeing, and people watching, and the food! Oh my, I've never eaten so much delicious food in my whole life."

"For someone as wild about Elvis as you are, it's good you finally got there."

"Yes, but I wear out quicker than I used to. I don't think I'll last too long tonight."

"Is your suitcase still in the car? I can get it for you."

"I don't need anything in there. I'll get it tomorrow. Did you run into any problems while I was gone?"

"No. And thank you again for letting me stay here."

"Tut, tut. Like I said, it put my mind at ease knowing there was someone here to keep an eye on things. How is the remodeling project coming along?"

"Oh, it's coming along."

"Well, I thought I'd be able to offer you a little more help, but I've been busy."

She paused, and if he hadn't known better, he'd have thought her cheery mood suddenly soured.

"Evelyn and Betty told me you'd ask for help if you needed it and in the meantime, I should mind my own business."

Brent just smiled, biting his tongue, arguing with his conscience, desperately searching for something appropriate yet non-incriminating to say. "I appreciate the offer, but it's a lot of sawing and hammering and such right now."

"I figured as much. I'm sure I'd just be in the way, but Jenny is coming up for a visit next weekend—oh, I mean the weekend after. She needs to work next Saturday to make up for being gone, but the following weekend she's taking off and coming up, and she's really eager to take a peek. She worries that the empty building will attract thieves or drug dealers or homeless people. I worried a bit about that myself. Someone breaking in and turning it into a meth lab or some such. The things young people do nowadays!"

Grace picked up one of the piles of mail that had been neatly stacked on the counter and went through it. "Mostly bills. Nothing here that won't wait until tomorrow. Are you staying the night?"

"No. I was just having a sandwich, then I'll pack and head out. You can go to bed. I'll lock up."

"I appreciate that. As much fun as the trip was, I'm looking forward to sleeping in my own bed. Good night, then. I'll see you next weekend."

Brent watched her leave, grateful for the success of her trip, reasoning that the better her life was going, the easier it would be to set her straight about his intentions for the store. If her daughter was coming for a visit, she'd understand how a second grocery store would never work in such a small town. Surely she'd be on his side. And at some point he really needed to make it clear he was not Elvis's illegitimate child.

On the other hand, who would have thought Elvis was a Packers fan?

40

YOU NEED SOME KIND OF THEME

Dana drove Binky's Silverado to the back of the store and parked next to Brent's F-150, backing into the stall so the item in the bed of the truck wouldn't be visible from the building.

Brent's was the only vehicle in the lot, as Dana had suspected would be the case at seven-thirty on a Saturday morning, since his work crew usually didn't get there until around eight.

She let herself in and wandered through the rooms following the mechanical sound of some tool. She found Brent in the southwest corner of the building fastening a shelving system to the wall with a cordless drill.

"Hey," she said, when the drill went quiet.

Brent glanced in her direction then turned back to his work.

"I've got a surprise for you," she said, putting a little melody into the words to make them sound more fun.

"I don't like surprises. At least not from you." He picked up a few screws, positioned a couple in his mouth, set one against a metal bracket and held it in place as he aimed the tip of the drill into it. He pulled the trigger, the drill whirred in a crescendo then came to a high-pitched stop as the screw hit its mark.

"Oh, come on. You are no fun."

"Sorry. Maybe you didn't notice, but," he mumbled, picking another screw from his mouth and positioning it, "I'm working."

"Can you *please* put that little noisemaker down for a few minutes? I want to show you something."

"Is it on your tongue?"

"No, you'll like this."

Dana waited. Whirrrr, thriiiiip! The last screw rammed into the metal bracket and she stuck her head between Brent and the shelf. "Have I not impressed the hell—I mean heck—out of you with my accounting skills?"

"Yes, you have, but obviously this isn't about accounting, therefore . . ." He let the statement hang as he picked up three more screws.

"Brent! Stop a minute! No wonder you're single!" For a brief moment she considered that her Aunt Kathy would be better off without this guy, but she'd gone to enough trouble at that point that she was going to see this little 'surprise' through to completion. She plopped on the floor, and he turned to look at her, letting out an obvious sigh of irritation.

"Fine. What?"

She popped up. "I really think you're going to love this. In fact I'll work half a day for free if you aren't impressed."

He groaned.

"Five minutes!"

Finally he set the drill down and took a few steps in her direction, but she looked back every couple of yards to make sure he was still following her. When they reached the back door she motioned for him to go first. That way he couldn't shove her out, lock the door, and go back to work before seeing what she'd brought him.

"Come on," she said, taking his hand and pulling him around to the back of Binky's truck. When they were in sight of it, she pointed. "There! Isn't that the coolest?"

She watched his face for the huge smile that should have appeared, but he just looked confused.

"It's a sign!" she said, irritated that he'd had no response.

"Yes, I can see that."

"Can't you just imagine that on the wall of the bait shop? Behind the checkout counter?"

He cocked his head.

"There are lots of old bait signs out there but most of them look cheap and hokey and tacky. Aunt . . . um . . . I thought this one looked appropriate, but nice. Tasteful . . . in a bait shop sort of way. Isn't it fantastic?"

He seemed hesitant to admit he was blown away by how perfect it was but finally said, "Yeah. I like it."

He walked around to the driver's side and took a few steps back, as if to get a longer-range view, then moved forward for a better look, opened the tailgate, and hopped up into the truck bed to examine it more closely. "Where did you get this?"

"My Aunt . . . I mean, I mean . . . well, I was thinking about, about remodeling the realty. You know, since now I'm doing the accounting work there, too . . . and . . . "

Crap. After all the rehearsing she had done, she'd still blown it. But maybe he hadn't noticed. Except that he was scowling, and obviously thinking about what she just said.

C'mon, Dana, recover!!!

"I thought I'd try to make it look more professional, more business-like, so I found this interior decorator and—"

"She's your *aunt*?!!"

Double crap.

"You were trying to set us up, weren't you? It's that Kathy Westby woman, right? I *thought* she was hitting on me."

"But she used to run a cafe in Green Bay. For years. I mean she did the ordering and decorating and hiring, and all that. She's really capable. She could run your bakery." Dana said the words really fast to get them all out before he interrupted her.

"Oh, so now you're doing my hiring for me. Not to mention that you *promised* to stay out of my love life."

"No, problem, buster, because you don't have a love life."

"You think you're so smart."

"I AM smart. And Kathy would be a perfect—"

"Hey! What makes you think you'd know who's perfect for me?!"

"Let me FINISH! I was saying she'd be a perfect person to hire. Not only could she help you with the interior decorating, WHICH YOU WILL NEED HELP WITH, but she could run the muckraking bakery for you, too."

He didn't respond, although based on the look on his face, he didn't really seem to be feeling positive about anything she'd said. OOO! She hated apologizing, but it looked like she'd really need to.

"Okay. Maybe I screwed up on the matchmaking thing. I'm s-s-sorry."

"What was that?" He bent his head in her direction and cupped his hand at his ear.

"I'M SORRY! And I'll stay out of your . . . your love life. No more matchmaking, I promise, but, seriously. You need some kind of theme for your place, and you're going to need some masculine touches and feminine touches, and you'll need to tie it all together. It's not going to be easy. You're almost finished with the building part, now you've got to focus on making it a place people want to come to, and be in, and support, and all that."

He still glared but seemed less determined to hate her.

"Okay. Let me explain. Kathy found the sign at an antique shop and she thought you might like it, but she was afraid you didn't like *her*, so she wanted me to show it to you. If you don't want it, it's okay. She told the owner she had a client who might be interested, but she couldn't be sure. He agreed to let her take it for a few days and bring it back if it didn't work."

He turned his attention to it again.

"How much is it?"

"It's a great deal!"

"How much???"

"One-hundred forty-nine dollars. And that's a deal."

"Whoa!"

"Tax included."

"It's just a sign."

"And . . . it's just what you need in the bait shop!"

"I'll think about it."

He looked at it again up close and then from a distance, not saying anything. Several minutes passed and the suspense was driving her nuts. She could tell he liked it, but maybe he was afraid to admit it.

"Do you want me to hang on to it? Let you think about it? Take it back?"

"No. Just leave it. I'll see what the guys say. Get a few more opinions."

"Okay," she said, in as neutral a tone as she could create, although the voice in her head screamed: *Great! He's going to keep it!* She was sorry she'd brought in Kathy's name. She should have thought that through more carefully. Kathy probably wouldn't get the job. On the other hand, *I didn't get fired!*

She took a breath to make sure her excitement wasn't obvious, then asked, "Where do you want it?" stifling her desire to shout: *I knew you'd love it!*

"I'll take it into the baitshop." He reached into the back of the truck, set it across the tailgate, jumped down, and pulled it off. "It's heavy."

"Well-made!"

He gave her a look as if to say he could see that, and she'd better not get pushy.

"When do I have to make my decision?"

She ran ahead to open the back door of the building. "Kathy said she'd get back to the owner by the end of the week."

"Okay. Remind me later in the week and I'll let you know."

She closed the door behind him and pumped her fist, but kept her triumphant "WOO-HOO!" to a whisper.

When she got back in the truck she remembered she was also supposed to give him Kathy's resume if he had a positive reaction to the bait sign. She pulled it off the dash and grabbed the truck handle but hesitated. Maybe it was better to leave well enough alone for the time being.

Hmmm . . . *Leaving something well enough alone.* That actually sounded kind of mature. And scary.

41

THE PERFECT STARTING POINT

Brent propped the sign against the wall in the bait shop, then pulled the plywood away from the new window installed earlier that week. The bright light coming in the south-facing room showed off the sign in all its fishy glory. Dana was right. It wasn't tacky; it was perfect. He'd seen similar signs but they always looked like they had been created by someone with more time than talent. He studied the colorful lures and the large mossy-green oval in the center which featured an open-mouthed fish twisting on a line in mid-air above water. Soon all this work would be finished and he'd be on the other end of that line.

As he put the plywood back so no one could see into the shop, he realized he'd have to start painting soon. He had held off because he didn't have a color scheme but as he noted the sign's mossy green and mustardy yellow, the tan background, and hints of orange, brown, and beige in the lures, he realized this could be the perfect starting point. He just wished someone other than Dana and that pushy Kathy Westby had brought it to him.

When CJ and Piper came in at eight o'clock he led them past the sign. "Whad'ya think?"

Piper shrugged, but CJ nodded. "Looks kind of old-fashioned but nicely done. Sort of classy."

"Yeah, I guess I like it, too," Piper said. "Where you gonna put it?"

"On the wall behind the counter. I'm thinking about putting this color scheme in the barbershop, too. Any thoughts?"

Piper responded with a big-eyed, overwhelmed look. "Don't ask me about decorating."

Brent turned to CJ who nodded again. "Yeah, I can see that," he said.

"The lady who might be renting the Green Bay salon after I leave came across some old green and gold chairs—Packers colors —that she was thinking about using. Apparently the barbershop they came from had been done up with signed footballs and other Packer stuff. The shop was near the stadium so that's where a lot of the players got their haircuts. And since the chairs I ordered were sent back I've been thinking maybe the Packers chairs would work for me."

"Sent back?" Piper asked.

"Oh . . . didn't I tell you guys that story?"

The look of confusion on their faces made it clear that he hadn't.

"They came the week you were here working, but you were all at lunch. I thought I'd make things less complicated by putting

Grace's address as my residence. But she still thinks I'm redoing the grocery store so she assumed they were coming to the wrong address and refused them. I didn't have my phone on me that day and I had transposed the letters in my email. I type fast and don't realize I'm spelling it B-R-N-E-T. All the letters are next to each other on the keyboard, and sometimes when I'm in a hurry I hit them in the wrong order. Anyway, when the company couldn't reach me, back they went."

"That must have cost some bucks," Piper said.

"No kidding. Almost three hundred to send them back. I was pissed off about it at the time, but seeing this sign and thinking about those green and gold chairs—supposedly they're in good shape, sitting in some basement somewhere—it seems like a Packers theme might be a cool idea. If I could get those chairs at a decent price I'd feel better about having lost so much shipping the other ones here and back."

Brent looked at the signboard again. Maybe he did need Kathy Westby's help. He'd just have to make it clear *he* wouldn't be part of the bargain. Besides, if he hired her to run the bakery, maybe he could get her decorating services at a discount, since it looked like his non-existent decorating budget was already in the hole by $149.

And if he was interested in those chairs he would have no choice but to get Monica Seaquist's phone number and ask her where she saw them.

42

THE CONVERSATION WAS OVER

Brent set the little piece of paper on his desk and rubbed his face. Why was this so difficult? He'd picked that piece of paper up, looked at it, then set it back down so many times he had the number memorized. He checked his watch and realized if he didn't call soon it would be too late. Simple question: *Where did you see the Packers barber chairs?* It wasn't that difficult.

But he also wanted to ask her to come along when he checked them out. And to let him take her out for coffee afterwards . . . and maybe take her to dinner a few days later.

So it *was* sort of like asking her out for a date. No wonder he was nervous. He had thought Lisa was nice and cute and fun, but compared to the way he felt about Monica Seaquist after having met her only twice . . . was this infatuation? And hadn't he accepted that being single was his fate?

But lately there were times he was lonely. Maybe Dana was right. Maybe he had been getting cranky and bachelor-y. Well, no. Dana *made* him cranky because she was Dana. Fixing him up with her aunt! She really had nerve. So there was another reason to pursue this relationship. He'd get Dana off his case and her aunt, too. As if he needed another reason.

He picked up the receiver, took a deep breath, and punched in Monica's number, his finger lingering in the air above the last digit before entering it. Seconds later he heard, "Hello?" and nerves hit again.

"Hello—"

He stopped short. Hello, Monica? Would that be proper? Or would Miss Seaquist be better? Ms.? Or Mrs.? Oh, hell! *Say something before she hangs up.*

"This is Brent Wallace. You were looking at renting my salon. I mean the one I'm renting . . . from Scotty . . . my landlord."

Oh, great. He sounded like an idiot. But to his relief, she said, "Yes, I remember."

"I hope it's okay that I called you. Scotty gave me your number. I wanted to know about those Packer barber chairs you had mentioned."

She explained where she had seen them and gave him a phone number.

"I don't suppose I could get you to come with me? Buy you a cup of coffee afterwards?"

No response.

"I'd pay you for your time."

She said she was rather busy these days.

"Oh. Sure. I understand. And of course, if there are only two or three, I wouldn't buy them unless you were sure you didn't want them."

She told him she wasn't interested in them. In fact, she was no longer interested in renting the salon, either.

His heart sank.

"Yes, well, it is a lot of work to run your own salon. I understand. But as long as you have a good client base, you could offer a few referral perks. That could help you bring in some new customers where you work now."

Hell, *he* might have to become a customer.

She thanked him for the advice.

"You're welcome. But I'd feel better checking out the chairs if you came with me. I hate to just call the guy out of the blue."

Her sigh, followed by a brisk, "I doubt that would be a problem," made it clear the conversation was over.

"Oh. Okay. Well, if I decide to buy them, I'll let you know."

As soon as the words left his mouth he realized he shouldn't have said them. For some reason she had apparently decided she disliked him. And realizing that, he had to ask himself if he had any interest at all in those Packer barber chairs other than as a way to connect with Monica Seaquist. He thought they'd hit it off the first time she came into the salon. Like maybe there was a little spark for her, too.

Or was he getting too old to read those things?

Of course he wanted the chairs, especially now that he was considering a green and gold theme for his shops. But when was the last time he gave a woman more than a passing thought? Maybe he could send her flowers. A bouquet with a note to thank her. But he should probably look at the chairs first. Maybe flowers were a little much. He didn't want her to think he was stalking her.

43

MICE!

Grace threw the load of wet clothes into the dryer and as she stepped back, a mouse scooted across the floor. She screeched and ran for the stairway, letting out a yelp when she banged into the dresser where Brent kept his work clothes. The scraping sound that followed—like a mouse scratching on wood—propelled her legs into a higher gear, and she took the stairs on a dead run. At the top she rammed the door open and dove for the closest kitchen chair, flopping into it with a shudder. She rubbed her upper right arm and lifted her sleeve to check the damage from running into the dresser. No blood. A little red mark. There'd be a bruise.

Once she caught her breath, she called Betty and asked to borrow her husband. "It's the mice. They're back. I don't know what it is about them. Not much scares me, but . . . ooo!" She shivered just thinking about it. "I was in the basement doing laundry, and one scooted across the floor. I headed for the steps, but I accidentally slammed into Harv's old hunting dresser, and I heard a scratching sound and—"

She never should have told Betty about her blood pressure. She listened for half a minute then butted in. "Of course I'm upset! Fine. I'll call you back in a few minutes."

She stood and got a glass of water, took several breaths, then called Betty again.

"Sorry. I'm feeling calmer, now. So if Frank could set a few traps, I'll ask Elvis to—" She returned to the chair and took a sip. "Oh, I don't think he cares if I call him that. It's sort of a nickname. So if Frank could just set them for me . . . I hate doing that, and they always snap when I try to put them down. Anyway, I think Elvis would check them on Friday. Okay. Thanks, dearie. Tell him to come in the back door. It's open. I'm recovering in the kitchen."

Grace put on a pot of coffee, making it extra strong for Frank. Ten minutes later he knocked and entered, carrying a small plastic bag. "So the little critters are back?"

"Awful things. I can't stand to look at them dead or alive. If I remember right, the traps are on the shelf across from the furnace."

"Thought I'd bring a few of my own along," he said, holding up the bag. "Already smeared with peanut butter. I'll set 'em all so you'll have a better chance of catching them. You'll have to watch where you step though."

"Just leave a path to the washing machine."

"Don't reach under anything without checking first. You storing any food down there? Mice usually aren't a problem this time of year."

"No. Just canned goods. I don't keep any other food down there. Oh . . . wait. Jenny brought me a sack of peanuts awhile ago. Oh dear. I forgot all about them."

"I suspect that would bring 'em in. Where is it?"

"By the outside cellar door. I was planning to shell them and store them in jars, but I completely forgot."

"I'll see if there's anything left of them."

"And would you check the dresser? The one against the wall on this side of the washing machine? I think they might be living in the drawers."

She listened to him run down the steps and couldn't help thinking that despite her general happiness with life, she wouldn't mind being twenty years younger.

As the coffee pot hissed the end of the brewing cycle, Frank charged up the stairs and entered the kitchen holding a tattered burlap bag. "Here's the culprit, or what's left of it. Shells scattered all over back there. I found your broom and cleaned them up. I'll toss the mess in your trash can on my way out."

Grace poured him a cup of coffee while he washed his hands at the sink.

"The mice must have made a nest somewhere," he said, taking a seat at the table. "Not in the dresser. I'm surprised you haven't noticed them before. It seems like they might have been down there awhile."

Grace shook her head. "Well, I haven't been looking for them, and since I got the dryer I hardly ever use that door." I don't know, Frank. Maybe I'm getting too old to be here alone. Since El . . . since Brent has been staying on the weekends, I realize how quiet it is the rest of the week. Maybe once he's settled and on his own, I'll put the place up for sale and move into an apartment or senior housing. I wouldn't mind being around a few more people. It's getting harder to handle all the maintenance and the lawn and such on my own."

"Aw, Grace, you're in better shape than a lot of people half your age," Frank said.

"Thanks, Frank, but you have to admit I don't need such a big house anymore. And if I fall and break a hip, then where will I be? I don't want to have to rely on other people. I had hoped Jenny would come back and live here with me, but she has her own life."

"Maybe Brent will want to buy the house, too."

"It's crossed my mind, but he's a single man. What would he want with such a big house? And he's already said he'd like a cabin in the woods."

"Wouldn't hurt to ask. 'Course you could always list with Pine Lake Realty."

She was about to give him a piece of her mind when she saw the smile on his face.

"Just teasing, Grace. Thanks for the coffee."

44

I BELIEVE IN LOVE

Dana pushed the door of Brent's salon open, bells sounded, and seconds later he came out of his office.

"Hi," she said, waving a few sheets of paper. "Got something for you. Since my hair is blonde now, I didn't think I'd be freaking anyone out. I also didn't see any cars in the parking lot, so I thought it would be safe."

He checked his watch. "I have a break for another twenty minutes or so. What are you doing here?"

"I'm heading over to check out some stuff in the Small Business Development Center. But I also wanted to drop this off for you. It's my aunt's—I mean—Kathy Westby's resume. And I need to tell her if you want that sign."

"Yeah. I'll take the sign."

"Do you want me to cut her a check?"

"Guess you'll have to."

"Might be nice to give her a finder's fee."

"What? But I didn't ask her to find it."

"Hey! I'm not talking a thousand dollars. Twenty-five. Consider it your first investment in employee relations."

"I never said I was going to hire her. Fifteen bucks. And next time ask first."

Dana rolled her eyes and handed him two sheets of paper.

"But this is for the bakery position. Is she still looking for work as an interior decorator?"

"Yeah. But I told you she also ran a cafe here in Green Bay for ten years."

"Okay. I'll look at this. But you need to tell her I have no time or interest in starting a relationship." He glared at her to make sure she understood.

"Yeah. Blah, blah, blah. Heard it all before. You're going to turn into a grumpy old man like my grandpa. When my Nanny Rae died, that was the end of him. I may not be the most normal person you know, but at least I believe in love. It would be good for you."

"Look. I'm more than twice your age, and since I've already been married, I have a good idea of what that's all about, so I don't understand why you think you'd be better at running my life than I am."

"Because I'm young and open to the world of possibility, and you're stuck in a rut."

"For all you know there just might be someone I'm interested in."

"REALLY? Cool. Who is it?"

"As if I'd tell you."

"You're probably just saying that to get me to stay out of your love life."

"That could be true, too."

"Fine. I'm leaving. Check over that resume. Kathy really knows her stuff, and if you ever decide you want to stop acting like you're as old as Grace, you should consider dating just to liven up your life a bit."

"You liven up my life about as much as I can handle."

She wasn't quite sure how to take that, but decided to put her own spin on it. She lifted her shoulders, cocked her head, put on a big smile, and said, "Thank you!"

Then she left and decided she'd go ahead with her plan. If it turned out well, she'd claim responsibility. If it backfired, she'd leave him in the dark.

45

SUAVE

Brent thanked the man for his time and said he'd call as soon as he'd shown the photos of the barber chairs to his interior decorator, but he was quite certain he'd take them. He couldn't help smiling. The man probably thought he was nuts to get that excited over a few old chairs. But ever since he'd made the appointment to see them, he had imagined calling Monica Sequist again, only this time he'd be prepared. He wouldn't sound so desperate. His idiotic responses had probably turned her off, but this time he'd be more . . . suave. Yes. More suave.

After pulling his car out on the road so he wouldn't block the man's driveway, he turned off the engine and dialed Monica's number. Since it was early Sunday afternoon he doubted she'd be at work. Although after their last conversation, he harbored a slight fear she might not answer, then chastised himself. He had to be more confident. *Suave.*

After three rings she picked up.

"Hi. It's Brent. Brent Wallace. I've just been looking at the chairs you told me about. I'm pretty sure they'll work for me. I just need to check with my interior decorator. I appreciate you telling me about them. Won't you let me buy you a cup of coffee?"

As soon as he said the words he thought it sounded less suave than he planned and more like begging, so he quickly added: "Since you're in the business, I wouldn't mind another opinion of my plans for the shop I'm setting up."

She told him she really wasn't qualified to give such an opinion, and buying her a cup of coffee wasn't necessary.

Hoping she was being polite, not dismissive, he said, "I know it's not necessary, but I'd like to."

She said she didn't have any free time, her tone of voice now brisk.

"Okay. Well, thanks for the tip. I think the chairs will work." The next word out of his mouth should have been good-bye, but against his better judgment, he looked for something else to extend the conversation. "Have you decided to stay at the salon you're at now?"

There was a brief pause and then . . . the phone went silent.

46 |

THE SCRATCHING SOUND

Brent parked in Grace's driveway the following Friday evening, got out, and looked across the street at the building. If he could hold her off for one more week, he'd be ready to surprise her. The grocery store's original plate glass window offered a spectacular view of the bakery, and if one peeked in now, as Grace might, it could look like part of a grocery store, so he hadn't been worried she'd discover the truth on her own. With the window of the bait shop boarded over, that wouldn't give anything away either.

Instead of an open corridor from the sidewalk, he'd put in a main entrance door. It not only served as an energy-saving airlock, but also allowed him to purchase cheaper entry doors for each shop. Since the design gave the impression of one store, it was another way to keep Grace from suspecting anything until he'd given her a tour. Although he felt bad for keeping her in the dark, at least he could control how the truth came out. Once she saw how great the shops looked, how could she not be impressed?

He knocked a few times on the back door, then let himself in, calling out to Grace that he was back.

"Hello, dear," she said, appearing a moment later. "I'm so glad you're here. I was hoping you could check on something for me."

"Glad to help. What do you need?"

"You go ahead and take your suitcase upstairs and get settled. I should at least let you catch your breath."

"I'm fine, Grace. I've been sitting in the car for over an hour. It's not time to take out the air conditioner yet, is it?"

She shook her head. "I have mice."

"Mice?"

She nodded. "Mice. In the basement. Jenny brought me some peanuts in a burlap bag a few months ago. I forgot about them, but the mice found them. I was down there earlier in the week and one ran across the room. It scared the dickens out of me, and I ran for the stairs and bumped into that dresser. There was a scratching sound. I thought there must have been mice in one of the drawers. You've been using it, right?"

"Yes, and I've never seen any evidence of mice. Of course, I haven't looked that carefully. Do you want me to set some traps?

"No, dear. Frank—you know, Betty's husband—came over and took care of that, but I was hoping you'd check them. I'm not squeamish about much. Spiders and snakes have never bothered me, but mice! Oooh!!" She shook her head, and Brent set his suitcase down.

"I'll go check them right now."

He headed down the steps, and Grace stayed at the top. "If you find any, fling them into the woodsy area in the backyard.

There's a cellar door off to the left. You can push that open and throw them out."

"Whoa," he hollered up to her a minute later. "You definitely have mice. Looks like the traps did their job."

"Be sure to check the dresser drawers. And check underneath it, too. Frank set eleven traps."

The incandescent lights provided enough illumination to determine no mice had been in the drawers, but it was too dark to see underneath them.

"Is there a flashlight down here somewhere?" he called up from the foot of the stairs.

"I have one up here. Just a minute."

He climbed the stairs and took the large lantern-style flashlight she handed him.

"It makes me sick to think they've been running around down there. Every so often I leave a basket of clothes on the floor. Ick! They probably crawled around in them."

"Your basement seems pretty sound. There are a few spots around the cellar door frame where they're probably coming in. I'll fill them in with some spray foam insulation, but for now I'll re-set a few traps by the door. Maybe that way we can catch them before they cause any trouble."

"Thank you!"

Back in the basement he checked the drawers and saw that, while for the moment they were mouse-free, the little rodents had definitely left signs of their visit in the form of droppings in the lower drawers. Next he shone the flashlight under the dresser where, just a few inches away, he saw that another invader had met its demise. Beyond that a trap closer to the wall had sprung with enough force to turn it on its side, but he couldn't reach it.

He found a broom and pushed it under the dresser, handle first, shoving the trap out. Shining the flashlight on it he discovered it wasn't a mousetrap, it was a small brown paper bag. The lost gift? He looked on top of the dresser and realized that when he tossed his towel up there, it must have pushed the bag off the back, and it got stuck between the wall and the dresser. When Grace bumped into it she must have dislodged it and it fell to the floor. That was probably the scratching sound she thought she'd heard. He recalled looking beneath the dresser but hadn't thought to look behind it.

The little brown bag had gotten dusty and dirty, but when he peeked inside he saw that the gift wrap was still pristine and hadn't ripped. Should he give it to Grace now?

"Are you okay, dear?"

"Fine," he said, shoving the bag into the top dresser drawer. "I found all eleven traps. Eight successful. I'll get rid of the ones I caught and re-set the traps. Do you have any peanut butter?"

"I'll bring it right down."

"No need. I'll come get it."

He made a quick decision not to tell her about the gift yet, but decided not to leave it in the drawer. She might check there. Or the mice might get to it. He decided to wrap one of his t-shirts around it, take it back upstairs, and store it in his suitcase.

And he'd tell Grace about the store this weekend. Absolutely. He just had to decide how. But now the gift would surely help.

47

SHE COULDN'T DO EVERYTHING

Brent closed the center drawer of the desk in the little office space he had set up in a corner of the storage area. The building's structural work was finished, the new windows and doors had been installed—a month later than he'd hoped—but considering all that had to be done, he was pleased. He had spray-painted the outside of the storage shed behind the shop but decided to save work on the inside until the following winter.

Within two weeks, construction would be completed, each shop fleshed out, filled in, and ready to be dressed up. He needed a face-to-face with Kathy Westby, and it had to be soon and here in the shops . . . definitely not in her home where she had turned their last meeting into a date. He considered asking Dana to handle this, too, but she would tell him he needed to make the final decisions and she couldn't do *everything*. She was probably right.

As weird as Dana was, she had already saved him thousands of dollars by getting him an operating loan at nearly two percent less than he'd hoped for and had saved him countless hours by pointing out all the ways an office manager would be useful. Then she became one. Next, she helped Kathy set up the bakery with used equipment, then helped her interview and hire two part-time workers. They'd set up a training session to begin on October 3rd, in anticipation of an October 10th opening, only a month away.

When Kathy agreed to run the bakery, she'd thrown in her interior decorating expertise for free. Just so she didn't plan to extract her "fee" some other way. He tapped her number on his phone, ready to set the boundaries from the start.

"We need to meet here in the shops," he began, then wondered if he was coming on too strong. She was a good person—just as Lisa was a good person—just not good for him. He softened his tone and continued. "The chairs I bought are here, and I want you to see them. I like the green and gold for a possible Packers theme for the barber and bait shop, and the same colors with the purple you showed me for the salon. As long as you think the purple will go with the chairs."

When she corrected his word choice, there was no hint of awkwardness. "I mean mulberry," he said, hoping she had forgotten how he reacted when she kissed him. He hadn't been rude, he'd just extricated himself from her grip—maybe with a little more intensity than necessary, since he'd practically leapt away from her—and left. She really was a nice person, just not his type. He didn't know how much clearer he could make that.

The following day, after a perfectly chaste and professional meeting, he thanked her for her help, gently ushered her out, and quickly closed the door. They had gone through each room, chosen the colors, and decided yes on the chairs for both salon and barbershop. She had shown him a set of framed pictures of baked goods which he had vetoed as dull and hideous although he had presented his opinion tactfully, following up with praise for the antique wrought iron baker's rack.

On her thrift and antique store runs, Kathy had picked up a variety of rolling pins to incorporate in the decor and several old-fashioned pottery bowls she planned to tip partway to spotlight items in the display cases. She had sketched out some ideas and showed him the fabric she'd use to create tablecloths. Although he had planned on four tables, after she made her case, he realized the layout with three was much more welcoming and appealing.

Clearly this woman, with her decorating skills and cafe-management experience, would be almost as much of an asset as Dana. She also seemed to accept that their relationship would be friendly but businesslike, although she had hinted that if he ever changed his mind he should let her know.

But why couldn't it have been Monica Seaquist who was so enchanted with him?

48

WHY ARE YOU HERE?

Brent stood back and looked at the antique sign hanging behind the checkout counter in the bait shop. It was still crooked. He stepped closer to adjust one end and realized he'd have to rehang it. Just then Dana popped into the room.

"Where did you come from?"

She gave him one of her weirder looks.

"I meant that I didn't hear you come in."

"Your truck's here and the back door was unlocked. Besides, we're practically family."

Practically family? He stared into space, once again struck speechless by what came out of her mouth, then turned back to the sign. "As long as you're here you can help me hang this thing straight."

"It should be a bit higher anyway."

"I thought art should hang at eye level."

"Brent, believe me. It's too low. Exchange places with me for a minute. And by the way, as much as I like this sign, it doesn't count as art."

He moved around to the front of the counter, and she positioned herself behind it.

"I see what you mean. Between the clerk and the counter a lot of the sign will be hidden." He took it down, set it on the counter, then pulled out the nails he'd pounded in the wall.

"Okay," he said, as he picked the sign up again. "Could you grab that pencil? Let me know when it's at a good height, and straight, then you can mark the two corners."

"And what do you say?"

He snorted. "PLEASE!"

She picked up the pencil and stepped several feet back from the counter.

"Why are you here?" he asked.

"Ah, Brent," she said, shaking her head. "I can always count on you for friendly conversation."

"The question remains." He repositioned the sign. "Is that straight?"

"Maybe . . . a little higher on the left. That's good."

"Okay, mark it." He watched her make a tiny dot. "No, you need to make a sideways mark with the pencil just above that corner, about an inch long so I can see it. *Thank* you."

"You're welcome. So . . . the reason I'm here. I was thinking that since you don't have any children, and I don't have a father, maybe you could be my . . . sort of . . . father."

He froze and nearly dropped the sign. After regaining his composure he turned to her, making his face state as clearly as possible that he thought she was nuts. Either she was really focused on making sure the sign was straight or she didn't want to meet his eyes, but she wouldn't look at him. He waited for her to say she was kidding, but when she didn't—and he realized *she* wasn't about to break the awkward silence—he said the only thing he could think of. "You already *have* a father. And can you please mark the other side?"

"Oh, right." She moved around him and drew a little line above that corner. "No. I really *don't* have a father."

There was something in her voice. Pain? Anger? Defiance? She was clearly waiting for him to say something, but he had no idea how to tell her he wasn't in the market for a daughter. He just kept holding up the sign and staring at it, even though she'd marked it, and it was heavy, and he needed to set it down. After several awkward—certainly on his part—seconds, she spoke.

"Yes, someone got my mom pregnant, but we've never met. I don't know anything about him. I guess it was a one-night stand." She sighed. "Let me look once more."

She moved around to the front of the counter, stepped back a few feet and moved her head side to side a couple of times. "Yeah. I think that's straight."

"Didn't your mother have to get financial support from him?" Brent realized he'd been holding his breath so he let it out, set the sign down, pounded in two nails, then hung it again.

"She said it wasn't worth the hassle. Or the humiliation."

"So you've never even met him?"

"Nope."

"But you're twenty-two years old. Why do you need a father now?" He turned to her, trying to look too inexperienced to be a father.

"For one thing, if Binky and I ever get married, there won't be anyone to walk me down the aisle."

He backed up several paces and looked at the sign. "Somehow I can't picture you having an actual walk-me-down-the-church-aisle sort of wedding."

"I didn't say what kind of aisle."

"True."

"So, what do you think?"

"I think it's a good height. It finally looks straight, too. Thanks."

"No. I mean about being my adopted . . . adoptive . . . father."

"You're serious?"

"Of course I'm serious. I wouldn't ask just anyone. You *do* realize this is an honor."

"I hadn't thought about it that way. And now that I have, I can't help but wonder why you would even ask me, *me*, of all people. I get the impression you think I'm a boring, old-fashioned fuddy-duddy who is overly involved with fishing and hunting and unable to get his own dates."

"Oh, of course. All those things. That's exactly why I think you'd make a good father. I mean, the truth is, I'm basically motherless, too, at this point, so I should have at least one parent I can count on."

"Surely your mother will come back and run the realty office after this fling is over."

Dana shook her head. "Nope. She just married her fling. He retired, he has money, and they're buying a place in Mexico where I guess she's retiring, too. She invited me to visit."

"So now you'll have a father."

"I cannot be a daughter to a cowboy-hat-wearing man who picks up and runs off with someone like my mother."

"I thought you liked your mother."

"I did. Right up until she ran off with someone she met on-line who wears cowboy hats."

"What if I discover a passion for cowboy hats? Then you won't want me to be your father, either."

"Fine. It was just a thought. Doesn't seem like you have much of a family and you're a flop with women. I just thought maybe you could start out with a daughter and work your way up."

"I am not a flop with women. I simply choose not to be surrounded by them every moment of my life. For nearly thirty years I've been cutting hair, working mainly with women, six days a week."

He could feel his heart rate soar as he let loose with words that felt like they'd been building for a long time, and once he got started he couldn't stop.

"Having just gotten *out* of a marriage, I know I could happily live without any more women in my life, but instead I am spending my weekends with a woman who acts like she wants to be my mother, working with an interior decorator who acts like she wants to be my girlfriend, and now . . ." he stomped, took a breath, and continued in a louder voice, ". . . you come in here acting like you want to be my daughter. Do you know why I am moving up here? Have you figured it out yet . . .?

By now he was practically screaming, but he didn't care. "BECAUSE I WANT TO GO FISHING AND HUNTING EVERY SECOND OF MY LIFE THAT I AM NOT WORK-ING, DURING WHICH TIME I AM SURROUNDED BY WOMEN."

He actually felt winded and realized he had crescendoed that harangue into a full-blown rant. She had really hit a nerve. At least he'd had the presence of mind to stop before he shouted that the one woman whose attention he would have welcomed wanted nothing to do with him.

"Okay. Well. It's been a thrill talking to you, as usual."

She did an about-face and walked out.

He turned in time to see her disappear through the door and thought about calling out an apology, but he meant what he'd said.

Still, he felt bad. He shouldn't have yelled at her.

He picked up the hammer and extra nails, and then, with a start, he remembered the unexplained box of chocolates Grace had found on her doorstep on Father's Day. A box wrapped in purple paper.

And then he felt really bad.

49

MORE THAN ONE REASON

Brent opened the door of the flower shop, noting that the sign listing their open hours meant he'd have only a few minutes to make a purchase. As he stepped inside he heard a voice bark out, "We're closing."

Brent spotted an old man at the back of the shop who stared at him as if he'd come in to rob the place. "I'll be quick. Do you have any deep purple, maybe almost-black flowers?"

The man closed his eyes, as if counting to ten or praying for patience, then hollered, "Mary! Come out here!" He gave Brent a look that suggested his entrance into the shop had completely ruined the day. The man walked past him, turned out the lights near the door and flipped the lock.

A plastic thermal curtain opened behind the counter and a youngish woman appeared. "Dad, wait a bit. Put the lights back on." She turned to Brent, her smile warm and sincere. "What were you looking for?"

"I'd like a small bouquet of darker-colored flowers. Maybe deep blue, or purple, almost black."

"Well, we have a few irises left. They're at the end of their bloom. Will you be giving them soon?"

"Tomorrow morning."

"Let me pick through them. I'll give you a discount. I should be able to find about half a dozen or so and I'll put some greenery with them to fill them out. Do you want them in a vase?"

Brent tried to imagine what kind of vase Dana would like. "Well, she's young and dresses weird, mostly in purple. As far as I can tell, she only shops at thrift stores. Her wardrobe seems to be mostly old prom dresses. That type of thing. And she has a lot of piercings and tattoos. Do you have anything frog-shaped?"

She laughed. "Sounds like a challenge. I'll see what I can find."

She disappeared behind the curtain, the lights went back on, and Brent walked around the shop, thinking about how he'd just described the old Dana. Although, despite the fact she had changed her outward appearance, inside she was still Dana. And somehow that was a relief.

As he let that thought go, he saw he'd ended up in front of a case with several pre-made bouquets. On a whim, and before he could talk himself out of it, he told the man he would also take the bouquet of daisies with the "Thank You" card attached on a spike.

The old man hobbled over, opened the case and took them out. "Could have done that yourself," he said, in an irritated monotone, and handed him the vase.

"Sorry. I didn't know I was allowed."

The old man was so grumpy. He probably didn't feel well. Brent watched him hobble back around the counter and disappear behind the curtain, thinking maybe there was more than one reason he was meant to stop at this particular flower shop today.

Minutes later the young woman appeared with a beautiful bouquet of deep purple irises, but rather than rising out of a tall vase, they'd been cut short and arranged with small white tulip-shaped flowers and some greenery in a squat, purplish, iridescent frog. It was unusual. And perfect.

"Thank you. That's so much better than what I'd imagined. And I'll take these, too," he said, setting the *Thank You* bouquet on the counter.

"Okay," she said, pulling a box from the floor behind her. "I'll prop these up so they don't tip over."

As she punched numbers into the cash register he took a fifty from his wallet. When the final number popped unto the screen he started to take out several ones, then changed his mind. He pulled out a couple of twenties, paired one with the fifty and handed it to her. After taking his change he set the second twenty on the counter and stepped away from the counter.

"Sir, you forgot—"

"That's for you," he said. Then he bowed, and blushed, and headed for the exit, where he flipped the lock, pushed the door open, and walked out into the beautiful evening.

50

HE HAD TO GIVE IT A TRY

Brent set the box holding the two flower arrangements on the seat beside him, wondering if it had been a mistake to purchase the second bouquet. Not only was he on the north end of town and far from Monica Seaquist's shop, but what was the likelihood she would even be there on a Friday night? Maybe he should take it to Grace. She was the one who really deserved a *Thank You* bouquet. In fact, even if Monica was still at work, maybe she wouldn't appreciate it. He had a sudden vision of her dumping the bouquet in the garbage.

But this was his last chance. He had to give it a try.

He started the engine and turned back toward town.

No one was at the reception desk, but one of the beauticians apologized to her client, set her scissors down, and came over.

"Can I help you?"

"I don't suppose Monica Seaquist is still here?"

"No, she's gone for the night."

"Is she working tomorrow?"

She flipped a page on the book on the desk, then shook her head. "Nope. Gone till Monday. Looks like her first appointment is at eight-thirty."

"I don't know if these will last. Can I leave them? Could you set them at her station?"

"Sure."

"May I borrow a pen?"

She handed him one, and he wrote on the card: *The chairs will work great for me!*

He was about to sign his name, but decided against it. She would know who they were from. There wasn't much more he could do.

51

MAYBE I DO

Brent placed the last of the lures in the bins and headed to the office where he popped a pod in the new single-serve coffee maker Kathy had donated "in the interest of sanity." He sniffed the result, took the coffee to his desk, sat, and pulled out his phone. He tapped in a number and seconds later Dana answered.

"Pine Lake Realty, your locally owned and operated real estate office."

"Hi, it's Brent."

"The old muckraker himself."

"You use that term a lot, but I don't think you use it correctly."

"I know what it means, but it has a good sound to it. Lots of crackle. It's my all-purpose swear word, put-down, and term of endearment rolled into one. What do you want?"

He couldn't help but notice the chill in her voice.

"Will you be in the office for awhile?"

"I promised Mom I'd be here Saturdays until noon through hunting season. I don't know why, but she's paying me, so . . ."

"Okay. I'll be right over."

"If it's work for the shops, you'll have to pay me overtime."

"Fine."

Her lack of expectation made his errand that much more fun. Seeing that crusty old man at the flower shop—and recalling his own nasty rant the last time he saw Dana—made him decide to be more aware of his attitude. After all, he was only seven minutes from his favorite walleye fishing spot. Which, granted, he hadn't taken much advantage of since starting the remodeling project, but that time would come. And maybe, whatever karma meant, Monica Seaquist's indifference was his own fault. Maybe he had to be a little nicer across the board. He planned to start right now and earn the karmic right to claim every walleye he could catch. Maybe eventually he could even look up Monica Seaquist and start all over.

He walked into the realty office and set the little Iris-bedecked frog on her desk.

"What's that?"

"It's a frog with an Iris growth."

"Hmmm . . . kind of cute. Who's it for?"

"My daughter."

"Thought you didn't have a daughter."

He shrugged. "Maybe I do."

Then he walked out, feeling a lot better than the last time he'd seen her.

52

THE TRUTH

Brent returned to his shops and did a quick walk-through. There was still much to be done, but he was ready to make things right with Grace.

Less than a minute later, he walked out the front entrance with the gift in his hand but had second thoughts. He took it back into the bakery and set it on one of the tables. Maybe it would be better to give it to Grace *after* he had shown her what he'd done with the old building.

As he stepped out onto the sidewalk the second time, he practically knocked over a woman passing by. He was about to apologize when he recognized her.

"What are you doing here?" he asked, realizing just as the words left his mouth that his tone probably sounded accusatory rather than shocked.

She stared, stuttered an "I, I . . .," then stopped.

"Did you follow me?" Brent asked, then nearly apologized, knowing that couldn't have been the case. Unless . . . the flowers? In his confusion he was unable to stop staring.

"I was wondering if you were following *me!*" she said.

"No. I've been here since last night."

They looked at each other for what seemed to Brent like several awkward minutes.

"Here . . . where?" she finally asked.

"I'm staying across the street until I find a place to live. This is where I'm moving to."

She looked beyond him to the building.

"I mean, this is my store. Well, shop . . . shops."

She still seemed confused.

"I'm the person who owns Brent's Sa—"

"I know who you are. I just don't understand what you're doing here."

"I'm going to work here."

"In a grocery store? I thought you were opening a salon."

"It's not a grocery store. It used to be, but now it's going to be Brent's Beauty, Barber, Bait, and Bakery." He couldn't help but smile, partly because Monica Seaquist was here, right in front of him, and partly because he was proud of what he had accomplished and, he realized, eager to show her.

"No. Mom said it was going to be re-opened as . . . I'm confused. I'm sure my mom said it was going to be a grocery store."

"Well, the lady who used to own it thinks that. So, are you from around here? You still haven't said what you're doing here."

"I'm visiting my mom." And then her hand went to her mouth and her eyes got big. "You're him!"

"Who?"

"The guy who looks like Elvis!"

"Oh, well, the lady who sold me this building thinks so. She must know your mom." Brent was feeling better about things all the time. How ironic that he'd practically given up on finding some excuse to see her again, and she was apparently from Pine Lake. What were the chances? Thank you, Lady Luck!

"I'm certain that the lady who sold you this building believed it was going to be re-opened as a grocery store."

Uh-oh. For some reason, she was really angry.

"No. I bought it to . . ." He started over, trying to sound self-assured, like someone who had come up with a great plan and was bringing it to fruition. Someone reliable. "I love to hunt and fish, but living in Green Bay, I never had much free time. I thought if I moved my business up here I'd be able to get out on the lake and in the woods a lot more often. But I didn't think running a salon would bring in enough income, so I decided to put in a separate barber shop, and a bait store and a bakery."

He expected her to be impressed by his cleverness, but the way her lips grew tight and her eyes collapsed into slits through which they glared at him, he realized his pronouncement had the opposite reaction.

The harsh expression on her face deepened, so he put on his cheeriest smile, hoping to lighten up the conversation again.

"You said your mother knows Mrs. Havisto, so you must have grown up around here."

"No. I never said that. You misunderstood. My mother *IS* Mrs. Havisto."

What??? What on earth was she talking about?

"But she told me she only has one daughter. I'm sure she said her name is Jenny. She went to Graceland with her a few weeks ago."

"She's always called me Jenny. My middle name is Jennifer."

His brain kicked into high gear, racing around thoughts, things he'd said, and things he assumed, and he stood there with his mouth open.

"Oh, boy, did I have you pegged. You think just because you're good-looking you can get away with anything."

"What—?"

"Don't play Mr. Innocent. You were flirting with me not two minutes before your girlfriend walked in—"

"Who?" he managed to interject but she kept on going.

"—and then you tried to take me out for coffee! I nearly fell for you. But I kept telling myself that guys like you think you can play the field, do what you please, and you don't care a bit about who you hurt—"

"But I—"

"And you lied to my mother who thinks the grocery store that she worked in with my father, that meant so much to the two of them, THAT EVEN I WORKED IN—"

Here she took in a deep breath and blew it back out, the force of her anger causing him to take a step backward. Conciliatory phrases raced through his mind, but none of them seemed equal to her wrath, so he just braced himself for the verbal tornado heading in his direction.

"—is going to be reopened, and she has her heart set on it being a grocery store again, while you turn it into some, some,

some . . . you're just a conceited . . . big-headed . . . small-hearted LIAR!"

"I don't have a girlfriend," he said, or meant to say, but later he realized he had been so taken aback by the kind of person she thought he was, maybe he had never said it out loud.

He watched her stomp away, cross the street, and head into Grace's house without so much as a second's hesitation. So, she was obviously Grace's daughter. But how had this all gone so sour? He'd been so happy to see her again and now . . . now?

Why hadn't he thought to ask her about the flowers he'd dropped off? Maybe that would have helped. Or maybe it would have made things worse, considering she thought he was some kind of playboy.

But why did she think he had a girlfriend? Who was she talking about? He thought back and then it hit him . . . oh . . . it was Kathy Westby. Kathy Westby, of course. Kathy had interrupted their lovely conversation when he was giving Monica a ride on the barber chair. When Kathy walked in and called out his name with that sing-song voice, Monica must have thought . . .

He remembered being irritated with Kathy at the time for ruining the moment, but he hadn't realized how it might look to Monica. Should he run across the street and tell her that woman was not his girlfriend, only his bakery manager and interior decorator? His *pushy* interior decorator, for whom he had no romantic feelings whatsoever?

And then he thought about her other accusation. Which was totally true. How could he not have told Grace the truth all this time? Except he had always intended to find a way to make her okay with it, and even if she wasn't, there was the gift from her husband to smooth things over. But now . . . now there was no way he could go to that house and . . . Grace probably knew by now. Monica—Jenny!—was probably at this very moment telling Grace how he had a girlfriend and yet he flirted with her and . . . and that there was *not* going to be a grocery store across the street.

What the hell was he going to do now? All his clothes were there. He'd been planning on sleeping there tonight.

And not just tonight! How could he ever set foot inside that house again? He'd have to find a room somewhere.

A room! Hell, he'd have to look for a new life. Grace would tell Evelyn and Betty, and before the day was out they'd probably round up a posse and kick him out of town. He would never have a customer! And as disappointing as that thought was, the fact that he had messed up his chance to connect with the woman he finally thought might be the one . . .

He stood there, in front of the building where—just a few months ago—he thought his dream of a lifetime would come true. But now that dream seemed . . . tainted. And the accusatory voices in his head were so loud.

He had to get off the sidewalk and out of the view of Grace's house, but he felt unable to move. Something demanded his attention, but he couldn't put his finger on it. He closed his eyes for a moment while some enterprising part of his brain beckoned him to a quiet corner and told him to think back on that conversation. *Remember,* it said. He tried to recreate the run-in with Monica, especially the part where he felt like the sun had suddenly appeared, albeit momentarily, as if bursting out from behind clouds. Because she had said . . . .what had she said? Her words came back to him: *I nearly fell for you.*

So she liked him, too?

She *had* liked him. And he had blown it.

He heard a muffler and turned to see the car pulling into the parking lot. The brakes squealed, and the car shuddered to a stop. How was that old heap still running? He asked himself the question several times as he walked over to the car, trying not to think about Monica Jennifer Seaquist and realizing that if Dana was coming over in the middle of a Saturday something must have gone really wrong.

And of course, he already knew that it had.

53 |

WHAT'S THE PROBLEM?

Dana waved. She wouldn't feel comfortable calling him 'Dad' so soon, and he probably wouldn't feel comfortable hearing it. They'd have to ease into the terminology, but surely the fact that he'd brought her *yes-you-can-be-my-daughter* flowers meant the idea was growing on him. As he came toward her, she got a little teary, but she figured she was allowed. This was a big deal, and she just knew she could count on him not to let her down.

He was almost across from her when the little teariness turned into more of a blubbering tearfest. She took the last three steps toward him in a rush and threw her arms around him.

"Thank you," she blurted in a high-voiced whisper.

He just stood there, probably in shock, she figured. But he didn't back away so she grabbed his arms and pulled them around her so that, whether he intended to or not, he was hugging her.

"You're welcome," he said, but not at all in the way she'd expected.

She pulled back and looked at him. "Oh. Did I? . . . did you *not* mean that I could be your sort-of-adopted daughter?"

"No. I mean yes, yes you can."

"Well, why do you have a look on your face that says you are considering jumping off a cliff?"

"I wouldn't do that. But I did just screw something up. Not with you though."

She looked at him, wiped her eyes, and her heart fell. "It's okay. I've gotten along without a dad all my life."

"NO! I'll be . . . I *want* to be . . . your—you know—adopted, I mean adoptive, dad." He took a breath and stood there like someone who'd just been told he had an incurable disease.

"Well I don't want you to be my adoptive dad if it's going to make you *that* unhappy." The tears were gone and she felt herself move back into fatherless mode.

"No. It's probably good for me to have someone as . . . as unusual as you in my life right now."

"I didn't ask to be your entertainment. I asked to be your daughter."

"Not entertainment. I just meant that you are always . . . you are always exactly who you are. Different, but, I like it."

"So you really did mean you'll be my sort-of-adoptive father?"

This time when he reassured her it was with a hug that *he* initiated. "Yes. I hereby sort of adopt you."

Now she knew he was sincere, and yet she also heard the undercurrent of sorrow. "What's wrong? I mean, now that we really *are* practically family, you can tell me. Maybe I can help. C'mon. Let's go sit on the bench out—"

"I can't."

"You can't what?"

"I can't sit out there where Grace can see me."

"She must know you're here, right? I mean, you stayed there last night, didn't you?"

He nodded.

"For muckrakin' sake, what's the problem?" She realized she'd put her hands on her hips and talked to him as though he were the kid and she was the parent. "Sorry. But I don't know what's going on. You're going to have to tell me. Unless you're hinting that it's none of my business."

He shrugged.

"Is it about the store?"

He nodded.

"Is it about Grace finding out it's not going to be a grocery store?"

He made a face like a four-year-old who had just broken his dump truck.

"I take it that's a *yes*."

He nodded.

"She can't stop you. Besides, the place looks great. Have you even shown it to her yet?"

He shook his head. "I was just going over to get her."

"And you're afraid to go alone? I'll go with you."

"No, it's not that."

"Well, I'm running out of guesses, so either you can tell me what the problem is, or tell me to go home, but we're not getting anywhere like this."

She hated feeling so helpless. When she first thought about asking him to be her sort-of-adopted-father, she figured she'd finally have someone else besides Binky to go to with all her troubles, but now Brent Wallace appeared to be the one who needed help. She looked around, wishing she could move one of those benches behind the store so they could have a good talk. He obviously needed to talk to somebody, and he must have decided she was acceptable, or he would have walked away by now.

"C'mon. Let's go sit in my car."

She didn't expect him to follow, but he trudged after her like a pitiful puppy on a leash. She got in on the driver's side and threw her purse, shawls, food wrappers, recent thrift store purchase bags, and Binky's coin collection in the backseat. Brent opened the door, climbed in, sat back, and sighed.

"I really don't know what to do," he said.

"You have to tell her."

"It's not just that. It's . . . do you remember me saying I may have found someone I liked?"

"Vaguely."

"It's Grace's daughter."

"Jenny?"

"Monica!"

"I thought she only had one daughter."

"Apparently that's true, and her name is Monica Jennifer Seaquist."

"Oh. I only ever heard her talk about her daughter as Jenny."

"I met her in Green Bay. She was thinking about renting the salon I'm leaving." He stopped and sighed again. "Talk about ironic. I don't know why I'm telling you this. This probably isn't the most appropriate topic for a newly minted father-daughter relationship."

"Just because you're old . . . older . . . than me, doesn't mean I can't understand. And considering that it's about you turning the grocery store into something else, well, I guess I do have *some* responsibility for the way it's turning out. I've heard a little about Jenny, but I've never met her. Couldn't you just go over there and explain everything to Grace, then call Jenny and tell her you like her?"

"First of all, Jenny's there right now. Probably crying and telling Grace what a terrible person I am."

"What are you talking about?"

"Well, in addition to the fact that she thinks I purposely and heartlessly lied to her mother about re-opening the grocery store, she also thinks I'm two-timing your Aunt Kathy."

Dana pulled her head back and scowled as if that sounded crazy.

"Kathy came in one time when Monica was looking at the salon. She opened the door and called out my name in this sing-song voice, like we were . . . you know . . . dating or involved or something. I was just irritated at the time because I'd made it clear to her I wasn't interested. But it must have sounded to Monica like we had some kind of relationship."

"Okay. My bad on that one. I knew Kathy was looking and, well, I knew you were single, so . . ."

Brent glared at her and shook his head.

"I'm sorry. Really. I thought I was doing you both a favor."

"No more matchmaking. Especially now that I'm your sort-of-father."

"Definitely no more of that. I promise! But I still don't understand why there's a problem. When did you see Jenny?"

"I just ran into her. Almost literally. I opened the door and walked out and I nearly knocked her over. I was so excited to see her because I've been trying to find a way to get to know her better . . . and then I find out that not only does she think I'm some kind of conceited playboy who just uses women, she also discovered I lied to her mom. And by now Grace probably thinks I'm a jerk, too."

He shrugged, and she grabbed his hand and shook it as if trying to jar some sense into him. "Hey! This is partly my doing. On both counts, I guess. I did think you needed help with women because . . . well . . . because you're a dork who wants to spend all his free time killing things. And I did say you didn't have to tell Grace how you were going to use that building."

She looked in the direction of Grace's house, the edge of the yard just visible from her vantage point. "Maybe I should have told her after the contract was signed. I know it was selfish on my part. I just wanted to sell the darn place. I wanted the money."

"I'm the adult here. Older adult. I'm the one who should have known better."

She looked at him, thinking how it was kind of sweet that he was acting the way she imagined a good father would act. But she also had to accept responsibility for her part in the deception, and as she thought about it, she realized that if what she had done was thoughtless, or even unethical, she wasn't a bit sorry. In fact, because Brent Wallace had come along and bought that building, she had found a job she loved, a direction for her life, and a sort-of-father, who was good enough for her, and she told him so.

"Thank you. I appreciate that. I do. But I also . . . I can't believe how much this is bothering me," he said. "I don't even believe in love-at-first-sight."

"Just because you don't believe in something doesn't mean it isn't a thing. You stay here. I'm going to talk to Grace."

"No. It's my problem. I can't let you do that."

"Well, based on what you said, I'm guessing that Jenny is screaming and Grace is crying, or vice versa . . . or they're planning your hanging, so let me go see what I can do. Grace and I have kind of come to terms on a few things, so . . . I'd like to give it a try. You can't see the porch from here. Hmmm . . . Nope! You got your phone?"

He nodded.

"Okay. You stay here. When I think it's a good time for you to show up, I'll call you."

She got out of the car and had taken a couple of steps when she heard him call out, "Wait!" She turned back.

"There's something I want you to take to her. Let me grab it."

She watched him head toward the front of the store then make a u-turn and head to the back.

This was not going to be fun.

She'd have to make it clear that she was the one who set up the son-of-Elvis ploy. And who told Brent that although Grace had wanted a grocery store there, he had no responsibility to re-open it. In fact, she'd have to explain that she had also told him he was practically obligated to do something else with it considering that no bank would lend him the money for—

Brent's fast-approaching footsteps cut her thought short and she watched him open a paper bag and pull out a small gift-wrapped package.

"Peace offering?" she asked

"No. It's from her husband." He showed Dana the tag. "I found it when I was cleaning up. It was in a locked box."

He turned the gift over in his hands a few times, thinking how giving it to her now might make him look like even more of a bastard, since clearly he'd have found it a long time ago.

"I couldn't find the key and had to cut the lock off with a wire cutter. I was going to give it to Grace today after I gave her a tour. I had hoped she would think the building had turned out so well, that she wouldn't even care that it wasn't a grocery store anymore. But if she didn't like what I'd done, I thought this would help. I actually found it right after I bought the building, but then I lost it. It had fallen . . . well it doesn't matter how I lost it, but I found it again recently. It seemed like perfect timing. Like it was meant to be. Now, considering what just happened, it's probably the worst timing possible. But it's hers. She should have it. So here."

54

THE GIFT

Grace peeked out on the front porch from the living room window, turned around, and walked back into the kitchen.

"Is it him?" Jenny asked.

"No. It's Dana. The realtor's daughter."

"She's ringing the doorbell again. Maybe you should see what she wants."

"Oh, she probably has a check for me. I can get it later. Right now, we need to talk about this." Grace sat and was about to put her hand on her daughter's when Elvis' voice rang out again.

"Mom! Answer the door. Talking won't change anything!"

"Well, I just think it's possible some of your information is wrong."

"But he said it. He just said it's not going to be a grocery store. And you were counting on that. And he's been living here rent-free while he—Oh, for Pete's sake, go answer the door!"

Grace pushed herself up from the chair and made her way to the door accompanied by 'A Hunk a Hunk of Burnin' Love,' when she had a sudden insight into a possible reason for her daughter's anger. She nearly turned around and headed back to the kitchen, but Dana seemed determined to wear out her doorbell. As she pulled the door open with her left hand, she held out her right.

"This isn't a good time, Dana. Just give me the check and—"

Dana plopped a small wrapped package into her hand.

"What's this?"

"If you let me come in, I owe you an explanation."

Grace looked at the package, wondering if it was meant to placate her as the result of another sum of money pilfered in some way. She scowled and gave Dana a sidelong look, tilting her head up in what felt to her like righteous indignation.

"I know what you're thinking, but I didn't steal anything. Anything else. The gift is from your husband."

Grace felt her heart thud, and her hand smacked her chest. "That's impossible! He's been gone over twenty years."

"Brent found it in the store. I guess it was hidden somewhere. He was headed over here to give it to you when he ran into Jenny."

Grace needed a few seconds to ponder the situation: Jenny seething in her kitchen, Brent finding a gift from Harv, Dana dressed relatively appropriately for a change in an actual shirt and jeans, her blonde hairdo without a beaded braid. She would definitely have the floor at her next visit with Evie and Betty.

Dana cleared her throat, but Grace still wasn't certain she should let her in. "Jenny said he's turning the building into . . . well, I forget exactly what she said, but not a grocery store."

"That's right."

"But our agreement was that El—that Brent would turn it into a grocery store. I made that clear."

"Okay, before you get too weirded out over this, let me say two things. First of all, with a very successful grocery store right around the corner, there's no way Brent could get a loan to open another one. Not for a town this small. And secondly, your husband, wherever he is now, has waited nearly twenty years to get that to you, so maybe you should open it. Then we'll talk."

Grace shook her head, still uncertain what to think about all this. She stared at the gift, then held it to her ear and shook it. "Well, come on in, then."

Grace led the way and when they got to the kitchen she made the introductions. "Jenny, this is Dana Novicki, Audrey's daughter." She nodded to her daughter. "And this, of course, is Jenny. She's a little upset right now."

"I can see that. I'm sorry we couldn't meet under better circumstances, Jenny. Must be something going around because Brent is pretty upset right now, too."

At the mention of his name, Grace noticed a slight jerk from Jenny. She decided not to jump to any conclusions just yet.

"Have a seat, Dana."

"Hmmm . . . I've never been in your kitchen."

Grace waited for her to comment on Elvis' role in the decor, but Dana just took a deep breath and smiled.

"I'm curious, too, Grace. Why don't you open your gift, then I'll try to explain what's happening across the street."

Grace shot her a dubious look, but Dana seemed pleasant enough. Grace returned to her seat next to Jenny and set the gift on the table. "Apparently El–, Brent, found this in the store. It's from Dad."

Jenny still looked close to tears but she turned her attention to the gift, and Grace shot brief glances in her direction as she read the tag. "*To my dearest Grace with love, Harv.*"

Grace took a conscious breath, imagining for just a moment that it had been Harv who handed her the gift. The love was still there, but the worst of the heart-rending pain had faded. Would this gift bring some of that heartache back? But how could she not open it?

She undid the wrapping to find a small white box. Harv had never been a jewelry-giving kind of guy. Maybe a watch? She lifted the cover to find a piece of paper rolled up like a scroll. As she unrolled it, ten one-hundred dollar bills fell out.

"Oh, my," Grace said, setting the bills to one side and pressing the paper flat. She read it to herself first.

"What's it say?" Jenny asked. "I mean, if it's not too personal."

"No. It's okay. I'll read it out loud. *'Dear Grace, This is a combination birthday card and thank you note for having made me the happiest man in the world. I'm grateful for your love, your laughter, your smile, and the way you always bring sunshine to the cloudiest day.'*"

She had to stop there, because she could almost hear him saying those very words. Jenny touched her arm, and Grace turned to her and smiled. "Sounds like Dad, doesn't it?" Jenny nodded, and Grace continued.

"*'Now I want to put some sunshine in your life. It's time we sold the store, my dearest one.'*"

At this Grace stopped, her mouth open in stunned disbelief. "*I* never heard him say anything like this." She stared at the paper a moment, shook her head, then returned to her reading.

"'*We have worked so hard for so many years and I wouldn't have changed a day of it, but I know you'd like to see more of the country, and I have to admit, I no longer enjoy running a business as much as I used to. It would be nice to have more than two days off in a row.*'" She nodded knowingly. "I definitely heard him say that." She pulled out the bottom part of the scroll and held it in place as she continued.

"'*Although what Gary's Groceries did to us when he first opened wasn't very neighborly, I've come to think of it as a blessing. I would never consider closing if this were the only grocery in town. And I have a confession to make. I toured Gary's store a few weeks ago and as difficult as it is to admit, I have to say he's doing a good job. Hard to believe, considering the hell-raiser he was, but the responsibility seems to have turned him around.*'"

"Wow. I can't believe Dad was ready to let Gary have all the grocery business in town."

"Well, dear. Now that I read this, I do recall there were several Sundays when Dad said he'd give anything to go back to bed. I thought it was just talk."

"Dad was older than you. He must have been sixty-eight when he wrote this. Most people are retired by then."

For a brief moment, Grace wondered if he would have lived longer if he'd retired earlier. On the other hand, if they had sold the store and then he passed, she would have had way too much empty time on her hands.

"Is that it?"

"No, there's more. *'Evie and Betty came to me last week and said how much you'd like to go to Graceland. Apparently you mentioned you wouldn't mind retiring while we're still young enough to travel and enjoy it. This was your father's store, so it's your decision, but I'm ready if you are—to close the store, to shop at Gary's, and to travel to Graceland and anywhere else you'd like to go. So here's something to get us started. Happy 60th birthday. With all my love, Harv.'"*

"Oh, Mom. That's so sweet." Jenny stood and bent over Grace with a teary hug. Grace looked up at Dana and saw a bit of glassiness in her eyes, too.

"That is sweet, Grace. You're lucky to have found someone who loved you so much," Dana said.

"And you're sounding wiser all the time, young lady," Grace said.

"Then let me explain something else. I talked to Paul Mendez from the bank. Not anything formal. I just ran into him one day and asked if they'd be willing to lend building or operating money to re-open Havisto's as a grocery store. He said that unless it would be very different from Gary's, like if it was all organic, or had some other focus, it was unlikely."

"I didn't think about that," Grace said.

"Now it's going to be Brent's Beauty, Barber, Bait and Bakery. Doesn't that have a catchy sound? We haven't had a decent bait shop in years. The cafe is for sale, and there's nowhere else in town for people to get together during the day. I admit that I was eager to sell the building, but Brent had a good idea. Besides, once you get to know him, he's not such a bad guy."

Dana turned to Jenny. "Based on that letter, it sounds like you were lucky enough to have a really great dad."

"Yeah. I still miss him. He was always patient and fun . . . and when Jeremy's—that's my son—when his father took off and abandoned us, Dad was right there. He was a good Grandpa. Took Jeremy fishing. Oh, Mom, remember how he used to play hide-and-seek in the aisles?"

Grace nodded, letting herself think of all the ways Harv had been a great father, an involved grandfather, and a wonderful husband. Then Dana broke into her thoughts.

"I never had a Dad. Obviously, someone contributed their sperm to the event . . . oh, sorry. Didn't mean to be gross."

"It's okay," Grace said, adding this information to the fact that Dana's mother had also left without much warning. "But you must have had some contact with him."

Dana shook her head. "Never met him, never heard about him. Saw a picture of him once. When I found it in a shoebox full of old photos Mom grabbed it, ripped it up, and threw it in the trash. She said as far as she was concerned it was a 'hit and run' and she wouldn't ever talk about it." She shrugged. "She was a pretty good mom. At least until Mr. Cowboy Hat came along."

To her surprise, Grace found herself trying to make Dana feel better. "Maybe you were better off without him."

"No doubt, but I still wished I had a dad. I used to get jealous of kids whose dads would pick them up after school, or teach them how to ride bikes. Or drive cars. All that stuff. Especially around here. It seemed like everyone had a good dad but me. I felt so different. Maybe that's why all this happened." She smiled and made a waterfall motion with her hands from her head down, then sat a bit taller in her chair and said: "But guess what went down this morning?"

Grace took notice of the sudden excitement in her voice.

"I got a dad! He's kind of dorky, and he's crabby a lot, but I think he's just been lonely. Then this morning he became my sort-of-adoptive father."

"Who would that be?"

"Brent!"

Grace watched her face light up while secretly stealing glances at Jenny, who suddenly looked pensive.

"He's loyal and honest, so I figured he'd make a good dad and wouldn't let me down. Although he is kind of hopeless with women. I tried to fix him up with my aunt, Kathy Westby."

"She's your aunt?" Grace asked. "The interior decorator?"

"Mmm-hmm. Interior decorator *and* recently hired bakery manager. Brent—I still call him that—Dad doesn't sound right yet—so after Brent found out what I did—I mean the match-making—he got really angry and made me promise never to do that again."

Grace kept a close eye on her. This was a much more poised and thoughtful Dana than she'd ever seen before, and yet she still suspected there was some underlying motive in her presence.

"I came over this morning to thank him for some flowers he gave me to celebrate becoming my dad, and he seemed really upset. Something about some woman he went head over heels for and he's been trying to get to know her, but she doesn't seem interested. He's so nerdy. He said he doesn't even believe in love-at-first-sight, so how could it possibly be happening to him?"

Now Grace knew there was something afoot. Despite the fact that Dana had just said she'd promised not to do any more matchmaking, Grace could have sworn that's exactly what was happening this very minute.

"He doesn't have a girlfriend?" Jenny asked.

"Nope. Only walleye. He likes walleye."

"Okay, maybe he doesn't have one here, but what if he has one in Green Bay?" Jenny pushed.

"Believe me. There are no women in that man's life right now, although, I swear to god, he is pining for the one that got away, whoever she is. Too bad. He'd make a good catch for someone."

"Well, maybe it's time I go see what Brent has done with the place," Grace said.

"But, Mom!" Jenny broke in. "Won't it be hard to see the store again knowing that the most important part of what you shared with Dad has been ruined?"

Grace thought about the letter, about Harv's wishes, about the fact that she'd had a wonderful life, and about how it was time to let this new generation take over.

"It probably hurt more seeing it the way it was when Brent bought it. I wish I had known about this little gift years ago, about how Harv felt. I guess I thought restoring it would help keep Harv's memory alive. Like I owed it to him. That seems silly now, since he was ready to give it up." Grace stood. "Do you think Brent's over there? Think we could get in?"

Dana whipped out her phone and punched in his number. "Hey. Could you meet us at the entrance? Grace and her daughter want to see what you've done with the place."

55

CONFESSIONS

Brent met them at the front door. "Hello, Grace. Ms. Seaquist." He noticed Dana, a few steps behind them, rolling her eyes. "This is the main entrance," he said as he motioned for the ladies to enter.

"It's not a funeral," Dana whispered as she passed him. "Lighten up! Try smiling."

He couldn't smile. It wasn't there, and he didn't think he could find it if he searched down to his toes. But he was conscious of every movement he made, every breath, every swallow.

He stepped ahead and pushed open the door to the bait shop, then pressed his back against it, allowing the others to walk in. He had intended to announce 'the bait shop', but no sound came out of his open mouth.

Grace looked around, nodding and smiling. "Very nice."

Brent felt like a piece of brittle glass, ready to shatter at any second. He couldn't think of a single word to say. Although there should have been some relief hearing Grace's comment, it didn't ease the guilt he felt for the deception with the store, nor the pain he felt for ruining his chances with Monica.

He was aware of her standing in front of a bin of lures and from the corner of his eye he noticed her pick one up. "I think Dad used to have some like this," she said, looking at Grace. "Mmmm. Brings back good memories."

Brent risked a glance at her face. He didn't mean to stare but the soft smile in her eyes and the slight tilt of her head left him feeling both that he was invading a bittersweet moment and that he'd become irretrievably caught in it. He focused on the lure then, but in his mind's eye that vision of her remained, etched in his memory.

Seconds later he became aware of the awkward silence and felt it was his responsibility to break it. "That's a Rapala," he said, grateful his tongue didn't stick to the roof of his parched mouth when he pronounced the 'L.' "Walleye love 'em."

His voice sounded weak, almost hoarse.

Dana surreptitiously elbowed Brent and pushed the corners of her mouth up with her forefingers. Brent shrugged. What was there to smile about? Her eyes grew big in frustration and she moved to a nearby shelf, as if she intended to look at something there. As she passed him she whispered, "I thought you'd be interested in making a *good* impression."

And then he fell apart.

"Grace! I'm sorry to have let you down after you've been so kind to me. I never meant to deceive you. It's just that I couldn't have re-opened the grocery store, so I—"

"Yes, I know. And thank goodness you didn't. I have a confession to make, too. When you first bought the place and

I thought you were turning it into a grocery store again, I was dead set on helping you every step of the way and . . . well . . . I know I told you a number of times that I've been busy, but the truth was that I just couldn't bear to be here."

She looked around the room and threw her arms out. "Too many memories. When I finally closed the store it was such a relief. It was hard walking in each morning knowing Harv wouldn't be there with me."

Turning to Brent she clasped her hands. "But I also felt such guilt, as if I were letting him down—almost betraying him—by not continuing to run the store after we had worked so hard to make it a success."

"Really?"

"Oh, yes. Didn't you wonder why I never came by? Do you remember right after you bought it I came over to give you that tour? I felt I owed it to you, but I just wanted to leave. The only other time I had been here since I signed the contract with Audrey was the day you showed up to look at it."

She stopped talking and looked around the room again, then took a deep breath and shook her head. "That's really why I came back to the store a second time that day. I kept thinking of that old saw about falling off the horse and how you're supposed to get right back on. When Evie invited us over for pie I knew I had given you her address, but I hoped if I came back a second time it might be easier, and a third time would be easier yet, and so on. But I don't think I slept a wink that night. I knew then that I'd have to let you bring it back on your own. And I kept hoping you'd change it enough so I wouldn't recognize it."

"You did? I wish you had told me. I've been dreading this day. I kept telling myself I had no choice, but I still felt I was letting you down."

"Well, I guess neither of us was being very honest."

"Oh, Grace. That's such a relief. You can't imagine," and he barely got the last syllable out when he was struck by an urge to give her a hug, which he acted on immediately.

"Wow. Two hugs in one day," Dana said. "Must be some kind of record for you, huh, Brent?" She told the two ladies that they'd had a father-daughter hug earlier. "With my new dad! It still sounds strange, but I like to say it. Dad! Is it too weird?"

Brent was so relieved, anything would have sounded wonderful.

56

DORKY

Dana tossed a clean set of sheets and pillowcases on the chair near the window and reached for the quilted bedspread, but Brent pulled it out of her hands.

"I can do that," he said. "I've been making my own bed for years."

Dana shrugged. "Fine with me. You'll probably do a better job than I would anyway."

"This is a nice big room. Great windows, nice view, its own bathroom. Isn't this where you usually sleep?"

She snorted. "Look at the walls," she said, and watched him survey the very feminine room done up in pastel wallpaper, a flowery bedspread, matching curtains, and white french provincial furniture. "Not exactly my style."

"Well, thanks. With Monica at Grace's house, I didn't feel right staying there."

"Yeah. You've said that about a hundred times already."

She could tell he was about to apologize so she put her hand up to stop him. "It's okay. I get it. I suppose I'd feel the same way under the circumstances. But you have to get over it. When Jenny comes up to visit her mom, there's a good chance you're going to run into her."

He nodded.

"And now she knows you're not some muckraking playboy, although for the life of me, I don't understand how she got that idea."

"Maybe because of your aunt?"

"No offense, Brent, but—hey, is it okay if I call you Dad? It's still awkward for me, too, but the only way to get around it is to start saying it."

"It's okay."

"Then, Dad, no offense . . . but you're not exactly the play-boy type. Kind of the opposite. If I had to describe you I'd say— well, actually, I have said—that you're kind of dorky and you're crabby a lot, but it's just because you're lonely." She couldn't help but smile at that, thinking how she had probably single-handedly rescued the mess Brent had gotten himself into. "In fact, that's exactly what I said to Grace and Jenny."

"Oh, thanks a lot."

"Come on. Jenny is just as nerdy as you are."

"She doesn't seem the least bit nerdy to me. She's a very . . . a very pretty woman."

"I didn't say she wasn't pretty. You're both good-looking enough to cause a lot of trouble, but you're also both too dorky to even consider it. You and Jenny are perfect for each other."

"Sometimes you act like the 16-year-old I thought you were when we met."

"Just make your bed, Dad, and I'll see you in the morning."

57

PRIDE

Grace set a cup of tea in front of Jenny and sat next to her. "You're pretty quiet."

"Oh, Mom, I just don't know what to think. I'm still angry at—I don't even want to say his name—at that guy for deceiving you."

"But I wasn't honest either."

"Are you being honest now? Because I heard you say, over and over, you wanted that building reopened as a grocery store."

"Yes, dear, I said it. I said it way too often, but it was out of guilt. And I should know better. Never do anything out of guilt. Or fear. You should do it out of love."

"But you *did* do it out of love. Love for Dad!"

"He was gone. What possible good did keeping the store open do for him?"

"You were honoring his memory! And *your* dad's memory!"

"But times change. People change. Things change. And I didn't want to. I wanted everything to be like it was when your dad was alive, but it couldn't be. And it was silly of me to try to keep it the same."

"So does that mean you're sorry you kept the store going?"

Grace needed a minute to think about that. She wanted to be truthful now, not just for Jenny's sake, but for her own sake as well.

"I guess I have to say I'm not sorry. It gave me something to do. But I wish I had kept it going in a different way. I was so afraid to change things. I didn't want to use computers because Dad and I never did. I didn't want to bring in organic foods, food from other cultures. I suppose somewhere in the back of my mind I decided I didn't have to because Gary was doing that, and I suppose if I ever thought it through, I would have realized that's part of the reason I refused to shop there. He was responding to what customers wanted. He was being a good businessman and I was being . . . I guess I was being stubborn and nostalgic."

She took a sip of tea and let out a little laugh.

"I remember once Evie asked if I had any soy sauce in the store. I said right back—probably in a snotty voice—'What do you need soy sauce for?' as if she were looking for some kind of poison. She told me about this recipe she wanted to try. I can't recall what I said about that, but I never brought it up again and neither did she."

She shook her head, appalled now at how she had reacted to Evelyn. "I bet a dollar to a donut she headed over to Gary's for it."

"But you loved working in the store. You always said that."

"I liked the customers. It was good for me to stay busy, but reminders of Harv were everywhere. Besides, I needed the money and there was nothing else I wanted to do. Not like you."

"Thank goodness I went to beauty school before I got married. After all these years, I can honestly say I still love working with hair."

"You were a natural. Every one of your dolls was always perfectly coifed. I never doubted you'd be a beautician."

"But sometimes I felt guilty that I wasn't willing to take over the store."

"I wouldn't have let you."

"What if I had insisted? What if I had said that I missed Pine Lake and I wanted to come home and run the store. Like you did for your dad."

"I would have known you were lying."

"Well, I do miss Pine Lake. I had to go to Green Bay to make money to support us, but I've never really been comfortable there. I'm a small town girl."

"There might be an opening up here."

"Really? At M and M?"

"No. Across the street."

"Oh, I could never work there."

"Why not?"

"Mom! This whole thing has been awkward enough. I'm not going to ask for a job. I have some pride."

"Pride isn't all it's cracked up to be. I suppose if I were truly honest I would have to say that keeping the store open was maybe fifty percent to honor Dad's memory and fifty percent stubborn pride, thinking that I wasn't going to let Gary get the best of us. Pride can keep a person from seeing things as they really are." She took another sip of tea. "Want a warm up?"

"No. I'll be peeing all night."

"Speaking of salons, did you decide to stay with Bon Tress?"

"I don't know. It costs a lot to rent the chair, but opening my own salon is complicated. I don't think I'm up to the business end of it. I just want to work with hair."

Grace got up and took two dishes from the cupboard then pulled a container of ice cream from the freezer. "I didn't get this from Gary's. Too stubborn. I picked this up from that truck that sets up every summer across from the gas station on the highway. It's not bad. Cheery Cheesecake. Not cherry. Cheery. Want some?"

Jenny looked over as her mom scooped a couple of mounds into one of the bowls.

"I guess so."

Grace filled the second bowl, put the empty container in the trash and brought the bowls to the table.

"This is one thing your dad used to splurge on. Remember that good ice cream he used to order? We'd never make a penny on it. The company sold all kinds of fancy frozen desserts and breakfast foods and such, but your dad wouldn't consider anything else. The delivery truck had to go out of its way, so they charged him top dollar. But he said a good bowl of ice cream was priceless. I loved him for that little splurge."

She took a spoonful and closed her eyes and smiled. "Not quite as good as what Dad used to get but close. Most nights after we left the store—even in winter—we'd have a bowl of ice cream together. Talk about the day. After he passed I never ordered from them again. It was too painful."

"Does it make you sad to be eating ice cream now?"

Grace shook her head. "No. For some reason, it's making me very happy."

58

BOUNDARIES

Dana pulled out a chair and plopped on it. "Wow, you're up already?!"

"I still have lots of work to do if we're going to open in three weeks." Brent picked up a plate from the counter and set it on the table.

"What are you eating?"

"Eggs. And toast."

"Where'd you get them?"

He gave her a look.

"Oh. Sorry. I guess that's obvious, I just meant . . . I mean, I was surprised because my refrigerator is pretty empty."

"I noticed. I ran to the grocery store."

"I usually just have a bowl of cereal for breakfast."

"There's a carton of eggs and a loaf of bread if you want to make something."

She shrugged. "I'll just have cereal."

"Whatever. Thanks for letting me stay here. I hope it's okay that I helped myself this morning."

"No problem. I'm glad you did because I'm not much of a cook. You can stay again tonight if you need to."

"I guess that would be best. I think Monica is staying over again. I need to start looking for something more permanent than Grace's house."

"You could move in here—"

"—now that we're practically family," he chimed in, matching her word for word. "I appreciate the offer, but I need my own space, and so do you."

"Whew! That's a relief. I thought I should offer. I like you and all, but we're still pretty different."

"Working together will be enough, don't you think?"

"Yeah!"

"The frog looks good." Brent nodded to the centerpiece.

Dana nodded and picked up a few iris petals that had fallen on the table. "Kind of replaces Percy. Where did you find it?"

"I lucked into the right place." He stood and carried his dishes to the sink and rinsed them. "Should I put these in the dishwasher?"

"Sure. Thanks."

"I'm surprised at how neat it is in here."

"Just because I dress weird doesn't mean I'm a slob."

"But you weren't wearing shoes the day we met, so I figured there were probably piles of stuff all over, and you couldn't find them."

"Nah. I hate wearing shoes. They were all in my closet. But I had to run to the office to get the keys so I was in kind of a hurry and I just forgot to put on a pair before I left. You'll notice I've had them on pretty regularly ever since."

"I did notice, and I thank you. Okay, time for me to get moving."

"Kathy and I will be at the bakery around noon. She finished the curtains so we'll put them up. Hmm . . . maybe not. We need to get blinds up first. But the tablecloths are ready."

"Where are you on the disposables?"

"Orders should be here tomorrow or Tuesday."

"Perfect. Training starts next week?"

"We changed it to this week. Wednesday, Thursday, and Friday so in case any problems came up, we'd have time to deal with them. One of the ladies is perfect, but we're not sure about the other one. We'll see how she does, but we have a backup plan."

"Then I'm off. Oh, I've got to call Lisa and make sure she still wants to buy our house."

"Hey, Brent. I mean, Dad . . ."

He had pulled out his phone, but looked up at her.

"You should think about hiring Jenny. I bet anything she'd like to move back up here."

"So why was she thinking about renting the salon in Green Bay?"

"But—"

"Tut, tut. You do remember that conversation we had about matchmaking, right? You promised!"

"Who said anything about matchmaking? I simply noticed the person you thought you might like to fall in love with is looking for a new, you know, like, work situation. I also know you think you're somehow going to run the beauty and barber shops by yourself and have plenty of time to go fishing, too."

"I said that stuff about falling for someone in confidence. I'm sorry I ever opened my mouth."

"No problem. But back to you needing to hire someone else."

"That's none of your business."

"That is totally my business as your accountant and office manager and, basically, muckraking CEO. I intend to be associated with a highly successful firm so as to improve my resume. I think I'll interview her."

"Who?"

"Jenny!"

"No. Stay out of this. I'll deal with it."

"You need another stylist or barber."

"Not yet. When I need one, I'll find one."

"There's not much of a pool up here."

"I said I'll take care of it."

"But you gave me permission to interview potential employees."

"Yes, for the bakery. But I know what it takes to be a good beautician."

"Work history, references, blah, blah, blah. Ooo! Almost ten. Gotta run. See you later."

59

INTENTIONS/INTRUSIONS

Brent stood at Grace's back door sucking air through clenched teeth. Should he knock? Just go in? They should have clarified the situation, but he'd been so relieved to discover Grace wasn't angry, he hadn't given any thought to retrieving his things. He ran his tongue across his teeth, wondering how bad his breath was.

He knocked, then pushed the door open and entered slowly. He heard Grace's voice in the distance and assumed they were upstairs. He'd get his things from the basement now, making plenty of noise in the process so Grace would hear him and come down. If Monica was staying again tonight, he'd have to figure out how to collect the rest of his clothes and suitcase from the bedroom. Either way, he needed to find out if he was still welcome after all that had happened.

He opened the basement door and stomped heavily down the stairs. He stuffed his work clothes in a trash bag, then stomped back up the stairs. He opened the door, walked into the kitchen, and came to a dead stop. In the chair closest to the kitchen range —where she had not been visible earlier—sat Monica.

"Oh. Sorry. I didn't know you were here."

Now he felt foolish for stomping. Monica probably thought he was angry. He couldn't read her face, but could tell she wasn't particularly thrilled to see him.

"I hoped Gr . . . your mom . . . would hear me. That's why I was hitting the steps so hard. I need to go upstairs and get my clothes and stuff, but I didn't want to intrude."

She folded her arms and leaned back in her chair, glaring at him, and he dropped his gaze.

"A little late for that, isn't it?"

He looked up, disappointed to still hear so much venom in her voice. He switched the bag of clothes to the other hand as he tried to think of some way to explain that he wasn't the ogre—or playboy—she imagined him to be.

"I appreciate being able to stay here. I had a cabin rented until November, but the owner's son burned the place down. Dana's the one who suggested your mom might be willing to rent a room. I wanted to pay her but she wouldn't let me give her any money. Except for meals."

Brent looked for a softening of Monica's attitude, but she muttered something, then lit into him again.

"That building was my mom's life. And I know for a fact it was sold on the condition it be turned back into a grocery store."

He moved the bag of work clothes to his other hand. He thought about putting the blame on Dana, but that wasn't right either. "When I bought the building, I didn't know that. I had the impression your mom wanted to see the store re-opened, but with Gary's just around the corner, I knew that could never happen. I agree that Dana should have made your mom's intentions clearer. It wasn't handled very well. But the building was deteriorating and at some point would be worthless, so Dana was doing what realtors are supposed to do. Sell! The realty was her mother's business, but she ran off and left Dana in charge. Dana had no experience beyond this one contract."

Monica still seemed coiled tight and ready to bite his head off. He gave her a chance to say something, but when she didn't, he continued.

"The only way Havisto's could have re-opened was if someone had the money to not only remodel and update the building—because no bank was willing to write a loan—but also purchase all new inventory and put Gary's Groceries out of business. Anyone with those resources wouldn't be looking at Pine Lake."

He tried to see it from her perspective and added: "Of course Dana was eager to sell the building, but she wasn't doing it out of spite, or to be mean. And I didn't buy it for those reasons either. For years I've been trying to figure out a way to spend more time on the lake and in the woods. That old building caught my eye. It was what I needed at the right price. I never intended to hurt anyone's feelings. Neither did Dana. She was looking at it as a realtor who had been hired to get the best price for someone. And as difficult as it must be for you to hear, the place really was in bad shape. I can't foretell the future, but I'm pretty sure that if Dana had waited for a buyer who would turn it into a grocery store again, it never would have sold."

"Okay, I get that she's young. Maybe I can even overlook the fact that the two of you completely ignored my mom's instructions to put a grocery store back in there, but—"

"If I can interrupt . . . sorry . . . but, honest, there was nothing in the listing contract about that."

"But Dana knew!"

"Her mother was the one who signed the contract with your mom, and she's not around."

"Whatever. The point is that you not only went against Mom's wishes, you took advantage of her because you look like Elvis Presley."

"I didn't set out to take advantage of her. Maybe other people think I look like Elvis Presley, but I don't think I do. Like I said, I had rented a cabin but it burned down, and there wasn't anything else available. I even put an ad in the local shopper. Until I stepped into this house—after I had bought the building—I had no idea your mom was this . . . this enamored of Elvis Presley, and I sure didn't come here thinking I'd use the way I look to mislead her."

"She apparently thinks you're his illegitimate son. And Dana is the one who gave her that idea, so am I wrong in thinking that you knew why she was so willing to rent to you?"

He shook his head and switched the bag to his other hand again. "Let me set this on the back porch."

He stepped out of the kitchen into the back foyer, opened the door, set the bag outside, and his phone rang.

"Hi, Lisa. Hey, I'm up north and . . . I'm in the middle of something. Let me call you later tonight."

He tucked the phone in his pocket, wondering what Lisa's news was. Had Ray changed his mind about marrying her? She sounded agitated. Damn, he didn't need that worry right now. He took a second to gather his thoughts and figure out what he'd say to Monica, and he returned to the kitchen.

She was gone.

60

MATCHMAKING

Grace opened the front door to grab the Sunday paper off the porch when Dana appeared at the base of the steps. "Hello, Dana. You're up bright and early."

"Lots to do. Is Jenny here?"

"Yes. She's in the kitchen."

"Can I talk to her?"

"May I ask why?"

"I want to interview her."

"What for?"

"A job."

"You mean a job across the street?"

"Yeah. In the beauty salon. Or the barbershop. Well, both I guess, although I suppose it would be mostly the salon. I think Brent wants the guys to be able to swear in the barbershop. Or something like that."

"Why are you doing the interview? Why not Brent?"

"Well, Grace, I'll be honest with you. I think something's trying to happen between your daughter and my sort-of-adopted-father. I think they'd be really great for each other, but it seems they're both too shy—and probably too embarrassed, or angry, or something—to do this on their own. So I figured we could just help them along. I can vouch for Brent. He's a good guy, even if he is a dork. And I get the impression Jenny is a pretty good person, too."

"Oh, I'll vouch for her."

"I figured you would. Is she still angry?"

"We haven't talked much this morning, but I imagine so."

"Okay. Well, I'm going to pretend we didn't have this conversation. But, as Brent's accountant and Chief Executive Officer, I'm authorized to—well, okay, let's just say I have not been officially-in-writing *prohibited* from—interviewing candidates for positions in his shops."

"Good enough for me."

"Before I go in, if you don't think I'm being too nosy, can I ask how things went after you left the tour across the street? Brent was such a mope I was afraid he was going to bust out crying."

"I think the thing that's really bothering her is that he . . . well, sorry, dear, but . . . *both* of you ignored my wishes."

"But that's just it. They were wishes. There wasn't anything in the contract that said how the building would be used."

"But your mother knew."

"And if she was still here, the building probably wouldn't have sold, and Jenny and Brent wouldn't have met. Any idiot can see they were made for each other. Sorry. I didn't mean that the way it sounded."

"I *have* grown fond of that young man."

"Yeah. He kinda grows on you."

"But Jenny isn't a pushover. She might need some time to get used to the idea that Havisto's won't be re-opened. On the other hand, she did say she misses Pine Lake, and that she's really a small town girl at heart. I could see her trying to get back here, but she has too much pride to ask for a job, so maybe it would be best if this idea sounded like it was all yours."

"At this point it is. I don't think Brent even thought about the possibility. I think he was still sort of in shock to discover that Jenny is your daughter."

"Well, come along. I've never been much of a matchmaker."

"And I'm not allowed, so we should make a great team."

RECALIBRATING

Grace had just turned toward the kitchen with Dana a few steps behind when Jenny stormed past and headed up the stairs, stopping half way to turn back and whisper in a loud and angry hiss, "I'll be in my room."

Seconds later a door slammed, and Grace turned back to Dana. "Doesn't look like a good day for an interview."

Dana shook her head. "Whew! I guess not. Okay. I'll be across the street. If anything changes call me."

After Dana left, Grace stood in the foyer wondering if she should go up and talk to Jenny. Before she had made up her mind, Brent came out from the kitchen.

"I'm not sure what I said, but I guess it was the wrong thing."

"I didn't know you were here."

"I wish I hadn't been. Apparently your daughter *really* hates me. I just came to get my stuff."

Grace took a closer look at his pained face, then swung her hand in an arc ending with a finger pointing to the kitchen. Brent did an about face and walked back in ahead of her.

"Have a seat, dear, and let's try to figure out where we are. Coffee?"

"I guess I could use a cup."

Grace shut the door between the kitchen and the rest of the house, pulled two Elvis mugs from the cupboard, filled them, and set one in front of Brent.

"I came by to get my work clothes and toothbrush and stuff. If Mon—I mean Jenny—is going to stay tonight, I'll get my things and stay with Dana. Unless you want me out for good. I can pack up everything right now, if you do."

"Oh, that's the last thing I want. I think Jenny will be here tonight, so if you could stay at Dana's that would probably be best. But after that you're welcome to stay."

"Do you want me to leave now and come back later after she's gone?"

Grace sighed. "She's in her room. I'm fairly sure she won't come out for awhile."

She sipped her coffee and held her mug up next to Brent's face. "I still see a resemblance, but now that I look close, it's not as strong."

"I didn't have a chance to clean up very well this morning."

"Regardless. I suspect you are not one of Elvis Presley's illegitimate sons."

Brent dropped his eyes, and Grace felt sorry for him. He seemed embarrassed by the whole Elvis thing. "I think that's pretty unlikely," he said.

"But it was fun to think that. It gave Evie and Betty and me something new to talk about. The idea that one of Elvis's sons was going to re-open the grocery store was so exciting. It's the best thing that has happened in years. Well, until I got the gift Harv left me."

"Oh, right. I wanted to explain about that. It was in that metal box in the old desk drawer. It had a padlock on it, and I couldn't find a key. I had to bring up a bolt cutter to get the box open, and there it was. The day I found it, you were gone. I intended to give it to you as soon as you got back. I set it on the dresser in the basement, but the next day I couldn't find it. I think when I threw my towels on top, it must have knocked it off the back and gotten lodged there. I looked all over but couldn't find it. I guess the day you bumped into the dresser it must have been knocked loose. When I checked the traps, there it was, underneath the dresser. I should have given it to you right away, but . . . "

He stopped and pulled in a deep breath. "I'm sort of ashamed to say this, but the truth is, I was hoping it would soften the blow when I finally got the courage to tell you what was happening with the store."

"And I shouldn't have been so stubborn about wanting to keep that building as a grocery store. You did a great job with it. Even if you aren't one of Elvis's sons."

"When I think back to the day you offered to let me stay, I was amazed you would open your house to a complete stranger. I know I'm not a bad guy, but you didn't."

"Well, if you hadn't looked like Elvis Presley, I probably wouldn't have. Dana set that up pretty well."

"I had no idea what she was doing. Or why she was telling me to wear that purple shirt and change my hair. I just wanted to buy the building, and Dana seemed to think that's what would make the sale, so . . ."

"Considering everything that's happened, I'm glad she noticed."

"She's not a bad kid. But after she told me you expected someone to re-open the grocery store, I should have come and told you the truth. I meant to. I had the words in my head, but every time I was about to explain, the phone rang or you left the room. Or I lost my courage. I'm sorry about that."

"Oh, I didn't bring up your resemblance to Elvis to wring an apology out of you. No, I think when it comes to apologies and honesty and so forth, we all share the blame. The reason I brought this up is because we all have expectations about how things should be. Jenny was counting on Havisto's reopening, too. For my sake, of course. So this is a shock to her, not to mention what happened in your salon in Green Bay with Kathy Westby."

Grace sipped her coffee, then looked at Brent, who seemed embarrassed at being reminded of that event. She took a deep breath. "Maybe I'm out of line here, but I'm going to explain a bit about Jenny's situation to help you understand why she's upset. She thought the world of her Dad and got the impression that Josh—he's the guy she married—was just like him. A hard worker, smart, sweet, enough of a handyman to take care of their cars and do little repairs around the house."

She stood and grabbed the coffee pot. "Warm-up?"

"Please."

As she filled Brent's cup she continued. "Josh got drunk the night Jenny told him she was pregnant. Didn't come home. When he showed up the next morning, he told her he didn't think he'd be a good father. She tried to make him see that they would be learning together, but a few days later he just up and left. She never heard from him again."

"He never even asked about the baby?"

Grace shook her head. "She waited a year, then filed for divorce as an abandoned spouse."

"So her opinion of men went downhill."

They sat quietly for several seconds, then Brent finished his coffee. "I didn't think I'd ever get married, but once all my friends had walked down the aisle, it just seemed like it was my turn, and Lisa, that's my wife—soon to be ex-wife—made it happen. But when I met Monica—is it okay if I call her Monica?"

"Of course."

"When I met her, I understood . . . I knew what a mistake I'd made with Lisa. She never was the right person for me. But I think maybe Monica is."

"On our trip to Graceland, she mentioned you. I didn't know it was you at the time, but she said she had met a guy. And she said he was cute and seemed nice, and even though they had only run into each other a couple of times, she thought they were clicking. Then it turned out he had a girlfriend."

"But I didn't. I don't. And now that she knows, why is she still so angry with me?"

"She apparently thinks she needs to watch out for me. She worries that you were taking advantage of me. And she doesn't think good-looking men can be trusted. Even if they could be, they wouldn't fall for her."

"Why not? She's beautiful. But that's not . . . the thing is, I felt more comfortable with her after five minutes than I felt with Lisa after eight years. I realize I don't even know her that well. But it seems like I do."

"Well, dear. I'd like to help you, but I'm going to stay out of it. I'll stick up for you every time, but I'm not going to do any matchmaking. Although I have to confess that about half an hour ago, that's exactly what I planned to do."

"So you think I have a chance?"

"I certainly hope so. I've thought of you as my son for months now. I wouldn't mind if you made it official. I hope that's not too forward of me."

"So I guess I have your blessing."

"Yes. But you're on your own. Just be patient. She's worth waiting for."

62 |

A PLAN

When Dana made the appointment to get her hair cut at Bon Tress, asking specifically for Monica Seaquist, she had given her name as Lana Novitny. She was afraid Jenny would cancel the appointment if she knew whose hair she was really going to cut.

Now, on a Thursday evening in mid-September, Dana took a seat in the waiting area. She pulled out her cell phone, surprised to see that in her eagerness to get there and save the day for Brent, she had arrived nearly fifteen minutes early. Just before seven-thirty, Jenny entered the waiting area, and the receptionist called out, "Lana?"

Dana, head down, began a silent slow count. When she got to eighteen, the receptionist stood and said, "Miss Novitny?" in a slightly louder voice.

Dana jumped up, putting a look of surprise on her face. "Sorry. I thought you said 'Lana."

"I did," the receptionist said. "I must have . . ."

She looked down at her desk, but by then Jenny had obviously figured out who she was, so Dana just said, "Hi. I'm here for a haircut."

"You don't need a—" Jenny stopped and glanced at the receptionist, who shrugged her confusion. After an awkward minute of silence, Jenny turned to her, apparently deciding not to make a scene, but making her feelings clear with a piercing glare. Another person who shouldn't play poker, Dana thought. Then Jenny shook her head and took off.

Dana looked around the salon as she mimicked Jenny's quick, punctuated steps. Uh-oh! Based on her pace, Jenny did not seem very happy about this. She'd hoped Jenny would see some irony, or at least a bit of humor in the situation, but maybe she should have given her real name. Jenny apparently already thought she was sneaky. Now she'd have to concentrate on keeping the conversation pleasant until the haircut was over and she could make the little speech she'd rehearsed on the way over: "Great haircut, Jenny. I'd like to offer you a job!"

"Quite a little factory they have here," she said, and Jenny stopped short, looked down for a couple of seconds, (trying to decide whether or not to respond to that, Dana guessed) then raced the last few steps to the back of the salon.

Jenny pulled out a towel, took it in both hands, then snapped it as she motioned to the barber chair. "If you're really here for a haircut."

Definitely some venom in that voice, Dana thought, but she made her own voice sound bright and cheery as she plopped in the chair. "Yup. Snip away."

"But that's not the only reason you're here."

"Why else do you think I'm here?" She studied Jenny's reflection in the mirror, and watched her pick up a plastic cape, give a disgusted shake of her head, and set it back down.

"C'mon. You've never been in this salon before."

"True. But I had to be in Green Bay today to fill out some paperwork, and since I really don't have the coloring to be a blonde, I decided to get some of this cut off and let it grow out."

She looked at herself in the mirror, fussing with her hair, trying to be as nonchalant and innocent as possible. "Nobody in Pine Lake is open this late, not that I'd let anyone there touch my hair anyway. And Brent's not open for business yet."

She casually shifted her glance from her own reflection to Jenny's as she said Brent's name, but didn't notice any reaction. "Just do your thing. I use regular U.S. currency like everyone else. Also, I'm a very good tipper."

Jenny squinted and stared at the mirror as if trying to make Dana disappear. "Fine," she said after an awkward minute. She pulled her fingers through Dana's hair. "What are you looking at here?"

"Well, I thought a Pixie cut would be kind of cute. What do you think?"

"I think you're here to lobby for the guy who ripped off my mom."

Dana cringed, noting that Jenny wouldn't even say Brent's name. "Ripped off? How do you mean?"

"I mean the two of you got together, dressed that guy—"

"You mean my dad, Brent."

"Oh, please! Save me the folksy attitude. You're two peas in a pod. This isn't a Hallmark movie; this is life . . . my mother's life and my dad's life, and even my life."

"Hey, hey! Wait a minute. I didn't come here to argue with you."

"Why *did* you come here?"

"I came here to, to—"

Dana realized she had underestimated Jenny's animosity toward Brent. And herself. She had hoped that after offering Jenny a job in Brent's salon, the rest of the matchmaking would fall into place. She turned toward Jenny, hoping a face-to-face explanation would sound more credible.

"Brent's not a playboy. He doesn't have a girlfriend, and he's a nice guy. And, by the way, if he knew I was here, he'd kill me. He made me promise not to get involved in any matchmaking."

"So that *is* what you're doing."

Crap! Caught between anger and embarrassment, she didn't know whether to yell or apologize, to lie or beg. She did a quick assessment and decided to try for flat-out honesty.

"I know I can't just talk you into changing your opinion. But it's the wrong opinion. And he's so muckraking miserable, it's driving me nuts. All I'm asking is that you give him a chance to take you out for something to eat. Heck, an ice cream cone. He never ripped off your mom. If you want to take out your anger on anyone, then I guess it should be me. Yes, I saw that he does kind of look like Elvis, and I knew your mom was nuts about the guy. But I didn't set out to ruin your lives."

She turned back to the mirror and studied Jenny's reflection. She was scowling, holding her body stiff, and Dana searched for a new approach.

"Do you realize what shape that building was in? How many offers we've had? And I mean good offers your mom refused because she was so set on her terms. Which, by the way, were totally unrealistic. No one, and I mean NO ONE was going to re-open that as a grocery store. Havisto's Market would have fallen to the ground. Your mom deserved to make some money from it. Besides, you saw what your dad wrote. He was ready to quit, and when your mom found that out last week, she was really relieved."

"That's not the point. You tricked her."

"Okay. For the sake of argument, let's say we did. *I* did. Brent had no idea I was trying to make him look like Elvis. That was all my doing. But what's the outcome? After eight years, the building finally sold. Brent has been a perfect tenant. He's been helpful. They get along. I think your mom likes him, and she has bragging rights among her friends for—"

"For a lie."

"Brent *was* adopted. He doesn't know who his parents are. He really *could* be Elvis's illegitimate son."

"I don't feel like cutting your hair." She stepped back. "Just get out of here."

Dana blew out a puff of air, pushed herself up out of the chair, and faced Jenny.

"I know I'm young. And I look weird to some people. But I wouldn't ask just anyone to be my adoptive dad. And, especially after this conversation, I don't understand why—and even more especially because all that guy has wanted to do most of his life is catch walleye—I don't understand why he can't stop thinking about you. But you'd be a fool to let him get away."

Dana turned and walked out of the salon, headed straight to her car, climbed in, and slammed the door. "Sorry, Dad. I really screwed this up," she said, and went over the confrontation, wondering if there was anything she could have done differently.

As she turned the key in the ignition, she looked over at the walleye decal she had bought for Brent's car to thank him for becoming her sort-of-adoptive dad.

It gave her an idea, and she drove away with a smile on her face.

63

A REVELATION

Grace was about to enter an eBay bid for a set of Elvis shot glasses when she had an epiphany. She sat for a minute to make sure it was a run-of-the-mill epiphany and not a heart attack. Then she shut down her computer.

Why was she buying more Elvis stuff? Whether or not Brent wanted to buy this house, it was time to sell. She still wasn't sure where she'd go. Not to that assisted living facility. That was for old people who acted old, not old people like her.

She stood and engaged in a bit of self-reflection. She was feeling fine. Her pulse was close to normal. There was no fever. Hmmm . . . She wasn't just feeling fine, she was feeling superb. Fantastic. Excited, even!

A wonderful sense of relief, of weightlessness, flowed through her. No more mice to fear. No more worries about when and what to paint, getting the garbage out on time, or replacing storm windows. It was almost October. She'd get Frank to help her and put the house on the market in the spring. Maybe even list with Pine Lake Realty since Dana was being true to her word, paying off her debt fifty dollars from each paycheck.

She hadn't told her yet, but once Dana paid back the eight-hundred-eighty dollars, Grace intended to end the payments. How could she—in good conscience—make her pay interest? The poor girl didn't even have a mother anymore, and Brent said she had become indispensable. A hard worker. Smart. Kept him from making some bad decisions.

Grace walked through her house, realizing the only thing standing in her way was finding a good home for Elvis.

64

FISHING?

Brent had been pushing hard all week and he needed a break. It was just after six on a Saturday morning. The sun would be coming up soon. He could get out to Little Pine Lake and be back by eleven, having had a few good hours of fishing before putting in a full day of work.

As he drove out of the parking lot he thought about the three-word message Dana had left on his phone: *Take her fishing.*

Monica's image appeared in his head again, the one where she was picking up the Rapala lure and thinking about her dad. It was as if she were standing right in front of him, as if he could just open his mouth and tell her, "that's the moment I knew..."

But Dana was crazy if she thought he'd ask Monica to go fishing. What kind of a first date was that? As if she'd even talk to him. Recalling their last confrontation in Grace's kitchen still made him cringe.

"So if you messed up, you have to fix it," Dana had said the night before. "You don't want to talk to me about this stuff, but I can see how much this is bothering you."

Monica had come to town for the weekend to attend a birthday party for an old friend, so he was at Dana's house again. She was still trying to convince him to take Monica fishing, but it was a terrible idea. As angry as Monica was with him, he couldn't imagine anything less relaxing than having her glare at him for a couple of hours.

He arrived at the lake, backed the boat into the water, watched the clouds roll across the sky, and got several bites on the line. But something was missing. At first he thought it was that he hadn't heard the crow in awhile. He hollered out a greeting, and the familiar caw came back to him like an echo, but he still felt empty. He reeled his line in and sat, bobbing on the water, all his fishing tackle out, a beautiful almost-fall morning that was exactly as he had pictured it could be just a few months earlier.

He cast his line out again but seconds later reeled it back in. The crow cawed "*Awwwww*" and Brent hollered, "Sorry, old pal. See you later."

After packing up and motoring to shore, he intended to trailer the boat and head back. But seven minutes later he was ringing Grace's doorbell, hands sweaty, nausea threatening. He checked his watch and let out a little groan. It was barely eight o'clock and he felt like a fool.

What the hell had he been thinking? He turned to leave but realized Grace would have heard the doorbell and was probably already on her way downstairs. He'd just explain . . . something.

Like maybe he couldn't find his . . . his what? And then the door opened.

"What do *you* want?" She took her hand away from the door and tightened her robe sash with harsh, deliberate moves. The look she gave him nearly made him do an about face, but he felt himself plant his feet.

"I have a few Rapalas in my fishing tackle box. I was wondering if you'd like to try one."

She stared at him, then put her hand back on the door. To steady herself? he wondered. Or was she about to slam it in his face?

"It's kind of early."

Had her voice softened? He took a breath and ventured: "This is the best time of day to catch walleye."

She looked at the floor for several seconds, then shifted her gaze to the doorknob. "That's what Dad used to say."

"I went out this morning, but it wasn't fun. All I could think about was you. I never meant to hurt you. I never meant to deceive your mom."

She didn't respond. But she did appear to be listening.

"My boat's still out on Little Pine Lake."

"Your boat is out in the water?"

Now she looked at him in surprise. Her tone had definitely changed, sounding more like what he remembered from the first couple of times she'd come into his salon.

"I still have lots of work to do on the shops, but we could fish for a couple of hours."

She looked at the floor again. He could see her thinking, could see the front of her robe move ever so slightly as she breathed.

"Mom really likes you," she said.

"I like her, too."

"It's hard to get used to the idea that Havisto's is gone forever."

"I'm sorry you had to find out that way. I tried to tell your mom my plans but, I swear, every time I got my courage up something happened. The phone rang, or she interrupted with some thought that caught me off guard. Or I chickened out. A few weeks ago I went over determined to get it off my chest but she was gone for the weekend. Visiting you. Although at the time I didn't realize her Jenny and my . . . I mean you . . . were the same person. When the remodeling got to a certain point I hoped that once she saw what I'd done, she'd be okay with it. Everyone told me how nice it looked. Even Evie and Betty were impressed. But they made me promise not to tell your mom they'd been there."

What was she thinking? He couldn't tell. Maybe he shouldn't have said all that. He decided to count to ten, and if she hadn't said anything by then, he'd leave. *One, two, three, four, five, six, sev—*

"I haven't been fishing since Dad passed. Let me get dressed."

65

FISHING

Brent checked the clock on the dash and realized they had been driving in silence awhile. He looked at her out of the corner of his eye. She was facing the window. He hadn't turned on the radio, thinking he'd ask what kind of music she liked, but now that seemed a silly way to begin a conversation. Then, to his relief, she broke the silence.

"It's amazing how little this road has changed since Dad and I used to drive it. I know it pretty well. Not because of fishing. Well, somewhat, but mostly because this is where he taught me to drive. We had a stick shift, and I just couldn't get the hang of it. He was so patient."

Now it was his turn to say something, but again, he didn't know what tone to take. Sorrow for her loss? Happiness that she was beside him? He felt the need to say something and finally decided Grace was the positive common denominator between them.

"It's obvious your mom still loves him. Sounds like he was a good father and a good husband."

"Better than the one I picked."

"I didn't do so well in that department either."

"You were married?"

How could he tell her that, legally, he still was? And then he remembered he still hadn't returned Lisa's call. Had he forgotten on purpose? If Ray changed his mind it might be more difficult to get Lisa to keep moving ahead with the divorce. He'd have to call her later today.

"Yes," he said. "But it was more like something that happened *to* me, not something I chose. All my friends had gotten married. One of them set us up on a blind date. Lisa kind of took over our courtship. Not that she was pushy, she just seemed to know what she was doing. She loves dressing up, going to parties. I guess she thought she could change me."

"So you got divorced?"

He didn't want to lie, but the truth would be difficult to understand, so he worked around it. "She started dating one of my best friends. It was a relief since we were no longer romantically involved. Now she's engaged, and I couldn't be happier for her."

"Are you sorry you married her?"

"I guess not. If everything hadn't happened exactly the way it did, I never would have met you."

He turned onto Little Pine Lake Road. "What about you? Are you sorry you got married?"

"Because of my son, Jeremy, no. But I never want to get married again. Too hard to trust people."

It made his verbal sins of omission more regrettable, but he wasn't willing to tell Monica the whole truth yet.

He pulled into the parking lot near the ramp and they got out.

"You really did leave your boat in the water."

"Not many people fish this lake. I was pretty sure it would be safe."

They walked to the boat in silence. When they got there, he put out his hand to help her, but she waved it away. He stepped in after her, untied the boat, then started the motor and drove out onto the water.

"I forgot how pretty it is out here," she said, when he had cut the motor. He could practically feel the warmth from her smile. Then the crow cawed its welcome.

"It's my favorite place to fish. When I first started coming here I didn't catch much, but I really liked the lake. It's so peaceful. I've seen eagles fly past, deer drinking at the shore over there by the woods. Did you notice the crow caw when I cut the motor? It welcomes me just about every time I come here. I've fished the lake enough now that I know the best spots and I almost always catch something. Quite a few times I caught the limit, so now I don't even go anywhere else."

"Well, it's close to the store."

"Seven minutes. That's what sold me on the building."

The crow cawed again. Brent hesitated, but then he cawed back, and Monica laughed.

Two hours later, he had caught one average-sized walleye but wouldn't have been happier if he had caught fifty. Grace had said he had to be patient. He should have told her it's the first thing you learn about fishing.

He glanced at Monica, as he had several times since they'd gotten out on the water. She seemed okay. Conversation had been sparse, and that was okay, too. It had been pleasant. Neutral. He could have stayed there with her like that—bobbing on the water, watching the ever-changing patterns of ripples on the lake, holding a fishing pole, being able to look at her whenever he wanted—for the rest of his life. But work awaited and he thought it best to leave while things were going relatively well.

"Hard to believe we've been out here two hours," he said, wondering what she was thinking.

She smiled and nodded but didn't say anything.

"Sorry to end it but I need to get back." He was about to start the motor, but first hollered, "Caw, caw." He waited but didn't hear anything and wondered if crows got jealous. Just as he put his hand on the key, a rattling caw filled the air like a blessing. He started the motor and headed back to shore.

"Anything I can do to help?" she asked as he tied the boat to the dock.

"Thanks. I've got it. It'll only take a few minutes. There's a trail through the woods over there if you want to take a short walk. I've seen deer and grouse in there."

"Okay."

She headed off, and he backed the trailer into the water and winched the boat onto it, relieved to be alone for a few minutes. As much as he had enjoyed being with her, he was also afraid he might say something wrong or stupid. Just so he didn't mess things up on the ride home.

She reappeared as he was doing a final check of the connections to the trailer. "Door's open," he said, and she climbed in the truck.

The first couple of miles neither of them spoke, then she said, "Dad didn't have his own boat, so anytime we went fishing we had to borrow one. We usually just made it out a couple of times a season, but it was always special. I think Dad would have gone more if it weren't for the store, but they kept it open such long hours."

"You worked there, too?"

"In high school, mostly. Then I moved to Green Bay and got my cosmetologist's license. Got married. Got pregnant. But apparently that wasn't in my husband's plan. He just . . . took off. I never heard from him again. I tried to find him, but . . ."

She was quiet for a minute and he wondered if he should say something, but then she continued.

"After Josh left, I moved back home for a few years and worked part-time in the grocery. Mom and Dad were so good to us. Once Jeremy was in school and I had saved a little money, I found the job at the salon in Green Bay and rented an apartment. Been there ever since."

He parked in front of Grace's house and grabbed the door handle, intending to walk around and open Monica's door, but she said, "Don't get out. I had a nice time."

"Me, too."

He thought she'd leave then, but she hesitated. He wanted to lean over and kiss her. Just on the cheek. As he took his hand off the steering wheel she pushed the door open. Seconds later she disappeared inside the house.

66 █

THE NEWS

Grace poured coffee and set out the kringle she'd made after Jenny left. Ever since the morning she'd introduced Evie and Betty to Brent, she'd begun making them again.

"We know you, Grace. You didn't invite us over just for coffee. You've got something up your sleeve," Evie said, cutting one of the pieces of kringle in half. "Whatever it is, I'm grateful. This might be your best one yet," she said, taking another bite.

"I added almond flavoring. It makes the cherry flavor stronger." Grace said.

"Nuh-uh. No changing the subject," Betty said.

"Okay. You're right. I want to sell my house."

She gave them a minute to digest the news. Betty's concern showed in the wrinkles on her forehead, and Evie shook her head. "You're not leaving town, are you?"

"I hope not. I haven't figured out what's next, I just know it's time to sell."

"Is Elvis going to buy it?" Betty asked.

"I think we all realize he is *not* Elvis's illegitimate son. As much fun as that was, I know it's probably not true. Although he is adopted. But still . . ."

"Well, you're the one who always calls him that, so now I've gotten used to thinking of him as Elvis." Betty said.

Evie grabbed the other half of the piece she'd cut. "Me, too. Goodness, I have to stop eating this."

"I can take it off the table."

"Wait!" Betty said, grabbing the plate. "One more small piece."

"I'm trying to remember to call him Brent," Grace said. "And I don't know if he'll buy the house, but either way, it's too big for me. I made the decision a few days ago, and even with all the kringle I've been eating I feel twenty pounds lighter."

"Come live with me," Evie said, reaching for the plate, then pulling her hand back.

Grace looked at her to be sure she was serious. "Do you mean that?"

"Of course. We can fight like sisters instead of friends. I've got the room. All on one floor. It's almost a shame to be taking up so much space by myself."

"Oh, Evie, that's nice of you to offer. I'd pay you rent."

"We can work something out. We probably should have moved in together years ago. It might have saved us both a lot of money. But . . ." She sucked in a breath. ". . . sorry, dear. No Elvis. *Please*? I guess you could put some of it in whichever bedroom you end up in, but I don't think he'd match the rest of my decor."

"Sad as it makes me, Evie, I think I'm ready to give him up, too. Nobody's going to want that much Elvis around. I just hope I can find a good home for him. All of him."

"You should write a book. You probably know more about him and his songs and movies than anyone else in the country," Betty said.

"Remember how embarrassed that tour guide was at Graceland?" Evie cut the corner off another piece of kringle and stuffed it in her mouth. "Okay, this has to go," she said, pushing the plate toward Grace.

Betty intercepted it, evening out the piece Evie had notched. "I felt sorry for him when people started asking you their questions instead of him. But he was very gracious about it." She picked up the plate of kringle and set it on the counter.

"Maybe I could give all my Elvis things to that museum."

"No offense, hon," Evie said. "But most of their stuff was owned by him. Most of your stuff was made for fans."

"True. Regardless, I'm getting rid of it. I'll think about your offer, Evie. But in the meantime I was hoping to hire Frank to help me spiffy up the place."

"Be my guest," Evie said. "He has so much time on his hands, he's driving me crazy."

"Why don't the two of you do some traveling?" Evie asked Betty.

"We're homebodies. Actually he needs a part-time job. He liked working at the bait shop. Well, at least he liked the money. Rebuilding cars is not a cheap hobby."

"He should talk to Brent."

"Why?" Betty asked, but Grace read her fake scowl.

"At ease, ladies. I know all about the store. Brent gave me a tour last week."

"Oh," Evie said with a sigh. "I was so afraid I'd let the cat out of the bag."

"How long have you two known?" Grace asked.

"A couple of months. Once when you went down to visit Jenny, we stopped at the store to check on the progress. We knew right away it wasn't going to be a grocery store. Elvis, I mean, Brent, explained the whole thing. He sounded so sorry about the way it all happened, too. Betty and I always did think you were nuts to hold out for someone to re-open it since Gary was doing so well. We thought you should have sold it years ago and let the buyers do whatever they wanted."

"Why didn't you say something?"

"We dropped hints here and there, but you weren't exactly open to the idea. In fact, I'm really curious as to why you seem to be taking it so well now."

"Because of Harv. Brent found a letter from him. Oh! I guess in all the craziness over the past few weeks, I forgot to tell you. It was hidden in a desk in the old storeroom, along with a thousand dollars. It was a gift he was apparently planning to give me on my sixtieth birthday. "

"A thousand dollars?" Betty's hand went to her chest and she sat upright.

"In the letter he said he was getting tired of running the store and was ready to quit if I was. He'd been saving up so we could travel. The money was to get us started. He wanted to take me to Graceland."

Evie put her hand on Grace's, and Betty leaned over and gave her a quick hug.

"That's so sweet," Evie said. "I'm sorry."

"Me, too, hon," Betty said. "What a shame. He must have passed soon after."

"Almost three weeks to the day before my sixtieth birthday."

"At least we got you to Graceland."

"Oh, Betty. You and Evie are the best. Since I couldn't go with Harv, I'm glad I got to go with you two. We always have been kind of like the Three Musketeers, haven't we?"

67

HOUSE PLANS

Brent ended the call, his mind churning with Lisa's news. He pushed away from his desk and headed out of the building. He crossed the street, pressed the doorbell, and imagined Grace pushing up off her couch. He hated to put her out but was still uncertain about protocol with Monica there.

"It's you! Why didn't you use the back door?"

"Is Monica still here?"

"No. She left shortly after you dropped her off. Come in."

He hesitated. "I'm here for two reasons. First to officially apologize for not being honest. We talked about it, but, I don't know if I . . ."

She waved her hand. "Water over the dam."

He smiled as he recalled hearing his grandmother say the same thing. "Yes, but I have another favor to ask. I need to make sure you don't feel I've taken advantage of your generosity before I ask for more of it."

"I was just on my way to the kitchen. Come join me."

She did a crisp about-face, and he closed the front door and followed her.

"Coffee?"

"Yes, please." He stopped at the kitchen entrance, still feeling the need for reassurance.

"Brent! Goodness. You remind me of a puppy that's just piddled on the rug. Now take a breath, sit, and be assured you are as welcome here as ever. In fact, I was about to call. I thought you might come for dinner."

"Sorry. I hope you didn't go out of your way."

"Leftovers! Chili and cornbread. In fact there's still some in the pan. I can have it warmed up in a couple of minutes."

"No, thank you. I ate."

"I know this . . . this . . . whatever it is between you and Jenny is causing you both a lot of misery, but nothing has changed between us. You're good people who got off to a bad start."

"That's the problem. We actually got off to a great start. Then I ruined it."

"Nothing is ruined." She shook her head, clearly frustrated. "Just wait 'til you're my age. If I took everything as seriously as you and Jenny do, I'd be dead."

"But it is serious. To me. I am very serious. I like her, but . . . is she afraid of me?"

"I don't think she's afraid of you."

"Okay, but it still seems like she's really holding back."

"If you want my opinion . . ."

"I do."

"I think she's afraid she'll fall for you and you'll leave. Like Josh did. It's about trust. She has a big, deep heart and big, deep feelings. She's leaning, dear, but until she's certain she can trust you, she's not going to fall. I told you before, you have to be patient. Don't give up."

"I won't give up, but I don't want her to think I'm stalking her, either."

Grace turned to the counter, poured two mugs of coffee and set them on the table. "Would you like a piece of pie to go with that?"

How about peace of mind, he thought.

"Jenny made it last night." She shook her head and laughed. "Way too much baking going on around here. I made kringle this morning, but Evie and Betty were over so I sent the rest home with them."

Brent nodded out of politeness, his thoughts focused on Monica, wondering how he could earn back her trust.

Grace moved back to the counter, cut a slice of pie, and stuck it in the microwave for several seconds. She pulled a carton of ice cream from the freezer, scooped out a generous serving, and plopped it on the pie.

"I had pretty much given up on finding anyone," he said. "I mean, the right one."

Grace set the pie in front of him and although he had been conscious of every move she made, once he actually looked at the pie, he was surprised to see it.

"Thank you."

"You're too young to have given up. And too good looking, if you don't mind hearing that from an old lady."

He felt his cheeks grow red. "There's never been a shortage of interested women. I mean . . . not to sound . . . you know . . . conceited."

"I know you're not a ladies' man, or a flirt, or any of those things. I think Jenny is beginning to see that, too, but she still doesn't understand why you don't have a girlfriend. And, pardon me . . . I don't mean to be nosy, but I don't get it either."

He picked up his fork and stared at the pie, the ice cream melting down the sides and making a creamy puddle on the plate. "When I was younger I dated a fair amount of women and most of them were nice, and fun, and I had a lot of good times, but they were all . . . well, not all, but let's say *most* of them were too noisy for me. And I don't just mean loud-noisy, but too . . . too intense, I guess. I think it's okay for women to make the first move, but . . . I'd like a chance to make the second move."

"I think I know what you mean."

"Kathy is a good example. Kathy Westby. The interior decorator. I probably needed an interior decorator from day one, and Kathy is good at it. But she was so . . . overwhelming. Maybe that's what I mean by noisy."

He took another bite of pie and grinned. "Actually, I just remembered something about the night I first looked at your building. I had caught a fish that day, and it was wriggling and flipping around, really struggling to get off the hook, and . . . well . . . that morning in a gas station this woman came right up to me and said . . . well, she embarrassed me. Not discreetly, either. There were other people in the store and after she said that, they all looked at me. I got so flustered I left without buying anything. So later when I caught that fish, I thought: That's how being around women makes me feel. Like they're fishing and I'm the fish. And I'm afraid to get hooked." He looked down at the pie. "But Monica never made me feel that way."

He took another bite. "Oh, boy. This is really delicious."

"Jenny always bakes when she's stressed. She's trying to sort out her feelings."

"The thing I like about her, I mean the thing that struck me right from the start was that she wasn't loud. She was just . . ." he shrugged. "She was different."

He set his fork down to let another thought come in. "I was giving her a ride in one of my salon chairs when she was looking at renting my shop. By 'ride' I mean I wanted to show her the hydraulics still worked, so I told her to hop on and I raised the chair, then lowered it. I can still bring back the sound of her laughter."

He remembered again. It seemed like each time he brought back that incident he fell for her a little bit more.

"And then there was that time in . . . that day in the bait shop . . . when you and Monica first saw it. There was something about the way she picked up that Rapala and said, 'Dad used to have some of these.' I could tell how much she loved her dad by the look on her face. And I thought . . ."

He realized he'd picked up his fork again and had been holding it in mid-air so he took another bite of pie, grateful he'd caught himself before finishing that last sentence.

"Sorry, Grace. I shouldn't be talking to you like this. I'm still not used to thinking about Monica as your daughter." He felt the heat rise on his face.

"Ice cream's all melted," Grace said, handing him a spoon. "I'm glad you feel comfortable talking to me. In fact, since you obviously have pretty strong feelings for my daughter, it's reassuring to know you're sincere. And don't worry. I won't repeat any of this conversation. I think she was building a picture of you in her mind, too, but I guess the day she saw Kathy Westby it shattered like a piece of glass. She needs time to replace it."

He scooped up the ice cream with the spoon and thought about how he could help her make a new picture. The fishing seemed like a good start, although she was really quiet when she left his truck that morning. On the other hand, Grace didn't seem to think there was a problem. He just needed to be patient.

"Thanks. I should have paid better attention to that pie. I don't think I did it justice."

"You're welcome," she said, setting his plate in the sink. "Now, you said you had another favor to ask."

"I do. But first I have to know it's okay for me to stay here awhile longer. I mean, when Monica's . . . Jenny's not here. I don't want her to feel she can't come home and relax in her old room."

"We can work something out."

"I could stay with Dana, too, although, despite how much she's grown on me, it's probably best that after we work together all day we don't end up spending the evening in the same house, too. I mean on a regular basis."

"No, I suppose not. But Jenny hasn't been coming up that often. During the summer she was taking care of a friend's dog on the weekends, so I only saw her a couple of times. She'll probably come up once in awhile now. No more than one weekend a month, I expect. So maybe those nights you could stay with Dana."

"Okay. Then, how do you think Monica would feel if she came home and found half of your garage filled with my stuff?"

"What do you mean?"

"The thing is, as I said, I'm still married. My wife filed for divorce, but there were some technical complications, and we're working on it. There's no problem but the paperwork is taking a bit of time. Anyway, she had been staying with her sister for the past few months . . . since . . . well, since she realized she was pretty serious about this friend of mine she's been dating. With my blessings. It sounds strange, but it's the truth. Anyway, because I've been up here so much lately, she moved back into our house."

Grace cocked her head, and he rushed to explain.

"We were never right for each other. She likes dressing up and going out. At first it was different, and fun. Lots of socializing. She was more like a good friend, but she wanted to get married. When she proposed I felt sort of lucky she was taking care of that part of my life.

"After the first year, it was clear we weren't going to have much of a marriage. But we'd put a lot of time and money into our house and neither of us wanted to leave. Or could afford to buy the other one out. The house has three bedrooms, so we each had our own space. Had our own lives. It worked really well.

"But the day I found out Lisa had gotten engaged, I realized I was free. That was the first time I seriously thought about moving up here and opening the beauty, barber, bait and bakery."

"And now your wife and her . . . her . . . fiancé . . . they want to buy you out?"

"Yeah. It's a big relief, but I also figured I wouldn't have to worry about it for awhile. Lisa said there's no rush. They know how busy I am, but I'd like to start moving things up here. I thought about using the shed, but it needs to be cleaned up. Painting made it look better on the outside, but the roof leaks and . . . well, I don't have time to take care of all that right now."

"Of course, you can use half of—"

She stopped mid-sentence, and Brent feared she'd thought of a reason it wouldn't work. "I could manage with the storage shed if it's a problem. Put some tar paper over the leak temporarily."

"No. That's not it. Would you consider buying?"

"The garage?"

"No. The house."

"This house?"

She nodded.

"I didn't know you were selling your house! I'll work out something with Dana until I can find a place. Forget I even asked about storing stuff here. Why didn't you tell me?"

"I just decided. When Evie and Betty were over this morning I told them. They were the first to know. You're the second."

"But you love it here. And all this Elvis stuff!? What will you do with it?"

"Haven't figured that out yet, but, I tell you, I haven't felt this certain about a decision in years."

"Where will you go?"

"Not sure about that either. Evie offered her place. She's got a three-bedroom ranch . . . I don't know. We'll see. But if *you* buy it, I'll feel like I can take my time leaving. If that would be okay with you. If you even want to buy it."

"I was thinking about building a little place in the woods, a little cabin I guess, but I don't see when I'm going to have time to build. And this is still close to the lake. And the shops. Gee, I have to think about it, but it sounds like it might not be a bad idea. Wow. You really want to sell?"

Grace nodded. "I guess I've been moving in the direction of this decision for quite awhile. I just didn't realize it."

68

AN ADVENTURE

Grace looked from Evie to Betty and back, not sure what to think about their idea. "You're serious?"

"Of course we're serious," Betty said. "Don't you think that's the best idea ever?"

"I guess I need to think about it."

"What's to think about?" Evie asked. "It's the perfect solution."

"For me, maybe, but what about Brent? It's his store. Stores. Shops, I mean."

"Oh, I bet he'll love it. Especially if Frank will do most of the work."

Grace shook her head. "First of all, I'm not so certain Brent will love it. And, Betty, that's going to take a *lot* of work. I mean, well, work and money. Why would Frank even want to do it?"

"Aha! That's the beauty of it. Remember I told you Frank has been driving me nuts roaming around the house? Well, at the beginning of September he offered to volunteer a few hours each week at the high school to help the more advanced kids in the construction classes. I think he really missed working with the kids, and the department was glad to have him. But here's the thing: Every year the class takes on a building or remodeling project. They had one scheduled, but the guy sold it or something, so suddenly they're without a plan. Frank was telling me about it and I got to thinking this would be perfect. I talked to Evie and she agreed, so I told Frank. He said it was exactly the type of thing they're looking for. He'll have to get approval, but he's pretty sure that won't be a problem."

"But I still don't understand who's going to pay for it."

"The kids will do the actual work for extra credit, and the school will supply the tools. Lumber yards donate materials to encourage kids to take these advanced classes hoping some of them will eventually become knowledgeable employees and customers. It will cost Brent something, but not nearly as much as if he had to pay for it all on his own.

"But once all the remodeling is done and the place is open, someone will have to be there. Someone will have to run it. Who's going to pay them?"

"It will have certain hours . . . like maybe noon to four or something like that each day. Maybe more in the summer and less in the winter. Maybe just Saturdays in the winter. We can work it out. The staff will be you and me and Evie."

Grace thought that suddenly Betty looked even younger than Frank. She hadn't seen her this excited in years. "But . . . us?"

"Oh, c'mon, Grace. Don't you think this will be the best Three Musketeers adventure ever? And you'll get to be the brains of the operation."

Grace pictured the scenario her friends had laid out before her, took a deep breath, and nodded. "Maybe it will work, but before you get too excited, I think you need to ask Brent."

"We're willing to go with you, but maybe it should seem like your idea."

Grace hesitated. They weren't spring chickens. On the other hand, Betty and Evie were absolutely giddy with excitement. How could she let them down?

She looked out the kitchen window for a minute or so, then nodded and raised her fist. "Okay. One for all, and all for one," she said, and with a "Here, here!" two more fists followed suit.

69

HIDING

Brent checked his watch, surprised to see so little time had passed. He finished hooking up the plumbing for the barbershop's sink and checked again. Not quite seven-thirty. If he remembered correctly Monica finished work at seven on Mondays. He didn't want to call until she'd gotten home and had a chance to relax, nor did he want to bother her too late.

He took his tools into the beauty salon intending to work on that sink next, but after several minutes he realized he was just sitting on the floor, wondering how he should go about asking her out. Would it be best to fish at Pine Lake again or offer to take her out on the bay? Although his boat was a little small for that.

Or maybe dinner would be better. Here? Or there?

He decided to call and after a few minutes of conversation he would start by saying he'd like to see her again. If she agreed, he'd let her choose how, when, and where.

Her phone rang until the machine picked up, but he hadn't been prepared for that possibility and ended the call without leaving a message. It had already been a long day, so he left everything as it was, locked up for the night, and headed back to Grace's house.

As he put his hand on the back door knob he became aware of several voices. He made out Dana's right away, then Grace's. It sounded like Kathy Westby was in there, too, although that didn't make sense. Then he heard giggling and was sure one of those high-pitched laughs belonged to Evie. If she was in Grace's kitchen, Betty was most likely in there, too.

A jolt of anxiety ran through him and he took his hand off the knob, turned around and tiptoed off the porch. As he passed the kitchen window he ducked to make sure they wouldn't see him. He wasn't eager to go back to work, but no way was he walking in on all those women.

And where were their cars? Confident they couldn't see him from her kitchen, he walked to the end of the block. Halfway down the side street he saw Betty's car, and the purple one sticking out behind it had to be Dana's, parked a foot and a half from the curb as usual. Obviously they didn't want him to know they were all at Grace's. So were they talking about him? He wasn't about to find out and walked back across the street.

With tools and parts already laid out, he picked up where he'd left off on the plumbing in the beauty salon. He got so involved he forgot about the posse in Grace's kitchen until he heard voices. Moments later Dana led the little band of ladies into the salon.

"There you are! We've been waiting for you."

His cheeks burned and he stuck his head under the sink, hollering out, "Gotta finish this last faucet." He fiddled around out of sight, making noise and even grunting at one point, until he worried they might think him rude. Still, he hated to leave the relative safety of the sink and face them. Obviously that meeting had been about him, and he was no match for the five of them.

"Brent, you're working too hard," Grace said when he popped out.

Her smile put him at ease, but they were all staring, and he was tempted to dive back under. "Lots to do yet," he said, kneeling back on his heels.

"We have an idea we want to pass by you," Kathy said, emphasizing her statement with a clap of her hands, and he noticed they all seemed pretty animated.

"Maybe you should tell him, Grace," Kathy said.

"I think it should come from you," Grace said.

"You're sure?"

"What's going on?" His heart banged in his chest.

"Well," Kathy began. "We have this idea."

70

A SOLUTION?

Dana let Kathy tell him the details, then she piped in, just as they had planned. "Isn't that a great idea, Dad?"

"Well, it's an idea," he said, and Dana could see he had his doubts.

"You don't like it?"

"It just seems like a lot of work for something so . . . unusual," Brent said.

"Aren't you one to talk!" Dana said. "I mean, I can see a beauty and barber shop. But bait and bakery?"

"I suppose so, but it doesn't sound as if you'll be selling anything. Will it be free?" Brent asked.

"I figured it would be," Dana said, looking to Grace.

"But there will be operating costs. Maintenance," Brent said.

He stood as he spoke, and Dana was afraid he might come up with an excuse to leave, so she jumped in. "There will be a small investment on your part, but with a big payoff."

"I suppose we could charge something. A dollar or two, maybe," Grace said. "But it's your place. What do you think?"

"I'm having a hard time envisioning it. Dana, maybe you could a little research. Run some numbers."

Dana shook her head. "It will solve so many problems. We don't need research. We should just go for it, as long as it's okay with you. It doesn't have to be forever, but for now it will tie up a lot of loose ends."

"Okay. I have my hands full as it is, so—"

"We don't need a thing from you right now except approval. Oh, and permission, of course."

"You said it would solve a lot of problems . . . like what?"

"It's obvious what a help it would be to me," Grace said.

"Frank will be out of my hair," Betty said.

"Kathy and I are looking forward to working together to set it up," Evie added.

"True, true," Kathy said. "I'm not saying it won't be a challenge to keep it from becoming tacky, but Evie has good taste and some great ideas. It will have to be fun and cheery. Whimsical, but classy. Then I think we can pull it off."

Brent looked at Dana, and she could tell he was considering it. "Duh. It will bring in more customers," she said. "Especially to the bakery."

"Looks like I'm outnumbered," Brent said.

"No. Your vote is the only one that counts," Dana said, thinking that if she put it that way, he'd be more agreeable to the plan. "It took a few days to grow on me, but, like Kathy said, if we keep it fun and whimsical, I think it will be a hit. And even if it isn't, what have we lost? We won't owe the remodeling crew anything. We'll just pull every thing down and make a run to the thrift store. If that's okay with Grace."

Grace gave her a thumbs up and Dana laughed. She and Grace had come a long way from mortal enemies to what she thought of as a grandmother/granddaughter relationship. Grace wasn't even going to make her pay interest on the money she'd taken. *Borrowed*, she silently corrected herself.

"As long as Kathy promises it won't be tacky and I don't have to put much time or money on the line, I guess it's okay with me," Brent said. "But I'm still having a hard time picturing it."

"Okay, Dad. Close your eyes. Now, imagine . . ."

71

TEARS

Grace pulled into the visitor's parking lot, turned off the engine, and grabbed her overnight bag off the passenger's seat. She opened the door, stepped out, and had second thoughts. What if she wasn't welcome after she said her piece? It could be awkward. She put her bag back in the car, locked the door, and headed to the building.

In the elevator she pressed the button for the third floor, her stomach in knots. Seconds later she stood in front of 3B, dreading the next several minutes, but certain this conversation needed to take place. She took a deep breath and knocked.

"Mom! What are you doing here? Is everything okay?"

"Yes, dear. Everything is fine. Wonderful, in fact."

"Did I forget something?"

"No. No, this is a surprise visit. I hope this isn't a bad time for you. I probably should have called."

Jenny shook her head. "It's okay, but . . . I know how you hate to drive in the dark so . . . I'm confused."

"We need to talk about a few things, and I thought it would be better to talk in person. I brought an overnight bag so I could stay, if it's okay with you."

"Sure. Where's your bag?"

"I left it in the car."

"Did something happen to Evie or Betty?"

"They're fine."

"Well, you're scaring me. You never just show up, so I can't help but think something is wrong, and you're afraid to tell me."

"Everything is fine. Better than fine. Everything is . . . as I said . . . wonderful. It's just that I've made some big decisions and I didn't want to tell you over the phone."

"What kind of decisions? You don't have . . . you're not sick, are you?"

"No. I just want to talk."

"Well, come in, then. Do you want me to run down and get your bag now?"

"No. That can wait."

"Coffee?" she asked as she turned toward the kitchen. "I have decaf. Or tea?"

"Tell you what. I'll get my bag while you make tea."

"And you're sure everything is alright? You're not going to spring any bad news on me?"

She shook her head. "Be right back."

Grace went over the two conversations in her head on the way down to the car. Telling her about selling the house wouldn't be a problem, but after that . . . well . . . the two things were connected. She just had to make certain she explained everything in such a way that Jenny knew these were her own decisions, made for her own good. That might be difficult.

Grace put her things in the spare bedroom, then returned to Jenny's living room. She sat in her favorite chair, the one Jeremy used to call "Grandma's chair," marveling at how much time had passed since those days—and yet how quickly things could change. She picked up the cup of tea from the side table and cradled it, glad to have something solid to hold on to.

"I'm waiting."

"Okay. Jenny . . . Jenny . . . the thing is . . . well . . . I'm getting older and—"

"Mom! What?? SAY IT."

"I'm selling the house."

"Our house?"

"Well, my house."

"The house *I* grew up in!"

This wasn't the way Grace wanted to begin this conversation. It had unfolded more calmly in her head.

"First the store and now our house? Did that guy talk you into this?"

"Jenny! Calm down. He had nothing to do with this decision. Well, maybe that's not true. Maybe he did, but in a good way."

"What? Did he just gently suggest that it might be good for him if you sold the house?"

"Why are you so angry with him?"

"I wasn't. I mean, I had gotten over that, but now this, after he lied about his plans for the store, so—"

"He didn't lie. Jenny, he's a good person who, if anything, was misled by Dana."

"In other words, the two of them pulled off this little stunt together."

"Dana . . . well, neither of them . . . acted maliciously. None of this was intended to hurt me. Or you. That old building never would have sold if the only thing it could have become is a grocery store. I should have realized that. Evie and Betty knew that years ago. They said they tried to talk sense into me but I wouldn't listen."

"But it was your building! You had a right to say how it would be used."

"There was nothing in the sales contract."

"Yes, but—"

"Jenny! This is *good* news. I'm thrilled. I'm relieved. I didn't realize what a burden that house was becoming until it occurred to me that I didn't have to keep living there. In fact when I told Brent I was thinking of selling he apologized for even being there and said he'd move his stuff out immediately. I'm the one who asked him if he'd be interested."

"So he *is* buying it?"

"He said he'd think about it. Nothing's definite."

"But not reopening the store is bad enough. If our house is gone, too, where will I . . . it's just that it feels like . . . like my life is . . . crumbling. That's my home, too."

"What is this?" Grace waved her arms.

"This is my apartment. It's not my home."

"It's Jeremy's home. He doesn't remember anything else."

"But it's just an apartment. Other people lived here and after I'm gone, someone else will move in. It doesn't have . . . it doesn't have the history our house has. I played in that yard. I went to school in that town. My class reunions happen there. And the store was . . . it was like part of our house. You can't let it all go."

"Jenny! I have to say I'm stunned at your reaction. I'm getting too old to be wandering around such a big house by myself. There's a lot of work to keeping it up."

She sipped her tea, wondering if she could have handled her announcement better. Although, based on Jenny's reaction, there was likely no way to make it acceptable.

"I remember you telling me you needed to work in Green Bay where the wages were better so you could make enough to retire someday. I assumed you'd come back to Pine Lake. But I never thought you'd want to move back into our house. You're used to an apartment. I assumed you'd find an apartment or a small house. My house is too big for one person. And never in my wildest dreams did it occur to me that you'd be hurt if I sold it."

"But, I told you! I'm not a city girl. I *do* want that house. I want it to be my home. I want to retire there. Please don't do this to me."

Grace looked at her daughter, who, despite the fact that she was in her early fifties and talking about retirement, sounded like a little girl again.

Grace had been sitting forward in her chair, but now she leaned back to think. She'd expected Jenny to be happy for her and in the excitement of that discussion, she would bring up Brent's name. *That's* where she feared the conversation would get rocky.

"Mom, I'm sorry. It's your house. It probably is getting to be a burden. But please think about this. You don't seem that old to me. I don't want you to get old."

"It's a little late for that. I *am* old, but I'm not ready to call it quits, either. If the house means that much to you . . ."

"No. It's okay. I know it's a lot to take care of."

"Considering that I've just upset you, maybe this isn't the best time, but it seems like there's a solution here. Why don't you see if Brent would have a job for you. If you moved back in with me, I'd definitely consider hanging on to it, as long as you'd be willing to help me keep it up."

Jenny looked down and Grace waited for her to say something. She waited until the silence grew awkward, then realized Jenny was crying. Grace rose from the chair and sat next to Jenny, putting her arm around her. "This isn't just about the house, is it?"

"I'm scared."

"Of what?"

"I like Brent. I do. But what if . . . what if I really fall for him and then he leaves? Like Josh did. What if he doesn't like Jeremy? I've been so strong all these years but all of a sudden I feel lost and scared and confused. Men like him don't like women like me."

"What are you talking about?"

"He's so handsome."

"He doesn't know that. Or maybe he knows that other people think that, but he doesn't get it."

"Regardless, it's true."

"He thinks you're beautiful."

"But I'm not."

"Well if he thinks you are, and he doesn't think he's handsome . . . do you see what I'm getting at here?"

"Josh really loved me. I know he did. But he left. All it took was a little baby and he left."

"He was afraid, Jenny. He was afraid he'd be the kind of father his own father was. You know that."

"I've been on my own for so long, and it's been okay. I've been okay. Jeremy and my job . . . and you . . . and my friends, have been my life. It's been enough. I've been happy. I just thought I'd work at the salon another ten or fifteen years, and then I'd come up and live with you and help you until . . ."

She grabbed a tissue and blew her nose.

"The reason I was looking into renting that other salon here was because I thought I could make more money. I could retire and move back home sooner. I wanted to walk across the street and get my groceries at the store again."

"In a town that small, with Gary's Groceries doing so well, how could anyone turn that back into a grocery store and make it? The bank wouldn't lend money for it in any case."

"That doesn't sound like you."

"I know. But this is the truth, Jenny. The honest to goodness truth. The thought that Havisto's will now be Brent's Beauty, Barber, Bait, and Bakery makes me feel like shouting for joy. I don't want that reminder. I feel so . . . unburdened. So light, and fresh, and . . . and even younger. I can't tell you what a relief it was to see Dad's words in that letter and to have permission to quit carrying the responsibility of making sure Havisto's reopened. Brent has been a godsend. I've grown to love him like a son. And I wouldn't mind having him as a son-in-law."

"Mom!"

"Don't tell me you haven't thought about it. He's said some very nice things about you."

"You really think he likes me?"

"I think you've made quite an impression on him."

72

FEARS

Brent opened the passenger side door of his pickup, deciding he could grab everything in one trip if he carefully stacked the boxes of supplies. He pulled out the pile and nudged the door closed with an elbow when his phone rang. He headed to the back of the building and balanced the pile against the wall as he opened the door, then raced to the bakery. He re-balanced the boxes on a counter and grabbed his phone, but the caller had hung up.

He recognized the number and returned the call.

"Oh, hi," she answered. "Sorry for not calling you back the last time. When you didn't answer just now I thought maybe you didn't want to talk to me any more."

"No. I mean, yes. Yes, I want to talk to you, but I couldn't get to my phone in time."

"I just called to tell you . . . I want you to know I'm scared."

"You're scared?"

"Yes. I am."

He wanted to tell her he was too, but he also didn't want her to think he was uncertain.

"Are you still there?" she asked.

"Yes. Sorry. I was trying to . . . I'm scared, too. But that doesn't mean I'm not certain about how I feel."

"How can you be certain? You hardly know me. And the last few times we've met I've been . . . I just haven't been myself. At least I don't feel like myself. I'm confused. And I'm afraid that if I let my feelings go where they want to go—"

"But don't you think we should try? I don't know if I can be the person you want in your life, but I promise I'll do my best. It might not always be easy. We're not teenagers. But I feel like I've been waiting for you my whole life."

"You're afraid, too?"

"Of course. I'm afraid I won't live up to your expectations. I'm afraid I'll disappoint you. I'm afraid I'll fall in love with you and mess up and . . ."

"So maybe we have to go slow."

"That sounds like a good idea. I'm willing to go as slow as you want. Just so we go."

"Okay. I think I need to hang up now. This is a lot for me. But . . . but thank you. Thank you for understanding."

"Thank you for coming into my salon that day. Meeting you has probably been the best thing that's ever happened to me."

"That worries me. I hope you're not expecting too much. I'm just an ordinary person."

"Me, too."

"But . . . I like being an ordinary person."

"So do I."

"It would be nice to find another ordinary person to be with."

"I'd like to apply for the position."

"Okay. Would you be available for an interview next weekend?"

"Name the time."

"I'll let you know."

"I'll be waiting."

73

CERTAINTY

Brent answered the salon's phone surprised to hear a man's voice, although every once in awhile one of his customers referred a shaggy son or grandson. The man asked if he could come in later on Friday or early Saturday. Brent found an opening, pencilled in the appointment, and didn't give it another thought beyond relief. Friday would be his last day in his Green Bay salon.

Just after seven-thirty Friday night, the front door bells jingled and he called out, "Be with you in a few minutes. Have a seat."

He combed out Donna Arneson's hair, fluffing and rearranging here and there as he looked from her hair to the mirror. She didn't tip worth a darn, but she'd been a loyal customer for nearly thirty years, and he'd never heard a nasty word out of her. He liked ending his Friday nights with her, but at least men's cuts didn't take long.

She paid with exact change as she always did, but instead of her usual two-dollar tip, she handed him a twenty. Then she took his right hand in her left, and patted it. She thanked him, and wished him good luck, her words barely more than a whisper. Then she left, without fanfare, and he watched her walk out, suddenly aware of how tiny she'd become. For the first time that day he stopped to think about how much of his life had been spent there.

Since he'd cut his time in the Green Bay salon down to a few days, depending on when he needed to be in Pine Lake for business, he hadn't had much time to reflect on his situation. But with Donna Arneson's kindness, the first bit of sadness threatened. He'd been regretting that he'd taken another appointment that night since it would have been fitting if she were his last customer. On the other hand, it was probably good not to have a lot of time to think about 'the end'.

A few minutes later, after he'd swept the floor and done a quick search of his work area to make sure everything was in order, he called out, "Come on in."

As the young man approached, Brent pulled a fresh apron off the counter and heard, "You won't need that."

"Pardon?"

"I said, you won't need that. I just want to talk to you for a few minutes."

Brent heard the undertones of a threat in his voice and took a step back from the chair. "Didn't you call for a haircut?"

"Yes, but as you can see, I really don't need one. I want to talk to you about Monica Seaquist."

"The woman who was thinking about renting here?"

"Yes. She's my mother."

"Oh." Brent breathed a sigh of relief and held out his hand. The man shook his head, putting Brent back on guard. He was trying to figure out exactly what to say next when the man—who seemed way too young to be taking such a threatening stance— scowled and took his own deep breath.

"I just want you to know that she is the best mom a person could have, and if you hurt her in any way, you'll be sorry."

Brent wondered exactly what this young man had in mind when he said the last three words but didn't dwell on that thought and answered quickly. "I would never, and I mean never, do anything to hurt your mom. I want to make her happy."

He took a few seconds to think, wondering what to say next, knowing he had to sound relaxed, yet certain about his feelings. "You must be Jeremy."

He nodded.

"Your mother's talked about you. Always with a lot of pride in her voice. I have no intention of coming between you in any way. Or ever hurting her. But I'll be honest: I think I want to spend the rest of my life with her. I won't rush her. We want to go slow and make sure this is the right thing for both of us. I'm not a playboy, or a heartbreaker, or anything like that. And if I ever do anything to upset her, even accidentally, you're welcome to set me straight."

His words seem to have taken some of the steam out of the young man's—Jeremy's—anger. He stared at Brent for a minute as if deciding whether or not to believe him.

They stood facing each other and Brent felt compelled to make his feelings clear. "I've never been so certain of anything in my life. As soon as I know she feels the same, I'm planning to ask her to marry me."

Jeremy seemed a bit surprised. Relieved? He nodded, turned around, and left.

Brent stood there—still somewhat stunned from the encounter—but, having met her son, he felt even more certain Monica Seaquist was the woman he had been waiting for.

74

"TRUTH IS LIKE THE SUN"

Grace pushed open the main door and bumped into a ladder.

"Whoa!" Dana shouted as she grabbed the top rung to steady herself. "Didn't you read the sign?"

"What sign?" Grace asked.

"Oops!" Kathy called out. "I grabbed it from the office but my phone rang, and I got distracted."

"Get that sign out there, now!"

Kathy ran off and Grace apologized to Dana for nearly knocking her off the ladder.

"Sorry, dear. Hmmm . . . That looks good."

"Is it straight? I made a line to put the stencils on, but now it looks crooked."

"Hard to tell from down here, but I think it's okay."

"Is it too high? Can you read it?"

Grace took a step back and read aloud, *"I was training to be an electrician. I suppose I got wired the wrong way 'round somewhere along the line."*

"Yeah, that's right," Dana said, craning her head back for another look at the stencils.

"Shouldn't Elvis's name be at the end of the quote? So people know who said it?"

"I'm putting off doing that. Brent's not exactly a fan."

"Living with me, he's probably had all the Elvis he can take."

"It's Brent's place, so I know I have to let him . . . well, at least let him *feel*, like he has the final say in all this. But, the more I think about it, the more I believe it will be a great draw. Great publicity. Something different. Pine Lake isn't exactly a well-known tourist destination. Besides, we had all these empty walls in this corridor. We needed to put something up here. Kathy and I agreed that slapping on paint wasn't the answer. This way it kind of ties in with the museum."

"How many quotes will there be?"

"Five on each wall. The letters are really big, but if we need to, we can fill in with photos."

"Have you talked Brent into dressing like Elvis?"

"I'll give you one guess."

"Maybe once everything falls into place he'll consider it."

Dana shrugged. "Maybe. But even if he doesn't it will be okay. He still looks enough like Elvis that people should get it. At least those who care."

"So he did agree to the name change, then?"

"Not exactly. We're still working on that, too, but bottom line, he wants this place to be a success. Once he realizes it will be a heck of a lot more successful if it's called Elvis's Beauty, Barber, Bait, and Bakery, I think he'll change his mind. In fact, I think once I convince him of that, I can talk him into dressing like Elvis, too. Or at least wearing his hair a different way. Now that he's admitted to being head over heels over Jenny, he *really* wants this to work."

"What's the latest on the shed?"

"Oh, man, those kids are muckrakin' crazy. I figured—you know—they're in high school, their hormones are going nuts, they're going to make a bunch of noise but nothing will get done. Wrong!" She jerked her body for emphasis, lost her balance for a second, hollered, "Ohhhh!!" and grabbed the ladder again.

"Be careful!"

"Sorry. Forgot where I was. Anyway, you can really see progress on the shed. I don't think you'll be able to start moving your Elvis stuff in there yet, but it's coming together."

"I'd better quit distracting you. Have you seen Brent?"

"He's in the office," Kathy said as she came back in from hanging the caution sign on the outside of the main door. "I have the stencils for the next quote. Want me to take a turn up there, Dana?"

"What's that one say?" Grace asked.

"*Truth is like the sun,*" Kathy read from a piece of paper. "*You can shut it out for awhile, but it ain't goin' away.*"

"He had a lot of good lines," Grace said. "My favorite is, '*I'm trying to keep a level head. You have to be careful out in the world. It's so easy to get turned.*' That's one of the things I liked about Elvis. It seemed important to him to be a decent person."

"Well, then you'll like another one we're putting up," Dana said. "It's something like, '*More than anything else, I want the folks back at home to think right of me.*'"

"That's my boy. Okay, I have to talk to Brent."

75

BACK AND FORTH

Brent looked up when he heard, "Knock, knock."

"Should I say 'come in,' or are you giving me the first line of a joke?"

Grace entered the room with a smile on her face. "I just wanted a word with you."

"Sure. Did you have a nice time in Green Bay?"

"I think so. Have you talked to Jenny?"

He hesitated, then finally ventured a tentative, "Why?"

"Because we talked about you. Sorry. It's none of my bus—"

He shook his head. "That's okay. She called yesterday afternoon. We had a great conversation."

"Good. Well, I wanted to talk about my offer. To sell the house to you."

"Of course."

"I'd like to take it back."

"Grace, it's your house. That's fine. I haven't had time to give it much thought anyway."

"No hard feelings?"

"Never."

"The thing is, Jenny wants it. I think she'd like to move back here. No, I know she wants to move back here, but now she's afraid that . . . well, I think she's afraid you'll take her coming back here as a sign that she wants to hurry things along in your relationship."

He shook his head. "I know it will take time, and I'm pretty sure we're on the same page with that. I'll have my hands full here for awhile, anyway."

"Would you also be willing to move out? She wouldn't want to push you out, but I'm pretty sure she won't move in if you're still living there. Appearances. Although, if she comes back I think I'll stay there awhile longer. I just don't know yet."

"No problem, Grace. Really. I'll find another place to live. I *can* stay with Dana for awhile if I need to. Once the shops open, she'll be back to more administrative work, so it's not like we'll be seeing each other all day."

"Well, thank you. I appreciate that. I'm still surprised. I thought Jenny was happy with her place in Green Bay, but she said that once Jeremy was settled in Milwaukee, moving back here was all she could think about. And that was even before she met you."

"It's a nice little town."

"There's something else."

"Sure."

"Have you offered Jenny a job? In the salon?"

"I haven't. I guess I didn't think to ask. But now that you mention it . . . wouldn't that have seemed kind of pushy? Like now *I'm* trying to make things happen too fast? Do you think I should ask her?"

"Remember the day Jenny stomped out of the kitchen?"

He nodded.

"Dana had come over planning to talk to her about working in the salon—"

"Which I specifically told her not to do!"

"When we saw Jenny's state of mind, we knew it was the wrong time. Jenny also told me that Dana came to her salon for a haircut, but it looked to Jenny like it was to lobby her on your behalf. When she told me, I didn't give it much thought, but I wonder if Dana actually went there to offer her a job."

"I had nothing to do with that. Either time."

"I didn't think so. And I'm guessing that's what Jenny realizes now, since you haven't said anything about it."

"Not that I wouldn't have. Offered her a job, I mean. In fact, if hiring her would help her move back here . . ."

"She'll definitely need to earn some money. I'm guessing she wasn't too friendly to Dana at the salon, so now I suppose she's a little sheepish about asking."

Brent jumped up and grabbed a chair from the corner of the room. "Sorry. I should have offered this earlier."

"Thanks. I thought I'd be in and out in a minute. I don't want to bother you."

"No bother. I'm glad you're telling me this."

"But just so you know, I'm going to pretend we didn't have this conversation. I don't want to go behind Jenny's back, but I know she's too shy and embarrassed to come right out and ask you for work. She especially doesn't want to use your interest in her to influence you. If she thought you were giving her special treatment, it would affect her own sense of integrity . . . and probably her feelings about your integrity."

"Now I'm confused. Do you think I should offer her a job or not?"

"I assume you're intending to work the beauty and barbershops alone?"

"Just at first. Until I see how busy I am. I assume I'll have some overlap in hours, but, maybe open the barbershop earlier. Seems like most of my women clients preferred later hours."

"Okay. Well, I think incorporating an Elvis theme will really make your businesses take off, so . . ."

Brent shook his head. "Elvis has been dead a long time. I hope all this isn't a waste of time and money."

"But if it doesn't work, you haven't lost anything. The shed will be remodeled and ready for some other use. On the other hand, if it does take off, you might have to hire more help. It would be the perfect opportunity to offer Jenny some hours. She'll want to pay me something for staying at the house. And, for her sake, I'll let her, but it won't be anywhere near what she paid for her apartment in Green Bay."

"You really think the Elvis connection will make a difference?"

"Elvis *is* a little better known than you are. I think, at least when you first open, there'll be a lot of action around here just because of the name. Then if you make a good impression, people will come back."

Brent took a deep breath. "Just so I don't have to dress like him. I know Dana wants me to, but that's not my personality. I can't be, you know, all sexy and . . . well, like Elvis was."

"No. But it will be a real draw to have an Elvis museum in a little town like Pine Lake. In summer I bet this place will go crazy. You might even bring back some of the old glory days when this was a hopping resort town."

"As long as you brought it up, are you really interested in running the museum? It could be a lot of work."

"Actually, I'm getting pretty excited about it."

76

A SIGN

Dana rushed in carrying a large package. "It's here," she shouted. "Oh! Am I interrupting?"

"No, dear," Grace said. "I was just about to leave."

"Well, hang on a second for the unveiling."

Dana propped the package against the wall and began ripping off the brown paper wrapping. Bit by bit the eighteen-inch letters became visible. As she tore off the last bit of paper on the left end, she looked over at Brent.

"What the . . .?" Brent scowled, and Dana gritted her teeth.

"Isn't it muckraking perfect?"

"Dana! That's not the sign I ordered."

"Well, it's the sign you *should* have ordered."

"No. It's supposed to say *Brent's* Beauty, Barber, Bait, and Bakery. In plain, ordinary letters, not . . . those . . . those crazy ones."

"But I thought we agreed you want this place to be a success."

"Of course, I do, but I—"

"Then you need to push the Elvis thing. And Elvis is definitely not plain and ordinary."

"And you need to remember that this is *my* business."

"Okay. The truth is, I knew I was taking a risk, so I also had the 'Brent' name made. I paid for the 'Elvis' part myself. It's connected by a few bolts on the back, so we can take it off and use the 'Brent' instead. But, if you want these businesses to take off, just think about it. Because the more successful it is, the more likely you are to need another stylist, and then Jenny can come and work for you, and you guys can get married, and—"

"Stop right there," Brent said, shooting out of his chair.

"I think I'll be going now," Grace said, rushing out the door.

"That was embarrassing!"

"Dad, you need to quit fooling around. Jenny is a real catch."

"That is none of your business."

"Yes it is. I want you to be happy and I know that being with Jenny would make you happy."

"Maybe Jenny doesn't want to be with . . . with someone like me."

"What are you talking about? I told you. You're two peas in a pod."

"We are not. Jenny is more, more . . . well, Jenny was married before."

"So? You were, too."

"No. I mean, she had an actual marriage to someone she really loved. She has more experience in this whole thing than I do. She's not going to rush into a relationship. She also has a son to think about."

"OMG! I'll have a BROTHER!!!!!!"

77

IF I WERE A FISH

Brent took Jenny's hand and helped her into the boat.

"Oh. You got another one of those turning seats."

She sat and he started the motor and drove out onto the lake, aiming for his favorite spot on the northwest end. He drove a little farther to where the lake narrowed into a cove, and the sun was just coming up over the trees. For years this had been his favorite place to be in the morning. He loved the gentle motion of the lake, the feeling of easing into the day. In this shady area he could see more clearly out onto the water and watch the criss-crossing waves make their mesmerizing designs.

He cut the engine, both eager to share his thoughts about what this—and she—meant to him and wanting to make the moment last. What was she thinking? The boat bobbed, rocking them in a gentle motion until he felt the silence becoming awkward. He wasn't sure what to say and was hesitant to break the spell. Then the crow did.

"CAW, CAW, CAW!"

"You weren't kidding! That crow really does welcome you."

He cawed back and she laughed.

He could have hugged that crow.

She twirled back and forth in the new boat seat. "These are really comfortable."

"When you spend a whole day on the lake, you really appreciate them."

He let out the breath he'd been holding. It looked like it was going to be a good morning.

"After I installed it, I got to thinking maybe it was a bad idea. I don't want you to think I'm being pushy."

"I suppose you fish with other people anyway."

"Nope. I don't. Or rarely, anyway. After being around people for so many hours all week, I like to come up here alone. It's usually just me and the crow."

Jenny gave a little start, and he realized what he'd just said.

"But I don't think of *you* as another person. I mean, not like that." He heaved a frustrated sigh. "I mean, I *like* being with you. You are the first woman, *young* woman, who doesn't make me feel like a . . ." He laughed. ". . . like a fish."

"Like a fish?"

"It seems like some women think . . . they think they'd like to get their hooks in me, so to speak. As if I were a fish."

She didn't respond, and he held his breath.

"Could I try one of those fathead minnows?"

"Sure. You want me to bait it for you?"

She nodded. "Dad said I should learn, but . . ."

He put the minnow on the hook and handed the rod back to her. She stood and cast the line out, then sat again. He'd paid too much for that extra padded comfort, but as she wriggled back against the seat with a smile on her face, he decided he'd gotten his money's worth.

"I like fishing," she said, squinting into the sun as she looked out on the water. "But I never catch much."

"Well, if I were a fish, I'd jump in the boat just to be with you."

She was quiet for a bit, but the hint of a smile put him at ease.

"When I met you," she said, "I liked you right away. But it seemed like there was this voice in my head that kept telling me to quit acting so ridiculous. That time I was sitting in your barber chair and you were raising it and bringing it back down . . . I think that was the most fun I've had in years. Or that kind of fun, anyway. I've had great times with my friends, and Jeremy has always been—even from the time he was little—a great, easy kid. A good companion. And I can't imagine having a better mom. But being in that chair, I felt . . . you made me feel . . . you made me feel special. For the first time since Josh left, I thought it might be fun to . . ."

He waited, but she didn't finish the sentence.

78

ROOM TO MOVE

Grace stood in the doorway of Evie's guest bedroom, overcome by a rush of emotion. Evie had taken all the pictures off the walls and the linens off the bed. Even the curtains were gone. She had never doubted that Evie's invitation to move in with her was serious, but she assumed it would be months, or maybe even a year, before that happened.

"Welcome to your potential new home," Evie said.

Grace gave her a hug and teared up. "You really meant it!"

"Of course I meant it. Whenever you're ready."

"Okay, but you can't sound so crazy when you call me," Grace said, wiping her eyes. "After you told me to get over here as fast as I could, I nearly called 911. I was afraid I'd find you on the floor, bleeding to death, or unconscious. Don't ever scare me like that again."

"Sorry! I was just so excited. You know how I love to decorate, but it never seemed worthwhile to update this room. Now that my grandkids are older they hardly ever stay overnight. I can't remember the last time anyone slept in here. So anytime I had a hankering to take on a remodeling project I picked a room *I'd* be spending time in. It will be fun to have you here. To have someone to talk to at breakfast and watch Jeopardy with. Like a forever sleepover."

She put her hand on Grace's arm. "I know that look, but don't worry. We're both used to living alone, but this is a big place. I promise you'll have all the privacy you need." Then she squeezed her arm. "We'll be like sisters who like each other."

"Just so you understand I'm not ready to move in yet. Jenny decided to move up here, but she thinks I'll still be living in my house."

Evie pulled her head back and scowled. "Have you *not* noticed how Brent looks at her? If that guy hasn't popped the question already, it's just around the corner."

"Even if he does, Jenny was hurt pretty bad when Josh left. She'll want to take this slowly. I can see something happening down the road, but not anytime soon."

"You want to place bets on it?" Evie's eyes grew big and her eyebrows headed for her hairline. "I say within the month there's an engagement ring on Jenny's finger."

"Well, maybe. But even if that happens, it would be awhile before the wedding."

"Didn't you tell me Brent was moving his things into the garage?"

"I thought he was. But now I'm not sure. Jenny will need the second stall."

"It seems strange that . . . well, that he'd look for another place when it's obvious how perfect this will all work out. Jenny and Brent there. You here."

"I'm butting out. Whatever happens, happens. In its own time."

"Regardless," Evie said, eyebrows raised, "it will be fun to redecorate. I'd love to help you pick out some colors and bedding and things. Then—whenever Brent does decide to pop the question and Jenny agrees—you'll be all set to move in." She stepped to the closet door and opened it. "See? Empty! It's just waiting for your things."

"But you can't tell Jenny about any of this. I don't want her to think I'm going behind her back. Apparently she's been planning on moving up here and living with me ever since Jeremy took that job in Milwaukee. She thought it would be ten years from now when she retired, but that's been her plan."

She thought about what Evie said. Maybe things were moving along . . . but Jenny was gun-shy and Brent was just plain shy. She had always assumed he'd leave at some point and had been dreading that day. It was so nice to hear footsteps on the stairs again, to sit across from someone at meals, and share easy conversation in the evenings.

She and Evie had always gotten along so well, there was no doubt they'd be compatible roommates. As much as she'd enjoy sharing a home with Jenny, maybe Evie was right. She wouldn't want Jenny to put off her plans with Brent because she felt obligated to keep her mom company.

"After I told her I was thinking about selling because it was getting to be too much for me, I guess she decided she needed to move back here sooner. I never realized how much it meant to her. She still thinks of it as "our" house, not my house. That's okay, but it was kind of a surprise."

Grace looked out the window, noticing how—as bare as it was—the sunlight filtering through the trees still made the room feel warm and cozy. But she didn't care for the blue walls. Maybe a muted green with a touch of grey. "Would it be okay if I painted?"

"We're starting from scratch!" Evie said, coming to her side again and settling an arm around her shoulder. "It'll be fun. You've been talking about remodeling for years. Now you have a blank slate. The sky's the limit. You could even put some Elvis in here if you wanted to."

"No. No more Elvis. I made my decision. The museum idea is perfect. And, the truth is, it's a relief."

Grace took a few seconds to ponder how it felt to say those words out loud. There was a bit of sadness mixed in with the relief. But here was a new beginning and at her age, new beginnings were exciting. "Remodeling a whole house was way too much to think about, but doing up a bedroom? I think I could handle that. You're better at decorating, so with your help, it could actually be fun."

"Of course. We'll get paint samples. You can use this bed or bring your bedroom set in. Change or keep whatever you want. It'll be exciting to see what we come up with!"

Grace nodded. In fact, maybe it would be better to get started on making this room hers in case Evie was right. She'd also have to find a way to let Jenny know that moving in with Evie was something she'd been looking forward to.

"Oh! I have a cake in the oven!"

Evie rushed off and Grace looked around the room. This would work. So many changes, and all because Brent had come into her life. She'd grown so fond of him. He reminded her of Harv: kind, patient, thoughtful. He'd take good care of Jenny. He'd make her happy.

She just had to get out of their way.

79

PASSED!

Brent kept his hand firmly on Monica's couch, now tipped against the wall of the elevator. As they made their way to the first floor, he told Jeremy he'd be happy to take him hunting sometime. "Or fishing. Did you ever get a chance to go with your grandpa?"

Jeremy broke into a smile. "Not very often. When we moved to Green Bay I was just a little kid. When I got older Grandpa and Grandma would take me for a week in summer. Then a couple of times Grandma would handle the store by herself for a few hours and Grandpa would take me out. Funny thing was, he didn't care a bit about fishing. I probably didn't notice that when I was younger, but one day—I think I was in high school— he actually forgot to bring the fishing poles. He didn't seem a bit upset. We just bobbed out on the water and talked about stuff. I think that's the time I remember best. We never stayed out long anyway. In fact, I'm sure we must have caught a fish or two at some point, but I don't remember ever bringing any home. Or cleaning them."

"It's not for everyone," Brent said, thinking how far he and Jeremy had already come. When Monica first told him Jeremy had insisted on helping her move her things to Pine Lake, Brent assumed there would be several hints, blatant or discreet, that he had better watch his step.

Which is exactly what he'd planned to do, bending backwards to reassure Jeremy that his intentions were honorable. After that first uncomfortable meeting in the salon, things had gone well. Jeremy was easy to be around, and Brent felt they were on their way to having a great relationship. Maybe some day Jeremy might even call him "Dad."

He took a moment to appreciate the irony. He'd never expected to be a father, but now it seemed possible that within a matter of months, he might end up with both a son and a daughter. Despite questionable first impressions, he couldn't have been more proud of either of them.

"The offer stands," Brent said. "As long as I'm free I'd be happy to take you out. I have plenty of hunting and fishing gear. You'd just need to bring the right clothes."

"With a new job I don't have a lot of free time, but I'll keep that in mind. Gotta make sure I can trust the guy my mom's hanging around with."

Brent laughed, thinking how Monica had likely been a savvy mom who had kept a close eye on her son and knew who his friends were. Now it was her son's turn to do a little worrying.

Of course, Brent would never let on that his mother had already told him he'd passed Jeremy's test. "Whatever that was," she'd said.

80

OLD FAITHFUL

Brent awoke early, eager to enjoy what might be his last chance to relax before the final push to get all the shops ready. A year earlier that would have meant a day alone on Little Pine Lake, but lately he and Monica hadn't had much time together, so he'd asked her to join him.

At first she had declined; she was scheduling appointments every day of the week to accommodate her Green Bay clients before she left Bon Tress. Although he appreciated her sense of responsibility, he was surprised to feel the disappointment more deeply than he'd expected.

Years earlier, when it became clear he and Lisa would never be more than good friends, he dove back into bachelorhood with relief. If love and marriage were that difficult and time-consuming, he'd been lucky to escape with minimal consequences and had learned his lesson. Few things thrilled him more than a day alone on the water or in the woods, but the social life of a married man—at least when Lisa was the wife—cut those opportunities in half. Even when one of his poker buddies joined him, conversation was minimal, and most of the camaraderie took place around a card table in the evening.

But Monica wasn't Lisa. She wasn't any of the women he had dated. He was pretty certain she was *the one.* Through the years he'd watched friends, relatives, and even clients struggle when it became clear their relationships wouldn't work. Although he hadn't given it a lot of thought in the past, recently he found himself thinking, comparing, and coming to the conclusion that he was old enough, had seen enough, and knew himself well enough that he could trust this feeling: he couldn't let her get away. He'd given up on love years ago, but love hadn't given up on him.

So when Monica called him mid-week to say she'd be at her mom's Saturday night and would like to join him Sunday morning, he became more confident of his plan for the day. On the spur of the moment, he'd even offered to take her and Grace to dinner Saturday evening, but with a full day of appointments, Monica doubted she'd get to Pine Lake until after eight.

When the alarm clock woke him Sunday morning, he lay in bed thinking about his plan, confident in his reasoning, but the timing was important, too. He'd have to see.

An hour later he headed out Dana's front door. She thought it was cool having his boat in her driveway and kept threatening to paint some kind of sign incorporating the name "Jenny" into it. So far she'd left it alone, but each morning as he headed to his truck, he checked it. He couldn't even threaten to fire her anymore because she knew exactly how much he depended on her.

But this morning when he noted the still-unadulterated Lund 1700 Pro Sport, he was disappointed. As strongly as he felt about making his relationship with Monica permanent, he hadn't had the courage to bring up the subject. If she saw her name on his boat, such a permanent-seeming development might at least start a conversation.

Or end a relationship. Monica had already said she was never getting married again. If he'd made any progress at all in changing her mind, he had to move carefully.

He hooked the trailer onto his truck and drove to Grace's house. He pulled up in front and before he even turned off the ignition, Monica came bouncing down the stairs, her hair caught up in a ponytail, a colorful jacket over her arm. As she came closer he was able to read the words on her sweatshirt: *World's Best Mom*. He couldn't help but smile as she made her way around the front of the truck, yanked open the passenger-side door, and hopped onto the truck's seat. Her light and airy mood buoyed Brent's spirits, and although he planned to ask how her week had been, the words suddenly seemed too ordinary for the moment.

"Lovely!" he said, surprised to hear the word come out of his mouth, but before he had a chance to regret it, she covered what he feared had been an awkward moment with a gentle laugh.

"I've thought many things about this sweatshirt, but never that it would earn a compliment like that."

He nearly told her he meant her, not the sweatshirt, but . . . she probably knew that's what he meant, and if he said it . . . ? He let it go, put the truck in gear and headed to Little Pine Lake.

Conversation came easy and as they arrived at the boat ramp, Monica brought up the sweatshirt again. "I think of this as my 'fun' shirt. There's a story to go with it," she said, then paused, as if going over some memory. Then she told him how Jeremy had taken over his friend's paper route and saved enough money to buy something for her. "But he didn't have a way to get to a store."

Brent pulled into the lot, put the truck in park, and turned to her, eager to hear the rest of the story.

"Later mom told me he called her to ask if she could take him shopping. When she came to Green Bay the weekend of my fortieth birthday, the two of them got all sneaky and left the apartment for a couple of hours. When they came back Jeremy was so secretive. I don't think he said three words the rest of the night. Probably afraid he'd spill the beans: he was only twelve at the time. I could tell they were up to something and was pretty sure it had to do with my birthday, but he'd also been talking about this Lego set he was saving up to buy. I thought he'd get me a bottle of cheap perfume or some little trinket with what-ever money was left over."

She turned to him. "Aren't you going to put the boat in?"

He smiled, realizing he'd gotten lost in her story, then shifted into reverse and backed up to the boat ramp. When he turned off the ignition his heart started banging in his chest. He'd come up with what had seemed like a wonderful plan but now doubts threatened. "Did he get the Lego set?"

"Well, Mom had made my favorite birthday cake. She always does. It's a cherry layer cake with homemade cherry pie filling in the middle and a cherry-studded cream cheese frosting. She brought it out and put four candles on it—one for each decade, she said—and then she lit them, and they sang Happy Birthday, and I blew out the candles. Then Jeremy got the biggest smile on his face and pulled a huge gift out from under the table. Nicely wrapped. He'd used about half a roll of tape."

She smiled, took a deep breath, and her voice softened. "I took off the paper, opened the box, and I couldn't believe it. He hadn't thought to take off the price tag. He'd spent all the paper route money he'd earned . . ." She turned away and faced the window, but he heard the tears in her voice. ". . . to buy this sweatshirt."

Suddenly the words were on the tip of his tongue, and he nearly popped the question, but caught himself just in time. He couldn't let her get away, but he also didn't want to scare her away.

No. It wasn't time yet.

He put the boat in the water and they sped across the lake. Within seconds of turning off engine, the crow cawed its welcome, and Monica turned to him and laughed, and immediately he felt better about everything.

"Ah! Old Faithful. At first when you told me about him, or it . . . whatever . . . I didn't believe you. But you're right. As soon as you turn off the engine, he caws. How long has that been happening?"

"At least five or six years, I guess. Maybe more. I don't remember when it started, but one day I realized it always seemed to give me that welcome. And to comment on the size of the fish I catch."

They bobbed on the water a few minutes and then, before he could talk himself out of it, he hollered out: "Hey, crow! What do you think of my girlfriend?"

There was no response, and although he hadn't expected one, it would have been pretty cool. He picked up one of the fishing poles and handed it to her. A few seconds later she leaned over, nudged him, and pointed to the sky.

"Is that him?"

Brent looked up and saw the crow coming from the woods. It flew over them in what seemed to be a lazy way, then landed in the willows on the north shore.

"CAW, CAW, CAW!"

"I think he likes you," Brent said.

Her smile took him back to the evening he'd given her a ride in the barber chair, and he wondered: *How do you thank a crow?*

81

LIVE A LITTLE

Dana, phone to her ear, did a quick scan of the bakery. "Sorry, gotta go. Still lots to do. Only five days 'til the grand opening. And don't forget. You promised! Before five. Love you! Bye!"

She rubbed a spot on the counter with her sleeve, then turned and nearly ran into Brent as he walked into the bakery.

"Oh my god, you look aMAzing!" she screamed.

"I feel like an idiot."

"No, really. You . . . wow. I can hardly believe it. You could be *him*!"

"Okay, let's get one thing straight. I will wear this getup on Saturdays *only*. So don't go getting any ideas in your head. Saturdays! ONLY!"

"Whatever. You look great today, and the photographer should be here any—"

"Photographer?"

"Yes. I told you. For their weekend events edition. It'll come out Wednesday."

"No! You said the paper was doing a *story*. I thought *you* wanted to see how I look in this."

She blew out a puff of air and made a face. "You think they're going to come up here and do a story on your GRAND OPEN-ING and NOT take pictures? Why do you think I insisted you get that sign hung?"

He groaned.

"It's called PUBLICITY! It's generally considered to be highly FAVORABLE for business. Some people actually PAY to have that kind of muckraking attention. Sheesh! You are SO lucky to have me."

Dana raised her eyebrows waiting for Brent to thank her, but she could see he was trying to deal with his uneasiness.

"Dad!" She grabbed his hands and gave them a little yank. "You can do this. You look fantastic. Let this happen. Let yourself actually LIVE a little."

Brent looked like he might vomit. He turned and walked away, and she called out after him, "Go set up the salon so it looks like you have a customer. I'll get Kathy to sit in your chair."

She thought back to the day she had asked him to be her Dad. It had thrown him off balance, but in the end he hadn't just risen to the occasion, he had leapt right over it and kept on going. It felt good to finally have a dad she could count on. She just knew he was going to make a great Elvis. And considering the fuss he'd put up when she told him how much it had cost to get the Elvis costume dry-cleaned, he probably wouldn't even throw up on it.

82

ALL MOVED IN

"I can't believe we did it! It's not even midnight," Grace said, taking a quick glance at her watch. "I never thought we'd finish tonight. And my Elvis things really look at home here. Not tacky at all."

"No," Evie said, straightening one of the photos on the wall. "Having a description under everything makes it look like a real museum."

"It *is* a real museum." Betty opened her arms wide, as if to make her point. "The Elvis Presley *Fan* Museum!"

"Putting the "Fan" in was a good idea." Grace said. "I don't think we'll have any legal trouble that way."

She looked around the newly-remodeled shed. The recently poured cement floors had been covered with a brown-toned, indoor-outdoor, shag-like carpet. A retro, multi-colored, geo-metric-patterned linoleum had been laid at the entrance. Dana had found a 1950's era gold couch and placed Grace's life-sized cloth Elvis on it. She also contributed a Polaroid Instant Snap camera, so for a dollar visitors could get a photo of themselves cuddled up to him.

Earlier that day, Grace remembered she had an old-fashioned record player and several of Elvis's albums stored in her attic. She'd asked Brent to get them down and bring them to the museum so his music could be playing in the background during open hours.

They had set out the souvenirs, memorabilia, and knick knacks on lower shelves along the walls. Above them, Kathy and Evie created several groupings of photos, posters, and album and magazine covers, enclosing them in painted geometric squares that were connected with lines mimicking the colors in the linoleum. They arranged the squares in chronological order, introducing each decade of Elvis's life with one of the photos that had previously hung along Grace's stairway.

"You two have done a great job making this look like it was planned. I just kept filling open spaces in my house. It makes a more impressive collection organized like this," Grace said.

"Are you nervous?" Evie asked.

"No, I feel at home here. I was worried that if people started asking questions about all this stuff—like when or where I got it—I'd get tongue-tied. But having some information by each piece will make it easier."

"And you're not sad?" Betty asked.

"No. Definitely not sad. Thrilled!" Grace said. "It will be so much fun to share my love of Elvis. And, thanks to you two, my house got a good cleaning in the bargain."

83

HURRY!

As the first Saturday in October dawned in Pine Lake, Elvis's Beauty, Barber, Bait & Bakery was already humming with activity. Alarm clocks previously set to six a.m. had been manually turned off long before that, due to varying combinations of excitement, anticipation, and anxiety.

Brent had started the coffee pot in the office at five-forty-five, and Grace put the second pot on at six-thirty. The doors wouldn't open until nine, but they'd all been through enough 'showtimes' to know there would be last-minute snarls. Despite the late night, everyone had arrived early, eager to start the big day.

Frank was already in the bait shop when Brent checked in. After working with the high school kids on the remodeling project, he'd decided he wasn't ready for retirement after all and offered to manage the bait shop. Although Brent had someone lined up for the job, an emergency knee replacement forced a change of plans. When Brent phoned Frank with an offer, he accepted on the spot. With his past experience, he was ready to go from day one.

Brent thought people would show up to satisfy their curiosity, grab a free donut, and leave. But Frank had a better sense of what the locals were thinking. The bait bins were bursting with lures, the minnow tanks were full of fatheads and shiners, and Frank had polished off his old spiels and was looking forward to "talking shop." Dana stopped by to give him a quick refresher course on using the cash register and credit card machine, then entered her number in his cell in case he had problems. He gave her a big smile, two thumbs up, and waved her off.

Kathy had arrived long before anyone else, opening the bakery door at four a.m. to turn on the ovens and fryers. By the time her crew arrived at seven, a batch of donuts and muffins were already cooling on the bakery shelves. When Brent caught a whiff of her progress he hustled in and asked her what the hell they were going to do with all that? Kathy shoved a donut in his face, turned him around, and pushed him out the door.

Dana planned to shuffle between the beauty salon and barber shops to answer questions, so Brent had given her an overview of the services and equipment Friday night. Afterwords he took a few minutes to appreciate the finished product. The green and gold chairs were still in excellent shape. Kathy had done a great job of making the barbershop look masculine, decorating with deeper hues of the colors on the sign in the bait shop. By toning down those same colors, she'd brought out a softer, more feminine look for the beauty salon.

Saturday morning Dana insisted on having appointment books ready, just in case. "If nothing else you'll get an idea of how many clients you might have and what times they like to come in. Who knows? Maybe you'll need to start Jenny out next week?"

Brent didn't respond, although when he scowled and pointed his finger at her, she shook her head, took on an innocent look and said, "I am not. You keep accusing me of being a matchmaker, but you're the one who's always reading stuff into what I'm saying." She took a quick peek at the clock on the wall. "No time to argue, Dad. You need to get dressed!"

He checked his watch, then remembered he needed to replace a light bulb in the museum. He still thought the project was a waste of time, energy, and money, but after all Grace had done for him, he felt obligated to go along with it and keep an open mind for her sake. He'd lost a storage room, but with the leaky roof, he wouldn't have used it anyway. He had his doubts when Frank and his high school crew showed up, imagining crooked walls, uneven floors, and potential lawsuits. But he'd underestimated their standards, skill level and professionalism. In less than a month they'd turned the old shed into a respectable home for the museum, even impressing the local building inspector.

Then Grace, Evie, and Betty took over, painting, decorating, and transforming the inside into a cheerful space, then hauling all the Elvis items across the street. The end result was an impressive and well-organized collection, a surprisingly tasteful tribute. Although Brent feared Grace might regret her decision, she seemed energized by the change. The way she dove into the preparations, he would have put her in her early seventies, rather than early eighties.

After rummaging around in the storeroom, he finally found the light bulbs and made a mental note to get that room organized. As he headed out the back door he looked up and realized he still hadn't hung the museum's entrance sign, which he'd hidden in Grace's basement.

He put the light bulb on a table just inside the door, then raced back to Grace's house. He ran down the stairs, grabbed the sign, and ripped off the packaging. It had come in just two days earlier and he hadn't had time to look at it. Now as he tore away the layers of cardboard and kraft paper, he held his breath.

Dana had offered to handle it but, after what had happened with the other sign, Brent wanted the final say and insisted on ordering it himself, then had forgotten to do so. He nearly confessed his oversight to Dana, but feared she'd think he'd done it on purpose. In a panic, he contacted the company that had made the Beauty, Barber, Bait & Bakery sign and gave them the dimensions and the wording. After a desperate, but unsuccessful bit of wrangling, he agreed to pay the hefty fee for a rush order.

When it came—just two days earlier—he'd hidden it in Grace's basement, thinking he'd wait until Dana had gone home Thursday night to put it up. But he'd forgotten to note it on his to-do list and now feared what he'd find, since he'd have no choice but to put it up and incur Dana's wrath if it didn't meet her expectations.

He ripped the last bit of paper away. The sign company had apparently looked back to the previous order and used the same crazy font for this sign. He stared at it for several seconds, remembering how he'd yelled at Dana when she'd unveiled the other sign.

It was his own fault, and now he had no choice but to bolt it up. He set it against the wall and stepped back, then shook his head, threw up his hands . . . and laughed.

Relief? Irony?

Whatever had brought on that reaction, he realized it was okay. It was all okay. He gave the the sign a big hug and raced up the stairs, out the back door, across the street, and to the former shed. He set it down in front of the building, took a few steps, then went back and turned the sign around. No one had noticed his oversight and he intended to keep it that way.

He tore back to the storeroom, found his cordless drill, clipped it onto his belt, then grabbed the 10-foot step ladder and lugged it back to the museum. Although the sign was fairly heavy, he managed to tuck it under one arm, climb the ladder, hoist it up, and hold it in place until he got the top middle screw in. He couldn't reach the ends of the sign so he tugged on it, saw it would hold, made sure it was straight, then climbed back down. He moved the ladder to each end and repeated the process until all the screws were in and the sign was secure.

Dana was probably having fits by now since she'd made him promise to be in his costume by eight-thirty and he'd already missed that deadline. He backed down the rungs, leapt off when he neared the bottom, folded the ladder, and remembered the light bulb. He propped the ladder against the museum, raced inside, screwed in the light bulb above the sink in the employees-only restroom, raced back out, grabbed the ladder, and headed back to the storeroom. He was almost there when he ran into Dana.

"There you are! OMG! Where is your costume?" she screamed. "Get dressed! NOW!!"

He gave her a quick salute, set the ladder up against the nearest wall, and took off on a dead run.

84

SHOWTIME

Brent pulled on the white, sequin-splattered jumpsuit, straightened the satiny gold vest he'd insisted on wearing underneath it (I am not showing that much chest!), and looked at himself in the mirror. Himself? Even the hair was unrecognizable.

The way Monica explained it—in what Brent was trying not to view as a betrayal on her part—Dana had shown her a few photos of Elvis, insisting that the more Brent looked like him, the easier it would be to play the part. Whether Monica believed Dana or she was just up for a challenge, she had agreed to recreate Elvis's hair on Brent's head.

He'd graciously grown it out, thinking that in itself was enough of a sacrifice. When Dana started talking about how he'd look good with his hair dyed a bit darker and the sideburns would perfectly frame his face, he put his foot down: "ONLY for the open house. NO sideburns!"

He thought he'd won that battle, but here he was staring at a head of unnaturally black hair and following Monica's instructions on how to use a little mousse to get a few strands to detach and hang loose on his forehead. No way this charade was going to bring in customers.

He looked in the mirror one more time, shrugged his shoulders, straightened the fancy belt with its huge gold buckle, and checked the time. Almost quarter to nine. He might as well get it over with.

He hurried out of Grace's house and noticed an unusual amount of traffic along South Street. As he stood at the curb waiting to cross, a horn beeped off to his left. When the car passed, a hand came out of the window with a thumbs-up, and he felt his face grow hot. Looking off to his right he saw a steady stream of cars turning into the parking lot which, he could see, was nearly full.

"There you are! C'mon," Dana hollered, holding the entrance door open for him. "Hurry up! I don't want anyone to see you until they come inside."

He tore through the front door and Dana grabbed his arm. "Before we open we want to get a picture of you by the beauty salon." He followed her, feeling very much like Brent Wallace in an Elvis costume. How could he possibly pull this off?

"Over here," Dana motioned. "Stand there." She moved him into the salon's doorway. "I think . . . maybe put your right hand up against the door frame and lean into it a little. And relax! You're a person, not a stick."

She stepped back, groaned, then grabbed his shoulders and shook them. "Loosen up a little. Remember, you're the essence of cool. People love you. Ladies swoon when they see you.

OMG! Smile! You're the King of Rock n' Roll!" She turned and hollered, "KATHY!!! Get over here with that camera!"

Kathy came running, yelling more orders at him. She snapped a handful of photos while Dana stood next to her, hands on her hips, tapping her foot. Finally, she yelled. "Okay! PLACES EVERYBODY! Elvis, you circulate. Just say 'Hello!' 'Welcome!' 'Thank you for coming!'. . . stuff like that. Like you're happy to see them."

Happy? He felt overwhelmed and stupid and miserable.

"Don't worry. You'll get the hang of it, Dad." She reached up and gave him a kiss on the cheek," and it was as if a spell had been broken.

He took a deep breath. Let his shoulders drop. It was just one day. Maybe he *could* get the hang of it.

Why not? Nothing else in this whole plan had turned out the way he had expected. Why not, just for today, let himself be Elvis Presley, King of Rock n' Roll, lady-killer, Mr.Smoothe.

Just for today. He was easing into Elvis when Dana came up behind him.

"Grace asked if maybe every hour or so you could come into the museum. She's guessing that's how long it will take for people to go through, so each new batch of fans will have a chance to meet Elvis. And they might ask for pictures with you, just so you know. You're okay with that, right?"

"Sure," he said. And the guy formerly known as Brent Wallace made himself smile.

Dana gave him a thumbs up. "I'll open the doors in a few minutes. I'm guessing there'll be a beeline for the donuts. First one is free, but if they want more, we're pricing them at two for a dollar, so we don't have to deal with change. We put a sign on the door and on each of the tables. Of course people are on the honor system, so we may not break even today, but as far as PR goes, it's still cheap."

He figured she was saying that for his benefit, but he no longer worried about how much this day was costing. Based on the parking lot this venture might just be a success, and at the very least, they knew that Elvis's, Beauty, Barber, Bait & Bakery was open for business.

Dana took off and motioned him to follow. "Frank's ready, and I think he'll be fine, but you might just check in every once in awhile to make sure. I will, too, depending on how many people are wandering around the salon and barbershop. Stay out of the bakery. That'll likely be a zoo, at least this morning."

She ran back into the salon and peeked out the side window. "Holy Guacamole! There are people everywhere. This is SO exciting. We made it happen!"

She gave him a quick hug. "Good luck! Circulate! Smile! What the hell . . . flirt a little! Okay, I'm going to open the front door."

He stopped by the bait shop to thank Frank for stepping in at the last minute. Frank cocked his head and shrugged his shoulders. "I'm actually looking forward to this," he said. "I didn't realize I missed it."

"Okay. We're on!" Brent said, as the swell of voices filled the front of the building. He turned toward the sound and moved off to the side as a flood of people rushed in.

85

THE BIG DAY

After a few awkward attempts, Brent eased into the role of Elvis. At first he just said "Hi," and held his hand out, but by the end of the first hour, "Hello, ma'am," rolled off his tongue, and his "Thank you very much," was getting rave reviews.

"Told you," Dana whispered in passing after watching the look on one woman's face. Friday afternoon she had pulled up a video of Elvis saying the phrase and made Brent repeat it until she was satisfied he could have passed for the King himself. As irritated as he'd been at the time—thinking they had way too much to do to be fooling around with *that*—of course she'd been right.

By noon he had added the lip sneer and a little swagger, to his, "Hello, I'm Elvis Presley," until Dana passed him again. "Just stick with the lip, hot shot," she whispered, with a shake of her head but a smile on her face.

He strolled through the museum every hour or so, amazed at how interested people were in what looked to him—having lived with it for a few months—like a load of carefully arranged miscellaneous items destined for the thrift store. What was even more surprising was overhearing Grace tell people that whatever they were interested in wasn't for sale. When he asked her about it she said someone had actually offered her fifty dollars for one of her supposedly 'autographed-by-Elvis' photos.

While his opinion hadn't changed, he was relieved to know that if at some point they decided to close the museum, she could probably make a decent amount of money by auctioning off some of the items. "Suppose I should get back. Are you doing okay?"

"Never better! People are so nice and they—"

"Excuse me." A lady had come up beside them, holding the miniature Cadillac that had been on Grace's end table. "Is this for sale?"

"This is a museum!" Brent said. "The only thing for sale here is a photo with Elvis. Oh! But not me!" He was about to explain about the Elvis on the couch when he was interrupted by a commotion at the entrance.

"There he is!" a woman yelled, and a group of ladies, all dressed in identical t-shirts ran toward him. As they got closer he saw a familiar face on the front of their bright blue t-shirts. They surrounded him in a semi-circle and turned their backs in what had obviously been a rehearsed move, although they needed a little work on their timing. But they stood still for a minute so he could read: *The Elvis Impersonator Bucket-List Brigade*, written in large blue letters, and, beneath in smaller letters: *Faithful Fans from Wausau, Wisconsin.*

He stood there, dumbstruck, all the confidence he'd managed to build up suddenly dwindling in the face of seven ladies in various shapes and sizes but with practically identical grins. They began chattering about how nice it was to meet him, and how he had done a great job looking the part, and asking variations on the question of whatever possessed him to open a beauty, barber, bait, and bakery. "Great idea!" one of the women said.

"Thank you," was all he could come up with, and then another woman stepped forward to explain.

"As you probably guessed by now, we're big fans." She swept her hand out across the semi-circle of women. "About six years ago a few of us went to an Elvis tribute. It was held in a small casino so we all got to talk to the impersonator. He was so nice and sweet, and so *authentic,* that we decided to form a little club and travel once a month to see an Elvis impersonator somewhere in Wisconsin. You're the first one who's owned a beauty, barber, bait, and bakery, so we *had* to come and meet you. We're going to call you B4 Elvis."

"I'm honored. It was nice of you to stop by, but I don't sing or do any stage work or anything like that."

"We didn't think you did but, heck, free donuts! We just thought we'd take a look around, for the fun of it. Lots of stuff here to see."

"Well, you should really meet Grace. All these things—"

"Did you say, *Grace?*"

"Yes. This all came from her house."

"Right here, dear," he heard, and Grace stepped up beside him.

"Is that your real name?" one of the ladies asked.

"It's on my birth certificate! I guess being an Elvis fan came naturally. Then I started collecting and—" She glanced around the room. "This was all in my house—which I did call Graceland —but I'm downsizing. Would you like a tour?"

"We'd love one," the woman who seemed to be the leader said, turning to Brent. "But first we'd like you to sign the backs of our shirts," she said, handing him a marker. "Just sign it 'B4 Elvis'," she said, and all the ladies turned their backs to him.

He walked away a little stunned by what had just happened. How did those ladies even find out about the shops? Had Dana advertised in Wausau, too?

Glancing back at the little group following Grace he noticed several people picking up plates, bowls, and other tableware off a shelf and looking on the bottom. Searching for price tags? He still hadn't changed the locks on the shed, but considering what he was hearing and seeing he decided to install a deadbolt the next day.

Back in the main building he felt a rumbling in his stomach and remembered that Kathy had put sandwiches and a fruit salad in the storeroom . . . and that Frank hadn't had a break since early morning.

"You've got a gold mine here!" Frank said, as Brent walked into the bait shop. "Look at this!" Frank opened the cash register and pointed to the little piles of bills, then lifted the drawer to reveal some fifties. "Guys keep saying it's about time we got a decent bait shop in Pine Lake." Then he closed the drawer and motioned to the back part of the shop. "Do you have some- one coming by soon to restock your tanks? Those shiners and fathead minnows are going like crazy. I think this place is gonna be a success."

"Wow. People are actually buying stuff? Yeah. I'll go grab some more stock, then you can take a break."

Back in the storeroom he filled a box with lures, peeked in the refrigerator, then decided to grab a sandwich and a cup of coffee. He made a note about the deadbolt and wrote 'thanks' beneath it, as a reminder to send a thank you note to everyone who had helped that day. And maybe a little bonus wouldn't be a bad idea either.

He headed to the bait shop, soon feeling envious of all the fishermen who were buying bait and making plans to use it. Back in May—when he'd put in the offer to buy Havisto's—he figured that within a few months he'd practically be living on the water. Now, almost five months later, he could count on one hand the number of times he'd been fishing since then.

On the other hand, was he unhappy? No. In fact, he was actually having fun. He didn't mind the flirting. Or at least he'd gotten more comfortable with it. Playing Elvis was probably good for him—not to mention ironic—considering that when he'd inadvertently taken on the role the first time, it led to Grace finally agreeing to sell the building. And now—

Frank's voice outside the bait shop interrupted the thought. "I'll grab him," Frank said walking in and motioning Brent to leave. "Thanks for the break," he said as he passed.

Brent stepped out into the corridor to see the owner of the lumber yard where he had picked up most of the materials for the mini-mall. "I hardly recognized you," the man said.

"Hey, thanks for all the materials you donated," Brent said, shaking his hand.

"How could I say no after all you bought from me to fix this place up. And thank *you* for the good 'PR'. I appreciate the mention on the sign, especially when the project turns out as attractive as the Elvis museum."

The sign had been Kathy and Evie's idea. They had created a large poster with the names of all the companies in Pine Lake that had contributed money or materials to the shop class for the museum project. They'd put it up beside the door so people saw it as they left the building. When Kathy suggested ordering something more permanent, Brent had said he'd think about it. He'd meant no, but he'd just changed his mind. Good will worked best when it moved in both directions.

By three o'clock the crowds were winding down, although every once in awhile there was a surge of activity. In the lulls he had a chance to reflect on the many hands he'd shaken. Locals introduced themselves and although he'd never remember all the names, he had recognized some of the faces from the gas station and the grocery store. Over time, he'd get to know them, maybe even join some club, or see if there were any poker games that needed an extra guy.

He took one more swing through the museum at quarter to five. Grace, Evie, and Betty were all sitting on the couch surrounding Elvis. He expected they'd be exhausted but as he got closer he heard their lively chatter. Apparently they were discussing the offers customers had made to purchase various items.

"I didn't realize some of these things were worth so much," Grace said.

"Are you rethinking the museum idea?" he asked.

"Oh, heavens, no! I haven't had this much fun and excitement in ages. No one I know—no offense ladies—wants to talk about Elvis anymore, but people come in here just to do that. Although a couple of times it seemed like people forgot this was a museum. I wasn't sure if we should start charging entrance fees, but asking people to pay a few bucks to come in and look around should make it clear that it's not a store."

"We need a sign telling people that nothing in here is for sale," Betty said. "One person actually got a little angry when I said that, as if we'd somehow deceived him."

"Charging a dollar for a Polaroid shot of someone sitting next to Elvis is about as complicated as I want to get. That and the entrance fees. We just need to make enough money to pay operating expenses, right?!"

"Yeah," Brent said. "But after hearing that people were offering pretty good money for some of the items, I decided to put a deadbolt on the door tomorrow. I don't think anybody would break in, but for a few bucks we can make this place more secure." He glanced at the clock over the dining table, featuring an Elvis whose upper lip showed a more exaggerated sneer than usual. "I think you can probably close up anytime now. The parking lot is just about empty."

"I'd like to tidy up a bit,' Grace said. "Then we'll head out."

When he got back inside the main building he heard Dana calling his name and followed the sound of her voice to the barber shop.

"There you are," she said. "Brent Wallace, this is my boyfriend, Binky. Binky Todd."

Brent felt a little sheepish in the Elvis costume, when Binky was still in work clothes, his carpenter's belt still wrapped around his waist. Binky held out his hand, calloused but clean, and gave Brent's a solid shake. "I wanted to go home and change, but Dana said I had to come before five."

"I wanted you to see how great this place looks," Dana said. "And to meet my Dad and show you how cool he is to dress up like this!"

"Well, I'm looking forward to changing out of this getup, too," Brent said. "Dana talks about you a lot, so it's good to put a name with a face."

Dana jerked. "Oh! Crap. It's five o'clock. I gotta close the front door. Be right back."

She took off and Binky's eyes followed her. "Dana talks about you a lot, too," he said after she was out of earshot. "You're the best thing that's happened to her in years. Well, except for me, maybe." He grinned. "After hearing her talk about you I thought you'd be about ten feet tall."

Brent shrugged, embarrassed, and a bit surprised. "Well . . . we got off to a rocky start. But, she kinda grows on you."

He nodded. "She's a lot of crazy on the outside, and sometimes she can't keep her quirkiness under control, but on the inside she's solid. The only time I've ever seen her upset was when her mom left. She kinda fell apart for awhile."

"Sounds like she ran off and left Dana with a little more responsibility than she was prepared for."

He nodded. "I met Dana at Cap's when her mom was still here. I'd see her around town. Always with a smile. She thought her mom was planning to move them to Green Bay, and she was excited about living in the big city. Then all of a sudden her mom was dating this weird guy online, and a few months later she headed out. It hit Dana pretty hard. Once in awhile she'd mention her mom, but she never dwelt on it. She's about the most positive person I know. Always upbeat, no matter what. We hit it off sand I started asking her out."

Dana had turned and was headed back in their direction.

"I don't know what it's like to have a daughter," Binky said, lowering his voice, "but I think you got one of the best."

86

THE CROW

Brent turned out the last of the lights. He was eager to get out of the sequined white jumpsuit and be plain old Brent again, but first he wanted a few minutes to himself. He made his way to the office then headed to his desk, winding around a cluttered mess of boxes, tools, spare parts, construction materials, and miscellaneous overflow from the storage room that had ended up there when the shed became a museum. There was still a lot of work to be done, but how far he'd come!

He thought back to the day he and Grace had first walked through the building, remembering how discouraged he'd been by what had suddenly looked like more than he could handle. What had almost been worse was the realization that he had deceived Grace. Although that had been Dana's doing, he'd still been so ashamed, especially after he'd gotten to know Grace and discovered what a sweet, kind, generous person she was.

Dana! At the time he couldn't have been more disgusted by how that obnoxious and underhanded sneak had roped him into her little scheme. The morning she handed him the keys to Hav-isto's, he'd been so relieved to be done with her. He had his little world all planned out: make peace with Grace, set up his shops, live in the woods, fish and hunt every minute he was free.

He had to smile. That Brent didn't have a clue.

Now, here he was, owner of what was on its way to be-coming a successful little enterprise, at least based on attendance and excitement over the Grand Opening. As much as he'd been dreading the day, it had turned out better than expected, thanks mostly to Dana. If she hadn't come along he probably wouldn't have such a comprehensive and well-thought-out business plan. How long would it have taken him to do the paper work to get the loan? He might have had the barber chairs he ordered, but if Dana hadn't taken the time to create a relationship with the lumber company and hardware stores, he might not have been able to get so many materials on credit. He and his crew would probably still be working on remodeling the building, and he'd be cutting hair in Grace's kitchen.

Except if Dana hadn't suggested calling Grace to see about renting a room he wouldn't even be living in Grace's house. As much as he'd ended up counting on Dana, the benefits worked both ways. Because of him she'd found purpose and meaning in her own life, not to mention an adoptive dad, who—if hesi-tant at first—was becoming more and more comfortable with the role.

Everything had unfolded so perfectly since that rocky begin-ning, as if it was all meant to be, even the incredible fact that he'd just spent a day playing Elvis Presley. It was still hard to believe Dana had talked him into wearing a white, sequined jumpsuit, not to mention letting a photographer take photos of him in that getup.

As with everything else she had tackled, her publicity campaign had been a success. They had been deluged with phone calls all week. Curious townspeople had peered in windows, and cars slowed as they passed by. People had come from around the area and—probably because of the newspaper article—had even driven up from Green Bay. The bakery had run out of donuts and muffins early, putting the fledgling crew to a real test. But thanks to Kathy's insistence that they buy far more supplies than he thought they'd need—and Mrs. Belisky's last-minute offer of help—they were able to produce double the amount planned for and kept up with demand.

Even the few problems that had arisen provided more comic relief than frustration, like the spray hose in the salon's shampoo unit that had sprung a leak. Fortunately a man in the salon at the time had grabbed a plastic cape, covered himself, and crouched down to get at the shutoff valve. Dana had given Brent an earful the next time he passed through. He probably shouldn't have pointed out she wasn't *that* wet, nor that she had just learned a valuable plumbing lesson. When she grabbed the hose on the other shampoo unit and aimed it in his direction, he laughed and hustled out of there. Knowing Dana, she would have soaked him.

He nearly made it to his desk when a light caught his attention on the break table: the coffee pot was still on. He turned it off, emptied the pot into the sink, rinsed it, and set it on the drainboard, then glanced at his watch. It was nearly six o'clock. The impromptu party that had sprung up at Grace's house was probably in full swing by now. He was eager to join them, but wanted a few more minutes to himself.

He grabbed a beer from the mini-fridge, pulled out the fancy new swivel chair Grace had given him as a grand opening gift, and sat at his desk. It was covered with sticky notes, mostly last-minute reminders. Flipping them into the wastebasket, he uncovered one with Kathy's sketch of a logo based on the Elvis sign. He had intended to have it imprinted on baseball caps to give away in the bait shop with any purchase over twenty-five dollars. Too bad he'd forgotten. It would have been fun handing them out to the ladies of the Elvis Impersonator Bucket-List Brigade. They would have gotten a kick out of that and probably would have insisted on getting their picture taken with him. He could almost hear Dana ranting about how he'd missed out on some good publicity.

Now he could also laugh about his stubborn refusal to change the shop's name to Elvis's Beauty, Barber, Bait & Bakery. When he was carrying the sign up the ladder, he had dropped it. It had landed on the 'Brent's' end and crumpled so that the 'B' and 'r' had turned in on themselves, leaving him no choice but to bolt up the 'Elvis's' piece instead. He had let loose with some energetic swearing at the time, but couldn't blame anyone else. Dana had cheerily pointed out that it would have been a really boring sign if he hadn't had that replacement part ready.

And after months of feeling guilty for deceiving Grace, she not only knew the truth about his plans, but was thrilled with the results, especially after learning her husband had been ready to let Havisto's Market go. What if he'd thrown that padlocked box out without ever looking inside?

He leafed through the appointment books Dana had left on his desk alongside an I-told-you-so note telling him to check out how many haircuts were already on the books. She'd added a P.S.: *hire Jenny*. He would let Dana think she had convinced him to do so, but he had already offered Jenny a job after Frank told him Pine Lake needed a decent barbershop almost as much as a bait shop.

Jenny! He'd made the switch. Monica was a beautiful name, but Jenny sounded softer, less formal, and suited her.

All in all, the day had turned out better than expected. He had feared no one would show up for the grand opening, the shops would fail, and he'd never make enough money to live up here and fish and hunt. Making money! That's what this move had originally been about. Making enough money so that he could hide away on the lake or in the woods. What he hadn't counted on was the warm welcome: the handshakes, the smiles, the pats on the back. He had never thought of becoming part of Pine Lake. In his mind, moving up here would involve two simple, distinct activities: the necessity of business, and the solitude of fishing and hunting.

He had nurtured his shyness over the years, whittling his social life down to one night of poker a week. He had turned away younger customers at the salon, preferring to interact with the older women whom he saw as non-threatening and less demanding. But now he felt different. More confident. More at ease. Pine Lake had turned out to be not just a spot to semi-retire and fish. It had become the home he had always wanted.

Could it be that he actually enjoyed this commotion? That by donning a sequined costume and pretending to be someone he wasn't, he had actually discovered someone he might like to be? Or maybe Jenny was the reason he felt like a better version of himself.

He'd wanted her there to share the day's excitement, but she was in Milwaukee with Jeremy where he was being honored for his volunteer work with an at-risk youth program. Considering how busy he'd been, he wouldn't have had time for her anyway, although the note she'd given him to be opened that morning was well worn after several readings.

He was feeling pretty worn out himself. It had been quite a day. Quite a week! Actually, it had been pretty crazy ever since that morning on Little Pine Lake when he started talking to the crow. In fact, if someone had come up to him six months ago and told him how his life was going to change—that he was going to semi-retire up north and fall in love—for real this time—he would have said they were nuts. He'd had a dream for years, but had never thought it would come true.

Now, things were falling into place. Jenny had moved into Grace's house, Grace would be moving in with Evie, Elvis had a new home at the museum, and Dana was in the process of closing the realty office and buying her mother's house. He had moved into the frilly bedroom there and insisted on paying rent, but warned Dana not to become dependent on it, because he was also setting up a line of credit with the bank. He had his eye on a certain familiar house.

His phone dinged and he read Dana's text: *Get your butt over here, Elvis!*

Be there in five minutes, he texted back.

He pulled Jenny's note from his pocket to read once more before he left to join the celebration at Grace's. As he opened it, he wondered how it was possible that after you had totally fallen in love with a person, you could somehow keep falling in love with them even more.

The note began with a request: would he be willing to take her fishing on her birthday . . . her eightieth birthday. At first that had thrown him. Did it mean she wasn't ready for a relationship, or that she wanted him to be in her life for a long time? The old Brent would have gone with the first thought, but the new Brent had sent her a text: *We should practice to make sure I'm ready for your eightieth birthday. Come fishing with me Sunday morning.*

A lake wasn't the most romantic place for a proposal, but she seemed as comfortable and relaxed on the water as he was. All day long—whenever he had a free moment—he had tried out different ways to ask the big question. Should he get down on one knee in the boat? Should he wait until he had a ring?

But so many things were in his favor. The Grand Opening had turned out better than expected. Tomorrow's forecast was perfect. The winds would be calm. Besides, he had a good luck charm.

The crow would be there.

ACKNOWLEDGEMENTS ▊

This could be a never-ending list, beginning with my parents, but with apologies to anyone I've left out I'm grateful to the following:

Gregg Malaczewski, my former hairdresser, for sharing his retirement plans and allowing me to steal the best parts. I'm indebted to him not only for the title and subtitle, but also for the many conversations that fed my imagination. Since it was thoughts of retirement that led to the book, I guess I have no right to be angry with him for retiring. Thank you! Gregg.

To the many readers—recent, early, and earlier—including:

My book club members: Kathryn Andrews, Barb Brown, Cheryl Cimbalo—who has provided extensive feedback on several of my novels—Elaine Hartman, Mary Hussey, Constance Hassett, Kathy Matchefts, and former member, Ann Renard.

My sisters: Carol Haag, Debbie Haag, and Diane Haag. They have listened, cheered, supported, advised, helped spread the word, and are the best sisters anyone could ask for.

Len Hansen, whose insightful comments prompted me to add much-needed chapters and also got me thinking about what I owe readers. Also to his wife, Mary Hansen, good friend, walking partner, and someone who always sees more in me than I see in myself.

The *very* early readers at Sunburst Condos. Kay Erickson was first to respond to my call for readers there, then passed the book along. When it kept moving from one person to another,

I started believing that maybe somebody besides my husband, family, and very close friends might like to read my stories.

I'm also indebted to:

Sharon Vincent, who continues to show incredible patience, persistence, and unfailing good humor. Although she's been a successful graphic designer for a number of years, I think she was born to put her artistic skills and great ideas to work on book covers.

Marie Clark, my editor, to whom I send a perfect manuscript that comes back even more perfecter. (errors mine ;)

And finally to you! My words just sit on the page until you come along and give them life. Thank you for reading!

AUTHOR'S NOTES

I end this novel with relief. While understanding it could never be perfect, I kept rewriting until I decided it was as good as I could reasonably make it.

Then I looked at it from the reader's point of view in light of a number of questions: What do I owe someone who spends six, eight, ten, twelve hours with this novel? What promises have I made in the first sentence, the first paragraph, the first chapter? With the characters? With the plot? With the cover!? Sharon Vincent created a fantastic invitation and I wanted the story within to live up to all that colorful quirkiness.

So I went back and looked it over. I found things to add, to subtract, to flesh out, to pare back. Now I believe it's as good as I can make it today. Tomorrow or the next day or five years from now when I read it again, I'll likely see changes I could have made. But today I'm satisfied. I hope you are too.